Praise for Jodi

"A brave, cutting-edge romance... This is a worthwhile read."

—*Library Journal* on *The Forbidden*

"Unpredictable and addictive." —*Booklist* on *The Forbidden*

"*The Forbidden* proves that Jodi Ellen Malpas is not only one of the romance genre's most talented authors, but also one of the bravest. In this raw and honest portrayal of forbidden love, Jodi delivers a sexy and passionate love story with characters to root for. *The Forbidden* is easily my favorite read of 2017!"

—Shelly Bell, author of *At His Mercy*, on *The Forbidden*

"*The Forbidden* is a gut-wrenching tale full of passion, angst, and heart! Not to be missed!"

—HarlequinJunkie.com on *The Forbidden*

"Every kiss, every sexy scene, every word between this pair owned a piece of my soul. I could read this book a hundred times and still react as if it was the first time."

—Audrey Carlan, #1 bestselling author of The Calendar Girl series on *The Protector*

"4.5 stars. Top Pick. Readers will love this book from the very beginning! The characters are so real and flawed that fans feel as if they're alongside them. Malpas' writing is also spot-on with emotions." —*RT Book Reviews* on *The Protector*

Also by Jodi Ellen Malpas

This Man

Beneath This Man

This Man Confessed

All I Am: Drew's Story

One Night: Promised

One Night: Denied

One Night: Unveiled

The Protector

The Forbidden

With THIS MAN

JODI ELLEN MALPAS

FOREVER
New York Boston

Forever
Hachette Book Group
1290 Avenue of the Americas
New York, NY 10104
forever-romance.com
twitter.com/foreverromance

First Edition: March 2018

Forever is an imprint of Grand Central Publishing.
The Forever name and logo are trademarks of Hachette Book Group, Inc.

The publisher is not responsible for websites (or their content) that are not owned by the publisher.

The Hachette Speakers Bureau provides a wide range of authors for speaking events. To find out more, go to www.hachettespeakersbureau.com or call (866) 376-6591.

Library of Congress Control Number: 2017957963

ISBN 978-1-5387-4519-9 (trade paperback edition)
ISBN 978-1-538-74518-2 (ebook edition)

Printed in the United States of America

LSC-C

10 9 8 7 6 5 4 3 2 1

For Jesse. Thank you for trampling my mind with your perfect kind of crazy.

And to Sara Burch, you're forever in our hearts. This one is for you.

With THIS MAN

Chapter 1

The pounding of my feet on the treadmill is rhythmic and comforting. The sound of Imagine Dragons' "Believer" on my iPhone is muffled by the pulse throbbing in my ears. The hammering of my heart tells me I'm alive. Not that I need to run until I can't feel my legs to achieve that anymore.

My pace increases, my breath beginning to become labored as my run turns into a sprint. Sweat is pouring down my bare chest as I watch the clock across the gym, eyeing the second hand slowly roll around the dial. *Two more minutes. Keep the pace for two more minutes.*

Yet when the time has ticked down and the machine automatically starts to slow, my legs do not. I smack my hand on the plus button to increase the pace again, my ego refusing to let me stop just yet. One more mile. I crank up the volume and sprint on for a while longer, pushing air steadily through my nose, roughly wiping away the sweat rolling down my forehead. Glancing down at the screen on the treadmill, I note my distance. Fifteen miles. Done.

I slam my fist on the button and let the machine work me down to a gentle jog, yanking the buds out of my ears and grabbing my T-shirt to wipe my wet face.

"You did it faster yesterday, you stubborn motherfucker."

My feet slow to a stop and I brace my hands on the handles, dropping my head while I work to level out my breathing. "Fuck you," I manage to wheeze, turning to face one of my oldest friends. John's shit-eating grin, the one that displays his gold tooth to its fullest, makes me want to knock it out.

He chuckles, low and rumbling, throwing a towel at my chest. "Still not come to terms with it, then?"

Stepping down off the treadmill, I wipe my soaked chest before shoving the towel back at him. "No idea what you're on about." I'm lying. I know exactly what the bastard is on about, and I'm sick to fucking death of being wound up about it. I'm not even sure how it's happened—where the time has gone. Because, Lord help me, I'm fifty this weekend. Fifty fucking years old. My ego is dented more each time I think about it.

I make my way over to the water cooler, John following behind.

"Fifty suits you."

I roll my eyes as I grab a cup and shove it under the tap. "Did you want something?"

Another mild chuckle sounds from behind me as I glug down the water and turn to face the smug bastard. I don't know what he's so tickled pink about. John's knocking on sixty, though you'd never know it. He's still in prime shape, not that I'd ever tell him so.

"The new weight machines are arriving later."

"You good to take care of that?" I ask, refilling my cup.

"No problem."

"Thanks." I glance around the gym floor of the health club I own, the space alive with music, sweat, and pounding hearts. Disciples' "Daylight" is booming, adrenaline pumping, shouts of encouragement ringing out. Turns out I missed owning a club after all. Not the sex and the indulgence of The Manor, but the community, the social aspect, and the day-to-day running of a business. So I opened a new business, this one not so secret but still pretty exclusive. JW's Fitness & Spa has gone from strength to strength since opening its doors six years ago.

"Where's Ava?"

John takes my empty cup from my hand and tosses it in the bin before wandering away. "In the office."

In the office? A smile spreads across my face as I take off across the gym, the thrumming of my pulse building again, except this time it's dropped into my shorts.

My pace quickens, and I bowl into the office, my plan mastered...and screech to a halt when I find no Ava. I scowl at the empty space and pull my phone from my pocket, dialing her as I stalk toward the desk.

"Hey," she answers, sounding a bit exasperated.

I don't ask why. At this moment in time, I'm really not interested. "Where are you?" I drop down into the chair at her desk.

"In the spa."

"You have three seconds to get your arse to your office," I tell her, smirking a little when I hear her gasp.

"I'm all the way across the club."

I shrug to myself. "Three," I whisper, kicking my feet up onto her desk and relaxing back.

"Jesse, I'm trying to sort out a disagreement between staff."

"Don't care. Two."

"Oh, for fuck's sake."

My jaw rolls with irritation. "You'll pay for that. One." The sound of her rushed steps seeps down the line, and I smile, victorious. "Ticktock," I say casually, reaching down to rearrange my jutting cock.

"We're at work."

I scoff. "Wherever, whenever." She knows that.

"You're very demanding, Jesse Ward." The huskiness of her voice forces me to inhale, deeply and controlled. Yes, she sometimes still runs away from me, but sometimes she runs to me. Like now. When she knows I'm charged and waiting in the office.

My eyes fall to the door, energy surging through me. *Come on, baby.* I hear her hustling down the corridor toward the office, and then the door swings open.

And there she is. My gorgeous wife. She looks no different from the day I met her. Sexy. Beautiful. The perfect mix of elegance and sass. "Zero, baby," I murmur, cutting our call and tossing my phone on her desk.

A familiar shiver bumps its way up my spine, and I smile, taking in every fucking perfect inch of her. She places a hand on the door frame, leaning into it as she chews her lip, eyes full of delight. Delight at seeing me. Her husband. The man she loves. "Good day?" she asks.

"It's better now," I admit. "Are you going to make it even better?"

Her greedy stare drinks me in. I love it. I love how she can't control her need to ogle me constantly, either. Yeah, so I'm fifty this weekend. So fucking what. I've still got it. I suddenly feel like the god she thinks I am. The god I *know* I am. "Well?" I prompt. She knows that there's only one right answer to this question.

She shrugs, playing it cool. Such a waste of her time. And mine.

"Don't play games with me, lady."

"You love our games."

"Not as much as I love being buried to the hilt inside you." I drop my feet from the desk and stand. "You're wasting valuable time. Come here."

"Come get me." She shuts the door behind her and flips the lock as I stalk forward, her eyes shining harder with each step I take. Her body tenses, preparing for my attack. Every nerve ending I have is alive and screaming for her. A swift dip and grab has her over my shoulder, and I'm on my way back to the desk.

She's laughing, her palms sliding under the waistband of my shorts onto my arse. She squeezes, digging her nails into the flesh. "You're all sweaty."

I lay her on the desk and spread myself all over her, pinning her in place with one hand while sliding her dress up her body as she wriggles defiantly. Pointlessly. "Stop fighting me, baby," I warn, pulling it up over her head and tossing the material aside before going for the knickers. I smile at the lace concealing her from me, reaching down with my mouth and taking the side between my teeth.

"Jesse!" she yells, head tossing back and forth, her body writhing.

I laugh under my breath. The play for power never gets old. "Who has the power?" I ask, ripping the material from her waist and spitting it out.

"You, you fucking control freak!"

"Watch your mouth!" I pull the cups of her bra down and shove my shorts down my thighs, freeing my raging hard-on.

Heavy eyes lift to mine as she sits up, takes hold of my cock, and executes a deadly stroke down the shaft. My torso folds, the sensation of her warm palm surrounding my flesh overwhelming. "Fuck, Ava," I choke out, resting my hands on her shoulders, my chin dropped to my chest. "I'm sure I could chase the moon and catch it when you're touching me." I'm pretty sure I could do *anything*. I'm invincible, indestructible. Yet I'm so utterly vulnerable, too.

She lowers back down to the desk and arches, her breathing shallow, her face damp and flushed. The sight is out of this world, the sounds magic. "Fuck me," she demands, impatient and eager. "Please, fuck me."

"Watch your mouth, Ava," I warn, taking her behind the knees and yanking her forward. "I have every intention of fucking you, wife. Hard. Fast."

The wonderful heat of her pussy is pulling me in like a magnet. The burning need in me intensifies. "Oh, Jesus, baby." I bend and kiss each nipple in turn before standing and ramming forward unforgivingly, panting like a motherfucker as she screams through the shock. It's always as good as the first time.

Her hands fly up over her head to cling onto the side of the desk. "Oh God!"

I grit my teeth, withdrawing and driving forward. Hard.

"Jesse!"

"You like that, lady?"

"Harder," she demands, her eyes wild. "Remind me."

"Of what?"

"Anything." She flexes her hips, egging me on. "Show me who has the power."

My smile is wide and satisfied as I watch her waiting for me to do as she's ordered. But I won't. Not until she says those three magic words. I abruptly stop and hold still, buried deep in her warmth, waiting. "Say it," I breathe, dropping my torso to hers and kissing the side of her mouth. "Give me what I want and I'll give you want *you* want."

Her face turns into mine, catching my lips sweetly. "I love you," she mumbles around our rolling tongues. "So much."

I smile against her lips and slowly push myself back up. "Hold on, baby."

Her entire body goes rigid, bracing herself for it. I don't hold back. Never will. I smash into her with brutal force over and over, spiking constant screams of ecstasy. It's like music to my ears. But I want to see how much she wants me, so I withdraw and place my palms on her knees, pushing her legs back, completely exposing her glistening pussy. She's throbbing. "Fucking beautiful," I whisper in awe. I slowly reenter her, dropping my head back and finding my pace, driving forward, plunging deep, rolling hard. "Come on, baby," I breathe, starting to sweat. "Find it."

More yells. More panting. My senses are in chaos. The blood that charges into my cock nearly knocks me to my knees, my grip of Ava's legs increasing as I thrust on. The signs of her impending orgasm are all there: wide, bright eyes and her fingers clawing into the wood. She's going, and one look down at her amazing breasts has me going with her. My torso tenses and convulses, a shock wave of pleasure chasing through my body. It's powerful. So fucking powerful. I come hard, shaking like a fucking leaf while Ava moans through her release, my fingers flexing on her knees. Good. Fucking. Lord.

"Shit," she breathes, going lax, her head falling to the side, her eyes closing. "Fucking hell, Jesse."

I release her knees and collapse onto her, making sure I remain tucked inside her, relishing in the consistent pulls of her walls around my surging dick. "Watch," I pant. "Your." Kissing her sweaty cheek, I relax all of my weight atop of her. "Mouth."

"You're good."

"I know."

"You're a pighead."

"I know."

"I love you."

I snuggle into her neck and sigh. "I know."

Her arms come around my back and hug me tightly to her. I'm home. Contentment flourishes within me. "I need to go pick the kids up from school."

"Hmmm..." I'm unable to muster any more strength to talk, let alone move. And then there's a knock at the door, and I grumble, lazily pushing myself up from her desk. "Same time tomorrow?"

She grins as she wriggles off the desk and starts putting herself back together, my pout growing with every piece of her skin that she's slowly covering. "Coming," she calls to the door, slipping her dress over her head.

I tuck myself into my shorts and sit on the couch across the room. "You already came."

She rolls her eyes at my cheeky grin and rushes to the door, having a quick faff with her hair before taking the handle. She's wasting her time. Her cheeks are glowing, her whole being looking freshly fucked. She swings the door open, and I know immediately who's on the other side when I see my wife's shoulders rise and tense.

"Cherry," Ava says flatly, turning on her heel and making her way back to her desk. She flashes me a look on her way, one that confirms what I already know. She doesn't like Cherry.

According to my wife, the woman has the hots for me. I don't know why this is news to Ava. Every woman has the hots for me.

"I'm just going to get the twins." Ava sweeps up her bag and throws it onto her shoulder. "What's up?"

Cherry struts into the office and places a file on Ava's desk. Her blond hair is twisted tightly into a bun high on her head, and her white shirt has a few too many buttons open, in my opinion. I'm not purposely looking. You just can't help but notice.

"The membership reports you asked for."

"Perfect. I'll look at them tomorrow." Ava makes her way to the door, casting her eyes over to me where I'm sprawled on the couch. "Walk me out." It's not a question.

I grin. My wife's feeling all possessive. Getting up from the couch, I fetch my T-shirt from Ava's desk and throw it on as I stride to the door. I don't miss Cherry's admiring stare as I pull the shirt down my torso, and neither does my wife.

"Let's go." I collect Ava and get us on our way before her claws come out.

"She fancies you," she grumbles, wrapping an arm around my waist. "If she wasn't so good at her job and I didn't need her so much, she'd be gone."

I laugh. "She's not done anything wrong."

"Yeah, she has. She looks at you."

I tug my wife more firmly into my side. "You can't trample staff for looking at me."

"What would you do if a male employee looked at me like that?"

Heat. It's instant in my veins, and it's not the satisfying kind. My growl is automatic, and she laughs, breaking away from me when we make it to the bottom of the stairs in the reception area.

"I don't think so, lady." I yank her back and crowd her with my arms. "Don't say shit that will make me crazy mad." I slam my lips on hers and devour her for a few mind-spinning moments. "See you at home." I bite her lip and pull away, smiling as I back up at her obvious daze. She's forgotten where she was heading. "Go pick up the kids," I remind her.

She shakes herself back to life and glances around the reception space. No one's paying any attention. They all know how we operate. This isn't just our normal anymore, it's our staff's normal. Has to be if they want to keep their jobs.

Off my wife goes, and I start counting down the minutes until I can go home and see my babies.

Chapter 2

As I ride my Ducati up the long driveway of our little manor, peace settles over me. Ava's car is in its usual place, the boot open. Coming to a stop next to her Mini, I pull off my helmet and scan the filthy vehicle. The black paintwork looks dusty, dull, and old. "You don't see dust on white," I mutter to myself. "And you can get more shopping bags into a Range Rover."

I may have forced the biggest, sturdiest vehicle on her one time, but she finally talked me around and got her faithful Mini back.

Ava appears at the front door, her steps faltering when she spots me by my bike. Holding her dark chocolate gaze, I rest my arse on the seat and my helmet on my lap, crossing my legs at the ankles. Well, isn't this the best welcome home a man could ask for? I take my time to admire her. She still looks freshly fucked. "My lady," I say, my tone automatically gravelly.

She brushes her hair over her shoulder. "My Lord."

I find myself shifting to adjust my growing hard-on behind the fly of my leathers. Her restrained grin tells me she knows of the activity she's spiked down there, and for a moment I consider once again how my wife must feel to know that she still, twelve years after we met, has this profound effect on me. I can't get enough of her.

She sashays slowly down the steps, watching me closely until she gets to the rear of her car. Then she reaches in, accentuating the swell of her curvy arse, and pulls out a Tesco bag. "Put the bag down," I tell her.

"Stop being so demanding." She feigns a sigh and swivels on her heels, swaying her arse as she saunters up the steps with the shopping bag hanging from her fingers. "I have your children to feed."

"And I have needs, lady," I call, dumping my helmet on the seat of my bike and going in pursuit of her. "Ava!"

I hear her laugh as she disappears through the doorway, and when I land in the kitchen, I find her standing with the bag at her feet. I pull to a stop and watch as she bends down slowly, seductively, and pulls some items from the bag. I grin when she waggles a cheeky eyebrow at me and flashes two jars of peanut butter. "I might let you lick it off me."

"Might let me?" I laugh, amused by her coyness. "Ava, you've been married to me for over a decade. Haven't you learned yet?"

"I have the power," she whispers, sliding the jars onto the worktop and pouting her full lips.

I find myself doubling over to stop my cock from breaking free of my leathers. "Ava, unless now is a good time to bend you over the worktop and fuck you blind, don't be teasing me." Jesus, I've had to control where I can take her since the twins were born. My willpower is wearing thin. Maybe it's my age. I shake that thought quickly away before it has a chance to ruin my mood.

"You need to talk to Maddie." Ava's statement comes from nowhere.

I scoff. Nope. No way, because I know exactly what my eleven-year-old daughter wants to talk about. "I'm not going over it again, Ava. End of."

"You need to learn how to deal with her before she divorces us."

"I know how to deal with her." I cough indignantly.

"Locking her in her room isn't dealing with her."

I scowl. "Don't exaggerate."

Ava laughs. It's condescending. She better wind her neck in or she'll be heading for a Retribution Fuck. "You threatened it just the other day."

I can't believe that I have to explain myself for the hundredth time. "Ava, she had on a pair of denim shorts that would have fit a Barbie doll. And she plans on going to the school party in them?" I laugh at the thought. "It isn't happening. Not while I'm alive."

My wife rolls her eyes. "They weren't that bad."

"She's eleven!"

"She's becoming a young lady."

"She's becoming a pain in my fucking arse, that's what she's becoming." Or a bigger one.

"You're being way over the top, Jesse."

Over the top? I don't think I am at all. "Ava, last week when I picked her up, some dirty little pervert was practically drooling over her as she walked from the school gates to my car." I feel the blood begin to boil in my veins, just recalling the incident. Had a fucking traffic warden not moved me from the restricted parking zone, I would have been out of my car and across the street faster than a roadrunner.

She smirks at me. "A dirty little pervert?"

"Yes. He's lucky I didn't shove his head down his pants so he couldn't ogle my daughter."

"And how old was this dirty little pervert?"

"I don't know." I brush her question aside, knowing exactly where we're heading here.

"I do." Ava laughs again, half-amused, half-exasperated. "He's eleven, Jesse. Just like Maddie. His name is Kyle and he's in Maddie's class. He has a crush, that's all."

I snort and head for the fridge. "He's a pervert," I state with utter finality, daring her to continue the discussion as I rummage through the top shelf looking for my Sun-Pat peanut butter. But I should know my defiant little temptress by now. And she dares to continue.

"Jacob has a crush on a girl," Ava says casually. I turn away from the fridge, seeing her collecting the jars of peanut butter off the counter and moving over to the cupboard. My boy has a crush? The only crush he has that I know of is a crush on football. The kid's mad for it. "Does that make *your* boy a pervert?"

My lips twist as I return to the fridge and continue searching for my comfort food. "Why are you doing this?"

"Because our children are growing up and you need to let them do that. Maddie's going to the school party, and you are not chaperoning her. It isn't cool to take your dad."

"She isn't damn well going without me," I snap, slamming the fridge door. "Where's my fucking Sun-Pat?" I swing around and find my wife holding out a new jar, her eyebrows high and knowing.

I swipe it from her grasp without so much as a thank-you and whip off the lid. My finger goes in, sweeps around the edge, and I plunge the big dollop into my mouth, still scowling at my wife, who is now shaking her head in dismay. She can shake her head all she likes. My daughter isn't going to the school party without me, and she definitely isn't going in those denim shorts.

"Where is Maddie, anyway?" I ask Ava's back, not missing the opportunity to relish the sight of her arse. That arse. I want to bite it.

"She's waiting for her daddy to get home so she can butter him up."

"Butter me up how?"

"Daddy!" Maddie's squeal of delight—a totally fake squeal, it should be noted—stops my questioning in its tracks. Oh no. She called me *Daddy*. Not *Dad*. I just know the puppy-dog eyes are coming.

I do the wisest thing I can. I put down my peanut butter and edge out of the kitchen without making eye contact. I'll be fucked. Screwed.

"I need to get changed." I bomb out of the door, hearing Maddie in pursuit.

"Daddy, wait!"

"I have things to do," I call behind me as I race up the stairs, catching a glimpse of her long chocolate hair bouncing over her shoulders as she chases after me. "Speak to Mum."

"Mum said I needed to speak to you!"

I just make it to the top when I feel something around my ankle. "Fuck!" I lose my footing and trip up the top step, crashing down to the carpet in a heap.

"Daddy, watch your mouth!"

"Maddie, for crying out loud!"

"Then don't run away from me, and face up to your responsibilities."

"Excuse me?" I roll over to my back and sit up, finding my girl lying across the final few steps of the staircase, her small hand still wrapped around my ankle, her head tilted far back to look up at me. She's already fluttering her lashes, the little minx. "My responsibilities?"

"Yes." She releases my foot and pushes herself to her feet, and I only mildly register that she has on jeans and a jumper. Long jeans and a long-sleeved jumper. This should please me, yet it doesn't. Because this is my little live wire of a daughter, and she's a little fucker when she wants to be. Like, all the time. And like now when I know she's only covered from top to toe because, in the words of her mother, she's trying to butter me up. It won't work.

Maddie sighs, shaking her head at me. "Dad—"

"Oh, so it's *Dad* now, is it?"

Her jaw tightens, and she looks at me in a way that only her mother can rival. Like she could cut off my dick with her glare. "It's not fair! All my friends are going, and their parents are okay with it. Why do you have to be the one to ruin all the fun?"

"Because I love you," I mutter, getting to my feet. "Because I know there are some idiot boys out there who will want to kiss you." What the fuck am I saying? The fact that my girl would probably rip off the balls of any potential kisser, probably better than even *I* could, is beside the point. It's my job to protect her.

"And stalk me," she retorts, making me recoil.

"What do you mean?" I don't like the smug look on her face. The look that suggests she has dirt on me. I narrow my eyes on her, waiting for it.

"Like you stalked Mum."

I gasp. "I didn't stalk your mother. I pursued her."

"She said it's the same thing, especially when the pursuing is done at Jesse Ward's level of pursuing."

"It's...no...she..." I huff and turn, marching to the master suite. I'm not arguing with a eleven-year-old. "Your mother loved me stalking her," I snap over my shoulder.

"You said you pursued her."

"Same thing." I slam the door to our dressing room behind me and yank my T-shirt over my head. "The girl will be the death of me," I mumble, chucking it in the wash basket.

Maddie barges in, forcing my hands to pause on the fly of my leathers. "I'm going to the party without you, and I will wear what I like."

"You are not going." I just manage to hold back my bad language. "End of."

"You're so mean!" she yells, her cheeks flushed with anger.

"I know!" I shove my hands into the waistband of my leathers, ready to push them down. "Are you scramming? Because I'm about to get naked."

Her pretty little face screws up in utter disgust. "Ewwww." She makes a hasty exit, leaving me looking down at my torso. Ewwww? The fucking cheek. I might be fifty soon, but I'm still fucking prime. Ask my wife. And every other woman on the planet. Ewwww?

I kick off my leathers and drop to the floor, smashing out fifty press-ups, muttering and cursing as I do. I should have stayed at the health club.

After yanking on some clean shorts, I turn to head downstairs, noticing a pile of clean laundry on the bed. I do what any decent husband would do: I gather it up and go back to the dressing room to put it away. I place my socks and boxers in the designated drawers, leaving me with a pile of Ava's knickers in my palm. I grin at the stacks of lace, unable to stop myself from bringing them to my nose and inhaling the clean smell of laundry mixed with Ava's lingering scent. I hum and close my eyes, planning tonight's intimate time. I see a Sense Fuck in the not too distant future. I'll make my wife see that it would be most unwise for us to let Maddie go to the school party without a chaperone.

"Dad?"

I swing around and find Jacob hovering at the doorway. His handsome face is quite alarmed. "Oh, hey." I quickly pull the lace away from my nose and smile awkwardly.

"Are you smelling Mum's knickers?"

I laugh like a twat, feeling the heat rise in my cheeks. My kids do fuck all for my ego. "Just checking they've been washed," I say, turning my back on him and opening Ava's knicker drawer.

"You're weird sometimes, Dad." Jacob sighs from behind me, and I cringe, but my cringe turns into a frown when I spot something in the corner of Ava's drawer. It's not the *something* that's the problem. It's the fact that it's in a different corner from this morning. I snarl at the diamond-embellished vibrator, or the Weapon of Mass Destruction, as my wife likes to call it, and slowly push the drawer closed. She isn't wrong. It *does* destroy. It destroys my fucking ego. Has she been using it without me? Giving her pleasure to a fucking machine?

Casting my grievance aside, just for now, I turn toward my boy. "What's up, mate?" I ask, wandering over to him and throwing my arm around his shoulders, walking us out of the dressing room.

"One of my friends from school, Sonny, has invited me to Old Trafford with his parents to watch United. They're playing Arsenal. Can I go?"

I smile to myself, looking down at Jacob as he looks up at me, all hopeful and with a little worry. I know what he's thinking. He's thinking that football is *our* thing, and I might not like him doing it with someone else. I take him training, I watch every match, I make a monthly point during the football season of a boys' day out, just me and him. All boys' stuff, where there are no women driving us nuts. "Sure you can."

"Thanks, Dad."

I lean down and sink my face into his mop of dirty blond hair. My boy. My beautiful, laid-back boy. "Hey," I say, releasing him from my clinch when something comes to me. "Mum mentioned something about a crush." I raise my eyebrows in question.

Jacob rolls his eyes and makes his way to his bedroom. "I don't have a crush, and if I did, I wouldn't tell Mum."

I grin. "Playing it cool, eh?" That's my boy.

"What, like you did with Mum?" He turns and catches me scowling. And another head shake. "I'm going to polish my trophies." He disappears into his bedroom, leaving me on the landing.

I zoom back to the dressing room, grab her vibrator, and head back out. A quick check of Maddie's room tells me she's sulking on her bed and will be lost in her mood for a good hour. A quick check of Jacob's room tells me he's already lined up his football trophies and will be lost in polishing those for at least two hours.

I hurry downstairs, brandishing Ava's vibrator like a sword in front of me. "How many times do we need to go over this?" I ask, entering the kitchen. "All of your pleasure comes from me."

I come to a screaming halt when I find that my wife isn't alone. Oh shit.

"Elizabeth!" I yelp, my hand frozen in midair.

"Oh... my... God," she breathes, looking at Ava in question. My wife's face is a picture of horror.

"Oh..." The vibrator glows at me, and I rush to hide it behind my back. "Always nice to see you, Mum."

Elizabeth sighs, turning to her daughter and kissing her cheek. "I'll call before I drop by next time, darling."

"Good idea," Ava mutters, her horrified face turning into an expression that suggests I'm in for it. My idiotic smile widens.

"I'll be on my way. Your father needs picking up from the golf course."

I wave at Ava's mother with my empty hand as she approaches me, shaking her head. "You're not staying?" I ask out of politeness. After all these years, we still have a love/hate thing going on.

"Don't pretend you want me to."

The vibrator behind my back feels like it's pulsing in my grasp, reminding me that I still have unfinished business to clear up with my wife. But then the device is suddenly snatched from my hand.

"What's this?" Maddie asks, holding up the huge dildo. Every muscle I have fails me, and I hear Ava and her mother gasp. My frozen state means Maddie has a chance to investigate her find, flicking at the buttons on the shaft. The vibrator jumps to life in her hand, and she screams, dropping it to the floor, where it proceeds to dance around our feet.

"What is that?" she cries.

"That's a weapon of mass destruction!" I blurt mindlessly, kicking it away.

"What's a weapon of mass destruction?"

"A bomb!" I grab Maddie and throw her over my shoulder, pelting out of the kitchen at top speed.

"Quick, Dad! Before it explodes!"

Fuck me, how do I get into these situations? I race up the stairs and burst into Maddie's room, throwing her on the bed in my usual fashion, and then watch as she giggles like girls do, brushing her hair from her face. Big, round, gorgeously dark eyes find me, and her giggles turn into hysterics as she rolls around on the bed clenching her tummy.

I drop down in an exhausted heap of dad next to her and pull her into my chest. "Come here, little lady," I sigh, taking the rare opportunity to grab a cuddle with my girl. She settles and lets me fuss over her for a few short minutes, still giggling every now and then. When she's gathered her breath, she breaks free from my hug and sits up, crossing her legs and looking at me for a few thoughtful moments.

"Daddy, please let me go to the party." She holds up praying hands in front of her face and juts out her bottom lip in an adorable pout. Doomed. Fucking doomed. "I'll let you approve my outfit."

I hitch an eyebrow, a little surprised by her willingness to negotiate. Pushing myself up onto my elbows, I ponder her suggestion for a few moments. She's being reasonable. I should try to follow her lead, no matter how much it pains me. I sigh and roll my eyes. That face always breaks down my determination. "I'm taking you there and picking you up. Ten o'clock at the very latest."

She squeals in delight and dives at me, tackling me back down to her bed. "Thank you, Daddy."

"You can ease off on the *Daddy* business now," I say, snatching another opportunity to have a hug. "And you *must* answer your phone when I call you or I'll be coming into the school to track you down."

"Can't you just text me?"

"No."

"Okay." She relents easily, understanding that she's reached her limit.

"And remember," I go on, keen to reinforce the rules. "It's illegal to kiss a boy until you're twenty-one."

She chuckles. "It's not illegal to kiss a boy, Dad."

"It really is."

"By *real* law or Dad's law?"

"Both."

"You're impossible."

"Maddie, do you want to go to the party or not?"

Her jaw tightens, and she draws in a long breath. "It is illegal to kiss boys before you're twenty-one," she says flatly, and I cock my head in a prompt for more. "By *real* law," she adds.

"Good girl." I kiss her forehead and get on my way, satisfied by a job well done. See? I can be reasonable. I don't know why everyone constantly barks on about my unwillingness to flex. I flex every day of my damn life.

Jacob emerges from his room, a tennis racket in his hand. "Where's Maddie?" he asks.

She appears with her own racket, now changed into some

ridiculously tiny sports shorts and a cropped T-shirt. They shoot off down the stairs. "We'll be on the court!"

"I'll join you soon," I shout at their backs. "Just as soon as I've dealt with your mother," I add quietly, pacing toward the stairs, hoping Elizabeth has buggered off so I can find out what's going on with that fucking vibrator.

I bump into my beautiful wife halfway down the stairs. The Weapon of Mass Destruction is in her hand, a condemning scowl on her face. She wants a scowling match? I'll win every time.

Stopping in my tracks, I curl my lip and growl under my breath, maintaining our staring deadlock. But, fuck me, it's hard when she looks so effortlessly gorgeous. So... mine.

I give my cock a mental pep talk, telling it to behave until I've vented. It fails, my shorts beginning to tent. It doesn't escape Ava's notice, her eyes dropping to my groin, her eyebrow curving as a lust I'm all too familiar with fills her eyes. We'll be having none of that. Not yet, anyway.

"Explain," I demand, shoving an accusing finger at the thing in her hand.

She pouts, looking at the device before slowly lifting her sparkling eyes back up to me, not missing the opportunity to drag her stare over my bare chest. There goes my cock again, lurching behind my shorts. A ghost of a smile curves her lips, and her eyes glimmer with mischief.

She casually slinks past me, and my body turns slowly, following her. She stops at our bedroom door. "Jesse?" she says in that low, husky voice that drives me wild.

"Yeah?" I answer, dragging the word out warily.

She puckers her lips and kisses thin air. "Fuck you." She rushes into the room and slams the door behind her.

What the fuck? "Ava!" I yell, stamping my way to the door. "Watch your fucking mouth!" I grab the handle and push all of my weight into the wood, jarring it a little. I can hear her laughing beyond. Oh, she wants to play, huh? I release the door and stand back. I could probably burn a hole through it with my glare. I take a deep breath and give her what I know she's asking for. "Three . . . ," I state coolly.

"I'm not letting you in."

"Two."

"Fuck off, Jesse."

My hackles rise, and I thump the door, spiking another teasing giggle from beyond. Oh, she's getting it. Hard. "One!"

"Screw you, Ward!"

My chest puffs out, and I stand back, locking and loading. "Zero, baby!" I yell, launching my shoulder into the door. It opens with ease, as I knew it would, Ava having wisely moved away in preparation for what she knew was coming. I catch her by the wrist before she even thinks to run. "Got you." I whirl her around and throw her up onto my shoulder, taking her to the bed. We land in a tatty tangle, and only a few seconds later, she's naked, my skin on her skin, my dick dancing. I find my place between her thighs and grab her cheeks, pushing my nose to hers. "I have two words for you."

"What are they?"

"*Retribution* and *Fuck*." I sink my face into her neck and bite her, licking and lapping at her flesh. "You ready, baby?" My eyes close in utter bliss, waiting for her sigh and the subtle, teasing flex of her hips.

"I want a boob job."

My eyes spring open, and I'm out of my happy place in her neck in a nanosecond. I need to see her face so I can gauge whether she's winding me up or not. As I stare down at my wife's beauty in utter shock, I quickly conclude that she's not winding me up at all. She's biting her lip nervously, and I'm pretty sure she's holding her breath. My cock shrivels to nothing.

"What the actual fuck, Ava?"

"I want a boob job," she repeats quietly.

"Forget it."

"Jesse..."

"No way." I push myself up to my knees, my gaze automatically falling to her boobs. The boobs I love. The boobs that give me hours of pleasure. Soft boobs. Natural boobs. *My* fucking boobs. I inwardly moan at the thought of someone taking a knife to them. "Hell will freeze over," I tell her. "You can get that idea *right* out of your head."

She follows my line of sight to her breasts and cups them. For once, watching Ava touch herself does nothing for my libido. What the hell is she thinking? "They need an injection of life," she muses, her chin on her chest as she inspects each one. "They're going south."

"The only thing that just went south is my dick." A cold shower couldn't have been as effective. "Like I said, not while I'm alive and breathing. Not even when I'm dead. I'll find a way to come back to life so I can trample your arse. Forget it, Ava. They're mine and I like them just the way they are."

"You really are being unreasonable," she mutters as I laugh my way into the bathroom and flip on the shower. "And they're actually *my* boobs, not yours."

That statement pulls me back to the door. She's staring at me defiantly. She knows she's not going to win this one but will try anyway, and piss me off even more in the fucking process. "How long has it been since I found you?" I ask.

"Twelve years," she spits back matter-of-factly, obviously holding back her eye roll.

"Then discussions over ownership are out of fucking date. We cleared up that small detail within weeks of knowing each other."

"Or so you told me." Her nostrils flare. "And year thirteen might be your unlucky year, Ward."

I jump back a little, startled. "What the fuck is that supposed to mean?"

"It means," she snipes, sitting up on the bed and folding her arms over her chest, "that year thirteen might be the year I leave you."

I gasp, horrified, despite the fact that her fingers go straight to her hair, playing with the strands. She's lying. It doesn't matter. She still has the nerve to say it. "Take that back right now."

"No."

"Ava."

"Fuck off."

"Mouth!" I steam forward, outraged, ready to put her back in her place. She tries to escape. She could have a mile head start and I'd catch her. Always will. She scrambles across the bed, aware that she's pushed me too far, and screams when I catch her ankle, dragging her back toward me. "Where do you think you're going?" I ask, flipping her over and straddling her stomach, arms pinned safely above her head with one hand.

"Get off me!"

I do the only thing there is to do. I look down at the sensitive spot by her hip, grinning evilly.

She stills. "Jesse, no."

I ignore her and go in for the kill, sinking my fingers into her tickle spot and going to town, digging, squeezing, and generally making it as unbearable as possible.

"Oh my God." She sucks in air and starts going loopy beneath me, bucking and screaming her displeasure. "No! I'll...pee..." She laughs uncontrollably, then shouts in vexation, "I'm going to wee myself!"

"Take it back now," I warn, not letting up. A bit of pee between husband and wife is no skin off my nose.

"I take it back!"

"Are you leaving me, wife?" I ask, giving her an extra-brutal squeeze.

"Never!" She gasps for breath, her body arching violently.

"I'm glad we've cleared that up." I release her and she jumps up off the bed, holding herself between her legs. "Knock yourself out, lady."

She pelts to the bathroom. "You bastard!" The door slams and I chuckle to myself, following behind, though less speedily than Ava. I walk in to find her sitting on the loo. She scowls at me. I grin.

Stepping into the shower, I start belting out a bit of Justin Timberlake, squeezing some gel onto the sponge. "How was your day, dear?" I ask.

"Fine." Grabbing her toothbrush, she slaps on some paste and starts scrubbing. "'ought... orrow... ate... am... ryone... irthday."

I look at her past the glass incredulously. "Wanna run that by me again?"

She spits out the paste. "On Saturday, everyone is coming around for your birthday barbeque."

"I'm not having a birthday barbeque," I say with utter finality, going back to scrubbing down. "We've discussed this."

"But—"

"No buts, Ava. I'm not celebrat..." I drift off, realizing that I was about to break my own rule: no mentioning the dreaded number.

"Celebrating the fact that you're turning fifty?" She cocks her head at me, her toothbrush going back into her mouth.

I flinch as I rub some shampoo into my hair. "I'm not turning fifty," I mutter, hearing her sigh. It's fine for her. She's still fresh as a daisy at thirty-eight. Thirty-fucking-eight! That's pretty much how old I was when I met Ava. Look how fast the years have whizzed by. If the next twelve years roll by as quickly, I'll be drawing my pension soon. My stomach churns with dread.

"You're still my god," Ava says softly, pulling my attention back to her. She's just outside the shower now, looking at me closely.

"I know."

"And you're still the handsomest man I've ever laid eyes on."

"I know." I shrug.

"And you still fuck like a god on steroids." She pushes her lips into the glass and kisses it.

"Yeah, I know." I meet her lips on the other side.

"Then what's the problem, you gorgeous god?"

"Nothing," I sigh. I'm being stupid, but fifty sounds so much older than forty-nine. I shut the shower off, and she moves back for me to get out, handing me a towel. I rub myself down and go to the mirror, looking myself up and down. Solid. It's all solid. As hard today as it was twelve years ago. And my face. Rough with four days' worth of stubble, and my skin is fresh. Quite honestly, I don't look much different. I know that. But it's more psychological. Fucking *fifty*.

A pair of arms comes around my waist, and her naked front pushes into my back, hugging me. "You're beautiful and all mine," she says, making me smile.

"That's my line."

She releases me and steps to the side, looking up at me. "Don't get a complex. It doesn't suit you."

I nod my agreement, kicking myself up the arse. What's up with me? I look good, my wife is wonderful, and my kids are the most beautiful creatures I've ever seen. I'm the luckiest man alive. I need to sort my shit out. I turn to the cupboard above the sink and grab down my deodorant. Ava's small pill packet catches my eye. "You taken your pill today?" I ask.

"Oh, I forgot. Pass them here."

"Really, Ava?" I grab them and thrust them into her hand. "Don't forget shit like that." I shudder.

She ignores my evident dread and pops one, swallowing it with some water. "So about the school party..."

"I've told her she can go," I say before messing with my hair and wandering back into the bedroom. "But I'm taking her there and collecting her afterward, and she better answer my calls or I'm going in." I pull some boxers on and snap the waistband. "So you can stop with your nagging."

"I don't nag," she spits indignantly.

"Not much."

"Do you want a slap, Ward?"

"Do you want a Sense Fuck, Mrs. Ward?" I cock my head expectantly and watch as the rush of desire returns swiftly to her cheeks. That look alone brings my dick back to life. Oh, damn, I need her again.

"Dad!" Jacob's voice invades the bedroom, and my cock shrivels to nothing. Ava sags, clearly disappointed that another Danger Fuck is now off the cards. Because the danger has just made its presence known. "Dad, you coming to play?"

"On my way, mate," I call, slipping on my shorts.

"Cock blocker," Ava grumbles, giving me her cheek when I approach.

I kiss her lightly around my smile, and she pushes her flesh onto my mouth. "Sleepy twilight sex by the pool tonight?"

Her eyes light up like sparkling diamonds. "Deal."

I grab my trainers and head for the door. "And the next time you use that dildo without me, there will be no loving for a whole week."

"What?" Her shock is clear.

"You heard."

"You couldn't live without it for a week either, Ward. You'll be punishing yourself more than me."

I smile, taking the stairs two at a time. She's right. "Then it'll be a week of Apology Fucks instead." Ava's mouth around my cock every day, two times a day for a week isn't something to be sniffed at.

"Fine by me."

I laugh and hurry to the courts.

Chapter 3

Happy birthday, dear Jesse! Happy birthday to you!"

The chanting of my closest family and friends is enough to make me want to go on a rampage to track down the key to eternal youth. I can't even see my fucking birthday cake through the raging fire atop of it. Fifty. How the fuck did this happen? Fifty! Maybe I could forget—God, would I love to forget—but my darling wife won't let me, and in addition to the forest fire cooking my cake, there are balloons and banners plastered all over the house and garden, just in case the fact that I'm an old bastard had escaped me.

"Anyone got a fire extinguisher handy?" I ask, sucking as much air into my lungs as I can manage. I'm gonna need it.

"Oh no," I hear Maddie breathe. "He's going to trample the cake."

I roll my eyes and blow out the candles while everyone has a laugh at my expense. Sam slaps me on the back and grins.

"Don't say a word," I warn before my friend can hit me with some sarcastic wisecrack. "You're no spring chicken yourself."

He laughs and cocks his head. I wish I could be as complacent about my age. "I'm a few years behind you, my man. Don't tar me with the same old brush."

"Fuck you."

"Jesse Ward!" Ava's mother cries, placing her hands over Maddie's ears while sharply nodding at her husband, Joseph, to take care of Jacob's. My father-in-law doesn't even bother, and instead ruffles my boy's hair on a smile filled with pride. Maddie shrugs her nan off and starts picking off the candles on my cake, counting them as she does, just to rub salt into my wounds. She gets to thirteen before a heavily pregnant Kate intervenes.

Ava's best friend smiles down at my girl, who's now looking up at her in question. "Let's not upset your dad any more," Kate says quietly, but not too quietly that I miss it. She flicks her eyes to mine, and the smile I had pointed at her swollen belly drops when I catch her smirking at me.

"This is the worst party ever." I huff my way to the kitchen to get a Bud, considering the benefits of getting blind drunk. And then I immediately scold myself for thinking such thoughts. Never. I pull the fridge open and make fast work of knocking the cap off a bottle.

"I'd ask you if you want something stronger, but I know you're not up for it," Sam says, wandering into the kitchen as I slam the fridge door.

"Don't tempt me." I knock back another glug as Drew joins us. His suit is so pristine, he couldn't have sat, bent, or even moved in it since he put it on. "Bit over the top for a BBQ, isn't it?" I ask.

"I have somewhere special to be after I've finished relishing in your misery." He moves past me to the fridge and helps himself to a beer, ignoring the look of surprise on my face. I glimpse at Sam, finding his expression matches mine.

Somewhere special? "What's more special than being with your mate on his fiftieth?" I bring my bottle to my lips as I watch Drew flip the cap off of his beer.

"I'm going to ask Raya to marry me." He barely whispers the words.

My snort of surprise sends my beer spraying so far, it hits every wall in my expansive kitchen. And Drew doesn't dodge it. I cough, choke, and sniff, while Sam laughs and Drew looks at me like he wants to rip my head off. He undoubtedly does. I've messed up his suit. He slams his bottle on the counter, nostrils flaring, though his face remains stoic. Married? Drew? There's no question he's found his girl in the beautiful Raya; I've never seen him so happy and settled, but . . . marriage? I just never imagined he'd venture down that road.

"Jesse," Drew snaps, brushing down his suit jacket. "For fuck's sake. Look!"

"I'm sorry." I snatch a tea towel off the side and chuck it at him.

"What's going on?" Kate waddles into the kitchen with some empty plates, Ava in tow.

"Drew's asking Raya to marry him," Sam and I declare in unison, making the girls pull to an abrupt stop before they both gasp, hands at their mouths, and then swoon all over Drew.

"Will you keep it down, she'll hear you," he mutters, throwing the tea towel with force at me before fighting the girls away. It smacks me in the face before I catch it.

"Hear what?" Raya asks, appearing in the kitchen with a dish balancing on one hand, a glass of wine in the other.

"Nothing!" we all sing, all grinning.

Drew rolls his eyes and collects his girl. "We're going."

"We are?" Raya slides the dish onto the counter, looking a bit bewildered as Drew takes her glass from her hand and leads her to the door. "What about Georgia?"

Drew tosses a smirk over his shoulder at me. "Uncle Jesse said she could stay."

"I did?"

"We did," Ava pipes up. "Have fun!" she calls, before moving into Kate's side. "Do you think he still has his cock pierced?" she whispers in Kate's ear.

What the fuck? I swing an incredulous look at my wife, whose mouth snaps shut quickly, her back going all straight as she looks at me, her lips pressed together. I give her an expectant look, and she shrugs, looking away guiltily. "Just what I've heard." She bites her lip, glancing at Kate, who chuckles, clutching her belly.

"Stop. I'll pee myself."

I glare at Ava. "How'd you know Drew has his cock pierced?"

She shrugs, all casual. "Like I said, just something I heard."

"I wonder who from," Sam muses, tossing an accusing look to Kate as he wanders over to her and gets as close as her stomach will allow. He has to lean forward to get his face in hers. "Explain."

"It was a surprise back then, that's all. I felt the need to share."

Sam slams a hard kiss on her cheek and then lowers his lips to the top of her stomach, dropping a kiss there, too. "Close your ears, sunshine," he whispers, looking back up at Kate. She's grinning. Sam's not. "Nice to know out of everything that could have stuck in your head from that night, it's my mate's dick."

I start chuckling again, perching on a stool to get comfy and enjoy the show. This party isn't turning out too bad after all. I fold my arms over my chest and swing my eyes from Sam's incredulous face to Kate's dismissive one. "Yeah, Kate," I goad as John sticks his head around the door.

"The kids have got the grandparents playing Twister. I'd prebook an ambulance if I were you."

"Come on." Ava tugs me from the stool and directs me out of the kitchen. "We have parents to rescue before they injure themselves."

"But I want to watch," I complain, looking over my shoulder, just catching Sam seizing Kate and swinging her back in his arms. She squeals a squeal that is definitely more delighted than scared. "Oh shit," she laughs. "I think I just wet myself."

"On second thought." I allow Ava to bully me out of the kitchen into the garden, where we find each one of our parents twisted into all kinds of mind-bending positions. I'm laughing again, harder when they all collapse in unison, creating a pile of puffing grandparents on the lawn.

"I'm too old for this." My dad creaks his way up to his feet before helping Mum up, too.

I clap my hands together, marching my way across the lawn to the enticing spotty game board. "Move aside, folks." I crack my knuckles and give the twins a mischievous grin. "The champion's here to defend his title."

"Here we go," Jacob sighs, booting his football away.

"I've had enough," Maddie declares.

"It's my birthday." I crouch and pull at the corners of the mat, clearing the plastic of wrinkles before kicking off my shoes. "You have to do what I say." I flip up the collar of my Ralph Lauren polo shirt. "Playing, Mrs. Ward?"

"Losing, Mr. Ward?"

I snort my thoughts on that. "I always win, baby. You should know that by now."

Ava pulls her hair up in a ponytail, pouting her lips. "Things could be about to change."

Another snort of laughter erupts from deep in my belly, backed up by the chuckles of our guests. Glad they think her statement is as hilarious as I do. "I'm blue," I announce as everyone backs up, giving us space. "Ava is red, Jacob is green, and Maddie is yellow. Who goes first?"

"The youngest goes first," Jacob pipes up. "Which is me."

"Only by two minutes!" Maddie protests.

I hold my hand up, halting the impending row. "Two minutes or two years, Jacob is the youngest."

"Jacob first." Ava moves in closer, her eyes narrowing to challenging slits. "Maddie's second, me third, and you, my dear husband, at a whooping fifty, will go last."

"Don't think you can distract me by taunting me," I warn, gesturing for Jacob to get on with things.

I focus on the game and, more importantly, winning it. John, Sam, and Kate join the small crowd with Drew's daughter, Georgia, and we all take our first move. It's all pretty straightforward, everyone stable, and everyone confident.

Ten minutes later, me, my wife, and our babies are a tatty tangle of arms and legs, and our audience is laughing. "Dad!" Maddie gripes. "Your big leg is in my way!"

"Good!" I laugh, not losing a scrap of focus.

"This way, Maddie." Sam crouches beside my girl, showing her the way to the spinner.

"No helping," I yell, turning my face and getting a mouthful of Ava's hair. I catch her eye and forget my grievance. I also forget my concentration, her boobs within licking distance.

"Don't even think about it, Ward," she whispers.

"Whenever, wherever, baby."

"Not while playing Twister with our kids in front of your parents."

My arms shake a little from the strain of holding myself up. It doesn't help that both Jacob and Maddie are leaning on me in one place or another, and Ava is virtually suspended over my torso. They're all being tactical, picking on me, but I won't break. No way. "You're doing this on purpose," I accuse. I close my eyes and focus, hearing clapping and encouragement from everyone, meaning Maddie just made her move and she's still in the game.

"Your go, Mum," the twins chant.

"Oh, if I can just stretch to reach the spinner." Ava's body pushes harder into mine.

Focus, focus, focus. Something soft and squishy presses against my mouth. Something I recognize. I open my eyes and come face-to-face with boobs. I can't help it. My mouth opens and I take a bite.

"Owww! Jesse!" She collapses on me, taking out the kids, too. "You big fat cheat!"

I laugh, rolling over and trapping Ava beneath me.

She huffs and puffs for effect for a few moments, making a pathetic effort to try to bat me away. The kids are muttering their disgust, our parents are tutting, and Kate and Sam are laughing with Georgia and John. But it's the woman I'm spread all over that has my attention. "You lose," I whisper, planting a light peck on her nose.

Her grin is instant, and so is the swelling of my heart. "No, I win." She grabs my hair and hauls me down to her lips, and I roll her off the mat onto the grass.

"We're having sleepy sex tonight," I tell her.

"Oh God!" Maddie squawks. "Mum! Dad! Please!"

We both laugh past each other's lips, but we don't ease up. Not now. Not ever.

Chapter 4

It's late. The kids are in bed, our guests have left, and I can hear Ava faffing in the kitchen. I wander through, stopping at the door to admire her for a few moments. She's getting the coffee machine loaded ready to flick on in the morning, something she does before bed most nights, as well as setting the kids' favorite breakfast cereals on the island. I wait until she's done and is rubbing cream into her hands before I quietly creep up behind her. I'm virtually silent, but she doesn't need to hear me to know I'm close. Her spine straightens, her hands pausing in their movements.

I push my front to her back and drop my mouth to her ear. "Get in the bedroom now," I order, quiet but stern.

She turns slowly, rubbing against me, the friction sending my body temperature through the roof. I scoop her up and cradle her in my arms, taking her mouth as I walk us to our room. She hums against my lips. I hum against hers. Fucking heaven.

Our lips don't part the entire way to the bedroom, and it's a challenge to give up our kiss when I make it to the bed. Dropping her down, I pull my T-shirt up over my head and throw it aside. Ava's teeth sink into her bottom lip, her gaze hungry.

"Like what you see?" I ask, confident of the answer. Call me an egomaniac. I couldn't give a fuck. I push my jeans down my thighs with my boxers, waiting for an answer. She's daydreaming. "Hey." I click my fingers, snapping her out of it. "Well?"

The tiniest of frowns mars her brow. "What did you say?"

I smile. Her question is a good enough answer for me. "I like your dress." I reach forward and tug at the silky black fabric, smiling when I hear her pull in a breath. "But it's a bit restrictive."

"Take it off," she demands, full of impatience. Her hunger for me only intensifies my hunger for her. But I still toy with her desperation. "What do you say?"

I see the need to fight me in her eyes, but my wife learned fast that giving me what I want gets her what she wants much quicker. "Please." Her plea is more than a plea. It's a fucking turn-on like no other. Her dress is gone in the space of a few short breaths. Her underwear even faster. Resting a fist on the mattress, I crawl up the length of her body, licking my way up her inside thigh, growling under my breath when I pass her sweet, soft, dripping pussy. Her groan stretches out forever, her spine arching, pushing her breasts upward. I circle her left nipple with a firm, slow lick. Fuck, she tastes good.

She sighs, her hands going to my head and wrestling with my hair. "You're a fucking god, Ward."

I bite down on her nipple in warning, but otherwise let her potty mouth pass, as I walk my fingers across her stomach and plunge them deep inside her core. "Oh, you're so fucking ready," I say as she cries out. I withdraw and settle myself atop of her, grabbing my aching cock and leveling it up. "Hard or soft, baby?"

"Soft," she sighs, all breathily and happily, her palms resting on my hips and pulling me down.

I sink in slowly, struggling to catch my breath as the pleasure ripples through me. "Like that?" I ask, hitting her deep.

"Just like that."

I withdraw, the feel of her walls stroking me forcing me to my forearms. "We are so fucking good together, lady."

"I know," she agrees, sinking her nails into my arse.

Her gaze finds mine, and I know that's exactly where it'll stay until I bring her to climax and she's forced to close her eyes. It's one of my favorite views. The passion and need on her face, her light pants heating my skin. It's debilitating.

This woman has me captivated every day of our lives together. Not just when I have her in my arms, or when I'm buried deep inside her. But with everything she does. Every time she looks at me, speaks to me, touches me. I'm the luckiest man alive, and I thank the Fates every minute of every day. I love her with a fierceness that gets stronger by the second.

"I love you, too," she whispers, reading my mind. "And I'm lucky, too." Her hands move from my arse and come up to my face, her thighs wrapping around my waist. She holds my face firmly as I maintain a careful, slow pace of my hips, rocking into her gently. "You are my life, Jesse Ward. You keep my heart beating."

I smile a small smile, nodding my understanding, keeping our eyes locked as I catch her lips. Our kiss mirrors the delicacy of our lovemaking until I slow it to nothing and our lips are simply touching. "And my heart will only ever beat for you," I whisper, balancing on the edge of explosion. "Are you there?"

"I'm there." Her face glowing up at me confirms it, and I thrust a fraction harder a few more times, carrying us over the edge together.

My body soaks up her trembles, the tremors going straight to my heart. It fills with feelings so strong I once again find myself trying to wrap my mind around the reality of our beautiful existence. I don't think I ever will.

We gasp into each other's faces, a million silent words of wonder bouncing back and forth between us. Neither of us needs to speak those words. We both know. I take her left hand from my cheek and kiss her wedding ring and then weave our fingers together, squeezing tightly and resting my face in her damp neck.

"Was it good for you?" I ask.

"Ish...," she sighs, and I smile against her throat, kissing lazily, small pecks here and there. "Tub-time?" she asks softly.

I hold still for a moment, thinking. Tub-time?

"I can hear those cogs kicking in." She laughs a little. She's right. Tub-time equals tub-*talk*. What does she want to talk about?

I pull my face from her throat and lift a questioning eyebrow. "Is there something you want to tell me?" My wife knows I'm at my weakest when she's naked, wet, and spread all over me.

"No, I just thought it would be nice to have a soak together."

Ava's wet nakedness slipping all over mine? I slip free from her tight warmth on a small hiss, my cock still twitching from the aftermath of my climax. "Bubbles?"

"Lots."

"Whatever my lady wants." I shoot up off the bed and head to the bathroom, flipping on the taps and pouring in a huge dose of bubble bath before swishing the water around. It seems to take fucking ages for the water to reach halfway up the side, and when I'm happy with the depth, I jump in, wafting the bubbles upward. "Ready!" I call.

Within a few seconds, I hear Ava laughing. "Where are you?"

I flap my hands, clearing some of the bubbles in front of my face, and grin when I find her standing by the door. "Your god awaits." I offer my hand, and she wanders over, still laughing, making a point of blowing some more bubbles from my nose as she lowers in front of me. I sigh a very fucking contented sigh as she settles between my thighs, my arms and lower legs wrapping her up tightly, my eyes closing in pure peace. The sensation of her palms stroking over the hairs on my legs is hypnotic. Utter fucking bliss.

It's silent for a few moments, gloriously silent and peaceful. Until Ava breaks it. "Jesse?"

"Hmmmm."

"About my boobs..."

My eyes flip open. I fucking knew it. Wants to soak with me in the bath? I scoff. "You mean the perfect boobs that your husband loves just the way they are? Those boobs?" I can't see her, but I know she'll have just pulled off an eye roll worthy of an award.

"Yes, those boobs."

"Forget it." I feel her shift under my hold. So I hold her tighter.

"Let me see you."

"No."

"Jesse." Water starts to splash around us until I'm forced to release her or risk flooding the bathroom.

"For fuck's sake," I breathe as she spins over, resting a palm on each of my pecs and bringing her front down to mine. The tips of our noses meet. I'm not going over this again. No way. Those boobs are fucking perfect. And, more to the point, they're mine. I nod my head to myself, determined to stand my ground, no matter how much she begs and no matter what she promises me. "No," I say firmly. "Not even for a million jars of Sun-Pat and *two* million Apology Fucks. No."

"But I hate them," she whines, pushing out her bottom lip. I reach down and sink my teeth into it. "Ouch!"

"The answer will always be no."

She wrenches herself free of my bite, hissing in pain as she does. Call me unreasonable, but it can't hurt as much as what she's suggesting. "Just listen."

My hands sacrifice her arse to cover my ears. "Definitely not."

"Jesse."

I close my eyes. "I'm not listening." I feel her lift from my body, obviously accepting that she's going to get nowhere. Good. I hope she's thinking about how unreasonable she's being. A boob job? I scoff to myself in my darkness. She's got more chance of me divorcing her.

When I've heard no sounds for a good few minutes, I assume she's given up and the coast is clear, so I gingerly open one eye to check I'm alone. I'm not. I'd snap my eyes closed again, but something in her hand just caught my eye. The shower hose? She's pulled it from the cubicle and has it pointed at me in the bath. I frown, suddenly noticing the water has drained from the tub. No! I try to get up quickly, slipping and sliding over the remaining bubbles coating the enamel of the bath. "Ava!" I'm hit with water. Freezing fucking cold shards of torture. "Fuck!" I lose my footing and crash to the bottom on the tub. "Ava, for fuck's sake!"

"Say you'll listen to me," she demands, moving in as far as the length of hose on the showerhead will allow, which is pretty fucking close.

My whole body goes into shock, leaving me at my evil wife's mercy. "Th-ree...," I chatter, wondering what I can do when I get to zero. I don't know, but it'll be bad. So fucking bad. "T-t-two..." I start to shake like a twat, unable to escape. Jesus, I feel like hypothermia is setting in. "Ava!"

"Will you listen?"

I can't even bring myself to get to zero. I'm too fucking cold. "Okay! For fuck's sake, okay!" The water shuts down in an instant, and I scramble from the bath and flop to my back on the floor, shivering. "Get me a towel, you evil witch." A soft bundle of cotton lands on my face, and I make quick work of scrubbing at my body. "Why would you do that?" I snap, incensed. "If my legs weren't frozen solid, you'd be getting the ultimate of all Retribution Fucks right now."

"I'll look forward to it," she snipes, putting the hose back in the shower. Then she wanders over to me, until she has one foot on either side of my chest. She lowers and plants her arse on my stomach, her hands on my pecs, and starts rubbing over my goose-bumped skin. "Let me warm you up."

"How kind." I need an oven, a quick ten minutes at 180 degrees. I'm cold to the bone.

"The surgeon said that a little—"

I choke on nothing. "You've seen a surgeon already?" Please, God, tell me it wasn't a man.

"You said you'd listen."

"And I fucking hate what I'm hearing, Ava." I push her off me and get to my feet, stomping away. "I can't even look at you." I head for the dressing room, where I rip down a clean T-shirt from a hanger. I don't know why; I always sleep naked, but I need something to do with my hands or I'm likely to strangle her beautiful neck. "If it was a bloke, don't tell me." I could throw up.

"Okay."

I swing around, outraged. "So it *was* a bloke you flashed my boobs to?"

She shrugs. "You just told me not to tell you."

"But you just bloody did! What the fuck, Ava?" I pull my T-shirt over my head and wrestle my arms through the sleeves, getting myself all caught up. "Fuck!"

"It's just a boob job."

I stop trying to get my T-shirt on, leaving me with my arms all bent and trapped somewhere around my neck area. Ava's fighting to hold back her smirk. "Just get a knife and kill me, because it'll hurt a lot fucking less than what you're suggesting." I realize my stupidity the moment the words have left my mouth. Ava's hint of a grin vanishes, and she recoils, her watery eyes dropping to my torso where two hefty scars mar my skin. I curse my idiotic arse to hell and back a thousand times over as I calmly untangle my arms and pull my T-shirt down my body, hiding my scars from my wife's sad eyes. "I'm sorry," I breathe, feeling nothing short of awful. Our story is epic, but I would rather it be missing that particular part.

"I would never hurt you," she says quietly, turning and walking away from me.

I ball my fist and slam it onto my forehead. "Baby, wait." I chase after her, grabbing her wrist and swinging her around. She doesn't fight me. She does the exact opposite, in fact. She launches herself at me and takes on her customary baby chimp hold of me, sinking her face deep into my neck. I couldn't feel any more terrible. "I'm sorry." I cling to her, feeling the wetness of her tears on my neck.

"I know it's been a long time." She hiccups over her words. "But just remembering how terrified I was when I thought I'd lost you makes me feel it all again. And I panic. Because look how in love I was with you back then. Look how much I needed you. Twelve years later, all of those feelings have multiplied by a million, and the thought of losing you cripples me, Jesse." She breathes in shakily.

I close my eyes and make sure I hold on to her that little bit tighter. "No one's going to take me away," I vow, meaning it with every fiber of my being.

"You talk like you're indestructible."

"I am. If I have you and the kids, nothing can touch me, Ava." I force her away and scan her face, wiping her cheeks of tears. We don't talk about the events of that day. Lauren is still locked up in a padded cell somewhere under constant assessment, and there's a restraining order in place in case that ever changes. Which, I'm advised, won't. Premeditated attempted murder, carefully plotted and very nearly carefully executed. No one will be seeing her for a very long time. "Don't cry, baby. I'm afraid you're stuck with me."

Reaching for my hair, she tugs on a huff mixed with a little chuckle. “That’s not funny.”

“Shut up and kiss me, woman.”

She’s on me like a lion, all parts of our horrid past pushed away, leaving room for only the good memories. The amazing memories. Memories that we build on every day of our beautiful existence together. Just us and our babies.

Chapter 5

As I dip and weave through the traffic on Park Lane the following week, the roof of my DB9 Volante down, the wind rushing past, I dial Drew to pass the time on my way to the health club. Just passing the time.

"Afternoon!" I greet, all chipper when he answers.

"Yes, what do you want?"

"That's no way to greet a friend." I grin to myself as I sail through an amber light and switch lanes, ignoring the honking of some knob in a Bentley.

"What do you want?" he repeats, sounding utterly bored by the conversation that hasn't even got off the ground yet. I'm about to remedy that.

"Just wondering how you're feeling now you're claimed for life."

"I was claimed for life before I put a ring on her finger."

I smile, all warm and fuzzy on the inside for my mate. We'd honestly lost all hope for the kinky fucker by the time Raya came into his life. "Congratulations, mate. I'm happy for you. So when's the big day?"

"A couple of months. Exact date to be confirmed."

"Shit, you're not messing around, are you?"

"Did you just say that?" He laughs, truly amused. "You had Ava down the aisle within weeks of *meeting* her."

I smile as I zip into my designated parking space outside the club and hop out, grabbing my sports bag from the boot. "Go big or go home. I've just got to the club. I'll catch you later." Hanging up, I jog into reception, looking around for John. "Hey, Gaby," I call to one of the girls who works the reception area. "You seen the big man?"

A neon-pink, clawlike talon points up the stairs to the gym floor. "Trying out the new weight machines."

I take the stairs two at a time, emerging into the open-plan gym at the top. It's quiet now, the mums all departed to go collect their kids from school. Another hour and it'll be crammed again after everyone has knocked off work. I spot John across the way and put my hand up when he nods to me as he loads weights onto the end of a bar. I hope I'm still lifting when I'm his age. He makes time every day in between helping us run this place so he can keep that huge body huge. He flicks his head, telling me he'll meet me in the office, so I make my way there.

I walk in and find Cherry at Ava's desk. Her head flicks up. "Jesse." She's up from her chair and quickly straightening out her skirt. "Ava asked me to check some invoices before she left to go get Maddie and Jacob. But if there's anything you need . . . ?"

I throw my bag on the couch. "I'm good."

"Tea? Coffee? Water?" She comes around the desk, smiling brightly. "Anything?"

I falter in my steps toward the filing cabinet, looking back with a curious brow. Was there suggestion in her words just then? "I'm good," I repeat, detecting a definite twinkle in her blue eyes.

"Well, if you think of something . . ." Her teeth sink into her bottom lip.

Is she coming on to me? She must be twenty years younger than me, and though it's a painful thought, I can't deny the small part of my ego that thrives on that. Yep. Still got it. But this woman needs to be told that I only have *it* for my wife.

"Cherry." I turn back toward her and make my way over, seeing her lip slip through her bite, her stance more confident. This needs nipping in the bud pretty damn quickly before Cherry is faced with the wrath of Ava. I shudder, but smile on the inside, too. I'm not the only possessive one in our relationship. "Perhaps we ought to—"

I'm cut dead when John strides in, his phone to his ear, talking to whoever is on the other end. "The part is missing and I want it here by morning." He hangs up and looks between me and Cherry. "All right?"

"Yeah, Cherry was just leaving."

She's off across the office fast, quickly closing the door behind her. "What was that about?" John takes a seat opposite Ava's desk, while I drop into her chair.

"I think Cherry has a crush."

John's low rumbling laugh grates on me. "God help her if Ava finds out. I'll have a word."

"Please do." I wake up Ava's screen and tap in her password, smiling as I do. THELORD3210. "Anything to report?" I ask, scanning my e-mails. John doesn't answer, and I lift my head, catching his straight face. I don't like that face. That's his ultra-serious face. "What's up?" I ask, wary.

"Sarah's back in town." That's it. That's all he says, sitting back in his chair quietly while I try to process what just came out of his mouth.

I'm still. And suddenly very hot, though I can't figure out whether it's from fear or anger. Oh, fuck. Shit is going to fly when Ava finds out. I haven't seen Sarah for years, and I have no desire to now. Memories are flooding forward, too many, too fast. I can't do this again. Uncle Carmichael, Rosie, Rebecca, the car accident.

There isn't a day goes by that I don't stop what I'm doing at some point and think about them all. But Sarah? I *never* think about her or what she tried to do to me and Ava. And I'm not about to now. My life is too perfect.

"Why?" is all I manage.

John's huge shoulders jump up on a shrug. "Things didn't work out for her in the States."

It didn't work out? I don't trust her. I gave her money. I gave her my blessing. But the one thing I couldn't give her was my love. I rake a hand through my hair, feeling so fucking stressed. "Tell her to stay away from me and my family."

"Already done. But this is Sarah, Jesse. I can't watch her every motherfucking second of the day."

I frown. "Where is she?"

John doesn't hold back his answer, pulling off his wraparounds so I can appreciate how serious he is. "Staying with me."

I balk at him, but his steely expression doesn't waver, his face poker straight. "Why the fuck would you do that?"

"She's broke, Jesse. And broken, too. What did you want me to do? Shut my door in her face?"

"Yes." I stand, my temper getting the better of me. "Fucking hell, John. Have you forgotten what she did to me and Ava?"

He's up out of his chair like lightning, his big body looming forward. "Shut the fuck up, you stupid motherfucker." He slams his fist into the wood. "You and Ava are exactly why she's staying at mine." I frown and he goes on. "I told her she can stay a few weeks until she gets herself back on her feet, but *only* if she stays out of your way."

I shrink a little. It's not something many people can make me do. Only two people, in fact. My wife, and this man right here. The man who has been by my side for over thirty years. My uncle's best friend, and now my best friend.

I feel a pang of guilt—not toward Sarah, but toward my oldest friend. He didn't ask for this. For all the decades this amazing man has been in my life, his loyalty has never once wavered. He's been a rock, looked out for me. I honestly don't know where I would be today without him. And here he is still doing right by me. "John—"

"Shut up." He gets up, slipping his wraparounds back on. "I'm taking care of it. I just didn't want to keep it from you."

"Thanks, big man."

"No need." He strides out of the office, and I try to breathe in some calm. I can't leave Ava in the dark over this. I grab my phone to call her, but an incoming call flashes up before I can dial. I frown down at the kids' school number, answering quickly. "Hello?"

"Mr. Ward, it's Mrs. Chilton, Maddie and Jacob's teacher."

My heartbeat naturally quickens as it always does when an unexpected call comes in from the school. I instantly think the worst—one of them has hurt themselves or maybe isn't feeling well. "Is everything okay? The kids?"

"Yes, yes, they're fine."

My lungs drain with relief, my head falling back on the chair. "Then why the call?"

"I'm sure it's nothing to worry about," she begins, obviously making me worry. All sorts of things start flying around in my head, starting with that dirty little pervert who's sweet on my girl.

"I'll decide that," I reply curtly.

"You see, your wife hasn't shown up to pick up the children from school. We've tried calling Mrs. Ward's mobile, but it's gone to voicemail each time. We've left a message."

"She's never late to collect the kids." I glance at my watch to see it's three forty-five, a good half hour since school finished.

"I know, Mr. Ward. Like I said, I'm sure she's simply got caught in traffic, and maybe her phone has died."

"I'm on my way." I hang up and race out the office, nearly

taking a startled Cherry from her feet on my way. "When did Ava leave?" I ask urgently over my shoulder as I sprint past her.

"Two thirty. The usual time." I fight my heart down from my throat, immediately dialing Ava as I run full pelt out of the health club. I land in the seat of my car heavily, and just like I dreaded, Ava's phone goes to voicemail. "Fuck!" I start my car and speed out of the car park, heading for the main road. Right or wrong, I skip the red light. I'm a thirty-minute drive from the school, twenty if I break the speed limit.

I try Ava's phone again, but once again get her voicemail, and my worry deepens with every minute that passes and I can't get hold of her. "Where are you, beautiful?" I hear Ava in my head telling me that I'm neurotic. Maybe I am. But nothing will ease my panic until I see with my own eyes that she's okay.

I join the road that'll take me to the kids' school, being able to pick up speed now the traffic is moving more freely. I try to pull up the app on my phone that tracks all our cars, but the damn thing won't load. "Fuck!" I dial Ava again, mentally demanding she answers. "Come on, come on."

"Hello?"

Relief. So much fucking relief. But the relief of actually getting an answer dies the second my brain registers that whoever has answered isn't Ava. "Who's this?"

"Who's this?"

"I'm the husband of the woman whose phone you have," I state curtly, my patience now completely evaporated.

"I apologize. The caller ID stated 'the Lord.'"

"Nickname," I mutter, slowly concluding that my silly wife has lost her phone and this lady has found it.

"Mr. Ward, is it? Your wife is Ava Ward?"

"How do you know my wife's name?" She has her phone, not her life story.

"Her driver's license."

It all becomes clear. "She's lost her bag." I sigh, more relief washing over me, yet my foot doesn't ease up on the accelerator.

"I'm afraid not, sir. My name is PC Barnes." She pauses for a few long seconds, giving me a moment to let that information settle. "Mr. Ward." Her voice has noticeably softened. Dread fills me. My heart speeds up. "I'm on the scene of a road traffic accident, and I believe your wife is one of the casualties."

My tongue thickens in my mouth. "What?"

"Sir..." Her words blend and warp, fading into nothing as I stare ahead at the road. An accident. Casualties. My wife. I see blue lights flashing in my mind's eye, bright and frightening, making me blink to clear them. But they don't fade and it takes me a second to figure out why. They're not in my mind's eye. They're in the distance.

Everything's a blur. Noise, movement, my heartbeat.

I hear the sirens.

I hear my car screeching to a stop.

I hear my car door slamming behind me as I eject myself from my seat.

I hear my feet pounding the road as I sprint toward the carnage up ahead, seeing Ava's mangled Mini upended on the opposite side of the road.

"Oh my God." I choke. Every window is shattered; the two front tires are missing, ripped from the body of the car. Skid marks zigzag the tarmac of the road before abruptly ending.

The world starts spinning, my breathing slowing. Crowds of people are blocking my path, and I fight my way through, shoving them to the side as I try to make it to the center of the madness. "Please, no," I wheeze, staggering mindlessly through the throngs of spectators. "Please, God, no."

A rough, broken sob rips through my body when I catch sight

of the gurney, and my legs buckle, bringing me to my knees. "No!" Straps circle her body, a breathing mask over her face. Blood is everywhere. She looks utterly broken, so fragile and damaged. My heart shreds in my chest. "God, no." The closer I get to her, the more damage I see.

"Sir, move aside!" a paramedic yells, wheeling Ava toward an ambulance.

"I'm her husband," I tell him, scanning her body, trying to comprehend the amount of blood soaking her. Her head is the worst, her long dark hair drenched in red. "Is she going to be okay?" It's all I can think to ask, and it's instinctual, because I don't know if anyone could be okay with this much blood loss. And when I get no answer from any of the rushing paramedics, it becomes clear that they agree with me. A lump in my throat expands as I jog alongside the gurney, tears brimming in my eyes. Her beautiful face is drained of color underneath the blood coating nearly every inch of her skin. "Hold on, baby," I demand softly. "Don't you dare leave me."

"Mr. Ward?"

I look across the bed, seeing a female police officer holding Ava's bag.

"PC Barnes. We spoke."

I nod, casting my eyes back to the ambulance where Ava is being hooked up to all kinds of machinery. "She didn't show up to pick up the kids from school," I whisper in a daze of ruin.

"Mr. Ward, come with me. We'll follow the ambulance."

"No, I'm going with Ava." I shake my head, harshly wiping away the tears.

"Mr. Ward." PC Barnes steps forward, her face soaked in sympathy that I just can't handle. It's wasted, because Ava's going to be okay. Damn it, she's going to be okay! I look away from the police officer, seeing urgent hands working on her lifeless body. "Your wife is in critical condition, Mr. Ward. You need to give the paramedics space to do their thing. I'll get you to the hospital just as fast."

I close my eyes, praying for some stability in my breaking world. This isn't the time to be throwing my weight around, though I'm desperate to go on a rampage until someone tells me she's going to be okay. She *has* to be okay. I can't exist without her. The thought alone punches a hole through my chest, and I'm forced to bend and brace my hands on my knees to breathe through the bolts of pain attacking me.

"Mr. Ward?"

I swallow and nod as I stare at the ground, my stomach turning. I could throw up. "Okay." I breathe, trying to focus on getting air into my lungs. But in my current state, I'm not capable of focusing on anything but my prayers.

"This way." PC Barnes rests her hand on my forearm, gently coaxing me from my daze. But it's the slam of the ambulance doors that brings me back to the circus surrounding me. I walk with purpose toward the police car, looking back at the mangled mess of metal that was Ava's Mini. "I'll have a colleague bring your car to the hospital. Do you have the keys?"

I mindlessly tap my pockets down in search of them. "They're in the car," I mutter.

"And you mentioned your children, Mr. Ward. Would you like me to have someone collect them?" She opens the passenger door for me, and I fall into the seat.

"The twins," I say to the windscreen. "I said I was on my way. They'll be wondering where I am." I start to root through my pocket for my phone. "Ava's friend. I'll call Ava's friend."

I dial Kate without thinking, so when she answers, I'm totally unprepared for what to say and my throat closes up on me, leaving Kate calling my name repeatedly in prompt. What do I say? Where do I start?

"Jesse, are you there?" she asks, now full-blown worried. "Hello? Jesse?"

PC Barnes gets into the car beside me and looks across at me, where I'm static, my phone hanging limply in my hand.

I cough, clearing my throat, but no matter how hard I try to speak, nothing comes. I can't talk. Can't speak the words. Can't tell Kate that her friend looks like she's at death's door. The blood. So much blood. "It's Ava..." My words fade, my eyes clouding over again. "I..."

PC Barnes takes my phone and switches on her sympathetic, professional tone, speaking calmly as she explains to Kate without too much detail that Ava has been involved in an accident and the twins need to be picked up from school. I hear Kate's gasp. I hear her agree without question or prying into details of Ava's condition. She knows.

"Ask her to call Ava's parents," I mumble. "And tell her to tell the twins that Mum's okay." I look across at the ambulance when the sirens come to life and invade my ears. "She's going to be okay."

After following my request, PC Barnes hangs up and starts the car, pulling out quickly and tailing the ambulance. I just stare at the back doors the whole way. It's the longest journey of my life.

Chapter 6

Touch and go.

The words whirl around in my head as I pace the corridor, desperate to be with Ava. If not for John holding me back, I would have burst through the doors into the operating room just to threaten the doctors with their life if they don't save her. Her parents have remained quiet and in shock, sitting on the hard plastic chairs in the corridor, Joseph comforting his wife each time the tears creep up on her and she falls apart. With each second that passes with no news, the ache in my heart intensifies. Such a deep ache.

I stop pacing and fall back against a wall, looking up to the tubular lighting of the corridor. She's been in there for hours. How much longer will they be? What are they doing that's taking so much time?

A hand lands on my shoulder, and Joseph offers a weak smile. "Kate's just texted. The twins are fine. She and Sam have been vague with them until we know what's going on. Kate said she'd keep them overnight and take them to school in the morning. I think it's best to try and keep things as normal as possible for now."

I nod, a barrage of guilt grabbing me. My thoughts have been so consumed with worry for Ava, I've hardly thought about the kids. What they must be thinking. How they must be feeling.

"Thanks, Joseph."

"Are you going to call them?"

Call them? Speak to them? I can't trust my voice to remain strong, and if I did, what would I say? "I'll text them."

He nods, understanding. "Elizabeth and I are going to get some fresh air and drinks. Do you want some water?"

"I'm fine."

"Get him some water." John intervenes, and I don't argue. I don't have the strength.

After Ava's parents have left us, John drags me over to a chair and forces me down to the seat. I land with a thud and feel immediately restless again. I need someone to come and tell me what the fuck is going on.

"She'll be all right." John's usually booming voice is soft and reassuring, though I take no reassurance from it. He didn't see the blood, her pale face, the wreck that was her car.

I drop my elbows to my knees and bury my face in my palms. "She has to be, John. Because if I don't have Ava, then I may as well be dead, too."

"Stop that, you stupid motherfucker." He physically shakes me by the shoulders. "You need to be strong. For the kids and Ava. Are you listening to me?" His voice gets louder until it's back to its usual penetrating rumble.

I nod. It's pathetic. But before I can respond, the doors to the operating room swing open and I'm up out of my seat like lightning.

"Doctor." My heart starts racing, my stomach doing somersaults.

"Mr. Ward, I'm Dr. Peters." His expression is solemn. "Please, take a seat." He points to the chair I've just vacated.

"No," I refuse point-blank. "I don't need to sit down." I hold my breath, begging to God that I really don't *need* to sit down. That what he's about to tell me won't rip my world apart, and therefore rip *me* apart.

The doctor relents easily, and John gets up, coming to stand close beside me. He's preparing. He's preparing to catch me when I collapse in devastation. "Mr. Ward, Ava has had a rather nasty blow to the head that has caused severe swelling on her brain."

I stare at the doctor's mouth moving, his words coming slowly and clearly, each one stabbing into my flesh.

"A nasty cut to her leg severed one of her main arteries, too. Between that and her head injury, she's lost nearly eighty percent of her blood volume, so we're working hard to replace it in a series of transfusions over the next twenty-four hours. Right now, she's stable but in critical condition. We'll do another CT scan in the morning to see if there is any improvement, but the extent of the damage will only be determined..." He fades off, clearing his throat. "When she comes around," he finishes meekly, and I just know he held back from adding *if*. *If* she comes around. My dark world becomes darker, my aching heart clenching painfully. "The rest of her injuries are pretty superficial. The odd laceration here and there, and X-rays have confirmed no broken bones. It seems her head took the worst."

My mind struggles to absorb the influx of information. "Damage," I whisper. "You said *damage*. You mean brain damage?"

"I can't rule it out, Mr. Ward. Ava is being transferred to the ICU." Just as he tells me that, the doors open again and two porters, along with a nurse, push a huge hospital bed into the corridor.

I cough on nothing, a low sob forcing me to cover my mouth.

"Motherfucker," John breathes in, shocked, his arm coming up around my shoulders to hold me upright. "She's going to be all right," he says again, but this time I can tell he doesn't really believe it. How could he? I can barely see her past all the tubes, wires, and machinery. But what I can see makes my heart slow to the point I think it might stop. My beautiful girl is grey, the blood loss obvious. My strong, feisty wife looks weak. So small and frail. She looks as broken as I feel. I have the fight of my life on my hands.

And I'm feeling like I'm on the cusp of the greatest loss I could ever face.

CHAPTER 7

A nasty blow to her head.

Swelling on her brain.

A coma.

Brain damage.

Blood transfusions.

Critical.

Each word is a stab in the chest. I've barely moved an inch from this chair. I've drifted in and out of sleep, and my hand has been in hers from the moment they allowed me into her room. It's like a fishbowl, two walls made up of windows, allowing everyone in ICU visual access to my wife. While her skin has taken on more color after the endless transfusions, she's still not awake. There are wires everywhere, machines surrounding her. There's barely enough room for me beside her bed. The CT scan yesterday evening revealed no improvement, just like yesterday morning's scan. No reduction of swelling, and though I'm trying to be hopeful, I know it's unlikely this morning's scan will show any signs of improvement, either.

It's been two days. I need to see my babies. I have to reassure them that Mummy's going to be okay, that she'll wake up soon and we'll all go home together. Even if I have no idea whether it's true. The sting at the back of my eyes forces me to close them before any more tears can escape. I've stalled letting them come here, hoping and praying that the doctors will give me news so I won't have to lie to my children. But the news I've hoped for hasn't come, and I can't stall any longer.

It's time to face my responsibilities and give my kids what they need.

Me. Their dad.

I'm just so fucking crushed that I can't give them their mum, too.

When my phone alerts me of a text from Elizabeth, I force myself to drop Ava's hand and get up out of the chair. My muscles scream their protest, my bones cracking. After dropping a soft kiss on Ava's forehead, I walk down the corridor to the café where I've arranged to meet her parents with the kids. I hear both of the twins before I see them. Two voices calling for me. I come to a stop, seeing their faces for the first time in too long. It takes everything in me not to drop to my knees. I'm fucking broken, but I can't let them see that.

Maddie and Jacob crash into me and throw their arms around my torso, cuddling me fiercely, each of their faces buried in my chest. The feel of them against me offers a mild comfort. For the most part, my dread has tripled, because now they're here. Now I have to be a man and comfort my babies once I've delivered the blow that I know will shatter their worlds.

"Where's Mum?" Jacob asks into my chest. "Nan says she's sick. Too sick to see us."

I close my eyes, clenching them tightly. "She's going to be okay." I grate the words, not just for the twins, but for me, too. "Trust your daddy. She is going to be okay."

"I want to see her." Maddie breaks away from me, her face blotchy from tears. "Please, Daddy."

This suddenly doesn't feel like a good idea. Ava doesn't look like herself. She doesn't look like their mum. I crouch down in front of her, taking my little girl's hand. "Darling, I don't think...she's..." I clear my throat, pulling myself together to get the words out even and strong. "Mum's not herself. She lost a lot of blood, so she's very pale. Very weak."

Maddie's chin trembles, and I look to Elizabeth, shaking my head. I can't let them see her like that. Look what it's done to me. I'm barely holding myself together.

"You can't stop us," Jacob yells, stepping back. "She's our mum."

My exhausted body lets me down, and before I can stop him, Jacob takes off down the corridor, Maddie quick on his heels. I drag myself up, watching as my boy slows to let his sister catch up before taking her hand and leading her on. The fact that they don't know exactly where Ava's room is won't faze my babies. Like their father, they are determined. They have a sixth sense when it comes to Ava, too. They'll sniff her out in no time at all.

I slowly follow, rounding the corner to find them standing at the glass window, staring into Ava's room, holding each other's hands. I study them silently, each of their faces a picture of pure shock. Then Maddie breaks down and Jacob turns into her, grabbing his sister and hugging her. The sight could bring me to my knees, and I once again have to find strength from somewhere to remain upright. It's in this moment that I realize my babies aren't really babies anymore. My eleven-year-old son is holding his own emotions in check so he can comfort his sister. My eyes well, and I quickly and roughly brush at them to clear my vision.

Elizabeth approaches, looking up at me with tightly pressed lips. I shake my head mildly, showing her the despair I'm fighting to hide from my children, and make my way over to them. My arms circle their shoulders, and I hold them tightly, absorbing the jerking of Maddie's body. I kiss the tops of their heads one after the other, over and over. "She'll be okay." I only just hold myself back from tagging *I promise* on the end, and it kills me to accept that my unwillingness to make that vow is because I never want to break a promise I make to my children. "Are you two listening to your dad? She will be okay." Those words, they're stupid but unstoppable. They are as good as a promise to my kids. Because Dad said so.

"Mr. Ward?"

I look up over the twins' heads. "Dr. Peters." With my kids still held securely in my arms, I cock my head, silently asking him if we need to be alone.

"It's good news, Mr. Ward."

Good news? I look through the window to Ava's seemingly lifeless body on the bed. She looks exactly the same as she has since coming out of surgery. Nonresponsive. No improvement. Good news?

"The scan we did this morning has shown the swelling has subsided considerably over the past twelve hours."

My head swings back toward him, the kids breaking away from me. He says it's good news, so why does he still look so serious? "And?" I question.

"It's still early days, and the extent of the damage won't be clear until she comes around. But it's a step in the right direction."

I know I should feel relieved, but the word *damage* is a constant in my mind, like they're priming me for something. "Thank you, Doctor." I end the conversation there, refraining from asking the questions I need to. Not in front of the kids. I look to Elizabeth, who moves toward us before I ask.

"I'll take them in," she says, gesturing the kids toward the entrance of Ava's room.

"They should talk to her," the doctor suggests. "Quietly, but they should talk to her."

Elizabeth takes the children into the room, leaving me alone with the doctor. "Damage," I say, returning my attention to him. "Tell me honestly, what's the probability?"

"It's impossible to say until she's awake. While she's in a coma, her brain is resting, giving it the best chance to heal."

I don't want to ask, and I won't. She *will* wake up. Of course she will wake up. "So what are you doing in the meantime?" I ask, unable to keep the curtness from my tone. It's all a load of ifs and buts. That's all I'm getting.

Through my fog of growing fury, I notice the doctor looking a little wary all of a sudden, backing up, and I realize I'm glaring at him, my jaw ticking, my body moving forward.

"Mr. Ward, we're doing all we can."

"And what if it's not enough?" Just as I utter the words, I hear the shrill shriek of Ava's mother, and I'm flying into the room like a bull, the doctor hot on my heels. I don't know whether to be elated or terrified by what I find. Ava is squirming around on the bed, sobbing and distressed.

"Mum!" Maddie cries, getting tugged back from the bed by an alarmed-looking Jacob. "Dad, what's wrong with her?"

I hadn't noticed the doctor passing me at the end of the bed, but he's now by Ava's bedside, pressing buttons, shifting machinery, hands working frantically around my girl. "Ava," he says urgently. "Ava, can you hear me?" He looks across to me, then nods to the children.

I understand his silent order, but I'm damned if I can move to follow it. My heart is going crazy in my chest, my legs full of lead. She looks like she's having the worst kind of nightmare. Or a seizure. Is it a seizure?

"Mr. Ward!"

The sharp snap of my name shocks me to life, and I grab my kids' hands, pulling them out of the room with me. I can't see Ava like this knowing there's fuck all I can do about it. I feel more helpless now than when she was unconscious.

I look back through the glass in a state of total shock.

"We should get coffee," Elizabeth suggests in an attempt to keep me busy while the doctors work on Ava.

I look down at each of my children in turn, Maddie first, her face tear-stained and red, and then Jacob. He's looking up at me, squeezing my big hand in his small one. They realign me, bring me back to where I should be. I stand taller and swallow down my shock. "Yes, let's get something to drink while the doctors do what they need to."

"Well, what are they doing?" Maddie looks back to Ava's room, and I quickly pull her back around, giving her a warning look. "Helping Mum." It takes everything in me not to look back myself. What I've already seen will haunt me forever.

* * *

After I force the kids to have some water and a sandwich, we go back to the ward in silence, my mind caught between dread and hope. I have no idea what I should be bracing myself for, what I should expect. And that scares me to death. The unknown. The lack of control.

When we arrive at Ava's room, the doctor is outside making notes. He looks up and smiles mildly, and the hope takes over the dread. "She's settled," he says. "Her eyes are open, she is perfectly aware of her surroundings, and she told me her name and date of birth."

"Oh, thank God." Elizabeth grabs my arm and squeezes, while I have to close my eyes to stop the tears of relief escaping.

Once I'm sure they're under control, I look down at my smiling babies. "What did I tell you?" I ask them seriously. "Always listen to your dad, you got that?" They both nod, cuddling into my chest as I mentally yell at myself for ever doubting it. I knew she wouldn't leave me. I knew she'd fight for me and the kids.

"She's just having some water and getting a few tubes removed," the doctor says. "We can go back in once the nurse has taken her vitals. I just need to run a few more tests, but you're welcome to join me in the room."

"Thank you," I breathe, squeezing the kids into me. "Thank you so much."

"You're welcome, Mr. Ward." He looks to the door when it opens and a nurse exits. "Shall we?"

I take a deep breath, suddenly a bit apprehensive. I haven't looked into my wife's eyes for nearly two days, and the thought of doing it now is making me a pathetic, nervous fool. What's wrong with me?

The nurse looks to Elizabeth as she passes us and smiles. "She's asking for her mum."

Elizabeth's hand goes to her chest on a mild whimper as she takes the lead, rushing to her daughter's bedside. A small part of me is happy for her. For the most part, I'm hurt that she hasn't asked for *me*, her husband, but I quickly put the silly slight aside and follow Elizabeth in with the children. I find my mother-in-law hunched over Ava on the bed, trying to hug her as best she can around the wires and tubes. I can hear the quiet sobs, and when I hear Ava's voice, I smile, not just because she sounds like my wife, if a little rough in the throat, but because she sounds totally with it.

"My head hurts," she complains.

"Oh, darling. Of course it hurts." Elizabeth's light laugh as she speaks is loaded with joy. "Look who's here." She moves away from Ava, opening up a direct path to me and the twins.

I move forward, desperate to look into those eyes, to touch her and feel her respond, even if it's just a light squeeze of my hand.

I've missed her so much. But when our eyes connect, Ava frowns, flicking her gaze to the children and then back to me. I stop, watching carefully as she seems to assess us. Where's the sparkle in those eyes I love so much? Where's the love? My heart slows to a faint thud in my chest, my joy fading with it. Something isn't right.

"Ava, do you know who this is?" the doctor asks warily.

My head swings toward him in horror. "Of course she does," I blurt. What is he suggesting?

The doctor ignores me and moves closer to Ava, whose eyes are still passing continuously between me and the kids. Still no sparkle. Still no love. "Ava, tell me your full name."

She doesn't hesitate. "Ava O'Shea."

I recoil, not quite sure what to make of this.

The doctor flicks a glance toward me. I don't know what to make of his look, either. "Ava, do you know who this man is?"

"What?" I blurt, my horror growing.

That horror reaches unspeakable heights when my wife slowly starts to shake her head. "No."

I gasp, suddenly struggling for breath. No?

"Oh my goodness," Elizabeth breathes, coming straight to me and claiming the children. "Come on, darlings. Let's go find your pap." She steers them out of the room, both of them looking back at me with confusion all over their faces.

And I just stand there, useless, staring into the eyes of the woman who rules my heart, trying to comprehend what's unfolding. "Ava." I barely get her name out, my mind frantically searching for words.

"Can you tell me how you crashed your car?" the doctor pushes on.

She shakes her head on a frown, reaching up to rub her forehead. But her eyes never leave mine. They're holding me frozen where I stand, taking me in.

"And this man isn't familiar to you?" Dr. Peters asks, making notes while he talks.

I hold my breath, begging she puts this right, praying that I didn't hear her correctly, that she's just confused. Of course she remembers me. I'm her husband. I'm the man who would lay down his life for her. She has to remember me!

She studies me for a few moments, looking me up and down, as if trying hard to place me. My heart cracks. "I don't recognize him." She looks down at the sheets, and the inevitable tears start to pinch the back of my stunned eyes.

"Do you have any children, Ava?"

"No." She almost laughs, quickly looking up at me again.

My world shatters into a million shards of devastation, and I stagger toward a nearby chair, sitting down before I fall. Her gaze follows me the entire way.

"You don't remember me?" I whisper the words.

"Should I?" she asks, her laughter gone and clear worry in her tone.

Her reply slays me. It turns my stomach and rips my broken heart from my chest. I want to scream at her, tell her that *yes*, yes, she should remember me. Everything we've been through. Everything we've done together. How much we love each other.

"Ava, this is your husband." The doctor points toward me where I'm slumped in the chair. "Jesse."

"But I'm not married," she argues, seeming to be getting frustrated. Frustrated? She's frustrated? I hate myself with a vengeance for concluding that she has no fucking idea. I positively *hate* myself. She doesn't remember me? Her husband. Her Lord.

I can't take this. I'm going to throw up. I dash out of the room and sprint down the corridor, thrusting the door to the men's open with force and falling into a cubicle. I haven't eaten for days, but that doesn't seem to be a problem for my stomach. I retch and cough over the toilet.

She's forgotten me. Forgotten our kids. What is this madness?

My body starts to ache with the force of my retching, and when I finally accept that there's nothing to bring up, I push myself up with too much effort and move to the sink to splash my face. I stare at myself in the mirror. I don't even recognize myself right now. I'm pasty, my eyes are sunken, and I look drained. I *am* drained. I was before Ava came around, and the small, momentary sliver of life I found when she opened her eyes has been cruelly snatched away.

What am I going to do? How do I fix this? The only thing in this world that keeps my heart beating doesn't know who I am.

A tap on the door prompts me to look past my frightful reflection. "Mr. Ward?" The doctor's voice has lost all the hope that filled it when Ava woke from her coma. Now it's back to sympathetic. "Mr. Ward, are you in there?" The door opens and Dr. Peters appears, his lips pressed tightly together when he finds me holding myself up by the basin.

"She doesn't remember me, her own husband, and not even our babies?" I swallow down the lump making me choke on every word, wondering why I'm posing it as a question. It's not like I heard her wrong. It's not like I didn't see the total blankness in her eyes when she looked at me and the twins.

The doctor enters the men's, shutting the door quietly and slowly behind him. Clearing his throat and plunging his hands into his pockets, he finds my eyes in the mirror. I can't turn to face him. My hands wedged against the edge of the basin are the only thing holding me up.

"Mr. Ward, it would seem your wife is suffering from amnestic syndrome."

"What?" I snap.

"Memory loss."

"No fucking shit, brainiac," I mutter. Is he just going to state the fucking obvious?

Ignoring my rudeness, he goes on. "Having chatted briefly with Ava, there appears to be a clear divide in her memory."

"What do you mean?" I ask, my forehead bunching.

"I mean, from what I have established thus far, there is an obvious cutoff point in her memory." He points to the side of his head. "The part of her brain that stores certain memories has been traumatized. Our ability to recall memories is a very complex process, without the added handicap of a brain trauma."

I close my eyes, trying to allow all the information to sink in. "What are you saying, doctor?" I ask outright.

"I'm saying your wife has lost the last sixteen years of her life."

"What?" I swing around to face him. "That's me. All of me, all of our time together. Are you telling me she won't remember any of it? Nothing?"

"The majority of patients who suffer from amnesia as a result of trauma will recover fully. How long that recovery takes depends on so much—the severity of the injury, the patient's frame of mind, their short-term and long-term memory."

"The majority of patients?" I ask, homing in on that part and that part alone.

"Ava is a young, healthy woman, Mr. Ward. The odds are in her favor."

"And if she doesn't fully recover?"

"The memories remain lost," he says bluntly, making me wince.

The kids' lives to this point. Me. She'll lose it all? "What about medication?"

"There is no physical or mental disorder present, Mr. Ward. She doesn't need medication. What she needs is her family to help her retrieve her lost memories. To support her. There are many therapy options we can consider, such as cognitive behavioral therapy, EMDR, energy psychology, neurofeedback, and maybe even hypnosis."

His spew of words means nothing to me. I'm lost in this crazy. "She doesn't even know who I am," I grate. "What am I supposed to do? Just take her home and hope she'll suddenly remember me?"

"It's all you can do, Mr. Ward. That and support her in any therapy sessions we decide to try in order to help." He takes the door handle, smiling mildly. "Ava realizes that she's forgotten things. That'll be both frustrating and upsetting, especially where her children are concerned. She might have issues with short-term memory, too, and daily life will take its toll. You need to be strong, Mr. Ward. You need to help her try to remember."

"I don't think a Reminder Fuck is going to suffice right now," I mumble.

"Pardon?" The doctor looks at me like I might be going loo-la. He could be right.

I shake my head and try to take in what he's said. Help her. Help her try to find the endless memories we share. I stand up straight and pull my shoulders back, a physical act of determination that I'm trying so hard to back up with mental determination. I can do this. I *have* to do this. There's no way I'm going to allow our history to slip away like it never happened. No way. I'll do anything.

"I'll do whatever it takes." I nod to myself and make my way to the door, passing the doctor without another word, now full to the brim with the mental determination I was missing only a moment ago. There's only one way to approach this. Gently. Patiently. Sensitively. Softly-softly. I blow out a breath, laughing at myself. Good God, this is going to be a battle like no other.

Chapter 8

As I approach her room, Ava is sitting up a little in the bed, her fingers twiddling with the thin white sheets. The wound on her head has been redressed, the bandage stark white against her dark hair. Her face is full of concentration, her eyes squinting every now and then. She's trying to remember, and it breaks my fucking heart to see it. It also renews my resolve. I'll die before I let her memories turn to dust.

I rap softly on the open door, prompting Ava to look up quickly. She winces, bringing her hand to the back of her neck and rubbing. I'm across the room like a bullet, forgetting everything gently-gently. "For fuck's sake, Ava, be careful!" I stop abruptly a few feet from her bed when she recoils, looking at me with wide, shocked eyes.

Oh shit. Too much? Every instinct is telling me to rub her neck for her, to chastise her for not taking care of herself and chastise her more when her inevitable feistiness kicks in.

But instead, and it fucking kills me, I back up, giving her a little space. "You should be careful," I say, an air of awkwardness already drenching the small room, and I've not even introduced myself.

Introduced myself? Do I need to do that? I frown at my feet, wondering what the fucking hell to say. *Oh hey, pleasure to meet you. I'm your husband. You call me the Lord. I'm a crazy, challenging, unreasonable pain in your arse; I'm possessive, I trample all over the place—your words, not mine—but by some fucking miracle, you love me nonetheless. We have sex. Lots of it, and you humor my need to have you wearing lace every day. Oh, did I mention that I owned a sex club one time? The Manor. It's now some swanky golf complex. We fell in love fast. Well, I did. You played hard to get. So I stalked you until you relented, because I knew there was something there. We just... we made so much fucking sense, but then my crazy past started to get in the way, and I thought it would be a good idea to try to hide it all from you. Oh, and I forgot one of the main points. I'm a recovering alcoholic. Before I met you, I drank and I fucked many women. That was my life. We've had some pretty shitty times, but the good far outweighed the bad, and you stuck by me through it all. I really don't deserve you, but you stayed with me despite all of my sins, and to top it all off, you gave me my babies. Two perfect babies. Did I mention I was married before you? No? Well, I was. I also had a little girl, but I lost her...*

I cough away the distress creeping up into my throat, the enormity of my situation slapping me hard in the face. I've always been in awe of Ava's ability to love me so fiercely. *Please, God, please.* I beg that she finds that ability again.

"So apparently you're my husband," she says quietly, an inappropriate tinge of humor lacing her statement.

I look up through my lashes, wondering if it's a good thing that she seems a bit amused by the fact that she has a husband. Then I catch sight of her frowning face and conclude that it's a bad thing. She's looking at me in... oh, fuck. Is that disappointment? Maybe she's not so surprised that she's married, just surprised that she's married to me.

"You look... taken aback." I move across to the chair and sit down calmly, watching as Ava starts to spin her wedding ring on her finger.

She shrugs a little. "I guess you're a little older than I imagined." Another frown. "Well, if I ever imagined I would be married."

Ouch! I shift on my chair, injured, though showing it would be selfish, given the state of my wife. "You're only as old as the woman you feel," I mutter pathetically instead.

"So how old am I?"

"Thirty-eight."

"I am?" She recoils, surprised. "Then how old are you?"

My lips press together, not prepared to reveal that little detail. It's like déjà fucking vu. "Twenty-one," I say coolly, trying not to scowl at her when her eyebrows jump up in surprise.

And she coughs. She fucking coughs. My scowl breaks free and my teeth grind, but I can't pull her up on it. "Twenty-one?"

I nod, confirming that I really am a twat.

"I might have lost my memory, but I haven't lost my eyesight."

Well, isn't she just full of compliments. "It's just a game we used to play."

"A game where you lied about your age?"

I laugh under my breath a little. "Pretty much." I neglect to mention the reason behind my tactics at the time, because I'm adopting the same tactic now. I don't want to put her off, and that's a killer of a thought at this stage in our lives.

I've been married to this woman for twelve fucking years, and I'm worried she might reject me. What kind of fucked-up nightmare am I in? Though, Lord knows, it's going to take a lot more asks to reach my real age on this occasion, and I definitely won't be sharing how she finally managed to extract the information from me all those years ago. I shudder, recalling the hellish few hours that she had me handcuffed to the bed.

I sigh and inch forward on the chair, scrubbing my hands through my hair. "Do you remember anything?" I ask, my eyes pleading with her. "Not one tiny thing, Ava?"

Her face fills with sadness, but I'm not sure if it's sadness for me or sadness for herself. She shakes her head, looking back down at her wedding ring. "I feel so misplaced." Her voice cracks, and one single tear splashes her forearm.

That's it. It's not natural for me to be sitting here. I get up and go to her, sitting on the edge of her bed and taking her hands in mine, avoiding going in for a full-on cuddle. It's ridiculous to think that I don't want to push my luck. With my own fucking wife. "You are not misplaced," I say calmly, seeing more tears fall. "Ava, look at me." My demand is way too harsh given our situation.

Not that it matters. She looks up at me, and our stares instantly lock, her brown eyes gazing deeply into mine as I squeeze her hands. Her lips part a fraction, and something appears in her eyes—something familiar. Desire. It's faint, but it's there, a small reaction, and I cling to it with everything I have.

"You feel that?" I whisper, starting to fiddle with her ring myself. Her slight nod forces me to swallow down my relief before it chokes me. "That's just the very beginning, Ava. That's just the spark that set our worlds alight." Determination is now running rampant through my veins, that small reaction driving it. "This head of yours." I gently stroke down her cheek, relishing her slight nuzzle into my palm. "It's been consumed by me for twelve years, lady. I'm not about to let you forget our story. I will make you remember. It's my mission objective. I'll do *anything*."

She sniffles, nodding, and everything tells me that she's accepting so easily because there's something inside telling her that she should trust me. That she belongs with me. "That smell," she says out of the blue, tugging me toward her. I go with ease, a little taken aback when she buries her face in my neck, no matter how amazing it feels to have her so close. She inhales deeply and I wrap my arms around her as best I can, not missing the opportunity she's instigated. "It's my favorite smell."

I smile and close my eyes. "I know."

Chapter 9

AVA

I don't recognize him. Not visually, anyway, but my body seems to know exactly who he is. It's like he's familiar to me, yet I can't place him. He's handsome, so very handsome; I can see it even through the sallowness of his skin and glaze of his tired eyes. His scent, a mix of fresh water and the freshest mint, is my favorite, though I don't think I've ever smelled it before. His face, cut with stress, is harsh but soft. His green eyes are sad but hopeful.

He looks at me like I'm his savior and his downfall. I feel lost. Lost and bewildered. I'm listening to what people are saying—the doctor, my mum—and it's impossible to comprehend what they're telling me. I'm married. I have eleven-year-old twins. I'm not in my early twenties, but in my late thirties. It's madness, and if it weren't for my mother, the woman I trust most in the world, backing up what the doctor's saying, I wouldn't believe it. I wouldn't believe the gaps they're filling in with wild tales of my love for this man and our life together.

We were married within a couple of months of knowing each other. I was pregnant within a few weeks. That doesn't sound like me. I've never been hasty when it comes to life-changing decisions, nor careless. I've always been independent and ambitious. The woman they are telling me I am doesn't sound like me.

Yet, this man who has been here almost constantly makes something inside me kick. My heart pumps faster when he is here. And my brain feels like it's trying to jump-start, trying to dislodge memories that I've lost. Memories of him? I'm a mother. I'm a wife. And I have no idea how I'm supposed to do either of those jobs.

I have to go home with a man I do not know. I have to take care of two children I do not know. Yet everything inside me is telling me to do it. The man, my husband, he radiates comfort. When he held me and let me cry into his chest, I suddenly didn't feel lost anymore. I felt safe, and I'm not sure if that feeling was spiked by my need for someone to just hold me and tell me everything was going to be okay, or if it was simply *him* that made me feel that way. Just him.

My husband.

Chapter 10

This is the stupidest idea you've ever had, Jesse, and you've had some pretty stupid ideas in your time." Elizabeth slams her empty coffee cup down on the table, enraged by my suggestion.

I don't flinch, maybe because I'm numb. But my *stupid idea* is the best chance of getting Ava better.

It's been three days since she woke up. Three days of tears, frustration, and hopelessness. For both of us.

I've sat in that room studying her, watching her mind spin, her eyes squint, her breaths turn shallow as she fights to regain her lost memories. She's seen a therapist who wants to continue the sessions once she leaves the hospital. Ava sounded noncommittal when she murmured her agreement and scheduled another appointment. I don't blame her. That hour was a stress-fest for both of us, each question posed by the therapist resulting in tears from Ava and further agony for me.

She can't remember anything about us.

The doctor says she's ready to go home, but she's going home with a man she's basically known for three days and a couple of kids who are strangers to her. The pain that thought spikes in my chest is excruciating, but that's how it is. I'm being brutally honest with myself *and* with Elizabeth.

Ava doesn't know us. It's my cold, hard reality.

"I don't want the kids to feel how I'm feeling, Elizabeth. I don't want them to see their mother looking at them like they're strangers, because it's fucking agony."

"But the doctor said she needs her family around her to help her remember."

I slam my fist on the table, my frustration getting the better of me. I only feel mildly guilty when Ava's mother jumps out of her chair. "She thinks she's twenty-two, for fuck's sake. She's still single in her head, just starting out in her career. Everything after that is gone, and I will move fucking mountains to make sure she finds me and the twins amid that chaos in her poor head."

I take a breath and sit back, leaving silence between us. It's a novelty to see my mother-in-law rendered speechless. "I'm asking you to take the children on holiday for me. Keep their minds busy. Let them be kids. I promise you, Elizabeth, I *swear*, I just know if I can spike memories of me and Ava, how we met, how we fell in love, the rest will follow naturally. You have to trust me. I've talked to the school. They're understanding and supportive, given the circumstances."

"How long do you want?"

I shrug. "A week. Maybe two. I don't know." Maybe all the time in the world won't be enough. Maybe the memories are gone forever. I inwardly flinch. No. I have to be positive. And there's no way on earth I'll survive very long without the kids around. "We'll stay in touch every day. Please, Elizabeth. I need this time."

Elizabeth's lips purse tightly. I realize she has difficulty letting someone else take charge of her daughter, she always has, but she needs to work with me this time. "And what are you planning to say to the children, because they think their mother is going home to them this evening?"

She will not make me question myself. I know what is best for my family. "I'll talk to them. They'll understand."

"You hope they'll understand, Jesse. Their worlds have been turned upside down, too. They need their father, as much as their mother."

I brush my hands over the overgrown stubble on my jaw, so fucking exhausted. Hasn't life thrown enough challenges my way? "And I'm going to get them *both* back," I vow. Because right now, Ava and I aren't ourselves.

Placing her handbag on her lap, Elizabeth studies me across the table, probably wondering where I might find the strength from, because I sure as shit look as beaten as I feel. "You look terrible."

Her insult is an acceptance without actually saying the words, and typical of my mother-in-law.

"Yeah, well, it's been a rough few days." I sigh, looking across the café when I spot Kate's red hair. She scans the space for a few seconds before she sees me and gives the same sympathetic smile she's given me every time I've seen her since Ava was admitted.

"Hey," she says when she arrives at our table. "Any news?"

"What, like if my wife knows who I am yet?" I ask, getting up from my chair. Neither of them answers my sarcastic question, both remaining silent and awkward. "I'm going to pick up the kids. Talk to them."

"Where are they?" Elizabeth asks.

"With my mum and dad." I give Elizabeth a kiss on the cheek, squeezing her arm in a sign of my thanks. I know she appreciates my gratitude when she squeezes mine in return. "I'll call you."

"Okay." She breaks away and heads toward Ava's room.

"I'll give her some time with Ava before I head down." Kate links arms with me. "Come on, I'll walk you to your car."

I let Kate's pregnant belly lead the way to the car park, trying to psych myself up for what lies ahead. It's a waste. Nothing can prepare me.

"Jesse, you should know there was a report in the local newspaper yesterday about the accident. They mentioned Ava, you, even the damn health club. And her memory loss." She shrugs when I throw her a questioning look. "They're asking for witnesses."

I sigh. "The police already told me she didn't have her seat belt on." I'm still so furious with her but unable to unleash it. "Apparently she was reaching into her bag for her phone." I swallow, batting back my anger. "She has Bluetooth. I don't know why she'd need her phone."

"A text. An e-mail."

I nod, though no excuse could make her recklessness okay. "Elizabeth and Joseph are taking the kids to the coast for a while," I tell Kate, feeling her look up at me in surprise. "This is too much for Ava, Kate," I start to explain, hoping she gets where I'm coming from. "I can see how overwhelmed she is. Me, the kids, sixteen years of missing memories from her life. You're one of the only people in her life that she actually knows right now."

"So what are you going to do?" Kate brings us to a stop and turns toward me. The huge Hospital sign past her on the side of the colossal building is glowing, despite it still being daylight. An important beacon. I'm sick of the sight of it. Unreasonably, I want to rip it from the bricks and set it alight.

"She might not ever get her memories back, Kate." I shrug and brace myself for what I'm about to say, daunted. "I'm a stranger to her. Just a man. So I have to go back to the beginning and try to make her fall in love with me again."

Kate places her hand on my arm. "You did it before. You can do it again."

I laugh a little under my breath, looking past Ava's best friend.

"I thank my lucky stars every day of my life that I found her, Kate. That for all my faults, she loved me." I smile a strained smile, one that's full of the sadness I feel. "It's a crazy miracle that she accepted me in the first place. I feel like she was my one-in-a-million chance. What if my chance has gone? What if I can't make her see?" I reach up to my chest and push my fist into my pecs, trying to stem the building pain. "It would be the end of me."

"Where's the Jesse Ward we all know and love?" Kate asks seriously, punching me lightly on the bicep.

"Love?" I ask on a slight hitch of an amused eyebrow.

"Yes, love," she retorts adamantly, following up her previous light punch with a not so light one. "Defeated doesn't suit you, Jesse. Ava didn't marry a quitter. In fact, I think you'll find she married you because you *didn't* quit. A man who doesn't give a shit what people think. A man who tramples anything in his sight to get what he wants. Do you want her back?"

I look at her, stunned. "What?"

"Your wife. Do you want her back?"

"Stupid fucking question," I mutter. "And ease off with the punching, will you?"

She ignores my scorn and points a finger in my face, forcing me to retreat or have it sinking into my eye socket. Kate's one of those people in this world who you can't help but respect, even if you don't always agree with her. And now she's pregnant, so I would be wise not to argue. "Then do what you do best and fight for her." Pulling her bag onto her shoulder, she battles to control her wobbling lip. "My best friend didn't marry a fucking pussy."

My eyes bug, and then I laugh a little. Call me what you like, but don't *ever* call me a fucking pussy. "Watch your fucking mouth," I mutter, loud but sheepishly, attracting the attention of many people in the vicinity, not that I'm much bothered by it.

Kate marches past me. Or as well as a heavily pregnant woman can march, which is more of a wobble. "Save it for your wife," she yells over her shoulder.

"I'm not a fucking pussy," I bark at an old man who's stupid enough to come too close. He nearly jumps out of his skin and hotfoots it away from me. There's no room for guilt. It was him or Kate, and Sam would skin me alive if I upset her.

I stalk to my car, yank the door open, and throw myself into the seat, looking into the rearview mirror. Jesus, Lord, the state of me. I'm not exactly enhancing my chances of succeeding in making my wife fall in love with me when I look like this. I need to straighten myself out. Desperately. And I need to do it before I pick up the kids. They need to see me looking as normal as possible, so when I explain to them what is happening, they will know that I am 100 percent together, and I need them to be, too.

Chapter 11

When I pull up outside my parents' home, a small bungalow nestled in an idyllic suburb on the outskirts of the city, the kids are out the door before I've had a chance to shut off the engine. The smile that crosses my face isn't forced. They're the only respite I have at the moment, the only peace in my rocky world, and while holding it together in front of them is adding to my exhaustion, I'm feeding off their love and their need to be close to me right now.

Jumping out of my car, I remove my shades and brace myself for their attack. They reach me at the same time, each finding their places in my side.

"Can we go now?" Maddie asks, looking up at me.

It's the question I was prepared for, yet the words I've practiced all morning disappear on me. "Let's head inside," I say, leading them toward the front door. "I need to talk to you guys."

"What is it?" Jacob's gone from my side in a heartbeat. "Is it Mum? Is she okay?"

"She's fine," I assure him, placing my hand on his mop of dirty blond hair and pulling him back into me. "I've been thinking, and I want to share my thoughts with you two."

"What about?" Maddie asks.

"Are you going to stop us going to the hospital again?" Jacob's tone is defensive. "You are, aren't you, Dad? Why? Doesn't Mum want to see us?"

My heart bleeds, and I hold him tighter into my side. "She's desperate to see you." I stretch the truth a little, if only for the sake of my kids. I've caught Ava a few times this week feeling her tummy, and I know every time she's had a shower she's been studying the small collection of stretch marks on her stomach, trying to get her head around the fact that she's a mother of eleven-year-old twins.

When I asked her if she wanted to see her children, I could sense the mental battle she was having in her head, and the tears flowed quickly after. Listening to my wife tell me that she didn't want to disappoint them tore my heart out. And when she begged me to help her remember them, getting herself in a state, crying and shouting, I decided what needed to be done. I need to tell her our story from the very beginning in the only way I know how. With actions. Where to start is the biggest question.

I look up to the front door and see my mum and dad standing on the porch watching us. Their faces are both sad. I know Mum can't bear seeing me like this. I try to disguise my devastation, but there's nothing a son can keep from his mother, whether he's ten or fifty.

I give my father a strained smile when he raises his hand, telling me he's got it covered, so diverting the kids away from the door, I walk them down to the garden and sit them on the bench overlooking his vegetable patch.

"She's trying so hard to get better for you both," I tell them. "And I need to help her do that."

"You mean remember us," Maddie corrects me, holding my hand as if she could fall down a hole if she let go of me. She's keeping me from falling down that hole, too.

I nod, not prepared to lie, and crouch down in front of them, squeezing their hands. "You see, there's a small part of Mum's brain that's not quite working properly at the moment."

"Because of the bang on her head?" Jacob asks.

"Yes, because of that. It's like the key's jammed, keeping the memories all locked up. I need to unjam that key."

Maddie's bottom lip starts to tremble, and her eyes fill with sad tears. "How could she forget us, Daddy?"

If at any point in my life I've wanted to rip my heart out and serve it at the feet of hope, then it's now. This moment, looking at my children who are so devastated. "She hasn't forgotten you," I tell them firmly, constricting my hold of their hands. "She's just momentarily misplaced her memories. I'm going to help her find them, I promise. Tell me you believe me. Tell me you trust your daddy."

Both of them nod, and I reach forward to yank them both into my chest, cuddling them with a force like no other. I'm strong. I need them to feel my strength.

"Nan and Pap are going to take you to the coast for a week or two while I help Mum, okay? You'll love it down in Newquay. You need to have some fun. Take Pap surfing and help Nan catch some sandworms."

"Pap can't surf," Jacob chuckles through his tears, the sound washing over me like the best kind of medicine. "And Nan's scared of sandworms."

I cluck his cheek. "Then make sure you hide one in her handbag."

"She'll know you told us to do it." Maddie rolls her red eyes before rubbing under them. "She'll curse you to hell again."

"I'm already going to hell in your nan's eyes." I rub some hair away from Maddie's face and ruffle Jacob's mop. "Look after them for your mum, yeah?"

Jacob moves in and takes his sister's hand, a sign of their solidarity and determination. My babies. "And you'll look after Mum? Help her?" he asks.

"I promise."

"How do we know she'll ever remember us?" Maddie, my little live wire, my spirited, defiant little madam, isn't as sure as her brother, and seeing her take the comfort Jacob is offering shreds me and warms me at the same time.

"Because your dad said she will," I cough through my closing throat. "And what your dad says is law."

"We know," they say in unison, looking at each other and smiling, as if silently agreeing that they trust me.

Which is good, because they should.

And I will *not* let them down.

Chapter 12

I arrive at the hospital to find Ava's doctor speaking with the head nurse. She nods, he nods, she speaks, he speaks, she frowns, he frowns.

"Everything okay?" I ask as I near.

"We were just going to call you."

I'm instantly worried. "Why?" I look across to Ava's room, seeing her sitting on the edge of the bed, dressed and waiting, her fingers spinning her wedding ring.

"Your wife was getting a little restless." He smiles fondly. "I told her I'd chase you up."

"I'm sorry, the children are going away with their grandparents," I tell him, watching as Ava looks up and spots me. I smile mildly, getting one in return. This is so weird, and the weirdness doesn't seem to be lessening one iota. "I had to make sure they had everything they needed." I return my attention to the doctor.

"The children are going away?" he asks, making it sound like I'm *sending* them away. It has my hackles rising, though I fight to rein myself in. I don't need anyone questioning my decision as their father, or as Ava's husband.

"They need some time out from this madness," I explain,

diplomatic and calm, though it takes everything out of me. "And if I'm going to help Ava remember us, I need to go back to the beginning of our story."

"Your story?"

I laugh under my breath. "Yes, our story. Let's just say it would make a cracking novel." My hand sweeps through my hair. "We're not your average couple, Doc." I sigh, thinking how best to word it so he has a chance of understanding. He'd need to know us to understand. He'd need to have seen what we've been through. "When I met my wife, it was like an atomic bomb went off in my chest." I avoid mentioning that it felt like an atomic bomb went off in my trousers, too. It's inappropriate. "It was like a part of my soul fused with a part of hers, and there was nothing I could do to stop it. It was the most incredible feeling." I look back into the room and find Ava's still staring at me. "Unforgettable," I whisper, watching her eyes fall to my lips. "Which makes this all the more difficult to accept, because how could she forget? Us. The intensity of our relationship and everything we've been through together?" I tear my gaze away from the woman who holds my life in her hands and return my attention to the doctor. "I'm scared to fucking death that those memories are gone forever."

He smiles like he understands, but he really doesn't. No one possibly could. "You'll make new memories."

I shake my head. "Nothing can replace them."

He nods this time, not countering me. "Here are the details of Ava's appointment." He hands me an envelope. "We removed the dressing on her head this morning. It's healing nicely, but keep it clean. The same with her leg. You have my number, Mr. Ward. Anything that might be worrying you, just call."

I take it and move past him, heading toward Ava's room. My body is heavy. It feels like I could be walking against a gale-force wind, the relentless gusts not only holding my body back, but catching in my throat, too, making breathing harder.

When I enter, I stand like a statue for a few seconds, at a loss for what comes next. "Bag," I blurt, rushing over to get it from beside her. "Are you okay to walk?" Any other day, I'd have picked her up without a word, whether she liked it or not. Quite frankly, all this asking is fucking alien. And I hate it.

She pushes herself up off the bed a little gingerly, and my instinct kicks in. I drop the bag immediately, desperate to ease Ava's struggle and help her to her feet.

She clings to me with both hands, one on each of my forearms as she straightens. I don't know whether it's because she needs to, or wants to. "Thank you."

"Don't ever thank me for looking after you, Ava." I don't mean to sound affronted, but it's unavoidable. "You are my wife. It's what I've been put on this earth to do."

She looks up at me, a small frown crossing her forehead, and I find myself holding my breath, waiting for her to tell me she remembers something—remembers me saying that before, because I know for damn sure I have. Or any recollection, no matter how small or insignificant she thinks it is. But when she shakes her head, I realize it's not coming.

I sigh deeply and get us moving, slowly but surely, constantly checking her for any signs of pain, or that this little trip is too much. She's focused forward, concentrating hard on the simple task of putting one foot in front of the other. It's so painful to watch her struggle. I can't do it.

I swing around to the nurses' station. "Are there any fucking wheelchairs around here?"

The nurse scans the area, clearly panicked. I can't even bring myself to feel bad. "They're all taken at the moment, sir. But if you don't mind waiting, I will try to track one down."

"Don't bother, I'll fucking carry her." Turning back to Ava, I find round, startled eyes. "I'm carrying you," I inform her, just out of courtesy, dipping and gently lifting her into my arms. She doesn't protest, which is a good job because I'm not watching her limp out of here.

She's studying me as I stride down the hall, probably assessing how tight my jaw is. I try to relax it, try to ease my strung muscles. I feel like I could explode with stress. With hope. With despair.

Up ahead, a pair of double doors swings open, a gurney being pushed out by a porter. And on the bed, a body, the face covered by a white sheet. I find my feet slowing and my eyes putting Ava there. On that bed. Dead.

My blood runs cold.

"Jesse?"

I jolt and look down to find my wife looking up at me with concern. I quickly shake away my morbid thoughts of what could have been. She's still here. With me. She might not be her normal self, but she's still here. I hold her tighter. I can't help it. "Come on, let's get you home."

"Home." She sighs, turning her eyes away from me. "Where is that again?"

"Anywhere I am," I say, letting my usual candidness where my wife's concerned creep back. Is she smiling a little? "Okay?" I ask, not wanting to presume she's finding me funny, or maybe recognizing little pieces of *us*. But what else could she be smiling at?

"You seem like the bossy type."

I laugh out loud, the burst of amusement completely unstoppable. "You have no idea, lady. No idea."

"I don't like being told what to do, just so you know."

"Oh, I know." I laugh again, feeling a small amount of pressure lifting from my shoulders. Only small, but...still. I look down and unleash my smile, the one I reserve only for her, the one she's not seen since she came around. It definitely has the desired effect, her body going a little lax in my arms. It's another small sign. "And just so you know, that'll soon change."

She scoffs. It's the sweetest sound, even if it's forced. "I don't think so."

My smile widens, because that right there was my wife. Defiant. Difficult.

Mine.

Hope flourishes within me.

Chapter 13

I watch her neck crane a little as we pull up the driveway to our home, her eyes taking in the grounds of our little manor. "I live here?" she asks, clearly astonished.

"*We* live here," I correct her, rolling to a stop. "Have done for nearly eleven years."

I jump out and round the car, leaving Ava still taking in her surroundings from the passenger seat. I open her door, but when she shows no sign of getting out of my Aston, I dip and reach across her to unclip her seat belt. My cheek brushes her lips innocently, and she freezes, breathing in sharply. I freeze, too, my face millimeters from hers. From my peripheral vision, I can see her lips are pressed together, her eyes wide.

Have I startled her? Set her heart racing with my closeness? Something tells me it's both. My eyes drop to her lips, instinct demanding me to just kiss her. Kiss her. Consume her. Maybe that'll trigger whatever it is that needs to be triggered.

But she turns away from me, and the hope flourishing inside me dies a little. I clear my throat and back off, giving her space to get out of the car, which she does quietly and slowly, ignoring my offered hand.

She takes slow, tentative steps toward the door—slow because of her injured leg, and tentative because, painfully for me, she's nervous. Every so often she peers over her shoulder at me. I say nothing, just follow her, feeling as hopeless as hopeless could be. I push the front door open and stand back, and she hovers on the threshold, looking around the entrance hall. I simply wait for her to find whatever courage she needs to enter. The kids' shoes are scattered in the corner, the small patch of marble tiles dull from the mud they've brought in from the garden. It's a small, silly sign of our family life, but it has Ava's undivided attention. Her home. Her hand comes up to her chest, and I see the pulses of it under her palm.

"Take your time," I murmur gently. She looks up at me and smiles a tiny smile before going back to taking in the space before her. She takes a step inside toward the collection of photographs lining the wall above the console table.

My heart thrums in my chest as she edges closer to the pictures. Her hand reaches up to one of us on our wedding day, her lip slipping between her teeth, biting it gently. Then she spends a while staring at one of me kneeling and kissing her pregnant tummy, her hand resting on her midriff as she does. She looks back to me and offers another small smile, which I return, so fucking nervous now, too. Then she finds one of my favorite pictures, one of the twins when they were toddlers, Jacob on my shoulders, Maddie on Ava's. We're on the terrace in Paradise. The blue sea behind us looks as alive as all of our eyes. The sun is as bright as my smile. Have any of these pictures spiked memories? Anything at all?

Closing the door quietly, I approach her, taking in the pictures myself. Pictures of us. Of our little family. Happiness and love are all over this wall. Everywhere I look, I'm finding things that could trigger something, and I hope so much that they do. And then there's my Ava Wall in the family room, all transferred from my penthouse at Lusso and added to over the years. Hundreds of pictures of the four of us. Maybe that will help, too. Because being in the hospital hasn't, the surroundings cold, clinical, and unfamiliar.

Her shoulders tense when I'm just a few feet behind her, and she looks back at me, her face so sad. She recalls nothing. "I wondered if I was in some kind of nightmare." She turns back toward the photos. "Or someone was playing a cruel joke on me. I woke up and was told I was married and I have children, and until now I didn't quite believe it." She points at the picture of us on our wedding day, her chin trembling. "That's me." Her voice breaks, and she looks at me, tears flooding her eyes. "With you."

I nod, trying to force down my own emotion. Jesus, nothing much breaks me, but my wife so distraught is guaranteed to cut me open. She looks back at the pictures, wiping at her eyes. "And that's me there, too." She points at a picture of the twins tackle hugging her on the trampoline in the garden. "With..." She hiccups over her words, sniffing back her sobs. "My children." Her shoulders start jumping, and she breaks down completely, covering her face with her hands.

I drop her bag and move in to comfort her, fighting back my own tears. "Come here." I pull her into my chest and cuddle her, looking up to the ceiling in despair. What the hell am I going to do? Her petite frame is jumping against me as she cries, her grief pouring out as her reality crashes down. "It'll be okay," I vow, dropping my head and burying my nose in her dark hair. "We'll be okay, I promise."

"Why can't I remember you? Why can't I remember my children?" She pushes me away violently, clenching her fists. "Why can't I remember?" she screams, shaking the house with the volume. "I need to remember! Please, help me remember!" She folds to the floor, landing on her knees, sobbing like I've never seen my wife sob before. The sight will torment me for the rest of my days. Fucking kills me.

I brush at my wet cheeks harshly and force myself to pull it together. She needs me to be together. Strong. Her husband. I scoop her up and cradle her in my arms, getting my own sense of comfort as she curls up into me and clings to me like her life depends on it. Like it's natural.

I walk us to the kitchen and sit down on a chair, holding her close to my chest while she lets it all out. What more can I do? Just be here. Hold her when she needs to be held. Tell her it'll be okay. I keep my face close to hers, hushing her quietly until she eventually calms down. It could be a minute. It could be an hour. Time means nothing at the moment.

"I'm sorry," she sniffs, wiping at a wet patch on my T-shirt.

"Don't be silly." I reach up and wipe her eyes, and she lets me, studying my face closely while I savor the tender moment. I'm so grateful that she's allowing me to comfort her like this. Does she realize that?

"Where are the children?" she asks, looking to the doorway, maybe listening for the sounds of kids.

"I've asked your mum and dad to take them to the coast. Just so you can settle in and get used to things."

"But they'll think I don't want them." I see panic on her face, and it strangely reassures me to know that she cares about how they must be feeling. She may not remember her children, but she still has a mother's instinct.

"They're fine, I promise you, Ava. I told them that I need time with you to help you remember some things."

Her eyes fall to my chest and flit across the material of my Ralph Lauren shirt. She's thinking. "I do want them," she says on a frown. "I know I want them." Looking up at me, she takes her hands to my shirt and fists the cotton. "I know they're mine."

I nod as I breathe in, my eyes glued to hers. "I know you know."

She returns my nod, thankful for my faith in her, as she smiles through a suppressed yawn. She's knackered. She needs to rest.

"You should get some sleep."

She looks down her front and then feels her ponytail. "I'd love a shower."

A shower. I've lost count of how many times we've showered together. The times I'm oblivious as I'm washing myself and that waft of cool air hits me, a sign my wife is about to join me under the spray. Now isn't going to be one of those times, and it hurts so bad.

"Sure." I stand and set her on her feet, backing up, reluctantly showing my intention to let her get on with it.

A tiny frown wrinkles her brow. "Where's the bathroom?"

I close my eyes briefly, gathering air into my dying lungs. Of course. She needs a tour of her own home.

"I'll show you." Resisting claiming her hand, I take the stairs, my feet heavy, my heart heavier as Ava follows, gazing around as she does.

I enter our suite, trying not to be nervous of showing my wife where we sleep. "The dressing room is through there," I say, pointing across the bedroom to the double doors. "And the bathroom is there."

Her dark gaze drags across my body as she passes me, taking tentative steps toward the dressing room. Uncertain whether I should, I follow, standing on the threshold as she absorbs the space. "You keep your underwear and nightwear in that chest," I tell her.

She slides open the top drawer and surveys the contents. Then she moves to the next, pulling out one of my favorite negligées, feeling it for a while before sifting through the rest of the drawer. "There's a lot of lace," she says quietly, making me smile a little. "Where are my cotton pajamas? The cozy stuff?"

"You like lace."

Her eyebrows slowly rise. "Clearly."

"And I do, too." I shrug when she shoots me an interested look. "A little."

"You buy all my underwear, don't you?"

"It's my favorite kind of shopping," I admit, unabashed.

She nods, slowly and unsurely, our eye contact never wavering. But the lust I always find so hard to control when we're alone together, especially when lace is thrown into the mix, isn't as strong today. Not for me, and not for her. It's brutal, but I know sex isn't going to fix this.

"So I guess I should put one of these on?" she finally asks.

I hate that it's a question. And I hate even more that I have to answer with the answer I don't want to give. "Wear what makes you comfortable." I push my shoulder off the door. "I'll leave you to shower. I have T-shirts in the drawer if you'd prefer."

I make my way downstairs, trying so hard not to feel defeated by such a trivial thing. Lace. It's trivial but means so much to both of us.

I grab a beer from the fridge, then make my way into the games room and plonk down heavily on one of the leather couches. Pulling my phone from my pocket, I find my Sonos app and put on some music, if only to kill the unbearable sound of my thoughts. Gnarls Barkley's "Crazy" comes on, and I don't bother changing it. It seems too apt.

My eyes fall to the bar in the corner, where every liquor known to man is stashed. Not for my enjoyment—I haven't touched the hard stuff for years—more for that of our guests when we entertain. But that vodka...

What I would do right now to escape from this nightmare. To get blind fucking drunk and pass out, and hopefully wake up to my life as it should be.

I tear my gaze away, drop my head back, and let my thoughts continue to torment me as the track goes on. Let the pain penetrate deeper, because she's upstairs showering alone. And I'm down here feeling useless.

I finish the bottle of beer but resist getting another, and go to the office. I sit at the desk and fire up the iMac, and then search through the files until I find what I'm looking for. The photos. Thousands snapped from the very beginning, to just recently at my fiftieth. Moments captured in time, faces smiling, and sometimes even scowling. Endless happy memories, every photograph loaded with love. I click through, my pain worsening with each image. How can she not remember any of this? How can she not remember me? I drop the mouse and scrub my hands down my rough face, feeling so fucking knackered—physically, emotionally. I need a shower, too.

I leave the folder open, ready to let Ava scroll through the years when she's ready, then drag myself upstairs. There's not a peep from our bedroom, and when I push into our room, I find Ava snuggled up in our bed. I can't help feeling hurt. She's always claimed it's impossible to get to sleep without lying on my chest. Then I feel a little hopeful, because she's wearing the lace instead of the T-shirt I offered. I ignore the fact that she has always slept naked. Baby steps.

After creeping to the bathroom, I take a quick, lonely shower, and then I trim my stubble, taking it down to the three days' worth that she loves so much. I spend only a few seconds taking in the man before me. I'm a fucking mess. I feel weak, disheartened, and sad. I've been in hell before, and I feel like I'm free-falling back there now. Why? Why is this happening? What did I do?

I brace my hands on the sink and breathe deeply, trying not to let the anger that's brewing erupt. I don't like it when things are out of my control, and right now, my world is spiraling into fucking bedlam. And there's nothing I can do about it, only hope. My shoulders rolling with the strain of keeping my temper contained, I growl, my teeth clenched, desperate to hit something.

I look up and face myself again. And before I realize what's happened, the mirror shatters and my knuckles split. It's okay, though. Now my reflection looks exactly how I feel.

Broken.

Chapter 14

I can't stand how quiet it is around here. I can't hear the kids tearing through the house, can't hear the coffee brewing, can't hear Ava shouting at the twins to get their little arses into gear for school. It's deadly silent.

I stare at the coffeemaker for a few seconds, feeling anger building. It's just a coffeemaker. But it's a coffeemaker that's always brewing when I get downstairs in the morning, because my wife has switched it on. It's her thing. That's what she does, and today she hasn't. Because she doesn't know.

I yank the cupboard open and search for the coffee. I don't even know how to work the fucking thing. Finally, I locate it, pour it in, and fiddle with the stupid fucking machine, cursing my way through it. I don't even know if I've done it right, but I switch it on, hoping for the best, and silently will it to hurry the hell up to rid the kitchen of the god-awful quiet.

I collect a cup, add milk, and then tap my fingers impatiently on the worktop while I wait, scowling down at my scuffed knuckles. My eyeballs feel like they're being scratched every time I blink, my lack of sleep catching up with me. I think I got an hour last night. An hour slumped in the chair by our bed, the rest of the night spent watching her sleep, desperate to crawl in behind her and cuddle her in my usual fierce way. But I dared not.

As I pour coffee, I hear my phone from across the kitchen. I fetch it and answer without looking at the screen. "Morning, Elizabeth."

"How are things? She settled in okay?" Her voice sounds as desperate as I'm feeling.

No. And *things* are fucking awful. "As well as can be expected," I say. "How are the twins?"

"Joseph has taken them to the driving range. We've got lots planned—surfing, crabbing, fishing."

I smile as I sip some caffeine down. "Thanks, Elizabeth. I really appreciate you doing this." I don't think I've ever sounded so sincere when speaking to my mother-in-law.

"Oh, Jesse." Her voice cracks under the pressure to remain strong, and for the first time in my existence, I wish she were here so I could give her a hug.

"Listen to me," I say as sternly as I can muster. "You've known me for twelve years, Elizabeth. So you should know that I'm not going to let those years slip away like they were never there."

She coughs over a little laugh, sniffling. "I know we're both terribly silly with our bickering, but you do know I adore you, Jesse Ward."

On the inside, I'm toasty warm with appreciation, and yes, I did know that deep down. But at the risk of breaking down, too, I'm forced to pull my arrogant self back to the surface. I can't cry on Ava's mother. She's depending on me. I can't cry on *anyone*. "Yeah, well, my heart belongs to another."

"Oh, stop." She laughs, and it's so good to hear. "You're still a menace."

"And you're still a pain in my fucking arse, *Mum*. Look after my babies."

"Okay." She doesn't argue, doesn't even question my order. "Keep in touch, won't you?"

"Every day," I assure her, hanging up and sliding my phone onto the counter, my shoulders immediately dropping. The energy to be strong is draining me. How long can I keep this up? On a sigh, I wander over to the fridge and pull it open, snatching down some peanut butter from the shelf. I remain where I am, just set on having a couple of scoops, something familiar and comforting in this foreign world.

A few minutes later, I'm halfway through the jar.

"Morning." Her soft, unsure voice hits me like a cricket bat in the back of the head, and I whirl around with my finger in my mouth to find her at the entrance to the kitchen, her hands playing nervously where they're linked together at her midriff. The lace nightwear has been covered with a cream satin dressing gown, her dark hair fanning her shoulders. She's a vision. And I can't touch her.

I suck my finger clean and swallow, quickly screwing the lid back on as she frowns down at my hands.

"Peanut butter?" she questions. Is that humor in her tone? Would now be a good time to tell her that one of her favorite pastimes is smothering her boobs in it and letting me indulge in my two favorite things all at once?

"It's a vice." I put it back in the fridge and grab some orange juice, pouring her a glass, nervous and shaky in my movements. "Did you sleep well?" Not once in nearly twelve years of marriage have I ever had to ask that question. Because I've always been right by her side, aware when she's sleeping peacefully or when she's fidgeting because something is on her mind.

"Not really." She pads toward me and takes the glass from my hands, smiling a little, before settling on a stool at the island. "It felt like something was missing." She looks away, as if ashamed to admit it. "I've concluded that it must have been you."

What? Hope flourishes within me again, and I'm not sure whether to welcome it or not. With no hope, there can be no disappointment. But I can't help it. Moving to the stool beside her, I take a seat. "Ava, you should know that—"

"Once I've had you, you're mine."

I nearly fall back off my stool. To hell with disappointment. Nothing could hold back the joy surging through my veins right now. "You remember?"

With her lips on the rim of her glass, her brow furrows a little. "I don't know where that came from."

"Inside you, Ava." I take her juice and place it on the counter, taking her hands in mine and squeezing tightly. "Way deep inside you."

She looks at me, tears in her eyes building again. Damn those fucking tears. "This is so frustrating." She squeezes my hand in return, wanting me to understand. She has to trust me. I do. I *really* do.

"I just stood in two children's bedrooms for fifteen minutes, demanding to remember them. I smelled the sheets of their beds and went through their drawers. Nothing." A lone tear rolls down her cheek, and I catch it with the pad of my thumb. It's no good. I lift her onto my lap, my body wrapped around hers. There's no resistance from her whatsoever. "I just want to bang my head repeatedly against a wall until it all comes back."

"You'll do no such thing, lady." My nose in her hair, I inhale, appreciative that she's letting me comfort her once again. Whether she wants it or needs it isn't something I'm wasting my thoughts on. Because *I* need it.

Sighing, she shuffles from my lap, forcing me to hold my breath and talk down my dick when she innocently rubs against me. There will be none of that, and I never, not ever, thought I would say that in my lifetime with her.

"What did you do to your hand?" she asks, running a light fingertip over the tops of my knuckles.

I shake my head and remove my hand from her touch, my silent way of telling her to leave it. I can see by the wariness in her eyes that she knows full well what happened to my hand. She must have seen the mirror. Or maybe she heard it shatter last night.

She doesn't push it. "What are we doing today?" she asks instead.

Yes. Back to the important business.

I get up and offer my hand, grateful when she takes it. "I've found all the photographs on the computer. I thought you could spend the morning going through those."

"The whole morning?" She lets me lead her into the study and help her sit at the desk.

"We have a lot of photographs." I wake up the screen, and we're immediately greeted by a picture of the four of us. It was in Paradise. The twins were toddlers. I was forty-two, and Ava a vision of stunning perfection at thirty. Maddie's in her arms, Jacob in mine. And we're kicking water at each other on the seashore, all of us laughing. It's a beautiful moment captured in time, natural and real.

I watch as she reaches forward and touches the screen lightly, her finger drifting across all four of our faces. "We're a really good-looking family," she muses to herself. "He looks like you. And she looks like me."

I say nothing, just kiss the top of her head and leave her to go through the endless shots of our happiness. I won't be able to watch her do that without breaking down.

* * *

Agony. It's pure fucking agony for the whole five hours she's in the office looking at pictures. I wonder constantly if anything has spiked any memory. And then I finally hear her crying and know that it hasn't.

I look up to the ceiling, squeezing my eyes closed, anguish settling deeply in my gut. Then I pull myself together and follow her cries to the family room. I find her on her knees at the foot of my Ava Wall. Her head is in her hands, her fists clawing at her temples as if she's trying to physically yank the memories free. Shit, she'll open her wound.

"Ava, baby." I run across the room, my heart tugging painfully as I gather her up. Every inch of the wall above us is covered with photographs and captions written by me, Ava, and the twins now, too. There have been days when I have come in here and chilled out on the couch and just stared at it all day, taking in the sheer magnificence. Nothing ever makes me smile harder than finding a new photograph and reading the words either Ava or one of the twins has put with it. It's one huge homage to my family, one of the most precious things in my life. And now it's a factor of my wife's desolation.

My eyes fall to the most recent picture, the one Jacob and Maddie put up nearly two weeks ago. It's me, my face moody as Ava kisses my cheek. The caption in Maddie's handwriting reads:

It's Dad's birthday. And he's real grumpy about it!

I swallow as I pull Ava closer to my chest and move to the couch, sitting and arranging her with ease on my lap. I quickly check her head, making sure she's not upset her wound, as she curls up so small, huddled and sobbing into me. I say nothing and just hold her for the next hour while she cries her heart out, curses out loud, shouts and screams, and sobs some more. My eyes are stinging from the silent tears I allow to escape while her head is buried in my chest, her fingers clawing at my T-shirt to hold on to me, like she's afraid I'll leave her alone in her darkness. Never. We're in this together. All the way to the end. I can't see any light at the end of this torturous tunnel, but I pray it's there somewhere.

Eventually, her sobbing subsides, though I don't push her to leave her hiding place, waiting patiently for her to brave facing the stranger who's holding her. "Zero, baby," Ava murmurs into my chest on a sniffle. I stiffen. "Why do I keep hearing those words?"

I push her away from my chest to find her eyes. They're red and swollen. "It's one of our games," I explain, and she frowns, encouraging me to go on. "I start at three, and when I get to zero—"

"What?"

I shrug, pushing on. "Sometimes I tickle the shit out of you, sometimes I kiss the living daylights out of you, and sometimes I put you in bed." That's about as delicate as I could be in explaining the countdown. "Ava, baby, it's just another part of our wonderful."

She smiles, just a little. But it's still a smile. "Ava, baby," she whispers, settling back into my chest, turning her face outward so her cheek is flat on my pec, her eyes staring across the room to the wall. "Whenever you say that, it sounds perfectly right. Whenever you hold me, it feels perfectly right. Whenever I look at you, I know you are mine. When I look at the kids, I don't recognize them, but something tells me to protect them. It all feels incredibly right."

"Because it is right," I reply, so relieved to hear that. It's a flash of the light in this darkness I'm searching for. "Everything about us is right."

"So why can't I remember?" Her voice cracks again, and not for the first time, I try to imagine her bleakness. Try to imagine what it must be like to feel so misplaced. I'm not sure it's fair to compare her struggle to mine. "You must be so frustrated, too," she sobs. "How long will it be until you give up on me?"

Give up? Jesus, she really doesn't know me anymore at all. Ignoring the pain in my heart is hard. Hearing her doubt my determination is a killer.

"You will remember," I vow. "You and I are a formidable force, Ava. Nothing has defeated us in the past, and I'm not about to let it now."

I take her wedding ring and bring it to my lips, kissing it gently, and she looks up at me with so much need in her eyes. It's need of another kind. Not a sexual need, but a need for me. Just me. To help her, to support her, to love her. To remind her. "I once told you that I wanted to look after you forever." I hold her eyes, never wavering. "I meant it, baby. Forever isn't over yet. Never will be, not for us. I love you. You are the best part of me, Ava. The greatest part. That can't be forgotten."

She blinks a few times, maybe a little taken aback. That hurts, too, because any other time I've told her how much I love her, she's just smiled and kissed me. "We must love each other an awful lot."

"It's pure bliss, baby," I begin quietly. "Total gratification." I lower my lips cautiously and peck her wet cheek lightly. "Absolute, complete, earth-shifting—"

"Universe-shaking love." She barely breathes those final words, but I hear them like they're being delivered through a megawatt speaker held at my ear.

"Yeah," I confirm, cool on the outside, but on the inside I'm constantly being carved up by the fact that she's saying things and she doesn't know why she's saying them. "I'm not going anywhere, and neither are you, do you hear me?"

She nods through more tears and crawls in closer to me, except this time her face goes into my neck and she breathes me in, her lips resting just perfectly on my skin as her hands slip under my T-shirt and feel me. "You always smell so good. Are you going to tell me how old you are now?"

"Twenty-two."

She chuckles, and I smile. "I can tell you make me happy."

"Good." I relax in my seat and we spend a few silent, blissful moments in our madness just snuggling, her hands skating over my chest, lightly touching me everywhere she can. Like she's reacquainting herself to the feel of me.

Chapter 15

We've been rattling around the quiet, empty house for two days, leaving only once so I could take her to therapy. We left the session after no spikes in her memory, and the hopelessness seemed to multiply by a million. I've forced myself into the spare bed each night, and hated it with a vengeance every time I've left her in our suite. Each time, she watches me as I go, and each time I've wondered if she really doesn't want me to leave. But there's no way I can ask her.

I keep seeing glimmers of a familiar look in her eyes, a pleased look, the look she used to give me every day of our lives. It's the look that tells me she wants me. The attraction she's never been able to hide. But now she's holding back. She's trying to fight it. Just like she did all those years ago when she walked into my office.

But this time, I can't charge her resistance down like a bull. I can't take what I want. I have to wait for it to be given to me, and it's killing me a little bit more each day.

I've been watching her, wondering what's going on in that mind of hers. And she's caught me doing it often, smiling a small smile each time. She's getting used to me. Weighing me up.

It's now nighttime again, and dread fills me as I walk her up to our room, the bed still unmade from this morning. I'd normally strip her down to her skin, lift her into bed, and crawl in behind her. But that fear of scaring her to death or being rejected stops me again. I don't know if I could take it. Yet walking out and leaving her kills me, too. Kate's words crawl into my mind. *Where's the Jesse Ward we all know and love?*

On that note...

"Arms up," I order Ava, taking the hem of her shirt.

She gazes up at me, a little surprised. There's uncertainty in her eyes, and she flinches when my fingers brush the flesh of her tummy. In return, I flinch, too, yet my reaction has nothing to do with the usual flame on my skin whenever I touch my wife, and everything to do with her wariness.

I drop her T-shirt and step back, giving her space, trying to control the agony in my chest before it puts me on my knees and has me begging. "Never mind. I'll give you some privacy." I turn before she catches sight of my watery eyes and take myself away from the one person in this world who brought me back to life. And the one person in the world who can finish me.

Closing the door behind me, I stalk away, aware that if I stop and try to gather myself, I'll either put a hole in the wall or crumple to the floor and cry my fucking heart out. I roughly brush at my damp eyes as I take the stairs, eager to put as much space between us as possible so that when I roar my frustration, she's not as likely to hear.

My pace quickens as I round the bottom of the stairs, and I stagger into the games room and shut the door behind me, falling against the wood, my body rolling with the effort it's taking to breathe. *Bang.* I smack the back of my head on the wood, squeezing my eyes shut, quaking with a fury I'm unable to control.

Why? Why is this happening? I've pushed her too far too soon.

The roar I've been suppressing since I escaped our room bubbles up from the pit of my stomach and explodes out of me, and I turn, throwing my fist into the door. The door doesn't splinter, but my already split knuckles split some more. It doesn't hurt. The only pain I feel is in my fractured heart. "Fuck!"

I stay where I am, forehead resting on the door, fists clenched, for as long as it takes me to cool down. It could be two minutes, it could be an hour. I don't know. I feel as though precious time is slipping like sand through an hourglass. Unstoppable.

It's the sound of my phone that eventually pulls me from the door. Feeling numb, I walk over to the table and swipe it up. It's Kate.

"Hey." I slump onto the couch and inspect my bloody fist.

"Everything okay?"

"My wife doesn't know who I am, Kate. So, no, everything isn't okay."

She doesn't reprimand me on my curtness. "No progress, then?"

I sigh, long and tiredly. "I keep getting glimmers of hope. Small things that make my heart leap with promise. And then they disappear, my hope dies, and I'm back to square one."

"I know it's not your forte, but you need to be patient, Jesse. Like the doctor said, there's a cog in her mind that's jammed."

"And it keeps jittering and then grinding to a stop again. It's so fucking frustrating."

"You're frustrated?" She laughs a little. "Imagine how Ava must be feeling, Jesse. She's woken up with a husband and two kids and sixteen years of her life missing."

Guilt. It sweeps right in and cripples me. "I know." I rub my forehead, like I can wipe away the stress. "I can see it all in there, Kate. It's all in there, I just need her to remember it." What if she never feels the connection and emotion she did when we met? No matter how much I might try to describe it to her, it won't be as intense and crippling as it was back then. How it always is. It won't bond us in the same way, and now more than ever I need that bond.

"She'll remember. Don't give up."

"Never," I vow, hoarse through the despair blocking my throat. Despair I'm quite sure I'm not hiding very well.

"How about dinner one night? All of us. Drew and Raya are game."

"Yeah," I agree half-heartedly. I'm not all that enthusiastic about sitting around a table with friends so they can see how much of a stranger I am to my wife. "Let me know when."

"I will. Keep it together, Jesse. It's no wonder she doesn't recognize you. I barely do myself." She hangs up with those words still lingering in the air.

"Jesus," I breathe, dropping my phone to the couch, so caught in conflict. I replay all those little glimmers of hope that Ava's given to me, words that have come from nowhere, but have been quickly snatched away with a frown or muddled look on her face. The soaring happiness followed quickly by unrelenting hurt.

My eyes fall to the drinks cabinet across the room again, the bottle of clear liquor enticing me, pulling me in with promises of respite. "Keep it together," I say to myself, forcing my heavy body up from the couch. I lock up the house and make my way upstairs, my eyes nailed to our bedroom door as I wander to the spare room. Another night without her sprawled all over my chest. Another night missing her warmth.

Another night with the biggest piece of me missing from my side.

Chapter 16

AVA

The past few days, all I've had to do is think. Think and go to therapy and think some more. I'm sick of thinking. I'm sick of the headaches from thinking too hard. The last I remember, I was dating a guy named Matt. I even remember talks of moving in together. So what happened? And what about the career I was working so hard for? I work for my husband. Live with my husband. It's obvious I'm always kept close by. Is that normal? Is it healthy?

I sigh and turn over in bed, catching sight of the clock on the table. It's eight o'clock. I can hear clatters and bangs coming from the kitchen. Last night he tried to undress me. I couldn't help but flinch when he touched my bare skin, not just because I was surprised. My flesh seemed to ignite, and though it was like nothing I'd felt before, somehow I know that I have. In that moment, I was alarmed by my reaction. Scared by it. I hardly know him. Yet my body does and it's telling me every single day. There's a connection. Something deep and almost debilitating. He's devastating.

I close my eyes and try to wrap my mind around all the signs that I love him. Not just the tangible proof—the pictures, the children, what people have told me. But the invisible proof. Like my skipping heart when I see him. Like my heated skin when he touches me. Like a strange urge inside me to be close to him. Something clicks whenever I am, like when he hugs me in those big arms. He's good at snuggling. He's good at comforting me. He's good at giving me space when I need it.

I stop that thought process right there and rewind. I don't think he's *really* very good at giving me space, and I really don't know if I want it. I can see the strain on his face whenever he leaves the bedroom. And I feel the strain within me. Something isn't right. *He* doesn't seem right, and that's a strange conclusion for me to reach when I don't *know* him.

Gingerly edging to the side of the bed, I wince as I stand, the muscle behind the healing cut on my leg pulling tight. I pull on a cream gown and head for the door. I want to know things, and I'm ready to ask. So he better be ready to tell.

Chapter 17

I'm making coffee again, creating as much noise as I can to fill the silence, when Ava marches into the kitchen. I'm taken aback by the determination written all over her face. Then she stops, her eyes sparkling a bit at the sight of my bare chest. As her gaze moves down, the sparkle fades and she points to my stomach. Or the two scars marring it. "What happened?"

I look down. I don't know why. "Nothing." I shake my head and return my attention to Ava, not prepared to go there yet. Besides, I know she didn't come stomping in here looking all resolute to talk about my scars. It's the first time she's seen them since the accident. "What's up?"

After a little shake of her own head, she rights her softened body, standing tall and confident. "Tell me how we met. I want you to tell me everything."

I cautiously lower my arse to a stool, torn between happiness that she's asked, and dread from the pressure of having to answer. It was all so intense and a huge whirlwind of feelings and emotion; the thought of explaining it is suddenly very daunting. "I don't know where to start, Ava," I admit as she joins me at the island. "I'm worried I won't do our story justice."

She breathes in a little, thinking, as her gaze flits across my face. "Then show me."

I laugh under my breath, but it's nervous. "I'm not sure you're ready for that." I don't want to freak her out when she's in such a mind-warp. This isn't like when we met. I can't go steamrolling in like I did back then. She's delicate now. Fragile. I feel like everything is hanging on my approach to this mess.

"Ready for what?"

I clench my eyes closed, swallowing. "My ways."

"Your ways?"

"Yes, my ways." I open my eyes and find hers. The mystification staring back at me only amplifies my worry.

She doesn't know what to make of that. Or of me.

"That's what you call it," I tell her. "My *ways*." I go on when she cocks a questioning head. "I'm unreasonable." I shrug. "Apparently." A deep breath helps me to go on. "A control freak." Another lame shrug. "Apparently." This is hard already, and I've not even skimmed the fucking surface. "I'm possessive and controlling and..." I press my lips together when her eyes widen a little. "Apparently," I add quietly.

"You just said *apparently* an awful lot."

"Apparently," I mumble, looking away from her, struggling to express what she needs to know. "For fuck's sake," I breathe, frustrated.

"You swear a lot, too."

I shoot my eyes to hers, finding a rather disapproving look. I could laugh, but I cough instead. "And you don't, for the record. Hardly ever, in fact." I refuse to feel guilty for telling her a barefaced lie. This could be the end of her potty mouth.

"I don't?"

I shake my head. "Never."

"Oh." She falls into thought again for a few moments, swallowing repeatedly until she takes in so much air, I'm worried about what might come from her mouth that requires so much preparation. "I *am* ready," she declares.

I'm lost. "Ready for what?"

"For you to show me." She bites down on her lip a little, gazing at me as I try to comprehend what she's asking me to do.

"I'm not sure, Ava."

"I *am* sure." She approaches me and lays her hands on my chest, forcing me to breathe deeply through the contact. "I have a huge, gaping hole in my head. It's where you and the children should be, and it's truly killing me that you're not there." She shoves me a little, bringing her face close to mine. "You're here, in my life, but you're not up here." Releasing one hand, she taps the side of her temple softly, though she still winces a little. Her move is a reminder to both of us that she needs to take it easy. Her visible wounds haven't healed yet, either. "And I just know that you should be. Seeing those photographs has only made that instinct stronger." Her voice cracks again, and I quickly take her hand back down from her head, holding it firmly in my grasp. "I need you to do whatever it takes."

Her fierce determination through her broken words staggers me. Then I remember who I'm faced with. I might be a stranger to her, but this is still my wife. The strongest woman I've ever met. She has to be, or I wouldn't be in her life, or she in mine. She tackled me before, took everything I had to throw at her.

"Whatever it takes?" I counter, just to hear her say it again. Just so I know we're on the same page.

"Whatever it takes," she confirms, nodding at the same time. She's giving me permission. Telling me it's okay to be... all of me?

"No pressure, then?" I quip, wondering where to start. The answer comes to me quickly. "Go take a shower. We're going on a little trip."

* * *

As I look up at the imposing building, I conclude that this is just as weird for me as it must be for Ava. The Manor is still The Manor, except now it's The Manor Golf Resort and Spa. The grounds are as spotless as they were when I sold the place, and the building as impressive.

"We met playing golf?" Ava asks, a little laughter in her tone. "How romantic."

"There wasn't much romantic about our first encounter, baby," I say, guiding her up the steps to the open doors, checking for her limp. It's there, if mild.

"There wasn't?" She sounds so disappointed, her head dropped far back, taking in the extraordinary structure. "You know, this could be your perfect opportunity to change that."

I skid to a stop, looking down at her, a little stunned. She remains quiet while I fish for a response to that. I have nothing, so I pull her on, my mind spinning into overdrive. Not about her hinting that maybe I should be romantic, but because she's shown a suggestive side, and I like it a lot. I shouldn't, however, take that subtle hint as a green light to ravage her. Not just yet, anyway.

"This way." I lead her into the bar, pick her up, and place her on a stool, trying to ignore the fact that despite the exterior of The Manor remaining the same, the interior has changed dramatically. It looks utterly shit. I gaze around, caught between resentment and reminiscence. The general layout is the same, though the décor is very different.

"Why are you scowling?" Ava asks. This will probably do nothing to help her remember. How could it when I barely recognize it myself?

"It just isn't how I remember," I tell her, pointing to the barman, who's kitted out in some green penguin suit that matches the rest of the décor. "Mario looked much better."

"Who's Mario?"

"My head barman."

"*Your* head barman?" she blurts.

"Oh yeah." I look down at her, smiling nervously. "I used to own this place."

"You owned a golf resort?" Her mouth hangs open as she takes a look around her. "The house, your flash Aston, this place. Are we rich?"

"We're comfortable," I say nonchalantly, hoping that is the end of that, for now, at least. The complexity of The Manor and how I came to own it isn't top of my priority list of things to tell her. It's *us* that's important.

I order two waters and quietly ask the barman if I can speak to the manager.

"Why did you sell it?"

"It wasn't a golf resort when I owned it," I say, fully aware that I've just opened the floodgates to an inquisition. I take the glass and pass it to her, waiting for the inevitable.

"Then what was it?" She takes a small sip, looking at me, waiting for an answer.

I stall, avoiding her gaze, like she might find the answer in my eyes. "Oh, look, a lovely painting of St. Andrews." I point my glass to a wall on the other side of the bar, where tasteful art used to hang.

She looks over her shoulder briefly, clearly not in the least bit interested. "What was this place when you owned it?" she repeats, leveling an expectant look on me.

This simple question has made me realize just how much there is for her to remember. Fucking hell, this is getting more daunting by the minute.

My arse drops to the seat of the stool next to Ava, and I sigh, long and defeated. "A sex club," I say quietly, not that there's anyone around to overhear.

"Pardon?" She coughs, her glass of water landing on the bar.

"It was an exclusive sex club for the rich and beautiful." I rest an elbow on the bar, propping my head in my hand.

Her lovely mouth is hanging open again. And I'm inwardly laughing. She's heard nothing yet, and for the first time, I wonder if there are certain things that I should hold back forever. Things that nearly broke us. Things that I would love to have wiped from her memory even before the accident. But that wouldn't be fair. Our story is our story, after all, and I have to have faith that she got past it back then, so she can get past it again.

"Wait." She retreats on her seat. "You said we met here." Her finger comes up and swirls the air around her head, comprehension beginning to dawn. The fear of her thoughts is endearing. "Tell me I didn't..."

"You didn't," I assure her on a small smile.

"Oh, thank God," she breathes, her hand coming up to her chest. "Finding out I'm married with kids is enough to wrap my brain around, without the added knowledge that I was a kinky bitch."

I laugh at her evident relief. "Oh, you're kinky, lady. And in a whole league of your own."

"What do you mean?" Her cheeks flush. I haven't seen embarrassment on my wife for years. It still looks good on her.

I relish in the sight, leaning in toward her to get close. "You're a teasing temptress, baby. A savage when you want to be."

"A savage?"

"Biting. Clawing." I smile a little at her growing shock. "Screaming, *really* loud. We're fucking perfect together."

Her blush gets even brighter, her eyes darting away from mine. "Oh."

I chuckle at her prudishness. "Well, this is a strange sight."

"What is?"

"My wife being all shy and reserved."

"Well, it's not every day you find out your husband owned a glamorous sex club."

"It's not every day your wife forgets who you are," I reply, with no hurt or harshness behind my words. It's just a factual statement. "We're both out of our comfort zone here, Ava."

She looks at me in quiet contemplation. "Why do I get the feeling that I'm about to experience something incredible?"

I smile and take her hand, helping her down from the stool. "Because you are. Because our story is truly incredible. Come on." I find the manager and have a quiet word while Ava stands in the entrance hall, staring up the sweeping staircase to the balcony landing. Just watching her there, taking everything in, looking so out of place, brings back so many memories. It's sweetly reminiscent, if a little painful. The sight is beautiful, but the feelings are ugly. I don't have the all-consuming intrigue and awe swirling within me like I did back then. I have anxiety instead.

I join Ava and stare up to the first floor, too. The doors off the landing are all closed—doors to guests' hotel rooms, as opposed to doors that lead to hours of pleasure.

"This way," I whisper in her ear, making her jump a little. I hold my hand out and smile when she takes it, walking us leisurely though what was The Manor. When we hit the ballroom, which is now a huge restaurant with a terrace onto the golf course, I look back, trying not to hope too much that any of this is familiar to her. It's a long shot, since it's so very different from how I remember it. "Our wedding breakfast was in this room," I say over my shoulder, leading her through the scattering of tables.

"Please tell me you sold this place before we got married."

"I can't." I return my attention forward, smiling when she

sighs. My smile stretches when I spot an elaborate spray of flowers in a huge glass vase with bursts of every color imaginable. I divert us to the table where it stands and scan the bouquet, spotting what I'm looking for. There's only one. But it doesn't matter. I only need one. I pluck the calla from the middle and turn, handing it to Ava.

She's unsure as she reaches for it, eyes flicking from me to the flower. "It's beautiful."

I smile mildly and pull her on. "Understated elegance," I say over my shoulder, relishing the beam she gives me in return. "They're your favorite flowers."

"Since when?"

"Since the day you met me," I tell her as we approach my office door, thinking I was quite romantic back then after all. I look up at the solid wooden door, my mind bombarded with so many memories, the most poignant and important being the first time that Ava O'Shea wandered in. I remember it like it could have been yesterday. I was hungover. Grumpy. Wishing I didn't have to endure the mundane meeting with an interior designer. Then John showed her in, and all headaches and irritability were forgotten. Instant intrigue, desire, and want replaced them. "Wait here," I order lightly, dropping her hand and opening the door, stepping into the vortex of memories.

Her head cranes around me, trying to see into the office. "Wait?"

"I want you to wait one minute and then knock on the door."

She laughs a little. "Why?"

"Because that's how it was when we met." I shut the door and spin around, taking in my office. "Really?" I ask thin air. What the fuck have they done to it? I rush across to the corner and drag the desk to where it should be. I haven't got time to rearrange the entire space to replicate what it was all those years ago, so this will have to do. I hear a knock and fall into the chair, quickly rolling up the sleeves of my shirt and roughing up my hair a little. "Come in," I call, grabbing a pen and jotting something down on a pad to the side. The sound of the door opening fills the office, and I look up to find she's poked her head around the door.

"I don't even know why I'm here," she says on a shrug, making me sag in the uncomfortable office chair.

"Just come in." I flap an impatient hand, beckoning her.

She shuts the door and stands across the office, looking around, a bit bewildered. "Nice."

"It was better when it was my office," I say, following her lead and taking the space in. I sniff my disgust and find my wife again. She's the only thing that looks right in here, even if she's staring at me a little blankly, her face asking me *what next?* Her dark hair, currently piled high in a messy knot, isn't as glossy, and her eyes aren't as shiny. But she still takes my breath away.

I get up from the chair and slowly round the desk, dragging my fingers across the wood. Then I rest my arse on the edge, crossing my legs at the ankles and my arms over my chest. Her eyes fall to my torso, and I smile to myself. "What do you see?" I ask, prompting her to look up through her lashes at me.

"What do you mean?"

"Here." I indicate down my tall frame, eyebrows raised in question. "What do you see?"

"I see you."

"Play the game, Ava," I warn—low and husky, instantly making her shift on her feet. That's more like it. She's fidgeting. Good. Let's get this fucking show on the road.

She breathes in, long and deep. She's finding the courage to say what she wants to say, and I silently will her on. "I see dirty blond hair," she begins, clearing her throat in order to continue, as if the silly act will wipe her voice of the lust that's growing. "Green eyes."

"And?"

"And a body to die for." She smiles shyly on a little shrug of one shoulder, color creeping into her cheeks again. "Which I'm guessing you must work hard for, given your age."

I just manage to keep my eyebrows from jumping up in surprise. "I don't work *that* hard," I clarify, thinking now would usually be a perfect time to start the countdown and warn her to take that back. But not now. "And you don't know how old I am," I point out.

"How old are you?"

"Twenty-three."

She laughs lightly, looking away. She's struggling to keep our eye contact, and I just know it's because she's finding it too intense to deal with. This is good.

"You think I'm handsome." I pose it as a statement, because I know it to be true. She might have lost her memory, but she can't have lost her taste in men. I'm her taste. Me. Only me.

"Devastatingly," she confesses, with no hesitance or shame, finding the strength she needs to lock eyes with me.

"Then we're off to a good start." I half smile, and so does she, more shifting of her feet happening.

"You're also cocky."

"You love my cockiness." I avoid telling her that she also loves my cock. It's too soon. Or is it? Then her eyes drop to my groin, as if she's read my mind, and my cock—the one she loves—shouts from behind my fly. I talk it down urgently. It's definitely too soon for that. I don't think her mind would cope, and especially not her healing body.

As I take measured steps toward her, her breathing gets more labored until she eventually gives up altogether and holds her breath. I reach her and dip, kissing her cheek lightly. "It's a pleasure," I whisper, smiling when she shudders from top to toe before snapping out of her trance and moving back. "You had the very same reaction the first time we met."

She puffs out a shot of disbelieving laughter, looking away, as if embarrassed by her reactions to me. "You...um...yes..." She shakes herself, and then winces, reaching up to her head and clenching the side. "You certainly have a presence," she finishes on a face screwed up in discomfort.

My guilt is instant. "This was too much too soon." I move in and pick her up, and she lets me, welcoming my offer of support.

"I have legs, you know," she says, settling her head on my shoulder.

"Yeah, yeah, you tell me most days." In one swift but careful move, I maneuver her body, guiding her legs to around my waist. "And this is more like it." Our faces are suddenly close again, her unsure eyes on mine. "You call it our baby chimp cuddle," I say quietly.

She smiles faintly, scanning my face, as if she can't get enough of it. "I'm guessing you didn't *actually* sweep me off my feet the first time we met, so what happened after you had me coming over all hot and bothered?"

"You ran."

"I ran?"

"Yes, you virtually threw yourself down the stairs to escape me. Well, after I'd shown you the extension and told you I liked your dress."

"The extension? You've lost me."

"I hired you to design the new rooms I had built here."

Realization floods her eyes, as well as a little happiness. Something has just clicked for her. "So that's why I was at a posh sex club!"

I nod and move over to a black leather couch, lowering and keeping Ava on my lap. "Tell me your last memory. What's the most recent thing you remember, Ava?" I take her hands and hold them on my chest, watching as she falls into thought, her forehead creasing in concentration. I wait patiently for her to try to find what she's looking for, soundlessly willing her on.

"I was working for a company called Rococo Union." Her lips twist as she looks up at me. "There was a man I was seeing. But it wasn't you."

I feel like a knife just plunged into my fucking heart, and though I fight not to show it, I know my nostrils are flaring dangerously. "Is that it? There's nothing else?" I try not to sound too hopeful. It's hard when I've never hoped for anything more. Just a little something for me to work on. "Anything?"

Her blank expression, the fact that she's stalling her answer, tells me she doesn't. "I'm sorry." She looks away, probably to avoid the disappointment on my face.

Her despondency kills me. I pull her forward, wrapping my arms around her shoulders. "It's fine."

"Take me home." She snuggles into me, and I feel her tears soaking through my shirt. "Please."

I'm up from the couch quickly, carrying her out, trying not to let myself feel defeated. It's still early days, and she's heard only a morsel of our tale. Yet she's exhausted by it already. But I won't quit. It isn't in my DNA, especially when it comes to this woman.

Chapter 18

I let us into our home and toss my car keys on the table in the hallway. Ava has been so quiet since we left The Manor, so thoughtful and pensive. And I just know that she's trying to wrap her mind around the fact that her husband once owned an exclusive sex club. I feel like my past—the secrets, the hard truths—is all rushing forward and drowning me again, albeit in an entirely different way. I've never felt so fucking helpless.

"Tell me about our first date," she says as she settles at the island and I get us some water from the fridge.

Our first date? Christ, I just know she's imagining something romantic like women do. All flowers and feelings and smiles. There was all of that, just not in the way she's probably expecting. "It's a little . . . unique." I take some water and shut the door, risking a peek over my shoulder.

"Unique?"

"Not much about our relationship is conventional. Never has been." I nibble on my bottom lip, wondering where to start. "We should go into the lounge where it's more comfortable." I hand her the water and pick her up without thought, carrying her to the crushed velvet couch by the fire in the lounge.

She doesn't say a word, but I can practically see her thoughts churning. It's slowly driving me mad, constantly trying to guess what's going through her mind. I can't go on like this. "What are you thinking?" I ask, setting her down on the sofa and joining her.

Pulling her feet up onto the couch on a little grimace of pain, prompting me to help lift her injured leg, she looks around the grandeur of our lounge. "I'm thinking this room has my name written all over it."

I know that's not what she was really thinking, but I humor her, also taking in the gold and crimson décor. It's my favorite room in the house, for that very reason. It is my wife through and through. "You were never one hundred percent happy with it." I don't know why. To me, it's perfect. But Ava always said there was something missing, and for the life of her she couldn't put her finger on it.

"The curtains need something on the header," she says out of the blue.

I shoot her a look, finding her staring at the drapes. "Like what?"

"Some decoration on the pencil pleats. A crystal here or there, maybe." She shakes her head and returns her attention to me. "What are you smiling at?"

"Nothing." I kick my feet up on the coffee table and relax back as best I can with her not in my arms anymore. I just want to yank her close. All this gently-gently is weird. Fucking painful.

"So, our first date?" she asks, pulling me out of my funk, my head dropping to the side to find her.

"It depends what you call a first date."

"Oh God, was I easy?"

I bark out a bout of laughter. Easy? I fucking wish. "Far from it. And it drove me wild."

"But I went on a date with you?"

"We'd had sex a fair few times by the time I actually took you out for dinner."

"I *was* easy." She grimaces, as if disappointed with herself. She shouldn't be. If anything, it was me who was disappointed that it took so long for her to finally give in to the pull that was driving us both to distraction. "I shouldn't be surprised since I know how quickly I fell pregnant." She shakes her head in dismay, and I keep my mouth firmly zipped closed. "But part of me was hoping you'd tell me we met, sparks flew, you asked me out, we dated for a time, we eventually fell into bed and made romantic love, and then when the time was right, you proposed. And we lived happily ever after."

It's as I thought. All sweet and light in that mind of hers. Idyllic fairy tales. Fucking hell, she's so far off the mark, she may as well be on another planet. "Not quite like that."

"Then like what?" She's hungry for information, keen to learn. I'm not sure I'm very keen to tell.

"Well, when you refused to entertain my..." I pause, wondering how best to position it. "Advances." That's diplomatic enough. "I had to get creative."

"I refused?" Her eyes take a little trip down my reclined body, clearly wondering why she turned me down. It plants another seed of hope that I pray won't be killed off before it has a chance to grow into something beautiful.

"Yes, and it's a question I asked myself many times, too." I smile when she finds it in herself to rip her stare away from my chest. "You're stubborn. Always have been, always will be."

She sniffs though doesn't argue, pressing on with her thirst for information. "Creative how?"

I open my mouth to tell her exactly how, and then think better of it. This needs careful approaching. "You refused to come back to The Manor to fulfill your designs, and I knew it was because you were wary of me, of the feelings you had. It was most frustrating."

I half scowl at her, and she half smiles in return. "So I promised I'd stay out of your way if you came back and finished the job." I can see her trying to cast her mind back. "But I didn't."

"Stay out of my way?"

I nod. "Staying away from you proved very ... tricky."

"You must have had a real crush."

"A crush?" I laugh. "An obsession would be more apt. You blew me back, with your beauty, your voice, your passion for your job. For the first time in years, I felt alive."

"Years?"

I knew we'd have to go over this, but ... God, it's not something I relish the thought of. "I was a bit of ... " I fade off, thinking how to make it sound less sordid. "A playboy."

"Well, that's not a surprise, since you owned a sex club." She's taking it rather well. It's a stark contrast to the reaction back in the day. If only she'd been this willing to listen and accept back then, when she discovered the communal room. I shudder, remembering the train wreck that ensued. "So you used to screw around?" she asks.

"Something like that."

"But you stopped when you met me?"

"I stopped," I say, hating myself for bending the truth. Positively *hating* myself. I'm being selective with what I tell her, and I know in my heart of hearts that it isn't fair.

"Why don't I believe you?" She tilts her head, scanning my worried face. "You're lying to me, aren't you?"

I close my eyes, stress creeping up on me, and swallow down my fear. I can't even appreciate the fact that she's reading me like a book, like she knows me inside out. "There was this one incident."

"You cheated on me?" She's up off the couch quickly, glaring down at me through the discomfort her sharp move has spiked. I'm about to be trampled, Ava-style.

"Not exactly." I grab her hand and encourage her back down, not releasing her when she fights to regain possession of her limb. "We weren't really..." Fuck, how can I put it? "Exclusively dating."

"But we were seeing each other?"

"I guess so. If that's what you want to call it."

"Well, I don't know, Jesse." She's getting more and more irate, and I have no idea how to handle it. Usually I'd pounce right back at her. We'd spar with words, and then we'd make friends in the bedroom. "Because I can't fucking remember, can I?" she seethes.

"Watch your fucking mouth!"

She recoils, disgust invading her face. "Excuse me?"

"I don't like it when you swear."

"Well, I don't like finding out that my husband has cheated on me."

Motherfucking God! I release my hold of her and sink my head into my palms, searching for some calm. I never dreamed we'd be going over this again. "Ava, I got myself in a bit of a state over what I felt for you. It wasn't healthy, the *intense* feelings so soon. So I walked away from you. I drank, a lot, and I screwed *two* women. And I didn't even finish, because all I could see was you. I spent two fucking days locked in my office wondering what the hell to do. Because you didn't know about The Manor. You didn't know about my history. You knew nothing, and I didn't have a clue how to tell you." This is fucking knackering me out. All of it. "So I threw all of my energy into making you fall in love with me in the hopes that you would accept it all when I found the courage to tell you. And you did, Ava." I grab her hand, ignoring her startled expression and soldiering on. "You accepted me because you were as hopelessly in love with me as I was with you. You couldn't be without me, either. You let me take the lead and you followed willingly. You let me lavish you with the attention and suffocation, because you knew it's what I needed. You learned how to deal with me, Ava, and you are the only person in this world who can." My voice cracks. "And now I feel like you're slipping away from me, and I don't have a fucking clue how to make it right."

She's still, quiet, looking increasingly startled. The silence is unbearable. Excruciating.

"Please, say something," I beg, pleading with my eyes as well as with my words. "I punished myself. You punished me. I can't go through that all over again."

"You punished yourself? How?"

I'm quickly shifting in my seat, dropping her and raking my hand through my hair. My actions speak volumes, even if my mouth refuses to.

"Jesse, how?" she presses, a certain sternness in her demand.

Does she realize she's reading my body language? For a woman who doesn't remember me, she's showing all the instinctive signs of *knowing* me. I wish I could appreciate that right now. I can't. I'm just more terrified by the prospect of ruining my chances before I've even really tried.

"I had myself whipped." I close my eyes as I tell her, unwilling to see the inevitable horror on her face. "It was either that or drink myself into oblivion."

"What?" she gasps. "Whipped? By who?"

I don't hesitate. Let's get this horror show over with. "Sarah."

"Who the hell is Sarah?"

"An old friend." I open my eyes and find Ava heaving before me. She's mad. It's a small blessing because it shows she cares. "You didn't like her much."

"I'm not surprised!" Pivoting, she walks to the French doors that lead to the garden and stands staring out across our land, arms folded over her chest. It's cloudy out there. Dull. Grey. Miserable.

Apt.

"Why would you do that?" she asks.

"I already told you. To punish myself."

She remains with her back to me, though I see her shoulders rise. An inhale of shock? Or an inhale of strength? "And this Sarah. Your *friend*. Is she still in your life?"

I'm thrown back to last week, the moment when John told me she'd returned to London. The moment when I went to call Ava to tell her but got a call from the school instead. The moment when my world shattered. "No," I vow, because she isn't. "She left, moved to the States when she realized there was only one woman in my life. You."

"That was good of her."

Her curtness stings, but I accept that it's all I can expect. "Sarah was my uncle's girlfriend," I explain. "They had a little girl together."

Ava turns to face me, all spite lost, astonishment replacing it. "But she was in love with you?"

I nod. "Uncle Carmichael owned The Manor before I did. I worked for him as a teenager. He introduced me to that lifestyle."

"Bloody hell, Jesse. Do your parents know?"

"Of course. That's why I didn't speak to them for years. We only reconciled when you came into my life." I pat the couch next to me. "Ava, come and sit down with me, please." I don't know if it's instinct or a sense of duty, but she does, settling warily. "I'm going to give you a shortened version because, frankly, it's so far in the past and there are so many other things I need to share with you, tell you, things that are more relevant to our lives now. Things that have made us happy. Things that have built us. Things that helped us get over the shitty stuff and brought us to now."

"But it's all part of our story, good or bad."

I can't argue with that. "But it's painful, Ava."

She reaches over and takes my hand. It's a natural display of comfort, and I'm so grateful for it. "Tell me."

I rub into my weary eyes with my spare hand, squeezing my other around hers. "I was a twin myself," I begin, and she smiles softly, changing the hold of our hands so her fingers are laced with mine, moving closer. "My brother was the good boy. The achiever. I was... well, a pain in my parents' arse, I see that now. I led him astray, and..." Fucking hell, I can feel a vise squeezing my heart, air being drained from my lungs. "We were out one night. Drinking. It was my idea. I encouraged him. Jacob walked into the road."

Her hand covers her mouth, realization hitting her. "Jacob," she mumbles.

I nod my confirmation of our son's name and my dead brother's. "Mum and Dad blamed me for Jake's death. I was a mess. I felt so guilty." Something tells me that I should hold back on my ex-wife and dead daughter right now. I'm already bombarding Ava with so much. So, right or wrong, I skip it and go straight to the beginning of my life at The Manor. Or the end of my life until Ava crashed into it. "I went off the rails. Took up residence at The Manor. Uncle Carmichael passed away, I inherited the place, and the rest is history."

Her cheeks puff out, her head shaking slowly, disbelieving. "I don't even know what to do with all of this."

"Do nothing. Say nothing," I tell her, pulling her closer. "When I met you, you pulled me out of the black hole I'd been trapped in for so long. You gave me new life and purpose. I felt good for the first time in years, and I wasn't about to let you refuse me those feelings."

"So you got *creative?*" Her eyebrow hitches a smidgen.

"Yes. I swear, I'd never worked so hard to get laid."

A small gasp followed by a playful slap of my upper arm

prompts a little laugh from me, and as a result, Ava rolls her eyes, not being able to help smiling herself. I pull her onto my lap, and she doesn't complain, coming with ease. "Was it good?" she asks. "When you finally got me into bed." Her lips seal tightly, as if she's bracing herself. She's wondered this before. She's looked at me and considered what it would be like to be intimate with me.

"You mean against a wall."

"Huh?"

This is better. This is the important stuff. The feelings, the connection, the out-of-this-world sex. "At Lusso."

Her frown is huge. "What's Lusso?"

"A complex on St. Katharine Docks. You were the designer. I bought the penthouse. That's how I heard your name and why I got you to The Manor. I liked what you did with it. Italian shit everywhere."

"Oh. So you did get me back to your apartment, then?"

"Not quite. I got you in the bathroom on launch night."

"I screwed you in the bathroom of a show home? Oh God!" Her forehead falls onto my chest and rolls from side to side in despair. "That's not like me. I don't do things like that."

I smile and wrap her in my arms, savoring the moment of her being so close. She wasn't like that. I know. That was one of the things I loved about her. Problem is, she's still that young woman in her mind. "It was incredible. The want thrumming from your body, mirroring mine. We were inevitable, baby. A spark just waiting to explode. And, trust me, we exploded."

I swallow, my face in her hair, my body coming to life just talking about that moment in our history. The moment she gave in. The moment the explosion happened.

As a result of my thoughts, my cock starts to stiffen, and it can't have escaped Ava's notice, since she's sitting on the damn thing. She better not move; I can't promise I'll be able to hold ba—

She shifts, and I suppress a growl, not very successfully. I'm iron behind my jeans. My veins are hot. My heart jumping. It's not a good place to be when any kind of Jesse-style fuck is off the table. Lips straight, she finds my eyes, and I see that dormant lust lingering in their depths. She swallows and drops her gaze to my lips. Fucking hell, I've never been so starving for her. Never been so desperate to take her. Never felt so paralyzed by desire. She's just staring at my mouth, her body now unmoving on my lap, her mind clearly racing. She wants to kiss me. Wants to taste me.

"Are you ready to stop fighting it now?" I ask, being catapulted back to Lusso when I finally got to take what I so badly wanted.

"I need all of you. Say I can have all of you." She immediately looks confused by her words, but I'm fucking elated, because even though she doesn't know where these words are coming from, they're coming, and that's really all the hope I can count on right now.

"You can have all of me," I tell her quietly, even though she already owns every fiber of my being.

She slowly drops forward until her lips gently meet mine. It's a beautiful moment, one, along with many others, that I will cherish for as long as I live. I don't take the lead, deciding that I should let her take it at her own pace, and I'm more than happy with her pace. It's slow. It's soft. It's gentle and loving and everything that it should be. It's everything that I feel.

The sofa melds around my back, and Ava melds into my front, my head resting back, my mouth and my tongue lax to easily follow her movements. My hands keep a firm hold of her hips, just enough to tell her that I'm here and I so desperately want to be. I haven't tasted her in over a week. It's the longest stretch I've ever gone without kissing her, feeling her, and maybe that is why every sense feels heightened. She tastes more potent; my skin feels hypersensitive to her touch. It's perfect. So perfect, I never want it to end.

"Are you okay?" I ask against her lips when she pauses a beat before resuming her exploration of my mouth, her palms holding my cheeks as if she's scared I'll move and break her flow.

"You are such a good kisser," she mumbles, pushing her front into me, not helping with the situation behind the fly of my jeans. Kissing, yeah, great, but I'm not sure if she's ready for more just yet. "It feels like we've done this a million times, got it down to a fine art."

"We *have* done it a million times," I say, quickly cursing myself when she breaks our lips and pulls away.

"Of course." Her cheeks are flushed, and I'm struggling to fathom whether it's with embarrassment or desire. "Sorry, I got a little carried away."

Oh, the strength it takes for me not to bark my frustration nearly breaks me. "Don't apologize," I order as softly as I can, taking her chin and directing her face to mine. "Thank you."

"For what?"

"For that amazing kiss."

She smiles, almost shyly. "Thank you, too." Her blush is heartbreaking because it signifies the loss of our time, and deeply gratifying because I can at least make her blush again. She was so used to me after all these years, nothing I said or did fazed her anymore.

"I want to take you out tomorrow," I tell her. "Do you think you can manage it?"

"Where are you taking me?"

Reaching for her hair, I push a stray lock over her shoulder. "A little trip down memory lane."

She says nothing, just smiles as I rise from the couch with her still attached to my front. Encouraging her to find her feet, I turn her by her shoulders and push her on. "Go get ready for dinner."

"Bossy again," she muses.

"Like I said, get used to it." I release her at the bottom of the stairs and watch as she takes them slowly, constantly glancing over her shoulder at me. I cock my head, lifting my eyebrows when she tries to hide a secret smile. "What's tickled you?" I call.

Her delicate shoulders jump up in a small shrug, but she doesn't say anything. She doesn't need to. She felt something powerful just then. Something in our kiss that reinforced the rightness of her being here with me. She was lost in that moment, and her mind was blank for all the right reasons.

Chapter 19

The next morning, I'm all set. I've called Dr. Peters to ensure I'm not pushing her too far, and he reassured me that my plan to revisit some of our past is a good idea. Just to take it easy with her, which was a stupid fucking thing to say. We also chatted briefly about all these small hints of memories, all the words, and he seemed thrilled by that. All in all, I'm feeling pretty good.

I know where we're going, what we're doing, and I'm really looking forward to it. That kiss last night. It was just a kiss, but it was earthmoving. I felt like she was breathing hope into me. It made sleeping alone again that little bit more bearable.

"What are you looking at?" I ask as Ava performs a full assessment of me in the hallway, her eyes roaming up and down my tall frame.

"You just don't seem the type to wear leather trousers." She's thinking so hard she's frowning. "Then again, you didn't seem the type to own a sex club, either." Looking up at me, she shrugs a little. "I guess they go hand in hand."

Laughter so rich and loud spills out of me. "It isn't what you think," I assure her, chuckling as I produce another set of leather trousers. "These are yours."

"Oh God, next you'll be pulling out a whip."

I recoil, my arm dropping limply to my side. "There's no whip."

"Oh shit." Her mouth snaps shut, her disposition quickly awkward. "I'm guessing whips are a no-go zone for us."

"It's not the most thrilling part of our history." I hand her the trousers, and she takes them, if a little cautiously, not because she's still wondering what we're doing and why she'll be wearing them, but because her mind is whirling about that horrid time.

"You told me that I punished you, too," she says, looking at the leather in her grasp. "You punished yourself by being whipped. So how did I punish you?"

I flinch, the cracking of leather across her back echoing through my skull like the perfect kind of torture. Though her reasoning at the time eventually made sense to me, it didn't make it any easier to accept. Anger sizzles, threatening to surface as I eye her with caution and collect my keys and shades. "I'd rather not revisit one of the most horrific moments in my life." My answer only seems to enhance her curiosity, and in true Ava style she pushes on.

"Something tells me that I didn't dump your arse for a few days. Or give you the silent treatment. So how did I punish you?"

"It's not important." I make my way to the door, eager to end this conversation. I'm a fool. Evading questions and distracting Ava in the early days of our relationship was what got me in such a mess in the first place. Haven't I learned?

"Your body language disagrees," she calls, pulling me to a stop at the door. "Tell me."

Tell her. Will she believe it? I didn't at the time, and I saw firsthand the nightmare unfolding before me. That bastard lashing her, her body hanging limply. I swallow and turn to face her, as well as facing up to my responsibility. "You weren't punishing me for sleeping with someone else."

She flinches at the reminder, and though the vision hurts, something sick inside me appreciates her reaction. Because it's another sign that she cares. The thought of me with another woman pains her. Even now, when she doesn't know me. "Then what was I punishing you for?"

"Having my guilt thrashed out of me. For hurting myself."

Another flinch. It's a minor reaction in contrast to the horror scene that played out in The Manor that awful day, but it still pricks at my skin relentlessly. Her jaw stiffens, her eyes becoming fierce. It's familiar, if unwelcome right now. "Tell me."

I match her stoic expression and spill. "You had yourself whipped, too." Her mouth falls open. "You let some scumbag shackle you half-naked and you let him whip you. Happy?"

"Do I fucking look happy?" she spits, throwing the trousers to the floor. "Why the hell would I do that?"

"Because," I say, unable to rein myself in, the anger that's lay dormant within me all these years racing to the surface unstoppably. I get my threatening face close to hers. She doesn't budge an inch, squaring up to me in return. My defiant little temptress. My angel. My Ava. Here she fucking is. "Because you wanted me to understand how much you loved me. Because you wanted me to feel how you felt when you found me being thrashed." My nostrils flare as she stares me down, our noses nearly touching, my body bent a little to make sure of it. "And it fucking worked."

Her jaw, so tight, is ticking wildly. She's mad. Whether she's mad because she knows deep inside that she really did do that, or if she's mad because she can't remember, isn't a question I'm bothered about in this moment. Because beyond the anger, I see a familiar, potent craving. I see that mixture of fury and desire. The need to rip a strip off me *and* rip my clothes off.

When we're angry with each other, the sex is even more passionate, crazy, and satisfying. It's all here before me now, yet I cannot be the one to make the first move. I can't push this. For the first time in our relationship, I'm depending on her to give me what I want, and, more importantly, what I need more than anything in the world. Our connection. Our chemistry.

"Kiss me," I demand. "Now."

"Fuck you."

"Watch your fucking mouth!" I bark, a secret smile hiding behind my straight face.

She doesn't try to hide hers. "Screw you."

"Three," I say lowly.

"Zero, baby." She lunges forward, smashing her lips to mine, her arms virtually strangling me as she climbs up my body. I stagger back, fucking chaos breaking out in my leather trousers—heat, blood, and solid flesh raging down there. She's unforgiving in her demand for my mouth. Harsh stabs of her tongue against mine, vicious tugs of my hair, deep, throaty groans of pleasure.

My back hits the door frame, jolting her in my arms, not that it distracts her from her mission. I can do nothing more than keep up with her pace, silently demanding her to start ridding us of clothes so I can lose myself in her. Find the peace I need. Relish the joining of our bodies.

Her hot, wet tongue circles my mouth, our heads tilting and turning constantly, taking other angles, pulling back, smashing together once again. It's madness. Disorderly. Absolutely incredible.

And then as quickly as it started, it stops. Like she could have been hit with a thousand volts of electricity, she catapults back, forcing me to release her before she dives clean out of my arms. "Oh my God," she sputters, brushing herself down, hands faffing everywhere, eyes avoiding mine. That kiss has wiped me of breath. I'm panting like I'm exhausted. "I don't know what came over me."

"Well it wasn't me," I mutter to myself, forcing back the

mental image of me doing exactly that. Coming all over her. Kneeling over her, her arms pinned down, my hand thrusting my cock in her face as she watches. My cum coating her lovely face. And her tongue licking it all up. *Fuck!* I physically rearrange myself, looking for room in my trousers to accommodate my raging hard-on. There's no room. Not in these damn things.

"Something got the better of me." She looks up at me. And I can see immediately that she gets it. Even if she doesn't *know* me, she gets it. The ridiculously strong attraction was the first stepping-stone to utter fucking perfection. And thank God she's not misplaced *that*.

"Yes, *I* got the better of you," I say, peeling my back away from the door frame. Ava darts surprised eyes at me. "Now, are you finished unraveling your knickers, lady?" I take her hand, scoop the trousers from the floor, and lead her out to the garages.

Pressing the button on the remote, I hold back while the door rolls open. "Bloody hell, Jesse!" She drops my hand and moves into the garage, motioning to the lines of cars and superbikes. "Are these all yours?"

Making my way over to the cabinet, I pull our helmets down from one of the shelves. "All ours."

"These must be worth hundreds of thousands."

"Which is why the garage is alarmed and the cars all have trackers."

"Trackers?" Her head tilts, somewhere between interest and worry. "Did you have a tracker on my car?"

"Of course." I don't beat around the bush. "A nice little app on my phone told me where you were at all times." I laugh when she snorts, disgusted. "Don't worry. You had the app too."

"I did?"

"Yes, you worry about me as much as I worry about you." I hold up the helmets.

"What are those for?"

"We're going swimming," I quip drily, pointing to her hands. "And those are your trunks."

Ava glances down at the leather trousers in her grasp, comprehension coming to her. She inhales quickly and swings toward my superbike, definitely thrilled by the prospect. "I'm going on that thing?"

I'm laughing again. "That's a little different from what you said the first time I took you for a ride."

"A ride?" Her eyebrow cocks with interest, extending my laughter. There's that suggestiveness in her again.

I approach her slowly, a little ominously, and dip, bringing our faces close. "You love riding the bike, but you love riding me even more."

Red creeps into her cheeks. It's such a satisfying sight, again taking me back to the early days when she was trying to hide how much she was floored by me. She tries to rectify her fluster. "I would challenge that, if I didn't know it to be true."

"Oh?" Interesting. "And how do you know?" She immediately starts to shift on the spot, and I grin, glancing down at her chest. Nipples like bullets. And I bet her knickers aren't too dry, either. All the signs thrill me. "Get your trousers on."

She smiles, steps back, and does as she's bid, and that's highly satisfying, too. All these natural instincts in her. It's hope. "Do I ride on my own?" she asks.

I scoff. "Never. Only ever with me."

"Why?" She's genuinely interested.

"Bikes are dangerous machines."

"So are cars," she counters quietly as she pulls her trousers up her legs. I still and flick her a glance. I can't help but think that had I enforced my demand to have her in a Range Rover, we wouldn't be in this nightmare right now. Judging by the state of her Mini, I'm surprised she's even alive. My veins instantly freeze on that thought. "Are you okay?"

"Yeah." I push on, demanding my mind to steer away from such sickening thoughts. I have her. She's here.

Once we're both covered in leather, I place her helmet over her head gently, smiling a smidgen while I fasten her chin strap. "I have déjà vu," she mumbles through her squished cheeks. "That's got to be a good thing, right?"

"I'm sure it is," I assure her, wriggling her helmet as gently as I can to check it's secure. "You look fucking hot."

"I know." She flexes her head from side to side. "And it's good to see you're wearing leathers, too." She freezes, as do I, both of us staring at each other. "Why did I say that?" She suddenly looks puzzled, and my hope dies, but only a little, because the doctor said he's pleased. All these little things here and there. There has to be a pinnacle moment that will bring it all rushing back. Something that will open the floodgates.

I go ahead and try to explain. "When we first met, I never wore leathers." Her eyes drop to my stomach. I know what she's thinking. She's thinking about the scars on my abdomen. She's thinking I must have sustained those injuries in an accident, and I don't put her straight. "You weren't happy about it," I finish gently, sweeping my arm out toward the bike in indication for her to hop on board.

She heads for the bike without thought or question. "I'm not surprised. You're not—"

"Indestructible, I know."

She stops for a beat, slowly looking over her shoulder and down to my stomach again. "This is so weird."

I laugh sarcastically. "Just a bit." Joining her, I throw my leg over the bike and settle in the seat. "Put your foot on..." My instruction fades off when I feel her front squished up behind me in the seat, her arms circling my midriff. "Okay, then."

"I feel like I should be, but I'm not even scared," she declares, snuggling closer. "Where are we going?"

Looking down at her hands linked over my stomach, feeling her head resting on my back, her body pushed tight to mine, brings me a little peace. Whether she knows it or not, she trusts me. I pull my helmet on and start up my Ducati 1299 Superleggera, giving it a few exhilarating revs. The roar is only amplified in the enclosed garage, and Ava's hold of me constricts. Had I not spoken to the doctor, this definitely wouldn't be happening. But she's comfortable. So comfortable. Besides, like I would let anything happen to her.

I kick up the stand and roll us out of the garage, taking it steadily to the main road. I ignore her demand for me to speed up. This ride will be slow and careful. Not something I'm really familiar with, but fast getting used to. Because I have to.

Chapter 20

With Ava nestled so snugly against my back, I may have gone the long way to my intended destination. I make no apologies for that. She's lucky I'm even letting her off the bike now. She swings elegantly but a little gingerly off the back, like she's done it a million times before, which she has. Then she unclips her helmet and pulls it off, tentatively shaking out her long dark waves.

Sweet mother of all things holy. My cock lunges like a depraved animal trying to escape a cage. It's not a bad comparison. It's been way too long since I've had sex. My balls are about to explode, and that moment back there in the hallway when she jumped on me hasn't helped my situation.

Next, she unzips her jacket, revealing her white casual T-shirt and a little cleavage. Not too much. Just a hint of the boobs I love so much. I shouldn't look. It's only slowly torturing me.

"Hey." My visor flips up, courtesy of Ava, and she scowls at me playfully. "Are you staring at my boobs?"

"What's it got to do with you?" I retort offhand, making her hover between light laughter and gawking at me.

"Because they're mine."

I snort and get off the bike. "There are plenty of things for me to remind you of, and this is one of the most important." I point my finger at her chest, then let it travel the entire length of her body. "All this is mine."

She slaps my hand away. "You're a pigheaded arsehole."

"Yeah, yeah," I sigh tiredly. "It's still all mine."

Huffing and puffing a few times, she flips me a scowl. For what point I don't know, maybe just to demonstrate her exasperation. It would be refreshing if it wasn't boring these days. Yet this little back-and-forth thing we have going on is strangely wonderful. "What are we doing here, anyway?" She looks across the grassy planes of Hyde Park.

"We're going for a walk. Or a mooch, as you like to put it."

"You mooch in shops. Not in parks."

"You don't like mooching in shops with me," I tell her.

"Why?"

"Because I trample all the dresses you like," I reply candidly as I take her helmet from her hand and put it with mine on the seat. "So I go shopping for you."

"You buy my clothes?" Horror is a blanket across her lovely face. "Control what I wear?"

"Pretty much, yes, and now isn't the time to try and change that." I offer my hand, and she takes it automatically. "We're happy as we are."

"You mean *you're* happy."

"Trust me, Ava. You are deliriously happy." I march on my way, not too quickly so she doesn't struggle to keep up. "Just tell me if you need a rest."

"I need a rest."

I move in front of her and dip, taking the backs of her thighs gently and hauling her onto my back. She yelps, but leaves me to my thing. "Better?"

"You're going to carry me all the way around the park?"

"Yes," I reply with utter finality, my pace picking up now that I haven't got to worry about wearing her out.

Her protests don't come. A question, however, does. "How old are you?" she asks, linking her arms around my neck and resting her chin on my shoulder.

"Twenty-four."

"Just tell me."

"No."

"Why?"

"Because I want you to find out for yourself."

"And how am I going to do that?"

I look out the corner of my eye, the edge of my lip lifting. "I'm sure you'll think of something." I see her mind immediately whirling. She's brainstorming. Good. Never in my life would I have imagined myself silently willing her to handcuff me and leave me at her mercy again. But now, I'd do *anything*. And now, I wouldn't get irate and lose the plot. I'd smile my damn way through the fucking torture. "Comfortable up there?" I ask, glancing to her face resting on my shoulder as I pace down the path.

Peeking at me, she nods discreetly before lowering her lips to my cheek and kissing me softly. "Very." I close my eyes and savor her affection, not knowing where it's come from, but unwilling to question it too deeply. Then she resumes her position, chin on my shoulder. "I could get very used to this."

"You already are, baby." I breathe in, then exhale slowly. "You already are." I continue down the path, feeling positive and actually quite excited about the rest of our day. That was easy affection, and I want more of it.

When we come to the exact spot I had planned, I gently lower her to her feet and point to the grass. "Lie down."

She laughs, caught between wariness and humor. "Why?"

"Because I told you to."

"And I always do what you tell me, do I?"

"I fucking wish," I mutter, lowering to the grass and putting myself on my back. I spread my arms and legs, imitating Ava's beat form the first time I took her for a run and she collapsed with exhaustion. "Familiar?" I ask.

"Should it be?"

I pout, disappointed. "Maybe I should drag you on a ten-mile run."

She splutters above me. "Are you serious? I'd be dead."

"You practically were the first time, but you soon got used to it. Now you're like Forrest Gump."

She glances down her body, taking in the good shape she's in. "Running clearly does nothing for my boobs."

I'm up on my elbows like lightning. "Oh no, lady." I laugh, though it's with dread rather than humor. "Don't even *think* about it." I shake my head furiously, daring her to defy me.

"They're not how I remember them," she muses, chin on her chest as she takes them in. Of all the things that aren't how she remembers, she's worried about her boobs?

"Your boobs are perfect."

"What's crawled up your arse?"

"You," I snap, reaching for her hand and tugging her down to the grass. A quick, expert maneuver has her beneath me in a flash. Trapped. And panting. My grin must be epic as I nestle my body between her thighs and claim her wrists, thrusting them up over her head. "You look good under me."

"You look good *over* me." Now she's grinning, too, and if I wasn't already on the ground, the impact of her voluntary affection would have knocked me on my arse. Something has shifted between us. Since that kiss last night, I feel like we're making progress, even if there are no monumental breakthroughs in her memory. She's receptive. I see she's curious about so much, not just the last sixteen years, but me. This man. This man who is her husband. This man who loves her with a fierceness that's debilitating for both of us.

She smiles, scanning my face, reading my thoughts. "Was that your chat-up line when we met?"

Her question brings on a crazy bout of laughter, my muscles forced to engage in order to hold me up and not squish her under me. "Not quite."

"What was it, then?" The true, almost excited curiosity in her eyes is another sucker punch to my heart. She thinks it'll be all romantic. Sweet and light. Make her swoon and go all giddy. I made her giddy all right. I remember it well. Her shock. Her disgust. But more the look in her eyes that told me she was wondering how loud she really would scream.

I cough my throat clear. "I'm not sure you're ready for that part."

"After everything you off-loaded already?" She snorts, and I growl. "Give me a break."

"I'll give you something," I whisper, flexing my groin into hers without thought.

"We're in the park," she whispers lustfully, with zero concern that we're actually in the park. She's saying what she thinks she should say.

"Wherever, whenever, baby. You know that." I don't wait for her to kiss me. I can see she wants me to, and the moment is too perfect to waste. So I gently drop my lips to hers and coax her mouth open softly, swallowing down the low, appreciative noises she makes.

"I'm learning fast." Her lips pass over mine at the same steady pace, and I smile against them. This is perfect.

"You like gentle Jesse?"

"I love gentle Jesse." She speaks between our kiss, totally indulging in my mouth. "Now tell me."

"Tell you what?" My mind has blanked on me, and I growl, annoyed, when she pulls away.

"Your chat-up line when we met." She sighs in exasperation.

"I asked you how loud you'd scream when I fucked you."

She starts laughing so hard, her whole body shakes, and while I'm a little stunned, I'm also delighted. And seeing her so amused is overwhelmingly rewarding.

"So how loud did I scream?" she asks, chuckling between each word.

"You nearly took off the roof of Lusso."

She's gone again, laughing like some demented person, eyes bursting with water, body losing all control. I could stay here all day and just admire it. Listen to her. "I'm glad you find it funny, lady." I wait, quite content watching her as she finds it in herself to calm down. I've really tickled her.

Regaining control of herself, she sighs deeply, flexing her hands a little for me to release them. As soon as I have, her arms are around my neck. "I just . . ." A deep breath. "I don't know. Everything you're telling me, how you are, how I am, how we are, just sounds so crazy. Yet my heart is telling me it's real. It's normal. Nothing feels wrong at all, just so incredibly right. Even the mad stuff."

I smile softly and brush some hair back off her face. "It's our normal, baby. I've always told you that."

"Our normal sounds pretty fucking perfect."

"Watch your mouth."

"Okay." She giggles and takes my lips once more, hungry for them since she tasted me last night. She can't get enough of me, and I'm not about to complain. I let her at me for as long as she wants, following her soft, swirling tempo. "We're probably gathering an audience." She's breathless. Good. Let me take some more of that breath.

"Fuck 'em." I take over the pace, every sound of pleasure that escapes her stroking my skin and warming it. I wouldn't be opposed to staying here for the rest of the day. But I reluctantly acknowledge that she needs to eat.

"You must be hungry." I pull back and trace the lines of her cheekbones, smiling at her swollen rosy lips.

"A little," she admits on a sigh. "I'm more thirsty."

"I know just the place." I press my fists into the ground on either side of her and push myself up, helping her to her feet. Pointing across the road to the coffeehouse, I take her hand and lead on. "You think you can walk that far?"

"No." She looks up at me, her lips pressed together cheekily. "You might need to carry me."

I say nothing and turn for her to climb onto my back again. We're perhaps only thirty paces from the café, an easy walk, even for Ava, but she wants me to carry her and I'm not about to refuse. She's playing. I love it.

With her face nestled close to mine, I walk us across the road and set her on her feet outside. "My lady," I say, pulling the door open and sweeping my arm out in gesture for her to lead on. I'm grinning. She's grinning. It's just one big grin-fest this afternoon.

"Why didn't you just woo me this romantically when we met?" she asks, passing through the door. "You know, instead of asking highly inappropriate questions."

I raise a brow as I follow her in. "How could I woo you when you refused to even have dinner with me? I was a desperate man. Besides, I eventually won your heart. Who cares how I did it?"

She laughs, bumping my shoulder as I flank her. I don't budge, but Ava wobbles a bit, forcing me to make a grab for her before she topples. "Ava!" I snap. "For fuck's sake, be careful!"

She startles, blinking rapidly at me in surprise as I hold her by the tops of her arms. "No need to make a scene." She glances around, as do I, seeing a few people looking our way. I couldn't give a flying fuck.

"Just be careful," I mutter, taking her hand and leading her on toward the counter, stuffing my hand in my pocket to find my wallet.

But I freeze, pulling Ava to an abrupt halt, too, my feeling fingers lying still on the leather of my wallet as I stare at what's captured my abrupt attention.

Sarah's eyes, clouded with surprise to match mine, flick between me and Ava. She was always a bit too fond of Botox and fillers, and it seems that love affair has grown in her absence. Growing old gracefully she is not. Her skin is too taut and her lips blown up to ridiculous proportions. She has a coffee in her hand, just turning to leave the café.

"Jesse?" Ava's hand lands gently on my forearm, and I rip my stare from Sarah and look down at my wife. "You okay?"

I cough, my head in chaos. "What do you want to drink?" I ask, slipping my arm over her shoulder and walking on, taking a wide berth around Sarah, hoping beyond all hope that Ava doesn't notice her. Sarah's body turns as we move, keeping her facing us. I feel my lips form a straight, warning line, silently threatening her to leave quietly and unnoticed. Her eyes are questioning, even if her face is poker straight.

We just make it to the counter when Ava turns away from me, directly toward Sarah. "I'll have a hot chocolate, please. I just need a tissue." She wanders off, literally rubbing shoulders with Sarah as she passes. My wife doesn't bat an eyelid at the woman who nearly tore us apart. Or one of the women. I watch in dread as Sarah's gaze follows her path to the nearby pile of napkins. She looks confused. John hasn't told her about Ava's accident? And then as Ava heads back, wiping her nose, her eyes fall straight onto Sarah. She frowns, eyeing Sarah as she stares. "That woman is staring at me,"

Ava says when she's returned to me, moving in closely to my side. "Do I know her?"

"No," I answer immediately, just as Sarah approaches. If looks could kill, Sarah would be dead on the spot. I just know my expression must be harboring all kinds of threats, but she heeds none.

"Jesse. Ava." She passes her eyes between us, and the atmosphere thickens in an instant. "Lovely to see you."

Ava looks up at me in question. I shake my head, returning to the counter and pulling Ava with me. I throw my order at the server, beginning to shake with the strength it's taking not to fly off the deep end. What the fuck is she playing at? Jesus, if Ava were herself, Sarah would probably be swimming in every coffee my wife could find and throw at her.

"Who is she?" Ava asks.

"It's not important," I all but snap, tossing a tenner on the counter and swiping up our drinks.

"Then why are you all bristly and mad?"

"I'm not." I place her hot chocolate in one hand and take her other, pulling her on, though she puts up a fight, trying to wrench herself from my grip. Damn her!

"Jesse, let go of me."

I do, but only because I don't want to hurt her. Though my relinquished hold causes her to stumble back again, and in the process of saving her from tumbling to the floor, I send our drinks there instead. "Ava, damn it, be careful with yourself!" I kick the cups aside and thank everything holy that she has leather trousers on, protecting her skin from the hot spray.

"Who is she?" Ava demands, standing firm, her eyes jumping from me to Sarah, completely ignoring the mess at our feet. "I don't have a good feeling about her. Tell me."

Jaw tight, I damn her to hell and back in my head. "We're

leaving," I grate, thrusting my hand to the door. "Now, Ava, or so help me God."

She snorts and turns toward Sarah. "Who are you?" she asks.

Sarah glances at me, absolutely perplexed, though once again she completely disregards my threatening look. "My name's Sarah."

Ava's body language changes in a nanosecond. She's now bristling as much as me. "Sarah?" Her eyes cast to mine. "Your *friend*, Sarah? Your uncle's girlfriend who's in love with you?" If I wasn't in such a pickle right now, I'd appreciate the fact that my wife clearly isn't happy about this. She looks fuming mad. "The woman who whipped you?"

Sarah, wary, steps back, so obviously confused by what's transpiring.

"Just go, Sarah. Now," I warn before it gets nasty, because God knows my wife is perfectly capable. Her spunk has only grown with her age. It's had to, if only to handle me.

Shoulders falling in defeat, Sarah finally turns and leaves the coffeehouse, and I brace myself for the wrath of my wife. "You said she wasn't in our lives anymore. Not even in the country."

"She wasn't."

"So are you telling me I've lost my mind as well as my memory? That I imagined that?" Her hand shoots toward the door that's slowly closing behind Sarah's back.

"She showed up last week," I confess. "I didn't get a chance to tell you."

She laughs, and it's full of sarcasm. "It wouldn't matter if you did, would it? Because I wouldn't fucking remember now, would I?"

"Watch your damn mouth, Ava." For God's sake, it's getting pottier.

A member of the café staff appears with a bucket and mop, looking at us nervously. I step out of the puddle of coffee and claim Ava.

"Get your hands off me," she spits, shrugging me off and

hobbling on. I sigh and follow. Now would be a good time for a Reminder Fuck. Just to remind her of her place.

I keep a safe distance behind her, not too far in case she staggers or trips again, as I follow her back across the park where we left my bike. I can see with each step she's getting slower, and her limp is more obvious. Though my stubborn little temptress won't ask for help. Tough. She's getting it. I pick up my pace and overtake her, dipping in invitation, rather than manhandling her into my hold in my usual fashion. She climbs straight onto my back, no question. "I'm only accepting because my leg is hurting," she mutters. "I'm still not talking to you."

I roll my eyes to myself. "Fine."

"Why didn't you bloody tell me?" she yells in my ear, making me flinch and wince and close my eyes. "It's bad enough that I can't remember a thing, and now I have to worry about someone trying to steal my husband?"

"No one is going to steal your husband," I say. Stupid woman. "Sarah means nothing to me. Never has."

"You clearly mean something to her. What does she want? Why is she here?"

"Ava," I sigh, thoroughly done with this conversation. But through my thick skin, I get that she's feeling vulnerable. It's my job to reassure her. "Unravel your knickers."

She completely ignores me, ranting on. "And are there any more witches ready to try and get their claws into you?"

"Ava, will you leave it?" I'm not growling, but I'm pretty damn close. *Keep your cool, Jesse. Keep your cool.*

"No. How am I supposed to know who to fight off if I can't remember any of them? You need to tell me."

Of all the things I want to remind her about, that isn't one. Besides, it would take too fucking long. I haven't the energy. "I said, drop it."

"And I said no. What am I sup—"

I stop, lower her, and pull her around my body so we're front to front, grabbing her cheeks. I catch her gasp of shock in my mouth when I kiss her hard, shutting her the hell up. I'm distracting her. Resorting to desperate tactics. It's something I won't apologize for. Besides, it seems she rather likes kissing me. Thank God. I lift her from her feet and continue walking, never dropping her lips. All the way back to my bike. "It was a lovely afternoon. Don't let anything spoil it." We have far more important things to deal with than Sarah or any ex. "Please."

Her face twists, her energy obviously wiped from the exertion of stressing, and her forehead falls to my chest. I cup the back of her head and massage into her hair, avoiding the site of her cut. "I'm tired," she moans.

And I feel guilty. I've pushed her too much. I take her helmet and gently push it onto her head, wondering if it would be unreasonable for me to demand she and the kids wear helmets while driving in the future. After the accident, nothing I demand to ensure their safety should be unreasonable, and she'd better accept that. "Come on. You need to eat."

I snap her visor down and plant a kiss on it before helping her onto the bike.

Chapter 21

I take her to a small bistro not far from our health club. She's obsessed with the eggs Benedict here, has been for years. So that's what I ordered her. But she's hardly touched a damn thing, picking and poking at the food on her plate. "Eat," I demand.

"I'm really not hungry." She drops her fork and pushes her full plate away before falling back on the chair.

My lips twist in displeasure. I'll force-feed her if I have to. I don't care where we are. "Here." I grab her fork and load it with some egg, holding it across the table to her. "Eat."

Eyes sulky, her jaw tight, she moves back some more. "I'm not hungry."

"And I'm not in the mood for your defiance." My head cocks in warning. "Eat."

"No."

"God damn it, Ava, you need to keep up your energy." I make a racket scraping my chair across the floor with me still sitting in it, so I'm beside her, closer, ready to pry her tight lips open to get this food inside her.

"Why? To deal with your unreasonable arse?"

I'd laugh if I wasn't so fucking livid. "Don't make me ask you again." I can feel myself starting to twitch in my seat. Today started so well, and now she's ruining it with something so silly as refusing to eat. Why can't she just fucking behave?

"What are you gonna do? Give me the countdown?" She blinks a few times, and then frowns.

"Yes, I would," I confirm, and she snorts indignantly. I drop my head, trying to cool the building irritation. Jesus, I'm getting too old for this shit. She's being defiant for the sake of it, to prove a point. "Ava." I look at her, ready to off-load every detail of her punishment when she's well, but my intended threats all die on my tongue when I spot something over the road. I crane my neck, zooming in. John's sitting outside a café up the street. He must be taking a break from the club.

I toss a few twenties on the table and claim a bewildered Ava from her chair. "This time, you got off. It won't happen again." I walk us toward my bike. "Wait here for me."

"Why, where are you going?"

"There's someone over there I need to have a quick word with. Stay put." I pass her helmet and jog off. "Hey, John!" I call.

His body goes rigid all of a sudden. Then he slowly looks over his shoulder, and I see worry on his face. "Everything okay?" I ask when I make it to him, rounding the table until I'm facing him.

"Yeah. What are you doing here?" He's shifting in his chair, his huge body all nervous. Something isn't right.

"I took Ava for lunch over the road."

"So where is she?"

I take a seat, resting my elbows on the table. "Waiting for me. I just saw Sarah."

He slowly removes his shades, revealing dangerous eyes. "Tell me she didn't seek you out." His nerves are gone, and now anger is apparent, his eyes blazing. It makes me smile on the inside, his loyalty and worry never faltering.

"We bumped into her in a coffee shop."

"We?"

"Yes, me and Ava. Of course, my wife didn't recognize her until Sarah introduced herself." My mouth twists, as does John's. "You didn't tell her about Ava's accident?"

"Not my news to tell. You know that woman. Give her an inch..."

I laugh under my breath. Sometimes you didn't even have to give her an inch. I gave her *nothing*, and she took a mile. Hundreds of them, in fact. "Well, she knows something is amiss, so expect to be questioned."

John tosses his glasses on the table, annoyed. "And what do you want me to tell her?"

"To stay away," I reply. "I don't care what else you tell her, but enforce that bit."

John nods, and then looks past my shoulder, prompting me to look, too. Ava is approaching, her limp now worse. Guilt racks me. "You'd better go," John says.

"Anyone would think you're trying to get rid of me." I push myself up from the seat and turn toward Ava when she makes it to us. "I'm sorry, baby. I'm just coming."

"How are you doing, girl?" John asks.

She doesn't answer, just moves closer to my side and looks up at me, searching for... I don't know. Then it occurs to me. Of course. "This is John," I say, motioning to his massive body in the small metal chair. "He's my oldest friend. He works at the club."

"Nice to meet you." Her words are quiet, tinged with an awkwardness that John doesn't miss, and I feel her flinch beside me. I look down and search her face. She looks a bit spaced out. And tired. So tired.

"I need to get Ava home." I wrap an arm around her shoulders and start leading her away. "Everything ticking over okay at the club?"

"S'all good." He slips his shades back on, and I realize I never did ask what he's doing sitting outside a café on his own. And with no drink?

I'm about to ask when a woman comes breezing out of the café with a tray, heading straight toward my friend. John shoots to his feet, pulling out the chair opposite him.

"Oh, thank you," the woman gushes, flashing him a bright smile as she takes her seat. "They didn't have lemon cake, so I got you scones." Her hair is a vivid shade of pink and pinned up wildly, her skirt long and floaty, her chunky-knit cardigan oversized. She looks perhaps early sixties, her face bright and cheery. I now notice the café, too. It's quaint, the tables old, distressed wood, the chairs industrial. And a little tin plant pot sits in the center of the table with heather bursting out of the top. How romantic.

"Thank you." John smiles, too, a big gold-toothed smile. What is this? Is what I think is happening actually happening? I take in the scene: him . . . and a woman. I have never, not *ever*, seen the big bloke with a lady. Ever.

I can feel the big kid in me rising to the surface, my need to tease him strong. He'll probably slug me one on the chin, but . . .

"Jesse?" Ava tugs on my arm. "What's wrong?"

"Nothing's wrong," I tell her, guiding her back toward the table. "But I'm probably going to be launched into orbit by John's fist." My smile's so big it hurts.

"Why?"

"Because he's with a woman."

"That's not his wife?"

"Oh no." I laugh. "He's never had one of those. No woman, in fact. Hey, big man," I say chirpily when we arrive by their table.

He grunts, reaching for his wraparounds and pulling them from his face again, giving me clear sight of his eyes and indication of his mood: prickly.

"You going to introduce us to your friend?" I cast my friendly, way-over-the-top smile onto his companion. "I'm Jesse." I extend my hand, and she's quick to stand and take it.

"Oh, I've heard a lot about you." She shakes enthusiastically, her spare hand cupping our joined hands. "I'm Elsie."

"What a pleasure, Elsie. Any friend of John's is a friend of mine. This is my wife, Ava." Releasing Elsie's hand, I pull Ava in some more as she smiles a small smile at Elsie.

"Nice to meet you."

The sympathetic look on Elsie's face tells me she knows Ava's situation. "And you, Ava."

"So how did you two meet?" I ask, getting a glimpse of John's gold tooth on his snarl. I've never seen the big guy so hostile. And nervous. It's a novelty.

"Oh." Elsie giggles and takes her seat, reaching across the table and patting John's hand. The big man is shrinking in his chair, and that just ramps up my curiosity. "I swore I'd never go on one of those dating website things, but I'm glad my friend talked me into it, else I would never have met John."

I swallow, nearly taking my tongue with it. "A dating website?" I splutter. John refuses to look at me. "You never said."

Slowly, his gaze lands on me with evil intentions. He doesn't have to speak a word. I'm copping it as soon as Elsie is out of the way. I can see a million threats in his narrowed eyes, all aimed at me.

Ava must sense his animosity, because she starts tugging my hand. "Let's leave them to it."

"Thank you, girl," John rumbles, eyes still on me. His are dangerous. Mine are dancing.

"We'll join you for a coffee." I pull out a chair for Ava, having way too much fun watching the impenetrable big man squirm in his seat. "You don't mind, do you, Elsie?"

"Of course not!" She moves her patchwork purse off the table. "How lovely to get to know some of John's friends."

The way John's looking at me, I can tell he's planning my demise. It'll be slow and painful. And it doesn't put me off one little bit.

I encourage Ava down into the chair, but she resists, somewhat reluctant. Maybe Elsie senses it, too, because she hops in and takes Ava's hand. "I was saying to John," she begins, smiling across the table at him. "I own a well-being center. Meditation, yoga, that kind of thing. It might help you, Ava. To relax the mind and find some inner calm during this difficult time." Her friendly face softens even more on my wife. "I hope you don't mind me saying so."

I nod thoughtfully to myself. Elsie looks like the bohemian type—all mind, body, and soul. But the only relaxing my wife needs to do should involve me. "That's—"

"You really think so?" Ava interrupts. "Because therapy isn't doing a thing."

"Why, yes!" Elsie looks excited by the prospect of helping Ava. "Meditation could be the perfect way to untangle all those thoughts and let the memories flow again. You should try it."

Ava looks up at me, hopeful, maybe even as excited as Elsie at the prospect. We have yoga teachers at the club. If she really wants to try it, then I'll get her on one of the classes. No sweat. "We'll look into it," I assure her, returning my attention to John, keen to get some more squirming out of him. "So, a dating website, huh?"

Slowly, purposely slowly, he takes his shades to his face and covers his fuck-you glare. "Haven't you got somewhere to be?"

"Nope." I raise my hand to signal the waitress, looking to Elsie. "Which site did you find him on, Elsie? Date a Moody Bastard? Free to a Good Home?" I chuckle when Ava smacks my arm, and Elsie giggles, too.

"It was Twilight Love, actually." Reaching across the table for his hand, she squeezes it affectionately. "I knew the moment I saw his profile picture that there was cotton wool under all that steel. And I was right."

"Awwww." I place my hand over my heart and turn gooey eyes onto John. "You big softy, you." He's going to lay me out soon.

"We should go," Ava says sternly, sensing the killer vibes emanating from John's big black body. She gives me a warning look to rival John's. "I'm tired, Jesse."

Just like that, I'm snapped out of my teasing mood. What am I thinking? She's exhausted. Shit. "We'll leave you two to it," I say, scanning Ava up and down.

"Good-bye," John grunts.

"It was lovely to meet you, Elsie." Ava pushes a smile through her exhaustion. "And thank you for your offer. I'll think about it."

"Of course. John will give you my number if you decide you'd like to try it."

As we wander over to the bike, Ava looks up at me, and I just know what's coming. "I think I'd like to try yoga."

"We'll talk about it when you're not so tired." I brush off her statement for now. We've argued enough today.

Chapter 22

When we get home, Ava doesn't head upstairs to take a nap. Instead, she goes straight to the kitchen and starts pulling open doors and drawers. I stand at the door watching her, unsure as to whether I should step in. I know exactly what she's doing. Since we saw Sarah, she's been visibly more stressed, swaying between worry and anger, and I can see her mind racing.

"How am I supposed to recognize a woman who tried to steal my husband if I don't even know where we keep the fucking mugs?" A door slams, and she stills, though her body is rolling, fired up by her anger.

"The mugs are in the top left-hand cupboard," I say quietly. "The plates in the bottom right-hand one. The knives and forks are in the drawer under the hob, and the breakfast cereals are in the pantry cupboard. In the morning, after I've made love to you, you come down and put on the coffee machine. Then you take a shower and get ready while it brews. You put a load of washing on around eight, and you make the kids' lunches. You rub moisturizer cream into your hands every time you get them wet, and you always put the dishwasher on before you leave to take the kids to school and go to work. After dinner, you let me tidy up. That's my job. To load the dishwasher while you help the kids with their homework. And when we're done, we snuggle on the couch and watch some TV before you load the coffee machine for the morning and get the kids' cereals laid out ready for when they're up. Then I carry you to bed and make love to you." I pause for a beat, finding it so hard to say such simple things without letting my voice crack. "You fall asleep on my chest. I know if something is on your mind because you're restless. Mostly, you don't move from my chest all night. And when you wake up, you roll off me and I spoon you, waiting for you to push your arse into me. Waiting for you to tell me you're ready to be woken up with some sleepy sex. And then we start all over again." I swallow and bite down on my back teeth, my devastation returning tenfold. All those simple things. Gone.

Ava slowly turns, and I see the river of tears pouring down her distraught, beautiful face. "I want to do it all. All those things. I want to do them all. I want my life back. With you. With the kids." Her voice is becoming distressed, and she takes the side of the worktop to hold herself up.

I'm across the kitchen and hugging her to me before I have a chance to think, letting her cry her despair into my T-shirt. My own tears tumble into her hair, our reality too much for both of us. All I can do is hold her. Be there for her. Love her. And all she can do is depend on me for . . . everything.

"Will you do something for me?" she whispers into the material of my T-shirt.

Stupid question. "Anything."

"Will you show me our wedding pictures again? Will you tell me who all the people are?"

I stall answering, but only because I don't know if I could take her breaking down some more. Seeing her so hopeless and fraught is soul crushing. "Sure," I answer, knowing I can't deny her that. "Want to do it now?"

She fists the material of my T-shirt, breathing in as she looks up at me. Her eyes. Her gorgeous dark brown eyes are welling, and I reach up to wipe under them. "Please."

"Come on." I lift her from her feet and gently help her get her legs around my waist. "Comfy?"

Her answer is her face in my neck and her arms circling my shoulders tightly.

Walking us to the study, I place her down on the couch and plump a cushion for her, helping her to get comfortable. Her small smile of thanks should please me. It doesn't. It hurts, because she should never have to thank me for being her husband.

I wander over to fetch the laptop and settle beside her, whirling my fingertip across the mouse pad. The screen comes to life, and I click the file for our wedding shots. A massive smile immediately spreads wide across my face. "Look how beautiful you are." So much fucking lace, I didn't know whether to worship her or rip it all off. "Do you know how hard it was for me to keep myself under control that day?"

"Well, no, since I can't remember a stupid... wait, are those handcuffs around our wrists?" Edging forward in her seat, she gets up close and personal with the screen. "They are. They're bloody handcuffs!"

I smile, smug. "Your mother wasn't best pleased."

Ava snorts, obviously imagining Elizabeth's reaction. "I can't believe you handcuffed me on our wedding day."

"Believe it." I point to the screen. "Hard evidence right there."

She's silent for a moment, observing as she relaxes into my side, her palm lying on my bicep. "Just tell me one thing."

"What?"

"Are you older than my mother?" She looks up at me seriously.

Is she fucking kidding me? If I didn't have a computer on my lap and her tucked into my side, I'd drop to the carpet and smash out fifty press-ups. Older than her mother? "Do I look older than your fucking mother?" The nerve. I feel a stressed sweat coming on. How old does she think I am?

"Well, Mum's early forties. I'm guessing you're there or thereabouts."

It takes me a few seconds to process her words, and then I realize... "Ava, your mother is sixty." Relief sends me dizzy. In her head, her parents are the same age they were in her last memory, and her last memory was when she was in her early twenties. "You're not in your early twenties anymore, baby."

"Oh yeah," she whispers, looking down at her stomach, remembering the stretch marks that tell her she's a mother, then to the boobs she's clearly not happy with.

"Look." I gently nudge her with my elbow before she falls into despondency, pointing at the screen. "You know who that is."

"Kate. She looks a bit miserable."

Ava's right. She looks like she's licking piss off a stinging nettle. Then I notice Dan and Sam in the background. And I remember. "She and Sam weren't talking," I tell her.

"Sam?" she questions, but then quickly holds up her hand to halt my explanation. "Kate's boyfriend!" She sounds almost excited. "Kate told me all about him in the hospital. I cannot believe she's pregnant!"

"That's right." I smile down at her gleaming eyes and then continue to walk her through all the guests at our wedding. It's a lot to absorb, but she seems to take it in stride.

"And this is Georgia," I continue when we're past the wedding shots.

"Raya's and Drew's daughter?"

"Drew's her father, yes. He's recently asked Raya to marry him. But Georgia's mother's name is Coral." I pause a beat, maybe thinking the name might spike something. Nothing. Her face is blank. "She tricked Drew into getting her pregnant because she was in love with me and tried to pass the baby off as mine." I quickly spit it all out and smile awkwardly when Ava swings disbelieving eyes onto me.

"What?" she asks, incredulous.

"We had some real interesting times, you and me."

She's silent, just staring at me with round eyes. "How the hell did our relationship survive all this?"

That gets my back right up, and my epic scowl must tell her so. "Because we were made for each other, that's why. Because I loved you and you loved me. We got through so much, and more, so I know we can get through this."

"You were a slut."

"*Was*. That changed the second I clapped eyes on you."

She sniffs, casually returning her attention to the screen. "Except the time you cheated on me."

For the love of all things calm, someone help me out! I breathe in and out slowly, forcing back my barrage of blue language and the temptation to deliver one huge fuck. I'm not sure which one would be most suitable for sarcasm. The Punishment Fuck, maybe? The Sense? I'm pondering that with far too much energy for a man in my situation, just punishing myself as a result. I need to pull this back to the important stuff.

"Let me tell you about the time I made an Ava éclair out of you." I settle a little, reliving that wonderful night. "I slathered you in chocolate and cream and licked it off to my heart's content. You stripped for me. It was sexy as fuck but hilarious watching you trying to gain the upper hand."

She looks up at me with a soft smile and a hint of sadness behind her eyes. She wants to remember so much, and I can see with perfect clarity that it's killing her that she can't, just as much as it's killing me.

"You've not heard the half of it, Ava," I tell her. "The things we've done, the times we've had. So many amazing memories."

"I know." Her hand reaches for my face and cups my cheek, smoothing down my bristle. "And even if I can't remember them right now, I love hearing you tell our story." She smiles. "Most of it, anyway."

I close my eyes and nuzzle a little into her palm, kissing the center. I don't want to get ahead of myself, but I feel like she's falling for me all over again. For the most part, being with each other today has been so easy and natural. Even the silly squabbles are *us*. Her reactions to me, in every way, are perfectly Ava and perfectly us. I ask myself if I would be satisfied with only finding her love again. Would it be enough without her memories? Of course, I'd make it enough. But part of our connection is everything we've shared since we met. The things that made us stronger. But it isn't just about the things that brought us closer and made us stronger. It's not just about piecing all that together for her and for me. There's one thing that she just *has* to remember. Or two things. Maddie and Jacob. I can't let those memories fade, no matter how many more we'll create. She has to have all of their years back. She just has to.

My phone rings and Ava reaches for it. Jacob's FaceTiming me, and as Ava stares down at his gorgeous face on my screen, I don't have the faintest idea what to do. I don't want to upset my boy and I don't want to upset Ava. I've spoken to the kids twice every day, but only when Ava has been in the shower.

"How come I can see his face?" she asks, and I stall, confused for a moment.

Then I remember that my girl isn't just missing sixteen years of memories. She's missing sixteen years of technology advancement. "It's FaceTime. Like a video call."

"Oh." Her bottom lip disappears between her teeth. "You

should answer," she says, handing me my ringing phone. "I want to see them."

I'm stunned. Happy but wary. "Are you sure?"

"Yes." She thrusts the phone at me. "Answer."

"I don't want to upset them, Ava," I say, hating myself for it. If I protect my kids, I hurt Ava. I can't win this one.

The phone rings off, and sad eyes glance up at my useless form. "Please." She's begging, and it's like a knife through my heart. "I need to see them. To speak to them." She swallows, shaking her head to herself. I know there's a part of her missing so much more than her memories and me. She's spent countless hours in their bedrooms, just lying on their beds, hoping it'll spike something. Maybe I was wrong to send them away. "It's an ache in here." Reaching up to her chest, she flattens her palm over her heart, and her wedding ring sparkles at me. "Today has been wonderful, and it would finish it off perfectly if I could see them."

My throat clogs with guilt, sadness, and too many other emotions to swallow down at once. How can I refuse her? I take the phone from her hand and dial Jacob, forcing back any signs of apprehension. I sit back on the couch and encourage Ava to come close as it rings and connects. And then he's there. My boy. His hair is damp and he's in a wetsuit. "Hey, buddy."

His face is halfway between excitement and uncertainty. "Mum?"

"Hey," Ava chirps, genuinely happy. She can see her boy's unease, and instinct is telling her to right it. My fucking heart booms in my chest.

There's a few bangs in the background, a door, I think, and Jacob is suddenly ambushed by his sister. "Is Mum there?" Maddie asks, a little frantic as she appears on the screen with Jacob. "Mum!" She has no unease, just pure excitement.

Ava leans forward to get closer, touching the screen with her fingertip. "How are you two? Having fun with Nan and Pap?"

"We've been surfing," Maddie tells her enthusiastically. "Well, me and Jacob did. Pap stuck to the boogie board." Ava laughs, and, God, I could cry. "Mum, did you get your memory back?" Maddie, bored of surf talk, asks the question I knew she would, while Jacob would only think it.

Ava smiles. "We've made progress." She looks up at me. "Haven't we, Dad?" Her look suggests I should pull it together. I quickly brush at my eyes and clear my throat.

"Great progress," I confirm.

"Tell us what you're doing," Jacob pipes up.

"Your dad took me out on his bike today," Ava begins. "We had a walk in the park, stopped at a café, and ate my favorite for lunch." She smiles, and I resist the urge to remind her that she didn't actually eat her favorite lunch. "Now we're looking at pictures from our wedding."

"And do you remember any of it?" Maddie's dark brown eyes, a mirror image of her mother's, glimmer with so much hope, I just can't see it dashed.

"There have been some things, yes," I jump in, putting my arm around Ava's shoulders and squeezing her closer. "Like your mum knows things, but she's not quite sure how she knows them."

"Like what?" Jacob asks.

"Like I knew how to ride on the back of Dad's bike. But I don't ever remember riding a bike before today. How cool is that?" Ava claps her hands excitedly. All I can see is sincerity in her. Nothing but a mother's desire to make sure her kids are happy and reassured, no matter what. Her way with them, even if she has no idea, is Ava through and through. It's inside her, and it isn't lost. "Then he took me on a romantic walk through the park to where we had one of our first dates."

Both of them look at each other on a roll of their eyes and mimic throwing up with their fingers in their mouths. I laugh, as does Ava. "What else did you remember?" Jacob presses on, done with the sloppy stuff.

"I remember some things your dad has said to me in the past. But enough of that. How is everything there?" Ava settles back on the couch and gets comfortable, chatting happily with our kids for a good ten minutes. And I remain where I am, content to watch her. I could leave the room and she wouldn't notice, and for the first time in my life, it doesn't hurt to know she wouldn't miss me if I were not here.

When she's done, she blows them both a kiss on a promise to call tomorrow, and sighs when she's hung up, looking down at the phone on a mild smile. It's a good few minutes before she snaps from her daydream and seeks me out.

"I didn't want to say good-bye, anyway," I tease quietly.

She laughs lightly and settles her head on my chest. "I'm sorry."

"Never apologize for loving our children more than me." I realize my error the second it's fallen from my big gob. Love me. Does she? Can she? *Will* she?

"I love you all the same," she argues quietly, pulling my stare down to the back of her head. There's unmistakable uncertainty in her tone.

"I don't expect you to wake up from a coma with no recollection of me and instantly be in love with me, Ava." Never has it hurt so bad to say something.

Turning onto her back slowly, her head on my lap, she looks up at me. "I love our children," she tells me, her hand on her heart. "I can feel it in here."

I place my hand over hers and squeeze, trying not to allow myself to be disappointed. A mother's instinct is stronger than anything else in existence. It might hurt, but it also injects me with more fortitude. If the next few days are anything like today, Sarah aside, then she'll be head over heels with me in no time.

I hope.

I pray.

There's no doubt the lust is there. I take comfort from the fact that this is how it started for us. That lust. That desire. The need to be all over each other. I see it in her now—the restraint it's taking to hold back, the overwhelming urge to ravish me. I have to let her go at her own pace, and that pace has accelerated satisfyingly today. But I know she's holding back, too, and I have a feeling deep inside me that it's because she's scared. She's scared of how she feels for me without even really knowing me. Just like she was scared all those years ago.

Ava tries to suppress a yawn, and makes a terrible job of it. "Time for bed." I get to my feet and help her up. "You must be exhausted."

She lets me lead her by her shoulders upstairs. I smile privately, but feel a little guilt creep up on me. She's overdoing things, and it's my fault.

The usual flurry of nerves descends the closer we get to our bedroom. Today has been a huge step forward. Would it be too much to ask...?

"Good night." She turns at the door and takes the handle, biting her lip as she moves back.

I die. Over and over inside, I die. "Good night." I turn quickly and make my way to the spare room before she can see the devastation on my face. Clearly it *is* too much to ask.

Closing the door softly behind me, I strip down to nothing and crawl into the unfamiliar bed. It's cold and lonely.

I toss and turn for hours, sleep nowhere to be found, not that it's much of a surprise. I'm about to give up and go put myself on the couch when I hear a stirring on the landing. Worried, I make to get up and go check on Ava, but the sound of the door handle stills me. Light creeps into the room through the small gap, and the silhouette of a body I'd recognize anywhere appears. I slowly ease down to my back. It's fucking ridiculous that my heart starts hammering. It's fucking ridiculous that I dare not move. It's fucking ridiculous that I'm nervous.

She pads on light feet across the room and gently pulls back the covers a little before crawling in beside me. I'm like a fucking statue, letting her lift my arm so she can burrow into my side. She settles, palm on my pec, cheek on my chest. It's one of the most beautiful moments of my life. So simple. But so significant. She can't sleep without me. I don't care that there's a barrier of lace between us. I don't care that she's technically in the wrong position. And then she sighs and she's on the move again, crawling onto my chest and spreading her body all over me, face in my neck. I smile, discreetly inhaling her into me, bringing my arm around her back and holding her to me.

Within minutes, I hear her soft breathing, and only minutes after that, my own eyes become heavy. The fact that the bed isn't ours and is lumpy is inconsequential. I could be lying on a bed of nails and be content. Because she's here. With her man.

Chapter 23

My sleepy brain is telling me not to move, though I'm not sure why. I'm aware that I'm curled around Ava's body, my front to her back, snug and tight. And I'm aware that I slept the best I have in over a week. I'm also aware of something growing between my groin and her arse. *That's* why I shouldn't move. But Ava doesn't get the warning. Her body starts to stretch, and she groans. *Oh, shit.* My muscles lock, my body freezes, and I hold my breath as she grinds her arse into me, causing all kinds of chaos in my cock and my head. Good God, what kind of torture is this?

Then she suddenly stills, my erection wedged between her thighs, my teeth grinding as I fight my way through the torturous sensitivity. "Oh . . . ," she breathes, shimmying a little, as if I'm not in enough fucking pain.

"Don't move, Ava," I warn. I'm so fucking hard, it could break off. "Please."

"Sorry."

"So you should be." I need to get out of this bed before the radar on my cock wins and finds its target. Half of me wants it to. Actually, the best part of me wants it to. I could fuck her memory back. I mentally slap myself for my unreasonable thought. But, then again, my lack of reason is one of the things Ava loves about me... right? *Jesus, Jesse, sort your shit out.*

Quiet falls, and she waits patiently while I focus on talking down my wayward dick. Five minutes later, I'm still iron. "It's no good," I finally admit. My cock has and always will have a mind of its own where my wife is concerned. "It won't go down." I relax and squeeze Ava closer, hoping that restricting the rampant little fucker might help.

"It's okay," Ava says, surprising me a little.

It is? What, my dick hard, or my dick where it is? Just a little nudge to the left and I'll be inside her. Would that be okay? *Shit, change the subject quickly.* "Couldn't you sleep?"

"No. Something wasn't..." She fades off, stilling. "Right."

"This. You didn't have this." I squeeze her tight, and she nods, sighing and settling again.

"This is nice."

"It would be better if you were naked," I say without thought, wondering just how much I want to physically hurt myself.

"Really?" She sounds truly surprised by that, and I frown at the back of her head. "Because I had a very good look at my body in the mirror last night, and, frankly, it isn't pretty."

My hard-on shrivels to nothing in a second as I stare incredulously at her hair.

"Stretch marks," she grumbles on. "Saggy boobs, and what the hell happened to my waistline?"

Is she playing some kind of cruel game? "Take that back," I all but growl in her hair. I won't have her speaking such bullshit. "Turn over." I bully her body over until she's facing me, a little alarmed. "Let's get one thing straight, lady." I wave an accusing finger up and down her reclined body. "All this here is mine, and I love it. Your boobs are perfect." I allow myself a brief glimpse at the mounds beneath her lace negligee, my mouth watering for a taste. "Your waistline is perfect, and the stretch marks you speak of make me smile every day. They're part of you, a part of us. I love them, almost as much as I love your boobs, and I love your boobs a lot. A *real* lot. And, for the record, so do you."

"I do?"

"Yes, you do." I nod sharply. I'm immoral. I don't care. "You love them because I love them. So are we done?"

"I guess so." Her eyes are wide, taken aback, though I sense some satisfaction somewhere inside her.

Her gaze drops down to my stomach, her teeth sinking into her lip and biting down. "What happened?" she asks, tracing a continuous line over my stomach, brushing over both scars.

I close my eyes and follow my instinct, confirming what she thinks she knows. "I had a motorcycle accident years ago." I hate myself for not telling her everything, though I'm quick to reassure myself that it's for the best. That shit could break her right now. I take her hand away from my stomach and move her fingers to my lips, kissing them sweetly. I haven't lost my master ability to distract my wife. Her eyes sparkle and she blinks rapidly. "Turn over," I order gently.

She obeys without a second of hesitation, spinning over as I grab my phone and put the Sonos on, letting the tracks shuffle. She wriggles back into my body, and my cock springs to life again just like that. And quiet falls. And I think about the spark of fire that I saw in her eyes before she turned away from me. And like an omen or something, a song that has been with us through good times and bad drifts from the speakers. Massive Attack's "Angel." I stiffen, wondering if it'll jolt anything in her.

"Jesse?" she says quietly, and I hum my acknowledgment, holding my breath in anticipation. But she doesn't say anything. Instead, she shuffles over again and stares me straight in the eyes. And I see her. My wife. The hunger for me that she can never keep at bay. The urge to tackle me and ravage me. The visibly potent desire that I'm faced with daily, from the moment she wakes to the moment she falls asleep in my arms. It's all staring back at me right now, and for the first time in our history together, I'm reluctant to give her what she clearly wants. What I *need*.

"What?" I whisper, brushing a lock of stray hair from her face as the music builds and takes over.

Without a word, she pushes me to my back and straddles my stomach. I swallow down some restraint when her bare arse meets my skin, the heat of her core against my flesh. She takes the bottom of her lace nightgown and pulls it up her body.

"Ava, what are you doing?" I ask, despite desperately wanting her to do it. Her boobs spring free, heavy and swollen, and I swallow again.

"I don't know." She tosses it aside and lowers her torso to mine, taking my cheeks. "But everything is telling me to do it."

"Are you sure?" Never have those words come from my mouth. Not ever. And my cock is seriously throbbing in protest at my reluctance.

Her answer is a kiss. A gentle kiss on the corner of my mouth. It's light and chaste, but the most consuming imaginable. My hands move to her back and skate across her smooth skin, my eyes closing in bliss. *Let her be. Let her take the lead and dictate our reunion.*

Relaxing into the mattress, I open my mouth when she licks the seam of my lips, her tongue soft and searching. Oh God, this is heaven. Holding back is a killer. Letting her control the pace is a battle like no other. Her bottom lifts from my stomach, and my cock springs up, skimming the heat between her legs. I jump. She jumps. I moan around our kiss, and she swallows it on a sigh. Her mouth seduces mine lazily as she lowers a fraction onto my weeping, eager cock. And like she was made just for me, which she was, she cushions me perfectly, gliding down my shaft with ease.

"Oh God," she breathes, and I smile around her lips, thrown into bliss.

The track, our track, continues to play, building to the crescendo. "No, baby. That's me."

She jerks and flies off my body, making me hiss from the sudden, unexpected withdrawal. "Fuck!" I cup myself, gritting my teeth, and find her sitting on the edge of the bed staring at the wall. What's happened? Didn't it feel right? "Ava, what's wrong, baby?"

I quickly shuffle to the edge of the bed and wrap an arm around her body, instantly getting a hint of her shaking form. She's trembling. "Ava, talk to me, please."

She shakes her head, looking up at me with eyes that are disturbed. "I had a flashback."

I try not to recoil. Is that good? "Of what?"

"I don't know." She looks at the carpet, her fingers twiddling in her lap. "It happened so quickly. Oh my God, please turn this music off." She looks around the room, as if searching for the stereo. "I can't bear it." Her hands cover her ears, and my damn heart splits.

I quickly find my phone and shut it off.

"Rowing boats," she mumbles, her forehead heavy. "That track. Your words. I saw rowing boats."

"Rowing boats?"

"Yes." She gets up and starts pacing the room, naked as can be, though she's too preoccupied to notice, or maybe give a toss. "Why the hell would I be seeing rowing boats?"

It clicks, falls into place. I get up and take her hand, leading her to our own bedroom. "This is why." I open the bedside table drawer and pull something out, handing it to her. She glances down at the book. "Giuseppe Cavalli," I tell her. "You had one of his pieces hung in the master suite of my penthouse at Lusso." I sit next to her and open the book to the page where the photograph is, eager for her to see, hoping it'll spike more than a flashback. "There." I point to the picture. "The original is hanging in our dining room. He was the master of light. You told me all about him when you gave me a guided tour of my new apartment. It was the first time we... well, made love."

"We did?"

"Yes." I frown. Haven't I told her this already? "In the bathroom at Lusso on launch night. I bought you this book." I flick to the back where the note still sits. "With this."

Ava pulls out the piece of paper and reads it aloud. " 'You're like a book I can't put down. I need to know more.' "

"Do you remember, baby?" I ask, watching her scan the words, hoping and praying she finds something to match the flashback.

Her eyes clench shut, as if she's desperately searching for any recollection. And I know she is. But when she sags and a tear falls, splashing the paper in her hand, I know she hasn't. "It was so vivid." She looks at me. "So real. I felt someone there with me, looking at the boats. It was you. I couldn't see you, but I *felt* you. Like I'm feeling you since I woke up after the accident. I feel you all the time, even when we're not touching. Even when you're not in the room."

I smile sadly and pull her onto my lap. "Time, baby. Give it time." While I'm reassuring her, I'm working hard to reassure myself. That flashback must have been fucking powerful to launch her off my body like that. Nothing can ever distract her from me, especially when I'm inside her. Facing the fact that there's a force more powerful than me in my wife's life right now is the hardest thing I've ever had to contend with. Because, of all the things in this world that can make her better, I just know I am her strongest chance.

Chapter 24

Three." I'm stalking my prey, closing in, watching as she backs away from me with a teasing smile on her face. "Two," I growl, picking up speed, laughing on the inside when she turns on a squeal and pelts off up the stairs. "One," I shout, taking them three at a time and bursting into our bedroom. She's standing on the far side, a can of squirty cream in one hand, a jar of chocolate spread in the other. And she's gloriously naked, except for the seductive smile she's wearing.

"Do your worst, Mr. Ward."

"Zero, baby."

I startle and jerk awake, frantically scanning my surroundings.

"Jesse?"

Ava comes into my vision, standing at the end of the bed in her dressing gown. "I must have dozed off again." I scrub at my face with my palms, wondering how I could be so tired after such a good night's sleep.

"I just spoke to Kate. She wants us to meet them for dinner tomorrow night."

I can think of nothing worse than putting myself in front of people and trying to smile. I just want to hide away in our little manor until things are back to normal. I'm on the cusp of suggesting we do exactly that, but Ava speaks first. "I'm looking forward to seeing her."

Of course she is. Ava's best friend is one of the only people she recognizes. And that fucking stings like a fuck-off-big Portuguese man-of-war. "Great." I smile through my false enthusiasm.

"I'm going to take a shower." She edges toward the bathroom, pointing to my phone on the bed. "The kids rang while you were asleep."

"Did you answer?" The thought of her staring blankly at my phone while it rang, their faces on my screen, is unbearable.

"Of course I answered." She seems almost offended. "They've been fishing today. Dad caught a ten-pound bream. Jacob sent the pictures through."

I reach for my phone, keen to see their faces. And I bark out a shot of laughter when Jacob appears on my screen, a huge fish hanging from his hand, an even bigger grin on his face. And then there's Maddie, eyes wide, looking at the bream like it could be a great white. "Look at them." My heart swells as I turn to Ava, her smile as bright as mine.

"Jacob looks so much like you in that picture." Ava's comment has me focusing on my boy once again. She's right. He does, more so than usual. "Handsome," she adds.

I shoot her a look, and she shrugs, a little shyly. "And Maddie looks just like you. Beautiful."

Her lips twist a little. If she dares challenge that. "It's quite scary, don't you think?"

"What? How similar they are to us?"

"Yes." She wanders over and looks down at the screen with me.

"Not scary," I counter, looking up at her with a wide smile. "They're lucky fucking kids."

She laughs, a genuine bent-over, stomach-clenching laugh. It's a sight to behold, and it has me grinning from ear to ear. "You're so pigheaded."

"So I'm told. Now get that gorgeous arse in the shower. I'll take you somewhere special after your therapy session."

"Actually, I was thinking of calling Elsie about her offer. Yoga might be the kind of thing I need. All this therapy is useless. I hate it. It just makes me feel crap and hopeless."

I get her point, completely. I hate seeing her looking so disheartened each time she's left a session. But... "We have yoga classes at the health club," I remind her. "If you want to do it, I'll get you on the classes." That way she'll still be close by.

"Yoga in a studio with thirty other people?" She wrinkles her nose at me. "It's not really the relaxation I had in mind. Elsie's classes sound far more therapeutic. One-on-one. What do you think?"

"I think yoga is yoga."

She gives me a roll of her eyes and heads for the bathroom. "But Elsie has this spiritual thing going on."

I grimace as I get up and follow her. "You're not going to go all hippie on me, are you?" I grin when she tuts dramatically. "Though if you want to stop wearing bras during the day, I'm down with that." Seizing her from in front of the mirror, I whirl her around, her gasp of lusty surprise like music to my ears.

"I'm being serious." She tries to force me away, and my disposition is quickly slighted as a result.

"So am I." I tug her back. "If you want to do yoga, we have a perfectly good health club for you to do it at. It makes sense for you to be at the club." Perfect fucking sense.

"So you can keep an eye on me."

"Exactly."

Her eyes narrow, pissed off. "I assume I had a life beyond you before the accident," she says, pointing a pout my way. "Or did you keep me nailed to your side permanently?"

I scoff. "I wish."

"I'm going to yoga at Elsie's well-being center, and you can't stop me."

She want to place bets on that? What's wrong with our club, if she wants to practice yoga? And what if her memories come flooding back while I'm not with her? Lord knows, if she suddenly remembers everything, it could certainly bring on a panic attack. I'm about to reaffirm my refusal to let her go, but I pull back, reminding myself that my life is practically hanging in the balance. I can't make her remember if she's not talking to me, and that's what's going to happen if I deny her this. Softly-softly. Patience.

"Fine." I spit the word out with force. "But I'm taking you and picking you up."

"I'd like to drive myself."

I laugh, loud and sharp. She's testing me now. "Don't push me, Ava. I've agreed to yoga. That's as much as you're getting." I push myself into her front and squeeze her tight. "End of.

"I'm driving myself." She pushes her hips into my groin. "End of."

Chapter 25

AVA

I'm torn between the need to keep him close and the need to desperately break away. To find some independence before I come to lean on him too much.

Yoga is the perfect place to start, just a couple of hours away from him. The big wide world is a scary place, but it's not going to get any less scary unless I push forward. So I'm going, and I don't care how much he sulks about it. And I'm driving myself.

Elsie was delighted to hear from me, and offered to let me join her this afternoon. I'm looking forward to it, and as I come down the stairs, feeling bright and positive, I see Jesse pacing the hallway. I don't let his clear displeasure break me down. "The keys?" I ask, pulling my bag onto my shoulder.

The scowl fired at me is fierce, as is his stance. The man can sulk, that much I've figured out. But his moody nature when things don't go his way is oddly endearing. Familiar. He grunts, looking me up and down, handing me a bunch of keys and a pretty pinky-gold thing.

I frown down at it. It's not much bigger than a credit card. "What's this?"

"Your phone."

"Oh." I smile and slip it into my bag and pull a hair tie out, securing my hair into a ponytail carefully.

"I'm not happy about this."

"No shit."

That scowl, it darkens, and my smile widens. "Don't push your luck."

"Don't push yours." I laugh, passing him and heading for the door. My shoulder brushes his arm, and before I know what's happened, I'm pressed against the nearest wall by his hard body. Damn, this man moves fast.

Getting up in my face, his green eyes almost dull, he growls, low and deep. His heart is clattering in his chest, the beats penetrating me. He's worried. Worried about being away from me? It might be unhealthy and unreasonable, but to me it's strangely comforting. Every move this man makes, everything he says, all his facial expressions and reactions, they all touch me somewhere deep, and my gut tells me it's all okay. Everything is fine. Instinct tells me how to react. My heart tells me how to love him. My mind tells me how to handle him.

I'm slowly putting it all together, figuring him out. He is the biggest part of who I am.

"I'll drive carefully." My instinct to reassure him is so natural. I'm wondering where it's coming from, since he's being completely unreasonable. "I'll be a couple of hours, at the most. I'll be back before you know it, I promise."

"And what if you aren't?" He's serious, his mind spinning with dread and the worst-case scenarios. "Do you know how long it took me to finally lengthen the reins I have on you? Years, Ava. Years of my fear battling with my reason."

"You have a reasonable side?" I ask, trying to throw some lightness into the mix. This is utterly ridiculous. I'm going to yoga for two hours, max.

His green eyes narrow into warning slits. "Sarcasm doesn't suit you, lady." He's not impressed, and like the sly bastard I've figured he is, he rolls those damn gorgeous hips into my groin, using his power over me like the weapon it is. "We need to make friends."

"Have we fallen out?" I laugh, trying to wriggle free, even though I know I'm going nowhere until he says so.

"Yes, we have." His eyes are now gleaming, hypnotizing, as he drops his mouth to my cheek and takes a light bite. He purrs, and I groan, having to stop myself from knocking my head against the wall behind me. What he can do to me, how he can make me feel, staggers me every time. "Stay with me."

My eyes close, the feel of his lovely lips trailing lazily all over my face debilitating me. He makes it to my mouth and laps his tongue far and wide, pushing me further up the wall. Oh my lord, he's a fucking god. My temperature is rising, my blood racing through my veins, my mind blitzed. And then I feel him smile around our kiss. I don't have to see it to know it's a smile full of satisfaction.

"No." I find some willpower and yank myself from my bliss, pushing him away, ignoring the animalistic growl. I'm learning his game. I pull my bag back onto my shoulder and get my breathing on track. Jesus Christ, every part of me wants him, wants to let him completely consume me, to make love to me. But I'm so nervous about that. My eyes drop to his groin. I felt it. Only briefly, but I felt it. It's fucking colossal, but it felt so bloody amazing, just that one stroke. I quickly realign my thoughts before I jump him. Would he like that? "I'm going to yoga."

"Then you'll be punished later, lady."

"Fine." I head for the door on a shake of my head, yet I smile to myself. Because I think I could be falling for the nutter.

As I take the steps down to the BMW, I pull myself together, tamp down my want, and focus on the afternoon ahead. Taking the handle of the door, I look back as I pull it open, finding Jesse at the front door, his shoulder leaning against the door frame, his big arms folded across his big chest. He's smiling. The crazy-arse loon.

Pivoting back toward the car, I only just stop myself from falling into the seat. Or onto Jesse's friend's lap. Not that there's much room with the huge black man taking up the driver's seat.

"What?" I blurt, righting myself and taking the top of the door.

He lifts his wraparounds and beams at me, flashing a gold tooth. "Afternoon, girl," he rumbles, thumbing to the other side of the car. "It's like the good old days, huh?"

My teeth clench with force that might crumble them, and I look up to find a very smug-looking man still holding position in the doorway. Unbelievable!

"It's you who will be getting punished!" I yell, stomping around to the passenger side. I haven't got time to argue; I'll be late for my first class, and I certainly won't be shifting the mountain of a man in the driver's seat.

"Look forward to it, lady!" he calls on an irritating chuckle, earning a scowl from me that rivals any that *he* dishes out.

I slam the door and face John. "I can't believe he's got you driving me."

John laughs, his huge sausage fingers gripping the wheel. "Girl, I drove you all over the place when you two first hooked up."

"It doesn't surprise me," I say, staring at his profile thoughtfully. "I have déjà vu," I muse quietly, and he smiles. He has a lovely smile, warm and reassuring.

"That doesn't surprise me, girl." His left hand leaves the wheel, extending toward me, his palm faceup. I lay mine in the huge shovel and he grips, firm but gentle. "Feeling overwhelmed?"

"By so much."

"But mostly him, yes?"

"He's an intense man."

"Like I've said to you a million times before, girl, only with you." Setting my hand in my lap, he takes his own back to the wheel. "You and those kids are his world, but you know that already. Ain't no man on this planet like Jesse Ward." He laughs under his breath a little, and I smile, sensing a fondness emanating from the big guy that feels somehow right.

"You're going to tell me to go easy on him, aren't you?"

"That motherfucker is fragile under all that bravado and muscle."

"He went through a lot. His brother, his uncle."

John hums, returning his full attention to the road. "Looking forward to your first session with Elsie?"

Is it me, or has he just swiftly changed the subject? I frown. "I am. Do you remember someone called Sarah?" I press my lips together, watching for his reaction.

"Of course."

"Did you know she's back?"

He casts his face slowly to mine. "I did." He's giving me nothing, so I continue to press lightly.

"Do I have anything to worry about?"

"Girl, there's not a woman dead or alive who would turn your husband's head."

"But he turns theirs," I point out, knowing deep down that it's not really my husband I need to worry about, but maybe a woman's desperation. Jesse is stunning. Tall, confident, strong, and a whole heap of other things.

"He doesn't see any of them." His look now is almost stern, like he's annoyed I'm letting something that's apparently trivial bother me. "Only you exist in that man's eyes, girl. Never forget that."

I sigh, staring out of the window as we drive the streets of London. And I scold myself because though my memories are a little lost, my instinct isn't. To Jesse Ward, I am life.

* * *

John drops me off with instructions to call him when I'm ready, and the first thing that hits me when I enter Elsie's studio is the sound of background music, which I quickly determine is whale calls. The place is warm, the walls made up of dark wooden panels, only a few tiny spotlights scattered in between the dozens of floor-standing plants. A few tie-dye tapestries hang from the walls, and a small fountain in the corner trickles calming water down the side of glistening grey rocks.

"Ava." Elsie's voice matches the scene perfectly, all calm and soothing. It's peaceful, tranquil, and I feel at ease. "How lovely to see you." Kissing me on both cheeks, she links arms with me and walks us to some bamboo doors, sliding them open. "This is where we'll practice." She practically floats across the room, her long white cover-up trailing the floor. Taking a mat from a hook on the wall, she lays it down for me. "Let me take your bag and we'll get started."

"Thank you." I give up my satchel and kneel. "I wasn't sure what to wear." I pull at my leggings.

"That's just fine. As long as you're comfortable."

Elsie pulls her cover-up over her head, revealing a toned, curvy figure dressed in a black leotard. I'm in slight awe; the woman must be in her sixties, and she looks amazing. Sitting on her bottom and crossing her legs with ease, she motions me to follow, which I do, a little nervous.

"Breathe in through your nose slowly, and out through your

mouth. In and out. In and out. Clear your mind, and let me take you on a journey to another world."

I wrestle to clear my mind, which is trickier than it probably should be, but it's been so full for days, fighting to find memories, trying to surmise what certain things mean. I squeeze my eyes shut and listen to Elsie's voice, quiet and soothing, guiding me through the process to achieve complete clear headspace.

Peace.

It settles over me like a warm blanket, and I fall into a trance, focusing on Elsie's quiet instructions as she guides me through some simple poses, ones that apparently cleanse the body of stress. And it works.

I follow her lead, accepting the help she offers when I struggle to get a few things right, my leg aching a bit in certain poses. Not too much, but enough for me to have to ask her to stop.

An hour later, I'm on my back, my legs up against a wall, my mind clear. "You did so well, Ava," Elsie says, helping me get my legs down. "I'll wait for you in reception. Take your time."

I slowly get to my feet, stretching. I feel like I've had a week's worth of sleep, my body and mind revitalized and fresh. That was so wonderful. I smile, despite not finding any memories, a new sense of hope and contentment flourishing as I collect my bag and make my way out of the studio, ready to thank Elsie from the bottom of my heart for suggesting this.

I find her sitting on a soft velvet chair, rubbing some cream into her hands. "Elsie, I can't thank you enough," I gush, so pleased. "I feel like a new woman already."

Elsie's face scrunches into a little impish grin as she stands and approaches, taking my hands. Her skin is soft, and the smell of sweet jasmine immediately hits my nose, seeming to add another layer of peace over me. Honestly, this woman, this place, it's like an amazing medicine.

"I told John this would be good for you. He's told me all about that man of yours." Her head tilts cheekily, and I laugh a little. "Passionate, but a little overbearing, yes?"

"A little," I admit, not wanting to bring him down too much. I know he's struggling, too. "He means well."

"Of course he does. He loves you with a fire in his soul. Now, will I be seeing you again?"

"God, yes. How much do I owe you for today?"

Her hand stops mine from going into my purse. "I don't charge friends," she says, looking past me when the door behind us opens. "Can I help you?"

I turn and see a woman gingerly entering. She shuts the door behind her, pulling her bag higher on her shoulder. "I was told you do yoga sessions here."

"Why yes, dear," Elsie glides across to her, her friendly smile almost sorry. "But I'm afraid I only teach one student at a time, and my schedule is rather full."

"Oh, I see." The woman looks sad now, too, and I find myself stepping forward.

"I don't mind sharing my session, Elsie," I say, smiling at the woman when her eyes sparkle hopefully. After all, I'm not paying. I feel bad for hogging a whole hour of Elsie's time, and she refuses to take my money.

"Are you sure, Ava?" Elsie takes my hand and squeezes.

I look to the woman and smile. "I'm sure she won't make much noise."

Elsie laughs, as does the woman. "I'm sorry, my name is Zara." She offers her hand. "You really don't have to do this."

"It's fine." I brush it off. To be fair, she looks like she could do with the serenity of this place, too. She looks a little sad. "I'm Ava."

"Lovely to meet you, Ava."

"I'll leave you two to see yourselves out." Elsie wanders back to the studio. "I need to prepare for my next session. See you Friday, then?"

"See you, Elsie," I call, turning back to Zara.

"I can't thank you enough," she gushes. "I recently moved to the city after a shitty breakup and I'm trying to keep myself busy in my spare time, and I could really do with trying to chill out. Breakups are stressful."

"You don't have to thank me. Today was my first session with Elsie. She is just wonderful. You'll love it."

"Can't wait. So I guess I'll see you on Friday."

"Do you fancy a coffee?" It comes from nowhere, startling me. But her face is so friendly and warm, and for the first time, I'm not frantically searching my head for the right things to say.

"Oh, that would be lovely. Are you sure? I don't want to keep you."

I laugh a little. "Trust me, there's nothing you're keeping me from." I link arms with her and we walk out onto the street, heading for the café up the road. "I'm sorry about your breakup."

"Don't be. I'm best rid of him." Zara smiles, though I sense a perpetual sadness lingering deep in her blue eyes. It's a sadness she's trying to hide from the world, and I can relate to that. I'm devastated that I can't find what I'm desperately looking for, and it's hard to keep my devastation from showing and tearing Jesse down, too. "The relationship was violent." She shrugs, like it's nothing.

"Oh my God, I'm so sorry."

"What doesn't break you makes you stronger. That's what they say, right?"

"Right," I agree wholeheartedly. I'm not broken. But I certainly don't feel any stronger at the moment. Call me mean, but hearing someone else's problems makes me feel mighty better about my own.

The conversation is coming easily. It's nice, normal. Zara isn't looking at me with sympathy, she isn't asking me pressing questions, searching my eyes for evidence of a memory like everyone around me does. She's just chatting to me like a normal woman would.

"Oh, excuse me," I say, pulling my phone from my pocket as we enter the coffeehouse. "I need to call someone." My thumb falters over the screen, and I stare down, not sure how to even use the thing. I've answered Jesse's phone, but that's only because the thing told me to swipe. So I swipe. And get asked for a code. "Never mind." I'll wait for John to call me. "I'll get these," I say, shrugging my coat off. "What would you like?"

"A latte would be lovely, thank you." Zara takes a seat while I order our drinks, pulling out my credit card and looking at the name across the front. Mrs. A. Ward. I'm prompted by the server to pay, and I come over hot. What's the PIN?

"It's contactless," he says, and I frown, catching a woman to my left tapping her card on the next machine. I follow her lead, raising my eyebrows when I see the machine tells me it's accepted. I smile, chuffed, and take the drinks, heading for the table and settling with Zara.

Crazy as it seems, I'm feeling a little rebellious, going off the normal course of my day. "So where did you live before you came here?" I ask.

"Newcastle." She shakes her head on a laugh. "I can't believe how expensive it is here!"

I find myself laughing, too, because I've been consistently shocked by inflation in my absent sixteen years. "Yeah, prices around these parts are no joke." I chink her coffee cup with mine. "How long have you been here?"

"Only a couple of months. Still settling in, but I really miss my dog."

"Oh no, what happened?"

"Rentals won't allow pets, so I lost him in the separation."

"Oh, that's crap. So do you have a job?"

"I do. Only started a month ago, but it's going great, and the potential to climb the ladder is just what I want."

"What do you do?" I sit back in my seat, riveted by the conversation, despite it being simple and normal and probably boring to some. But it's different.

"I specialize in commercial property interiors. It sounds rather boring, I know, but I'm passionate about it and that's what matters, right?"

"I used to be an interior designer." I sound utterly unimpressed with myself. I used to be. Now? Now I don't know what I do.

"Oh you did?" Her eyes light up as she sits forward in her chair. "Private?" she asks, and I nod, telling the stupid lump in my throat to fuck off. "And you don't anymore?"

I shrug, trying to sound nonchalant. "My husband owns a health club. After I had the kids and some time off, it made sense for me to work there." At least, that's what I assume.

As Zara rests back in her chair, she takes a sip of her coffee, thoughtful. "Well, if you ever decide to dip a toe back into that world, I know my company is *always* looking for talented designers in all sectors."

What is that inside me? Excitement? "Really?"

"Sure!" She matches my beam. "I can put you in touch with my manager, if you'd like?"

"I'd love that. Let me give you my number." That excitement doubles as Zara fetches her phone and gets ready for me to reel the digits off, looking up at me in prompt. "It's..." I fade off, rummaging through every corner of my mind for my own phone number. "It's..."

Zara chuckles. "I never remember mine, either." She taps at the screen of her phone and turns it toward me. I see her name in her contacts and her number. "Call me and we can save them."

I look down at my phone. It's asking me for a code again.

"Your birthday?" Zara prompts, and I glance up, finding her smiling softly.

I have no idea. Am I that predictable? My date of birth isn't the number that comes to mind, though. So I tap in the first four digits that do: 3210. The screen lights up, a dozen icons glaring at me. "Here." I hand it over. "It's probably easier for you to enter it rather than reel it off to me."

Without question, Zara quickly and keenly taps her number into my phone and connects the call, letting her phone ring once before hanging up and saving my number.

"Perfect," I declare as she hands it back and I slip it into my bag. She smiles. It's such a warm smile. Friendly and accepting, and it makes me feel so at ease.

We chat about almost anything for the next hour, almost anything except my recent accident. She doesn't need to know that, and it's a relief to have it off my mind for a while. Just talking. Getting to know someone. Someone who I'm not already *supposed* to know. I'm so wrapped up in the chatter, I completely lose track of time.

"Goodness, where did the time go?" Zara laughs, getting up from her chair. "I was supposed to be at a hair appointment fifteen minutes ago to sort out this mop."

Her hair looks just fine, long, dark, glossy waves that make her blue eyes more striking. "Don't you work on Mondays?"

"I usually work from home a few days a week, so I get a bit of freedom to sneak to yoga and the salon." She winks, and I laugh. "I'll see you Friday?"

"Sure." We walk to the door together, and as soon as I make it to the pavement, I spot Jesse's Aston up the road through the trees lining the street. Oh no. John must have called him. I quickly find my phone and cringe. Missed calls, texts, and voicemails crowd the locked screen. I shrink a little. "My husband is waiting for me."

"Oh, where?" Zara looks where I point, having to bend to get Jesse's car in her sights. "That fine man pacing the pavement?" She gives me a playful look. "You lucky thing, you."

"Oh, behave." I laugh, and she does, too, giving me a quick peck on the cheek. "Have fun at the salon," I call as she jogs off.

I smile, thinking that I like Zara. My smile is short-lived, though, when I turn to find Jesse stalking down the street in my direction, looking nothing short of murderous.

What's his problem?

"Where the fuck have you been?" he barks, positively shaking with rage. "I've been going out of my fucking mind, lady!" He seizes my hand harshly, and I look back to see if Zara is still around, because I know just what she would think if she saw this little episode.

What the hell is he doing? "Get your hands off me!" I snap, shoving him away. "I went for a fucking coffee."

His face is that of pure shock. And not because I went for coffee. "Mouth!"

"Fuck you, you heathen." I barge past him, attempting to stomp to the car, but my leg is aching badly now. This? This ridiculously over-the-top reaction, just because I went for a coffee? The man has a screw loose.

"God damn it, Ava!" He's coming after me fast, fueled by his rage. I don't care. He can't stop me going for coffee, and come to think of it...

"I'm going back to work." I must be fucking loo-la. Why would I goad him like this? Why would I poke the fucking bear?

He lands in front of me as I step into the road, every inch of his tall frame vibrating. I square my shoulders and lift my chin, displaying all of the grit I feel. "Over my dead body," he whispers lowly, getting his face close to mine. I don't back up. Never. "You're not ready to go back to work."

"No, I'm not ready to go back to *your* work. Because I haven't got a fucking clue what I'm doing! As soon as I can, I'll be applying for a job where I do know what I'm doing." It's then, after the onslaught of my shouts, I realize that I haven't just poked the bear, I may as well have stabbed the beast.

His chest slowly inflates, his face getting redder and redder. I wisely back up now, ready for the beast to explode. But what will come first? Because there are two issues here, my language, and the fact that I'm threatening to get myself another job. He won't let me work anywhere except with him? How stupid!

"Watch your fucking mouth!" he booms, practically silencing the entire street with the volume. Maybe even the whole of London. "And the day you get another job is the day you put me six feet under."

"Don't fucking tempt me." I take a wide berth around him, aware of him close behind. *I'll* be the one six feet under at this rate. With stress.

I yank the car door open and throw myself into the seat heavily, wincing as I do. I hurt. Everywhere. I turn my face away when he lands in the driver's side, his force putting mine to shame. "I've had a million heart attacks in the past hour!"

"And a seizure. And a stroke, by the look on your face. I had a coffee, for crying out loud. Aren't I allowed that?"

"Who with?" He revs his Aston hard, the car sounding as angry as him. "Because I rang Kate looking for you, and you weren't with her."

"I have other friends, too, you know."

"Like who?" He roars off down the road, throwing me back in my seat. Oh, he's mad all right. Good. So am I. Who does he think he is?

"A friend from yoga," I tell him snootily, not willing to elaborate. Call me pathetic, but I kind of like the idea of having someone all to myself. "You're driving like an idiot." I clench the side of my seat when he zooms through an amber light, cutting someone off when he switches lanes. We get honked at, and Jesse proceeds to flip the finger, not once, but twice, hurling a barrage of abuse out the window. Jesus Christ, the man is a fucking lunatic.

"Given my accident," I say, quietly alarmed by his recklessness. "I'm surprised you're being so careless." The brakes screech, and we're suddenly crawling along the road at a snail's pace. "Now you're just being stupid." I fire him a filthy look, but note very quickly that he's not being stupid at all. He's being serious, his brow all crinkled in silent thought. And I know those thoughts are of the day he found my mangled car before he found my mangled body. I can see the flashbacks in his rapidly dulling eyes, his anger morphing into pain. And that pain finds its way into my heart and makes me feel like the worst person in the world.

Damn it. I close my eyes briefly and sigh, reaching for his hand where it's squeezing the wheel, his knuckles white. He lets me pry his fingers free and bring his hand to my lap, where I cup it with my other, holding it tightly.

"I'm sorry," I say, a million strands of regret woven between the two small words. There's that instinct again. The one that desperately wants to ease his pain. To make him calmer. To give him what he needs.

He pulls the car over to the side of the road and takes his hands back, scrubbing them down his face slowly and harshly. The evidence of a tear streaks his bristly cheek. Oh God. What have I done? He looks on the verge of breaking down. I unclip my belt and crawl across the center console, onto his lap, pulling his hands away from his face. Deep green eyes overflowing with dread gaze back at me. "You need to chill out, Jesse."

"I'll chill out if you stop trying to kill me dead." He's serious, yet the crack in his voice is clear. His true fear is sobering. And, I realize, I shouldn't toy with that.

"Be quiet and kiss me," I demand, taking the reins, doing what I'm fast learning he needs me to do. And I don't have to ask him twice. I'm taken in a kiss that's full of appreciation as he sighs his thanks into my mouth and settles beneath me. His heart settles too, lowering to a soft thrum in his chest, reverberating against mine.

"And to be clear," he mumbles, and I roll my eyes behind my lids, knowing exactly what's coming. "You're not getting another job." I don't argue. Not now, though I plan on breaking him down gently over the coming weeks. Even I know I'm not ready to go back to work yet. His head falls back against the headrest, his face serious. "Why didn't you call me? Text me? Anything."

I look away, a bit embarrassed. "I don't know how to use that stupid phone." I can feel a lump growing in my throat. It's so stupid.

My jaw is clenched and my face pulled to his. His face is agony. "I'm sorry for being unreasonable."

I feel immediately better. "So you're going to let me work elsewhere?"

"No," he says simply, with no apology. "That'll never happen." The confidence in his voice almost makes me believe him myself. We'll see. It is what it is, and he is what he is. Neurotic.

And I am what I am.

Falling in love with him.

Chapter 26

After my heart attack of yesterday, I kept Ava at home today and gave her an in-depth tutorial on how to use her phone. I only let her leave the house to keep her therapy session, and I drove her, waited, and brought her home. And she didn't argue. Fucking hell, I've never been so panicked. The whole time she was missing, I tried to reason with myself. Tried to keep myself calm. It didn't work. I was terrified, and then when I found her, that terror turned into anger. I couldn't hold back. But what was she thinking disappearing like that? It's taken a whole twenty-four hours to get my heartbeats back to a safe level.

Now I'm waiting for her in the hallway so we can meet the gang for dinner. I pace, back and forth, over and over. Where the hell is she? I glance down at my Rolex and sigh. Normally, I'd be up there helping her along in my own little way, but nothing about our lives feels normal anymore.

Wandering over to the mirror, I take in my Wentworth grey three-piece, pulling in the jacket and straightening my blue tie. "Perfect, Jesse," I say to myself, smoothing my hair into place. My hand pauses mid-fix. My suit might be dapper, my body carrying it well, but I look tired. Exhausted, in fact. Jesus, I've aged ten years in two weeks. I groan and blink my green eyes, feeling at my tidy scruff. Stress appears embedded in my skin, clouding my eyes. I actually look my age, and that fucking sucks when you're fifty. Pulling my phone from my pocket, I dial my mum.

She's quick to answer. "Jesse? Everything okay?"

"Yeah, Mum. We're getting there." The last thing I want to do is give her more cause for concern than there is, and there's already a lot. "I need to ask you a question."

"What?"

"Answer truthfully."

"Of course."

"How old do I look?"

There's a slight pause, and then she starts chuckling. "Darling boy, you don't look a day over forty."

I catch myself in the mirror again, scoffing under my breath. "You're just saying that to make me feel better."

"You're tired, son."

"Fucking knackered."

"Jesse Ward, watch your language."

"Sorry," I grunt and continue faffing with my hair. "How's Dad?"

"Worried." She doesn't beat around the bush. She doesn't need to. Everyone is *worried*. "How is Ava? Any improvement?"

"A little," I admit, wishing I could tell her there's been a mammoth breakthrough. "The doctor's been encouraged by the small signs we've seen so far."

"That's good. You must be pleased."

I hum half-heartedly, telling myself once again that I'm expecting too much too quickly. "I have to go, Mum. I'm taking Ava out for dinner."

"Oh, how lovely!" She sounds thrilled. "Bet you're looking forward to that."

Not really. "I am. It's like we're dating again."

"Then make sure you woo her."

"Are you giving me relationship advice?" I ask, hitching a sardonic eyebrow. I've known my wife for over twelve years. I do not need tips on how to woo her.

"Well, we've all heard of your persistence in the early days of your relationship."

"I already told you, Ava exaggerates. I'll call you tomorrow." I hang up, ready to yell my impatience up the stairs, but my phone rings again. I answer without looking. "Hello?"

"Jesse?" Sarah's voice sinks into my ear and burns my brain.

"How did you get my number?" I'm instantly angry. Fucking fuming. Doesn't she know what's good for her? I hear the bedroom door closing. "Don't call me again, Sarah."

"But I need—"

I hang up on her, working hard to cool myself down before Ava questions my pent-up state. *Be cool. Be calm.* Then I catch sight of my wife. "What the fuck, Ava?" It just tumbles out of my mouth but, Lord have mercy, what the fuck is she wearing? I gawk, studying the little red number, every little thread. It doesn't take me long.

"What?" She brushes down the front of her dress with her palms. I'm hoping to get some kind of horrified gasp when she sees the dress clinging to her lithe body, thinking maybe she missed the full-length mirror on the way out of the dressing room. But there's no gasp. Just a questioning, curved eyebrow as she looks back up at my twitching form.

What? *What?* Let's start with the length of the damn thing.

"Where did you find that?" I ask.

"It was at the back of my wardrobe."

I snort. At the back of her wardrobe hidden from me. When did she get it? When was she planning on wearing it? Shit, has she already? "You're not wearing that."

Her head tilts, making her long hair skim her half-exposed boobs on one side. "Yes, I am."

"Over my dead, decomposed body, Ava. You and I have a deal," I tell her, marching up the stairs toward her, set on turning her right around and sending her back to the bedroom in disgrace.

Her eyes follow me all the way until I'm before her, her face plain confused. "What deal?"

"You wear what I tell you to wear." I take her shoulders to turn her, but get shrugged off on a scoff.

She's off down the stairs before I've realized she's missing from my grasp, leaving me a big bag of incredulous man at the top. "I'm changing the deal," she calls, fixing an earring in her ear as she goes.

Excuse me? I fly off down the stairs after her. "You can't change the deal."

"I just did." She disappears into the kitchen as I round the bottom of the stairs at one hundred miles an hour, skidding my way around the corner after her.

I find her collecting her purse off the island. Her face is begging me to challenge her. Oh, I challenge. Doesn't she know me at all? My brain spasms at that thought, and I boot it away before I can spend too much time agonizing over the fact that she doesn't at the moment. Well, she soon will. "The dress goes."

She lifts her dress even higher up her thigh, and I recoil at her sheer insolence. And cheek. And bravery. "The dress is staying." She looks down herself again. "It pulls me in at all the right places."

She doesn't need pulling in. What she needs is a dress at least a foot longer. Ordinarily, she knows I can't be held responsible for my actions if some stupid prick makes an inappropriate or rude remark, and the chance of that happening when she's wearing a dress like this is multiplied by a million.

"What are you gonna do, anyway?" Another challenge, and I have to stop myself from laughing.

"You really shouldn't ask me that question. I'm not above doing it again." I walk over to the drawer and pull it open, searching through the utensils. Give me strength, that dress barely covers her arse.

"The scissors are in the other drawer," she says, so matter-of-factly, almost casually.

"What?" I nearly chop my fingers off when I slam the drawer shut, swinging around to face her. How did she know I was searching for the scissors?

Looking a little blank, she lifts her arm and points to a drawer. "That one."

I'm no longer shaking with anger, I'm shaking with excitement, but I force myself into something close to nonchalance. It's fucking hard. This is colossal. I move slowly toward the drawer and place my hand on it, never removing my eyes from hers. "This one?"

She nods and I pull it open, blindly reaching inside for the scissors. Pulling them out, I calmly shut the drawer. And she frowns. "Why are you looking for the scissors, anyway?"

I refuse to let her sudden confusion beat me down. What just happened was another glimmer of hope. Lifting them in the air, I point them at the offending red dress and snip the air. "Are you going to remove the dress, or am I cutting it off?" I tilt my head, a little serious, but mostly playfully. Truth be told, I'd let her wear the dress now. My mood has changed considerably.

Comprehension slams into her, her jaw dropping. "Oh my God, you cut off my dress?" Her hands come to the sides of her head and press against her temples, like she could be trying to squeeze the memory to the front. "What kind of unreasonable arsehole are you?"

"The one you love," I declare, walking forward, snip-snipping at the air, a cunning smirk pulling at my lips. "Remove the dress."

"Fuck you, Jesse." She's absolutely outraged. It's sweetly reminiscent. "Jesus, did I actually let you do that?"

"Yes. You were too distracted by all my handsome glory to notice what I was doing until it was too late."

She snorts. "I've never met such an egomaniac."

"Yes, you have." I continue to stalk forward, ready to pounce when she bolts. "And you married him."

"I must have been mad."

I take no offense, don't let her claim faze me, since there's absolutely no conviction in her tone. Just lust. "Crazy mad," I whisper, smiling when she starts taking steps back, trying to keep some distance between us.

"Crazy mad," she murmurs in reply, her eyes clouding over with a ton of desire. "You are the crazy-mad one." Her arse meets the worktop, her retreat blocked. I reach her and press my front to hers, dipping to put my mouth at her ear.

"Take it off."

"No." She's being defiant for the sake of it, playing the game. She knows one way or another this dress is coming off.

"You're heading for a Retribution Fuck."

Startled, she looks up at me, my promise snapping her out of her trance. I immediately kick myself. Too much? Ava laughs somewhere between bewilderment and amusement. "What the hell is a Retribution Fuck?"

I feel heat in my cheeks, and she hasn't missed it, her gaze jumping from my bristly face to my eyes. There are so many mind-bending things for her to get her head around. The time has come to address the fucks. While the styles of fucks I lay on my wife were perfectly understood between us, I never imagined what it must sound like to a stranger. And, right now, painfully, my wife is practically a stranger. Great. So we're going to have a conversation about fucks. Why didn't I keep my stupid mouth shut and focus on getting that dress off?

I take in air, wary of her half smile. She might not be smiling in a minute. "Want to sit down?"

"Do I need to?"

"Probably," I admit, reluctantly moving from her path.

She moves across to the chair and slowly lowers, her eyes always on me. "So, the Retribution Fuck?"

"It's like a punishment, I guess." I shrug and put the stupid scissors away.

She looks horrified, and every reason for me to be worried about this conversation is confirmed. "You punish me?"

"Yes, but you like it."

"I like being punished?"

Damn it. How can I explain this so it makes any sense at all? "It's a game," I start, having a quick nibble on my lip before I go on. "A power play. You've always humored me." Fucking hell, what do I sound like? "The handcuffs..."

Her neck recoils sharply, and she hisses, reaching for her head on a wince. Guilt tears me up inside, and I move in to ease her, but come to an abrupt halt when she raises her hand, warning me off. "Handcuffs? Again with the handcuffs. You didn't just use them as a gimmick on our wedding day?"

Fucking hell. I shrug sheepishly. "It's all part of the game."

Ava looks away, her hand still on her head, rubbing lightly. "Who has the power?" she murmurs meekly.

Another jolt of life sparks within me, and I quickly put myself on the stool in front of her, taking her hands from her head and holding them firmly. "Me." I swap her hands for her cheeks and plant a kiss on her lips. "Always me."

"But something tells me it's actually me," she says against my lips, and I smile like a madman, because she's right.

"You keep telling yourself that, lady." I rub her nose with mine.

"So you punish me." She takes my hands from her cheeks and interlaces our fingers. "What for?"

"Not doing as you're told. And sometimes I utilize the Reminder Fuck, just to remind you of your place."

Eyes wider still, she just stares at me. "The Retribution. The Reminder. All sounds lovely." The sarcasm in her tone is potent. "What other fucks do we have?"

"I think your favorite is the Truth."

"Why?"

"Well, *you* get to handcuff *me*, usually when I'm asleep." I scowl at her. I can't help it. "And you use your position of power to extract information from me."

Her eyebrow lifts, her eyes looking me up and down. She's imagining restraining me. It's both thrilling and terrifying. Especially when there's so much more about us for her to learn. I decide here and now that, in actual fact, I'd hate it if Ava laid a Truth Fuck on me again. I make a mental note to find the cuffs and hide them somewhere she'll never find them.

"Then there's the Apology," I continue.

"Who's apologizing?" she asks quickly, though I know she knows.

"You."

"What for?"

"Usually being defiant."

She laughs again. "Like wearing an unsuitable dress?"

"Exactly like that."

"So are you going to make me apologize?"

Jesus, I'd love nothing more. My dick is screaming at me to let her. "I'm not sure you're up for that just yet."

"Why? What do you make me do?" Her face is becoming more horrified by the second.

Make her? I don't make her do a damn thing. Wouldn't dream of it. My lips press together. Jesus Christ, I must sound like a monster. I cough and glance down at my groin, and Ava flies up from her stool. "Are you fucking kidding me, Ward?"

More sparks, more life. She called me *Ward*. She only ever calls me that when she's spitting mad with me. And what do I do when she swears? "Watch your fucking mouth!" I bellow, knocking her back a few steps with the force.

"Fuck off!" she snaps, stomping off out of the kitchen.

Shit, I love her so fucking much. I go after her, hearing her indignant huffs and puffs as she stamps up the stairs. "Ava," I call, running up behind her, three steps at a time.

"Fuck you! You're a hypocritical wanker, Ward. Watch my mouth? Why don't you watch yours!"

I notice a small limp in her last few steps. "You called me *Ward*!" I rush to explain, and she stops. "You always call me *Ward* when you're cranky with me."

She slowly turns, her thoughtful face coming into sight. "I imagine I call you *Ward* all the time," she mutters.

"A few times a day," I admit, my shoulders jumping up casually. "Mostly you humor my needy side." I extend my hand from a few steps below her, resigning myself to the fact that, today, the dress can stay. She just better hold me back if some pervert has a wandering eye. "And the thing I need most of all is you."

Her body softens, her sigh definitely dreamy. "And then you're all romantic."

I smile, and I know it's shy. "I've been known to have my moments."

"Like?" The interest in her voice thrills me. She's craving

information, and I'm more than happy to give it. "We have romantic fucks too, you know."

She laughs lightly. "Well that's a relief."

"There's sleepy twilight sex. And sleepy sex. And the Compromise Fuck. We had loads of those when you were expecting the twins."

"And what does a Compromise Fuck entail?"

"A little rough, a lot of gentle. And, for the record, lady, you were the one who wanted the rough." I nod when she huffs a light breeze of surprised laughter. "And then there's the Quiet Fuck. Usually when we've stayed at your parents'."

Her light laughter turns quickly into hard laughter. "You gag me, don't you?"

"You can't keep your pleasure quiet, Ava. What can I say?" I shrug around a cocky grin, and she shakes her head in dismay.

"Go on," she urges.

I take a step up, bringing us to eye level. "The Proposal Fuck was quite romantic."

"You asked me to marry you during sex?"

"Actually, you were handcuffed to the bed and I didn't release you until you accepted."

She's now on the verge of falling to her arse in amusement. I know it's a lot to take on board. But at least she's laughing and not raging anymore. "I can't believe what I'm hearing."

"Believe it, baby. But if it makes you feel better, I did propose again. On my knee. In front of your parents."

Satisfaction flourishes before my very eyes. She looks dreamy, one hand moving to her chest. This pleases her. I know how much her parents' opinion means to her. I try to behave around them. I try real hard. I don't always succeed, but still. It's the thought that counts.

"It was my birthday. You couldn't say no."

A smile pulls at the side of her mouth. "And how old were you?"

"Twenty-five."

Softly chuckling, she glances away, clearly coming to terms with all of this. Her life. My life. Our life. "Wait." She looks back to me. "Why did you propose twice?"

All the contentment flowing through my veins turns to acid, my lips forming a straight, annoyed line. I'm not annoyed with her, more with myself. "We'd had a disagreement."

"Really? I can't imagine what there could have been for us to disagree about."

There it is. That sarcasm. "Sarcasm—"

"Doesn't suit me. I know. Why did you propose twice?"

"Can we get back to the fucks?"

Her head tilts in impatience. "Tell me."

I can't go over this again, and I'm not afraid to tell her so. "It doesn't matter. Just know I punished myself and you punished me, too."

Comprehension dawns fast, and she flinches, as if she could be being hit with the motherfucking whip in her mind. "So you cheated on me when we were engaged?"

"God, no!" I blurt, disgusted by the suggestion. Give me strength. I won't insult her and tell her we barely knew each other, nor will I argue my case in any way. It's done. I can't change it. I hate myself every day for it, but it's done. "You found out when we were engaged. That's why I proposed to you again. Properly. I was trying to show you that I could be the man you needed, as well as the man you wanted."

"Oh" is her only acknowledgment.

Good. Let's move on. On to the most utilized fuck in our lives. "The Danger Fuck is our favorite these days."

"What's that?"

"When the kids are within a mile radius." Her smile's back. And so is mine. "Can we go for dinner now?"

"Depends." Her nose lifts, and she waits for me to ask for confirmation of what exactly our date depends on.

I don't need to ask. On a dramatic roll of my eyes, I pick her up, mindful of that limp, and carry her down the stairs. "You can wear the stupid fucking dress."

She grins, victorious, and loops her hands over my neck. "Wasn't so hard, was it?"

"We've not left the house yet. And you should have worn flats instead of heels. I saw you limping."

"I wasn't limping."

"Are you arguing with me?"

"Yes."

I wrinkle my nose and nuzzle hers. "Are you wearing lace under that red thing?"

"I didn't have much choice. There's nothing *but* lace in my knicker drawer."

"Good." I carry her out and put her in my Aston, pulling the belt across her body. She doesn't protest, just lets me do my thing and buckle her up. "We're late," I muse, checking my Rolex as I shut the door and round the car. Falling into the driver's seat, I start her up and rev a few times.

"That's your fault for having so many fucks to explain." She goes to the mirror and applies a little gloss to her lips. "Which was your favorite, by the way?"

I laugh, loud and sharp as I put the stereo on and Glass Animals' "Youth" fills the car. "All except the Truth." I turn up the volume and zoom off, reminding myself to find those handcuffs and hide them.

Chapter 27

As expected, the gang is waiting for us when we arrive, all sitting around a table in the corner, two spaces left for me and Ava.

As soon as Kate spots us, she scrambles up from her chair and takes Ava in a hug, getting as close as her baby bump will allow. "So good to see you."

"We're still young in my head." Ava sighs, and Kate starts giggling.

"How's yoga going?"

"Great. I met a girl, Zara—she's so lovely—and she mentioned that the firm she works for is always looking for new interior designers. I might look into it."

I scowl. Over my dead body.

"That's fab," Kate says, flicking me a cautious look as my wife pulls away and tugs that ridiculous dress down her thighs.

I scowl again, this time at the racy red number, wondering what I was thinking letting her wear it, and pull out Ava's chair. "Sit," I order, earning a collection of incredulous looks from all angles of the table. "Please," I add through my ticking jaw.

Ava lowers to the seat, the tension obviously thick, not because of my beef with the dress, and not because she's talking about a job she isn't going to be applying for. It's the first time the guys have seen Ava since the accident. Sam, Drew, and Raya all look a bit nervous, none of them obviously knowing what to say to her.

Ava must sense it, because she flicks me a nervous look and then sighs, returning her attention back to our quiet friends. "Nice to meet you," she chirps.

The guys laugh, and the tension lessens as a result of her joke. "Drinks?" I flick my arm in the air, summoning a waiter.

Everyone throws their orders at me for alcohol, excluding Kate, but *in*cluding my wife. I don't think so. "Water, please," I tell the waiter as I indicate to Kate and my wife. "For me, too. And wine for Raya." I nod across to her.

"Make it a bottle," Drew pipes in quietly.

Ava's hand meets my forearm as she leans across, speaking quietly. "I'd like wine." She thinks I didn't hear her. I heard her perfectly. Louder than everyone else who virtually shouted their order to me.

Smiling tightly at the waiter, who's paused scribbling on his pad, looking at me, I turn toward my wife. "You're not having it." My tone is a warning, and she would do well to take notice. As I slowly swivel back toward the waiter, I catch the faces of our friends. All of them are silent. Watching. Nervous. "Water," I reiterate, taking my napkin and laying it across my lap. Silence. Eyes dodging me and Ava. Awkward vibes. I start chewing my lip, peeking out of the corner of my eye. The look of pure disgust on my wife's face actually makes me wince. Shit, she looks livid.

"You'd better order me some wine, Ward." She comes close, eyes full of fire, making me slowly lean back. I hear Sam cough through a laugh, and Drew snorts. Wankers. They should be backing me up. She just came out the other side of a horrific car incident. She's not at full health. Drinking alcohol would be daft, and it would be highly irresponsible for me to let her. "Now," she adds on a growl that rivals mine.

"It's not safe," I argue quietly. "The last thing you need is alcohol fuzzing your already pickled mind."

"Pickled?" She coughs over my lame choice of word. "My mind isn't pickled, Jesse. Order me some wine, or so help me God..."

"So help you God *what*?"

"I...I don't know." She stutters over a few more words before clearly finding the one she's looking for. "Divorce," she spits scathingly. The whole table gasps, me the loudest, and Ava shoots our friends a surprised look. "What?"

Kate shakes her head mildly, warningly, and Sam blows out his cheeks. "Red flag. Bull on the loose. That's all I'm saying." He disappears into his glass, while I fight to maintain my temper before it sends me off around the restaurant in a whirlwind. Divorce? That damn fucking word is banned from our lives.

"Well." Ava shrugs, nonchalant, though I can sense her buried wariness. "I only want a glass of wine."

I can feel the pressure in my head building, my body rolling where I sit.

"Oh, here we go," Drew says quietly, taking his glass, as if it could protect him from the imminent explosion.

I bolt forward in my chair. "Take that back," I demand.

She flies forward, too, matching my threat, the defiant thing that she is. "Order me wine."

"No."

She quickly has hold of my jaw, squeezing hard. "Do it."

A staring deadlock that would put all others that have come before to shame holds us in our positions for what seems like forever. I'm mad, so fucking mad, but deep inside, past that madness, is happiness. She's always known when to let me win, and now isn't one of those times. She's finding her feet. Getting to know *us*. It takes a lot. A fucking lot, but... "Fine. You can have one glass," I relent, thinking she's on to a good one and she better appreciate it.

"We'll see."

"We will," I agree, prying her fingers from my jaw, maintaining my glare.

"Are you done?" Kate sighs, accepting the bottle of white when the waiter approaches, making quick work of pouring for Raya, and then Ava before I change my mind. She doesn't miss my eye on the side of Ava's glass, watching the level. "Though I have to say," Kate goes on, nodding at Ava to seize the goods before it's swiped away by the madman sitting next to her, "it's kind of nice to see you're still you." Toasting us across the table, she sips her water.

"So when's the wedding?" Ava asks Raya, pulling the table back to some light chitchat. My glare hardens when she takes her glass and peeks at me on a hidden grin as she takes her first sip. She'll pay for that.

I put myself into the conversation, but my attention is never far from Ava's wineglass. It's been weeks since she had a drink, and we need to be careful of any reaction with the meds she's on. A few sips will be like a few bottles.

"Excuse me," Ava announces as she stands. "I need the ladies."

I sit up straight, contemplating escorting her as she leaves us. Is that a limp? Or is it a drunken wobble? I don't know, and I need to be sure. Either way, she could do with my help. I make to stand.

"Jesse," Kate calls across the table. "Leave her."

"But—"

"Leave. Her." Her order is almost a warning. Like I'd ever take any notice. Except this time I do. I don't know why, but I do. My eyes pass from the table to Ava's back a few times as she gets farther and farther away from me. I'm so torn.

"I'd listen," Sam says, pointing to his girlfriend's pregnant belly with his beer. "Honestly, man. I'd listen."

"What if she stumbles?" I say to Kate, a clear vivid flashback of her delicate head coming into my mind. There's blood. Lots of blood. I wince.

"She's had one glass of wine. Now, sit."

"Come on, Jesse." Drew joins in the persuasion party. "Know your limits, mate."

I drop to the chair with a thud. "I know fuck all anymore," I admit, my head finding my hands. "I don't know if she'll ever remember me, the kids, our life. I know nothing, and it's breaking my fucking heart." I will myself not to cry, try so fucking hard, but that one traitorous tear drops to the table, seeming to make a bang when it lands on the cloth. My strength is waning. I'm finally crumbling for everyone to see. Kate's next to me in a heartbeat, followed quickly by Raya on the other side. Two women rushing to comfort the big baby.

"Don't let your frustration beat you," Raya tells me, nudging my shoulder playfully. "There's no way she could forget what you two have. Not forever."

"Are you being over the top?" Kate pipes in, spiking light laughter from my supposed best mates. "Smothering her?"

"No," I assure her. "Jesus, I'm sleeping in the spare bed. I even let her wear that fucking ridiculous dress. And now she's drinking wine when I really don't think she should be. So you can't tell me I'm being too suffocating." I leave out the rampage I went on yesterday when she went missing. They don't need to know that bit. I sniff and grab my water, so wishing I could swap it for something stronger. A lot stronger.

"She'll get there. Keep at it," Sam offers on a rare smile of support.

"Yeah." I swallow down my frustration and straighten myself

out. What the fuck has gotten into me? Blubbering like a baby in front of friends. "Here she is." I brush at my eyes quickly as Kate and Raya return to their chairs.

"Don't worry," Drew says. "We won't tell her you've been crying."

"Fuck you," I spit. "I do believe you bawled one time when you thought a certain blonde had fucked off to Australia and left your sadistic arse."

Drew shrivels on the spot, and Raya chuckles. "How cute."

I pull out Ava's chair, and she graciously accepts, looking at me as she lowers. "Okay?"

I tug her closer, and she leans in, naturally coming until my lips are pressed to her cheek. "I'm sorry," I breathe across her skin. "I worry, that's all."

She pulls back and smiles softly, reaching for my cheek and caressing it lightly. "I have you with me, so I'll be fine, right?"

Never have those words sounded so comforting. Whether she's saying them because she's learning fast once again that I need to hear them is a moot point. "Right," I confirm. "We need to make friends. Kiss me."

She doesn't question my order. And I know it's instinct rather than her being wise or trying to pacify me. Her kiss is just a lingering peck, only light, but still. I'm swallowed whole, caught in the moment. Until a cough interrupts my bliss. Peeking across the table, I find everyone watching us. Waiting. Smiling.

Ava starts faffing with her napkin as I return to my chair, smiling at the sudden color of her cheeks. "Sorry," she murmurs, her eyes darting everywhere except at our friends.

No one is fazed. No one but Ava. They all know us. We might not be *wholly* us at this particular moment in our lives, but I can tell my friends are as pleased to see tiny hints of the normal Jesse and Ava.

We all order from the menu, the chat coming easier now. Observing Ava as Kate tells her stories from recent years is more pleasurable than I anticipated. As our meals land on the table, I watch for the next half hour as Ava pushes the food around her plate, drinking far more than she is eating.

"More wine?" Kate mumbles around her chili-infused dish, the hottest on the menu, nodding at Ava's glass. Am I the only one here concerned about the amount of alcohol falling down my wife's throat?

Semi-scowling to myself, I lean toward Ava. "Take it easy, baby. You're still fragile."

She rolls her eyes, patting my hand. It's so fucking condescending. "I'm fine," she assures me.

An hour later, she is not fine, and I'm fucking furious with myself for backing down. I don't trample all over the place for the fun of it. There are always perfectly sound reasons for me insisting on something, and the reason I didn't want her to drink is evident as Ava wobbles her way up from her chair. Kate better not try to stop me this time. Tossing a scowl to each of my friends, just so they know I'm holding each of them accountable, I take Ava's elbow and escort her to the ladies.

"I'm not drunk." She hiccups and giggles. "Well, not much."

"Be quiet," I grumble, letting myself into the restroom with her and pushing a stall door open. "In you go."

I fill the door as opposed to closing her in, holding one of her hands while she pulls her knickers down with the other. "What are you smiling at?" she asks, lowering to the loo as she beams up at me, squinting through drunken eyes.

"I'm just surprised you haven't ordered me out."

She's thoughtful for a beat. "I didn't even think of it. Besides, we've had babies together. I assume you were there for the birth."

My cheeks burn with the stretch of my grin, fond memories of the day my babies were born coming back to me like it could have happened yesterday. Where has that time gone? "It was the most beautiful day of my life." And stressful. I pull off some tissue and pass it to her, then help her up when she's finished. "I think it's time to go home."

"Oh, but I've had a lovely evening," she whines, letting me guide her to the sink. "Listening to all the stories."

Yes, it's been lovely, but not once has she shown even a hint of retrieving her memory, and I've been looking very closely for something. Anything. Just another glimmer. "It's late." I flip the tap on and put her hands under. "And you've had more than enough to drink."

"Bossy boots." She giggles as I roll my eyes and take her hands to the towel. "Can I have one more glass before we go?"

"No." I hold her waist and guide her out of the toilets, back to the table. "We're going now." I hold Ava with one arm while retrieving my wallet with the other and grabbing some notes with my teeth.

Ava takes them from my mouth before I have a chance to spit them out. "He won't let me have another drink," she grumbles, tossing the money on the table. "What a bore."

"One more for the road, Jesse," Kate pleads, batting her lashes. "She's just a little tipsy."

"A little tipsy is too tipsy."

"I'm having fun," Ava retorts indignantly. "It's not like there's much else to be happy about right now. I'm married to man who I don't know, I don't recognize my children, and I'm missing sixteen years of my life."

Everyone shrinks at the table. I ignore them, and I also ignore my wife, taking her shoulders while biting my tongue. "Say goodbye," I grate.

"Bye!"

Turning her steadily, I proceed to guide her drunken bones out of the restaurant. I need to turn this around before I lose my rag. I'm so close. "You're heading for a Retribution Fuck, lady." I open the door and give her a deadly serious face when she looks up at me through lowered lashes. She's imagining it. Me fucking her stupid while she's handcuffed to our bed. "What else are you imagining?" I ask her cockily, wanting her to know that I'm fully aware of where her inebriated mind is at.

"Nothing," she squeaks, moving past me through the door, her hips not swaying in their usual fashion, more jolting. That limp is getting worse. I'm hiding all of her heels when we get home. And I should mention it to her doctor.

I'm about to swoop in and remove her from her feet, when she stops abruptly, causing my front to collide with her back, knocking her forward a few steps. I catch her elbow and curse her. "For fuck's sake, Ava."

She pays no attention to my irritation, her focus remaining forward. "Matt?" she says.

My neck cracks with the speed I lift my head, and my hand automatically moves from Ava's elbow to her waist. I also step forward and close the mere inch of space between her back and my front. Anger races to the surface. It's made worse by the fact that she recognizes the wanker she was with before she met me. It's a fucking kick in the teeth. A baseball bat to my gut. And it only fans the flames of my anger.

Time hasn't been kind to Ava's ex-boyfriend. Not kind at all, though I can tell by the way he's drinking in my wife that he thinks otherwise where she's concerned. Fucking hell, hold me back.

"Ava?" He moves forward, oblivious to me looming beyond. I'm head and shoulders above Ava; you can't fucking miss me unless something more pleasurable is stealing all of your attention, and my wife, especially in that ridiculously short red thing, is definitely a more pleasurable sight than me. My face is twitching, caught between snarling, growling, and glaring. "Wow, you look amazing."

She shifts before me. Is she trying to break away from me? Or is she nervous? I don't know, and I like the thought of neither, so I lock my hand tighter on her waist. She's going nowhere. But Matt is if he doesn't fuck off. Like into space when I launch him there with my fist.

"Thanks, Matt." Ava looks back at me, though I can't tell if her look is wary or warning. My eyes are preoccupied burning holes through her arse-wipe ex. Just hearing her say his name causes all kinds of fury within me.

"I read in the paper that you were involved in an accident. Sounded pretty bad." Matt keeps his focus on Ava. "Though I have to say, you're looking very well."

"I'm getting there. You're looking good yourself. How have you been?"

Seriously? I'm expected to stand here like a spare part while my wife and her ex-boyfriend have a fond reunion? Not happening. Over my dead fucking body. Or maybe it'll be over Matt's because, I swear, I will fucking kill him.

"We're leaving." I tug Ava on, keeping my deadly stare trained on Matt as I escort her away. He finally looks at me, and I will him to have a little think about what happened the last time he came sniffing around my wife.

"That was rude, Jesse," Ava argues pointlessly as I walk us to the car.

I stop her and bend, bringing myself to her eye level. "You don't remember what he did to you, but I do."

Instant bitterness travels in waves across her face, and I fear it's not bitterness toward her ex, but toward me. "What did he do?" she asks, all cocky.

"He cheated on you. You lived with him, Ava, and you moved out when you found out he'd cheated on you. He's an arsehole." I see surprise on her face, and definitely hurt. Over him?

"So he cheated on me, you cheated on me." She laughs wickedly. "What the fucking hell is wrong with me? And since I'm supposed to love you madly, your transgressions hurt more! So the only arsehole I see right now is *you*, Jesse. Just you! And I fucking hate you!" I can tell she regrets the words almost immediately by the quick press of her lips together, plus her small step back away from me.

But I don't think she will ever appreciate how much it really does hurt. I think I'd rather take another knife to my stomach. She hates me?

"I'm putting your cruelty down to too much alcohol. Get in the car. Now." I sound possessed, and I don't give a fucking shit.

Without another word, she slides into the passenger seat and buckles up, not taking her wary eyes from me as I slam her door and stalk around the front of the car. Throwing myself in with force, I start the engine and screech off recklessly, fighting to cool my burning rage. It's bad enough she recognized him—bad enough that the last man she remembers in her life was that scumbag. But her words?

I look down at my white knuckles gripping the steering wheel, the strength of my hold doing nothing to stop my shakes. I'm fucking livid. Her hateful claim has put me in psycho territory. It's been years since my temper has reached these heights. Years since I flew off the handle and went on a rampage of destruction. I feel like every shitty thing is coming to a head. I'm at boiling point.

And she knows it.

Chapter 28

The entire drive home Ava's fingers remained clawed into the leather of her seat. It didn't make me take my foot off the pedal. Either the car took the heat of my anger, or Ava did, and shouting and screaming at her wouldn't have helped either of us.

I'm surprised my Aston's door doesn't drop to the gravel driveway on a scream of pain after I've viciously slammed it shut. Ava's out of the car far quicker than I expected she could manage, hobbling to the door.

I hurry to catch up, my instinct to help her taking over and taming my anger. "I can walk." She bats my hands away as I try to pick her up. "Leave me alone."

I will never leave her alone. Leaving her alone would be as good as giving up, and where my wife is concerned, I never give up. As gently as I can, I lunge in and swipe her from her feet, lifting her over my shoulder. "Forget it, lady." The smashing of her fists into my back are a sign of her trying to make a stand more than a means of escape. We both know she's going nowhere until I release her.

"I said leave me alone!" she screams, half-vexed, half-hysterical.

It's exactly how I feel inside. I absorb each blow, pacing toward the door. "Jesse!"

"Shut the fuck up, Ava," I warn, kicking the door open once I've unlocked it.

"You're an animal!"

"Story of my fucking life where you're concerned." I lower her to her feet. The fists that were smacking pointlessly at my back begin pounding at my chest. And I just stand, motionless, letting her vent and thrash out, screaming her frustration.

If only I had the same kind of outlet. Something to beat and pound and scream at. But I don't, so I savor her brutal smashes of my torso, hoping that at the same time she beats the frustration out of me, too.

She goes for it mercilessly, her strength fueled by her despair.

And I'm fine with it. I'd be her punching bag for the rest of my miserable days if it would make her feel even the tiniest bit better. Because, ultimately, while I'm in pieces trying to navigate my way through this unfamiliar, painful territory, the love of my life is in more despair. While I have our memories to cling to, she does not. While I have our children's faces to picture during this nightmare, every moment of their short lives to remember, she does not. While I have hope and recognize the glimmers of her recollections, she does not.

My thoughts take over, anger burning my insides as she continues to scream and punch. "Go on!" I roar, and she startles, moving back. "Fucking hit me, Ava! It can't feel any worse than how I'm hurting here." I smash my fist into my chest. "So hit me!"

I close my eyes as she comes at me again. And while she's lashing out, I think about how powerful our love is. Not as powerful as I always thought, because if it was, surely it would shine through anything. Even this.

It takes me a few seconds to realize that she's stopped thumping me, and when I open my eyes, I find her heaving before me, her hair a crazy mess around her face, her eyes wild. We stare at each other for a few moments, me expressionless, Ava clearly shocked by her outburst. Or shocked that I've stood here and accepted it. Because what the fuck else would I do? Retaliate? Hit her back? Her thinking that might be a possibility makes me feel sick. Makes me want to hurt myself to demonstrate that I'd take everything before I'd let anything cause her pain.

Just seeing her before me looking so lost and hopeless, clearly wondering what I'm thinking, and me *knowing* what she's thinking, only amplifies my despair. And my anger. I can't take this.

I leave her to compose herself in the hallway while I stalk through the house to the games room, my mind set on one thing. The one thing that will numb me. The one thing that will take me away from my nightmare. My eyes home in on the bottle set on the bar; the respite that just a few swigs could give me is too tempting to pass up. I shrug my suit jacket off and toss it to the carpet, then yank my tie loose and pop open the top button of my collar, too.

My eyes still on that bottle, my hand goes through my hair roughly. Long-lost memories of the alcohol-induced haze of nothingness return full force. I need that nothingness right now. Because if this is how my life is going to feel from now on, then I'm out. I'm done.

I swipe up the bottle of vodka and pull out the cork, my breathing labored. A bead of sweat starts trickling down my forehead, and I roughly wipe it away as I bring the bottle to my lips. Just one sip. That's all it'll take. One swallow to start numbing the pain.

Nostrils flaring, I knock back my first big gulp and gasp, the liquor burning down my dry throat. It hits my stomach hard, and my thoughts go back to the days when I was lost in a haze of drink and women. I see myself naked. With endless women, all women who aren't my wife.

"Jesse!" Ava's stricken voice pierces my flashback, pulling me away from the decadent days of The Manor, back to my reality. Her glassy eyes hold me in place. Beautiful eyes, the chocolate eyes that put me under a spell and never let me go. "You shouldn't be drinking," she pants, still breathless from her episode in the hallway.

I look down at the bottle, except this time I don't see an escape. Now I see poison. Now I see the coward's choice. Now I see real damage. She's right; I shouldn't be drinking it. But most importantly, she knows I shouldn't be drinking it. "Why?" I ask quietly, looking back to her. "Why shouldn't I be drinking it, Ava?"

Her mouth opens and closes, her mind clearly straining to find the answer. I don't want to admit that the answer she's looking for isn't there. I don't want to accept that she won't find it. Her statement was just another one of those pointless glimmers of hope.

Her blankness shoves me over the edge, and I lose my shit, frustration and despair getting the better of me. "Why, Ava?" I roar. "Why shouldn't I be drinking the fucking vodka?"

"I don't know," she sobs, her shoulders shaking uncontrollably, emotion finally taking the place of her frustration. "I don't know." She buries her face in hands, hiding from our reality.

Seeing her so broken is harder than dealing with the frustration. Seeing her so utterly helpless shreds my heart. This is lower than any depths of hell I thought I'd seen.

"Fuck!" I flip, throwing the bottle at the wall ferociously before I do something stupid like down the rest. Shards of glass fly like shrapnel, the devil's juice spraying every wall.

"I shouldn't drink it because I'm a fucking alcoholic!" I boom. "Because before I met you, all I did was drink myself into oblivion and fuck anything with a fucking pulse. That's why!" I stagger back, my back hitting the wall, my breathing shot. I can't control my body. My mouth.

My fucking tears.

Though I can still see her shock through the water distorting my sight.

"You gave me a reason to stop, Ava." I heave where I stand, feeling like my life's rapidly escaping my control altogether. "You made my heart start beating again. And now you're not here anymore and I don't know if I can go on without you."

My knees buckle, and I slide down the wall like a sack of shit, hitting the floor on a thud. I'm past holding it all in. I'm so past trying to be the strong one. Because without Ava, I'm the weakest man alive, and I feel like I'm without her now. My elbows hit my knees, my face going into my palms and hiding. I can't bear the shock on her face. Can't stand the fact that she's seeing me like this.

"Just go to bed," I beg, needing her to leave me alone in my misery. "Just go."

I feel cold. Lonely.

And then . . . not.

Her hand slides onto my neck, and I look up to find her kneeling before me, teary eyes staring into mine. "I'm going nowhere." Edging her way closer, she places her palms on my knees and pushes them apart, moving between them. "Because even though I don't know where I am, I feel like I'm at home. Even though I'm struggling to wrap my mind around you"—more tears tumble as she squeezes my knees—"I know you're mine. I know I'm your heart. Because even though I don't *know* you, I know that when I think of you gone, it hurts really bad just here." Taking my hand, she pushes it into her chest. Her heart is thundering. Like mine.

"Ava, I'm a broken man." I feel fucking awful admitting it.

"The thought of you losing every memory we've had together cripples me."

"I know you're stronger than this. I know you're more determined. You promised you wouldn't give up on me."

My heart constricts. "Baby, I haven't given up." I sigh and gesture her closer, and she comes with ease, letting me pull her onto my lap and cuddle her. "I'm just having a minor relapse."

She snuggles close, and my world evens out a little. "Don't have a relapse again, please."

"Then you need to start doing as you're told."

"Never," she argues. "Because I know I never normally do, do I?"

I smile through my sadness. "You don't."

We remain bunched up on the floor for a while, quiet, both of us calming, our bodies recovering from our shakes. Then Ava breaks out of my hold, placing her lips on my cheek and inhaling. "Come to bed?"

I swallow, hating that it sounds like an unsure question. "I'd love to." I'll cuddle her all night. Keep her close. No sex, no *anything*, just contact. I *need* contact.

"Thank you."

"Don't thank me," I scold her gently. "Never thank me for loving you."

"Because it was what you were put on this earth to do." Her bottom lip quivers over every word, and I gulp down the melon-sized lump in my throat and yank her back into me.

"That's right." Suffocating her with my hold, I sink my face into her hair and fight to keep more emotion at bay. "This dress is still ridiculous," I croak.

"I forget I'm thirty-eight now."

"So you were just being stubborn, yes?" I don't need confirmation. I know my wife better than she knows herself.

She nods into my chest. "I don't have the figure I did when I was in my early twenties."

I scoff at that, getting us up from the floor and lifting her into my arms. "You're more beautiful every day. End of." We'll be having none of that nonsense.

"You're obliged to say that."

"I'm obliged to say nothing, lady." I take the stairs and enter our bedroom. "But, as you know, you are obliged to do as I say." I place her on her feet and automatically turn her around, taking the zip of her dress. "Understand?"

She nods and remains still as I unfasten her, my eyes falling down her back with the zip. As I push the material aside, I hold my breath, bracing myself for the vision of her exposed back.

"Perfect," I sigh, letting the red material drop to the floor. The black lace underwear underneath fits her perfectly. Fuck. I don't think that cuddle I was hoping for will be enough. Will she let me?

My hands reach for the clasp of her bra. One flick releases the catch, and I notice her shoulders lift an inch. I move in close and slide my forearm around her waist, resting my chin on her shoulder. "I want to make love to you," I whisper, and she tenses, but not from fear. It's from anticipation. "I want to peel this lace off your body and take my time exploring every inch of you." I drag the straps of her bra down her arms until it tumbles to the floor. "I need you, Ava. More than I've ever needed you." Kissing her cheek lightly, I relish the feel of her pushing closer into me. "Let me show you how much I love you."

She turns slowly and lifts her chin to see me, and without a word she starts to unbutton my shirt, one by one, slowly and purposefully, a million emotions dancing in her dreamy eyes. Fear. Hope. But most of all, need. For me.

I realize I need to be gentle. Slow and patient, thoughtful and caring. More so than ever before. So I let her undress me at her own speed, resisting the urge to rip my clothes from my body and toss her on the bed. "Want some help?" I ask, just so she knows I'm open to all options.

She glances up at me, and I see apprehension in her gaze. And I realize that even though she's desperate for me, she doesn't know what this will be like. She doesn't know how explosive we are together, whether hard and raw or slow and loving.

"Don't be nervous." I take her wrists, instantly feeling her tremble. "We don't have to do this." Never has it taken so much energy to say just a few words.

"But I want to." Her gaze drops from mine, down my torso, her teeth sinking into her lip. "I really want to."

Forcing her way out of my hold, she pushes my shirt from my shoulders and places her hands on my pecs. My body feels like it's just gone up in flames, and my hands twitch, desperate to grab her. Ravage her. Kiss her. Make love to her. The look in her eyes tells me she's aware of all this. She knows.

"I *really* want to." She reinforces her claim with a hard kiss on the lips, and I'm instantly overwhelmed by it, my palm going to the back of her head, gently pushing her closer, my mouth opening, inviting her in.

Her hands are everywhere. Our kiss is bordering clumsy. I can feel my control slipping. This is what desperation does to me. It makes me urgent, makes me want to take her hard and fast, to stake my claim, mark my territory, show her how good we are. But now isn't the time for me to get carried away.

I slow the tempo of our kiss. I don't need to give her instruction. Her hands find the fly of my trousers, and I kick off my shoes. I help her slide my trousers off, keeping up our kiss, and then walk her back to the bed. I take her down to the mattress and gently tug her up to the top. Our lips are still sealed, our tongues dancing slowly, breathing each other's breath.

I don't think she's ever tasted so good, even with the hints of alcohol mixed between us. I come down to rest over her, taking my arms up over her head, leaving her hands free to roam my back, my arse, and eventually my face. She is lost. Consumed. I force myself to break our kiss, just to prove to myself that she'll hate the loss.

"Jesse," she pants, her hands grabbing at my hair trying to get me back on her mouth. Then her legs lock around my waist, a demonstration that she's not letting me go anywhere. "Why are you stopping?" She blinks repeatedly, and the egomaniac inside me likes to think that it's because she's struggling with my magnificence so close up.

"I just want to look at you for a moment knowing that I'll be inside you again very soon."

Her lips purse, her hands going to the waistband of my boxers. She pushes them over the rise of my arse. "How does a man of your age stay in such good shape?" She cheekily pinches my bum, and I flinch on an epic grin.

"Lot and lots of sex."

A small giggle escapes her, and her short nails sink into the flesh of my arse. I grit my teeth, enduring the sharp pain. "I'll have to take your word for it."

"You'd *better* take my word for it." I raise my eyebrows in warning as her hand glides softly through my hair, her eyes following.

"Because it's so good?"

"The sex? Yes."

"I'm afraid I need proof, Mr. Ward." Her brown eyes land on mine with a bang, and the blood that's been steadily filling my cock gushes in. Her lips press together, her hips flexing up, pushing into my colossal erection. "Oh my," she breathes.

"You've felt nothing yet, lady." Down I go, lips crashing to hers, slow and steady suddenly forgotten. Wild hands feel down my thighs and start pulling impatiently at my boxers. I can fully appreciate her eagerness, taking my own hands to her knickers, but rather than trying to shove them down her legs, I rip them right off.

She inhales sharply but quickly adopts my method, tugging at my boxers. I hear a rip, but they're still a barrier between my flesh and hers. "Fuck," I mutter, taking over, giving them a few brutal yanks.

And then there is nothing but skin. Nothing but the friction of my flesh rubbing all over hers as we writhe together, our lips and tongues clashing, our moans and hungry gasps blending, drenching the room.

"I need to be inside you now," I tell her, shifting my hips to get the angle right.

It doesn't take much guidance from Ava to get my cock resting at her throbbing entrance. She sucks in air and holds it, and I pull back to get her in my sights. Eyes on hers, I nudge forward a fraction, resisting the urge to pound straight in. "You ready, baby?"

"God, yeah." She can hardly talk through her want, but she can move, rolling her hips up and taking a bit more of me.

"Oh Jesus." My head drops limply, the feel of only a little bit of her stripping me of control. I thrust forward on a yell and hold still.

"You fit me just right." She threads her hands through the hair at my nape and tugs me back onto her lips. "So fucking right."

"Watch your mouth, Ava."

"No."

"Okay." She could swear until she's blue in the face and I'm red, and I wouldn't give a shit. Because now. Now is *everything*.

"Move." She sinks her nails into my arse again, egging me on. "Oh God, please move. You feel so good."

I'm not the kind of man to disappoint, especially my wife. Nuzzling her cheek, I take her hands from my arse and thrust them up on the pillow, raising a little to get her in my sights. She's panting. Wanting. Loving the feel of me inside her. I jolt my hips teasingly. "You want gentle Jesse, baby?" I lick my lips, savoring the sight of her sweating. "Or should I rip you clean in two?"

She inhales, somewhere between shock and delight. "Which do I prefer?"

"Depends on your mood. What are you in the mood for, gorgeous wife?" Another thrust, short and sharp, makes her tense, snap her mouth shut, and hold her breath.

"Just take me away from our nightmare for a while. I don't care how. Just do it."

I waver on the edge of despondency. Our nightmare. She wants to escape. Then she bumps her hips, too, and that despondency sinks in a pleasure like no other. "I'm introducing a new fuck to our relationship, baby." Dipping, I kiss her hard, pulling away before she has a chance to engage her mouth and keep me there. "We'll call it the Reunion Fuck."

And that fuck is going to be my new favorite. I swivel my hips, grinding deeply. I flex my hands over her wrists, but keep them where they are, withdrawing from the amazing warmth of her pussy and gliding gently back in. My body is craving a nice hard fuck, but my mind won't allow it. "I'm going to make the softest love to you."

She melts beneath me, and the wobble of her lip tells me she likes my idea. "Okay."

I lower my face, catching her mouth gently as I start a measured, delicate rock of my hips, making sure my drives are slow and exact, my tongue following suit. I release her hands and let her feel me. I let her control our kiss, tolerating the loss of her lips from time to time when she lazily throws her head around on the pillow, sighing, moaning, struggling to keep her eyes open. She's floating away, caught in the moment. A moment with me. I ensure my rhythm is consistent, ensure she's held in a perfect state of pleasure. I've never seen anything so stunning, and I find myself focusing more on her losing herself rather than my own pleasure. It's no loss. Nothing could ever beat this.

My wet skin peels away from her chest as I lift and brace myself on my forearms, needing a better view. Her eyes follow mine, her hands reaching for my face and holding me. Our hips are in perfect sync, her rolling up, me rolling down, each plunge achieving the deepest depths.

"I can see why I fell in love with you," she whispers, grazing her palms over my stubble.

"Because I'm an Adonis in bed?"

"*And* out of bed." Her voice gets higher, and then she moans her way back down to a level tone, her eyes blinking slowly. "You're the perfect mix of man. Big, strong, passionate, devoted. You love with everything you have."

"And I'm nothing without you."

"And everything with me." I'm pulled down, her face sinking into my neck, and we take the final stretch to release holding each other tight, breathing in time together, moving as one.

Our climax hits simultaneously. I don't yell. Neither does she. I don't buck or jolt. Neither does she. We roll through our pleasure calmly and quietly, the only frantic, crazy thing happening being the hammering of both our hearts. I'm alive. So is she. Everything else can be fixed. I'm sure of it.

"You want me to move?" I ask against the wet flesh of her neck, mindful that I'm now limp and probably very heavy.

"No." Arms coming straight around my shoulders, legs around my waist, she locks me up tightly in her hold. "I want you to stay exactly where you are all night." She turns her face into mine and finds my lips. "Because this is where you are supposed to be. With no space between us."

Locked together.

Touching everywhere. Her lips resting on mine, my lungs inhaling her breath.

"Jesse?" she murmurs sleepily in my ear, and I hum my prompt for her to go on. "I think I'm falling in love with you."

CHAPTER 29

Just call me a domestic god.

I'm getting used to this stupid coffee machine now. I'm also getting used to the fact that it's not ready for me to drink when I get up in the morning. Ava has finally been sleeping well, and waking her come morning is out of the question. So I've taken over her jobs.

I flick the machine on and open the pantry cupboard, pulling down the cereals and setting them on the side for the kids. It's only when I'm on my way back to the coffee machine that I realize what I've done. The gaping hole in my existence grows, and like they've sensed I'm missing them, my phone rings and I rush over to answer. I smile when I see my boy's face lighting up the screen.

Answering, I prop it up by the cooker and continue with Ava's breakfast. "Are you cooking eggs, Dad?" Jacob asks in greeting. The sea in the background looks amazing, the rush of the waves loud but calming. A holiday. I could do with one of those.

"Sure am, buddy." I tap the spatula on the edge of the pan before lifting to show him. "I'm making your mum breakfast in bed." I feel like I've been born again, injected with energy. Last night was one of the most amazing nights of my life. And better still, I know my wife feels the same.

"Remember she likes a runny yolk," Jacob reminds me, having me looking down at the pan and the two very *un*runny yolks. He must catch my frown. "Do scrambled," he tells me. "And salmon. You know that's one of her favorites."

"I have no salmon," I grumble, thinking I need to get my arse to the supermarket pronto. We're low on everything. But grocery shopping is hardly the romantic date I had planned for later. I hear Jacob sigh, and I shrug, because that's what I do. "How's Maddie?" I ask.

"She met a friend. She's down the beach now."

A friend? "Nice. What's her name?"

"Hugo."

The pan clatters to the stove, my hand catching the burner. "Motherfucker!" I yelp and start jumping around, clasping my hand tightly to stem the pain. "You bastard!" Fucking hell. My knuckles are still sporting the aftermath of my lash out on the mirror and door. Now this? I shake it out, grimacing in pain. "Fuck, that hurts."

"Jesse Ward!" The sound of my mother-in-law's voice penetrates my senses, and I fly over to my phone, just catching Jacob rolling his eyes as Ava's mother pushes him from the camera. Her face appears, very displeased.

"Hugo's a girl's name." I state it as a fact. "Isn't it?"

"Hugo is a boy," she says flippantly. I don't appreciate it. "Just the grandson of some friends. We had dinner with them last night."

I get my face up close and personal with the screen, noting Elizabeth backing away. My baby girl is on the coast without me there to make sure no little twerps sniff around her. "I'm relying on you, Elizabeth."

"To do what? Trample in your absence?"

"Yes!" I look down at my hand and see a blister developing. "Keep him away from my daughter," I warn, swiping up my phone and making my way to the sink. "Boys can't be trusted. How old is the little shit?"

"Thirteen."

I drop my phone in the sink. "Thirteen?" Oh my God! "Elizabeth, this—" I'm interrupted mid-rant when someone takes my hand, I peek to the side to find Ava inspecting the burn. She shakes her head, takes my phone from the sink, and props it up against the backsplash.

"Hi, Mum." She flips on the tap and forces my hand under the flow of cold water. I hiss as she looks at me out the corner of her eye, her expression telling me it's my own damn fault.

"Hi, darling!" Elizabeth, understandably, looks delighted to see her daughter.

Too bad. I seize the phone while Ava tends to my hand, keeping it steady under the water. "So, this boy."

"What boy?" Ava pipes up, leaning and grabbing a towel off the side.

I ignore her and press Elizabeth for details. "Keep him away from my daughter."

"Oh, stop overreacting." My mother-in-law sighs. She just can't help undermining me, the fucking pain in the arse that she is. "She's growing up, Jesse. You need to let her."

I think I might explode. How long would it take me to get to Newquay? "Elizabeth—" The phone is gone from my hand speedily, Ava whipping it away and wandering off. I stare at her back incredulously.

"Are the kids okay, Mum?" she asks, looking over her shoulder, giving me a stare that dares me to hijack my phone. It's a fucking conspiracy. All of them ganging up against me. "Good. And, yes."

Ava pouts. "He's being very attentive and caring. I'm feeling better by the day."

I don't want to smile. Not when I'm so pent up and stressed, but before I know it I'm grinning like a loon. She's feeling great. I was, too, until my mother-in-law ruined it. I huff and plonk my arse on a stool, scowling down at my injured, towel-wrapped hand. Perfect. Fucking perfect.

"I'm looking forward to seeing you, too." Ava joins me, holding up the bath towel that's wrapped around her as she sits on the stool. I don't know what comes over me. One minute she's covered in white fluffy material, the next she's covered in... nothing. The towel hits the floor and Ava gasps, shooting shocked eyes at me. And I just grin. Big, wide, and satisfied, making a meal of relaxing on my stool and looking her up and down, up and down, up... and... down.

I breathe in and exhale loudly. "Breakfast's looking mighty fine," I muse, earning a few playful slaps across the head. I laugh my way through it as she scrambles for her towel. Silly girl. I whip it away and run around the other side of the island, waving it teasingly.

"Ava, you're naked!" Elizabeth screeches.

"Damn FaceTime." I shake my head mockingly, throwing the towel over my shoulders. "You're naked, baby."

Her scowl is award worthy. And so is my smirk. "I have to go, Mum. Give the kids a kiss for me." She disconnects the call and points the phone at me. "You're in trouble, Ward."

"Oh, goody." I rub my hands together. "Bring it on, baby. Bring. It. On."

Her attempts to hide the twitch in her lips fails miserably. "You're much older than me. I'm thinking speed isn't your thing these days."

Much older? "You haven't seen me chase the boys away from our daughter. I'm a fucking greyhound."

Eyes narrowed, she steps to the left. And I step to the right. "I'll catch you," she warns.

Good. I hope she does. "And what will you do to me then?"

"That's for me to know."

"And I'm gonna find out." I dart out of the kitchen, towel billowing behind me, and as soon as I'm out of her sight, I drop to the floor and lie down on my back.

She comes half hobbling out of the kitchen, yelping when she trips over my foot. I catch her perfectly and bring her softly down onto my chest. "Seems you caught me, Mrs. Ward."

"Don't humor me." She presses her palms into my pecs, intending to push herself away but getting completely distracted by the vast expanse of my naked chest instead, her eyes sparkling with delight. The grins are coming thick and fast this morning.

"Earth to Ava," I whisper, knocking her out of her mesmerized state.

"You know," she sighs, keeping her eyes on mine as she lowers her lips to my pec and drops a lingering kiss there, "I think even if I were still young, I'd want to do you."

Laughter rumbles up from my toes, jolting her on my chest. I feel her grin against my skin, her hands splayed and feeling me. Once I've pulled myself back around, I roll us, trapping her naked body beneath mine. She hisses, and I bolt up, worried. "It's fine." She sinks her hands into my hair and plays with the strands. "The floor's cold on my back. How's your hand?"

My eyes narrow, aware she's trying to divert the attention onto me. "My hand is fine." I flex it a little, testing my own claim. A little sore, but that's all.

Moving her hands to my arse, she sinks her nails into the material of my boxers, circling her hips up on a sultry hum.

My cock wakes up, and I lift my hips to make room for it between us, the ache instant. I groan, dropping my head. I need to rein myself in. "I've taken up far too much of your energy over the past couple of days." Motorbike rides, dinner, arguing . . . sex.

"But—"

"No buts." Begrudgingly, I rise, helping Ava up and wrapping her in the towel, ignoring her grumbling. "You need to eat." Her shoulders slump, and while I'm beyond thrilled that she's struggling to contain her want, I'm aware of how much I've taken out of her, even if she won't admit it. I turn her and lead her back to the kitchen, sitting her down before serving up her eggs. Questionable eggs. "Eat," I order, putting the fork in her hand and grabbing my phone. I just need to make a call. I dial John and leave the kitchen. "Sarah rang me last night," I tell him quietly when I'm out of earshot, looking over my shoulder.

"What the fuck?" He's not happy. Good. Neither am I. "I've fucking told her."

"Well, you can tell her again."

He grunts his confirmation. "I will. I have. But she's insisting she needs to talk to you."

"That ain't happening. The woman's poison."

"I know that. You know that. But Sarah's just as stubborn as ever." He sighs. "I'll speak to her. How's Ava?"

"She's good. The club?"

"S'all good," he confirms. "You concentrate on your girl."

"Thanks, John." I smile as I hang up, and quickly take the opportunity to call Elizabeth back while Ava's eating her breakfast. "Hey,"

She sighs. "Jesse Ward, I am not—"

"Shut up, woman. I've not called about the little shit. I wanted to talk to you about Ava and the kids."

"Oh? Everything okay?"

"Yes, actually. Really good. And the kids?" I don't need to ask. I can see it on their faces every time we talk. They're fine.

"They're great. Full of questions, but they just need reassurance. Speaking to Ava has helped."

I smile. "I know it's been a week already, but our first few days here were spent in tears. I'm seeing progress now, Elizabeth." It pains me to say it, and I miss the twins terribly, but... "Can you give me a little more time?"

She doesn't hesitate. "We were thinking of heading back on Monday."

"I love you, Mum."

"Shut up, you menace." She hangs up as I head back to the kitchen and take a stool next to Ava, noticing she's not touched a bit of her breakfast.

I nudge her when she places her fork down, flipping her a warning look as I slide my phone onto the counter, ready to commence force-feeding my wife. "Stop staring at it and eat."

She sighs and loads her fork with a miniscule bit of egg. "Who was that?"

"John." I get up and pour some coffee. "I was just checking up on the club."

"Can I see it?" She pops some breakfast in her mouth and chews slowly, watching me.

"See what?"

"The club."

"Sure. You eat all your breakfast and I'll take you after your therapy session."

The flare of exasperation in her eyes makes me smile. "Like a good little wife?"

Resting my elbows on the island across from her, I smile the smile I reserve only for her. "Exactly like that." I blow her a little kiss and start clearing up the kitchen. Maybe a visit to our health club will jog something in that muddled mind of hers.

Chapter 30

The car park is jam-packed. I spot Drew's car in one of the reserved bays and pull up next to it, quickly making my way around the car to help Ava out. She's quiet as I walk her to the modern building. It couldn't look more different from The Manor. The club is still luxurious, but nowhere near as ostentatious. The reception area is buzzing when we enter.

"Is that a salon?" Ava asks, pointing to one of the four shop fronts on the first floor. "And a beauty parlor?"

"Yes, and Raya operates from that one there."

"What does she do?" Ava lets me take her hand, seeming a bit overwhelmed by the place already.

"Sports therapy." I nod to one of the girls on reception who quickly lets us through the turnstiles. "And that one over there is a health food store."

"It's like health heaven," she says, smiling awkwardly when the girls on reception all wave hello. "And I work here?"

"You sound disappointed." When we arrive at the juice bar, I spot Drew through the glass window that overlooks the pool area. He's at the top of the diving board giving Georgia instructions.

"Well, I've always dreamed of owning my own design company," Ava says.

"You gave up work to have the twins." It was way before the twins came, but how Ava came to leave her employment at Rococo Union isn't something I'm going into. I often wonder whether that prick Mikael still owns it, or if he sold it off as soon as my wife quit. "When the kids started school full-time you decided you wanted to have an input here."

A doubtful look lands on me. "I decided, or you made me?"

"You decided," I confirm, and order her favorite power shake. "In your words, I'm crap at organizing financial stuff and you weren't about to let someone else do it."

"So you pay me?" She accepts the shake, eyeing it suspiciously.

"Handsomely," I reply, my voice suggestive and low.

She tosses me a playful filthy look. "Very funny."

"You're a director, Ava. Like I said, *we* own it."

I can tell she's happy about that, her lovely lips taking the straw and sipping thoughtfully as she gazes around the bar, where laptops clutter tables and people chat post-workout. "Hmmm, this is lush."

"Glad your taste hasn't changed," I say, motioning her to the stairs that lead to the gym floor.

Her face is suddenly bright and chirpy as she flanks me, her lips stuck to the straw. "That would have been a bit of a shock for you, wouldn't it?"

"What would?"

"Well, if I came around and didn't fancy you." She titters as we take the stairs, amused.

"So you fancy me?" I say, sounding casual and unaffected.

"You're all right, I suppose."

The nerve. I nudge her and she chuckles, coming to a stop at the top of the stairs when the gym floor comes into view. "Wow."

Turning slowly on the spot, she takes in the vast space. It could take her a while. A Bodypump class is happening on the grid across the way, a team of serious weight trainers are lifting in the corner, a group of women are speed cycling at the far back. And then the glass-fronted studios are all full, one class or another happening in each. All the endorphins bouncing around the place are sinking into my skin, and I wish I could hit the treadmill. Exercise has always been a blessing to me, a perfect way to alleviate stress. And now, when I'm the most stressed I've ever been, I haven't had the opportunity to expel it.

Many people pass us, clients and staff, all saying hello, smiling, clearly pleased to see us. But Ava doesn't recognize any of them. She just smiles awkwardly, becoming increasingly uncomfortable by the second.

"I'm here every day?" she asks, her tone not cluing me in on whether that pleases her or daunts her. I'm hoping it pleases her, and then maybe she'll lose that silly idea of working elsewhere.

"Yes, with me."

She seizes my hand without prompt, clinging to it harshly. "It's very loud."

Shit, she's right. It's banging, nothing unusual, but Ava's head is delicate. I pull her on, keen to get us away from the pumping gym floor to somewhere quieter. "Here." Opening the door to her office, I usher her in and shut out the noise. That's better. She probably couldn't hear herself think.

She wanders in quietly, taking in the space that she frequents daily, my eager eyes looking for some recognition on her face. She finds the picture frame on the desk and lifts it, smiling down at the photograph of us all. It's just another piece of evidence that this is real, that she's not about to wake up at any moment and discover she's been trapped in a dream. "Your office is very nice," she says, setting the frame down.

My office? "This isn't my office, Ava," I say, taking my usual spot on the couch by the window. "This is *your* office."

Her eyes widen a fraction, going on another little journey around the space. "Mine?" she questions, obviously thrown.

Reclining, I smile at her wonder. "Yours."

I watch as she pulls her chair out from her desk and sits down, tugging open a few drawers. She takes something out and flashes it to me on a grin. Setting the red nail polish on the top, she sits back, and I smile, thinking she looks as sexy as ever when she's behind that desk. "I feel very important."

"You are." I kick my ankle up onto my knee and rest my elbow on the back of the couch.

"So where's your office?"

"I'm sitting on it."

Her smile is given through a frown. "You work from that couch?"

"Yes."

"And what work do you do from there?" She kicks her feet up onto the desk, while I kick mine up onto the couch, lying back, arms behind my head, all comfy. I wish she could see what I see when I'm in here. I see us on every available surface. Me between her legs. God, how many times have I taken her on that desk?

"The only work I get done while I'm in here is admiring my wife. It's a very important part of my day."

"Slacking on the job? The boss isn't setting a very good example."

I'm thoroughly amused by her words. "Ava, everyone around here knows that it is *you* who's boss. Not me."

"That's absurd." She picks up a pen and starts to fiddle with it, weaving it through her fingers in feigned concentration. "You're a control freak. I can't image you let me take the reins in your fancy health club."

"I'm only a control freak when it comes to you. And it's *our* health club."

She nods, thoughtful, gazing around. "So while I'm slaving away, you just lie there looking pretty, do you?"

I lift my head a little, eyebrows high. "You think I look pretty?" I'm playing it all cool, but inside I want to jump up and rock out to a bit of J. Timberlake. She's being rather open with her attraction today. Almost blatant. Almost suggestive.

It's no wonder she has a headache: her eye rolls are constant *and* impressive. "How do I concentrate with you loitering around?" She goes into another drawer and pulls out a few files, frowning at them. Then a calculator that she sets to the side. And, finally, a nail file. She looks delighted with her find as she takes it to her nails.

"I leave you to work." Fuck, what was I thinking bringing us in here? All my intentions to make her take it easy are forgotten. Lost. She's sitting there in her pretty little sundress and flip-flops, her hair a mess of loose waves, her face makeup-free, and she looks fucking edible. And that desk is calling. I throw my legs off the couch, getting up, and stride toward her.

The side-to-side motion of the file slows as I near, her eyes lifting up my tall frame to my face. "You're not lying down now." She points the file at me, as if I might have missed the fact that I've got myself to my feet. "Does that mean you're going to do some work?"

"Oh, yes." I sit on the edge of her desk, my gaze never wavering from hers. "I'm going to do some work all right."

Breath hitching. Body subtly fidgeting. Eyes filing with hunger. Nipples hardening against the material of her dress. My eyes drop to her crotch, my head tilting. She's wet, too. I can smell it from here.

"Behave," she all but squeaks, going back to filing her nails, doing a terrible job of feigning coolness.

She's on fire. I can practically see the flames on her skin. And all of these reactions have the usual effect on me. *She* has her usual effect on me. This woman makes my veins burn. Makes my eyes sting just looking at her. Makes my heart surge with adoration.

"See, that's always been a problem for me, Ava." I place the tip of my finger on the shiny wood of her desk and drag it lazily across the surface. "I've never been able to behave when it comes to you."

"Wherever, whenever," she murmurs, lust spilling over every word. "We've had sex in this office, haven't we?"

"The couch, the floor, the desk, against the door." I take her feet from the desk and use them to pull her closer on her rolling chair, smiling when she sticks herself to the back. Plucking the file from between her limp fingers, I flick it across her desk and lower her feet to the floor, straddling her lap and placing a palm on either side of her head. "I have many fond memories in this office, baby. I wish you had them, too." I dip, touching her nose with mine, loving the feel of her breathy pants hitting my face. "But I'm going to love making more." I place my hand between her thighs, going in for the kill. I'm too wound up to resist. Last night has only made me hungrier for her. And besides, I know my wife well enough to know when she wants it, and she wants it now. "Spread them."

Her legs split open immediately, and before I have the chance to kiss her, she's kissing me. I'm attacked with brutal force, her body up out of the chair faster than is wise, yet I'm in no position to stop her. I sit her on the desk, putting myself between her thighs. While her mouth devours mine, her frantic hands work the button of my fly, yanking impatiently, small growls backing up her frustrated, fumbling fingers. I smile around our kiss, my grip of her hair gentle, contradicting her force. I rip my lips away from her, finding her eyes. She looks drunk.

I draw back and pull up my T-shirt over my head. "Who has the power, baby?"

"You," she murmurs, reaching for the waist of my jeans and tugging me forward. Her hand soon finds my cock, pulling it free and squeezing gently. I'm so fucking thrilled that she still knows that. Still feels it. Still wants me with a craving she can't control. I am her god.

Jesus. This woman rules me. Controls me. She keeps my blood chasing through my veins, my heart beating, my soul pure. And right now, she doesn't even know it. She needs reacquainting with the feelings that always cripple us. That take us to heights no one could ever understand. The feelings that make us *us*. I think she's more or less there already. Even before this moment. Even before we made love. Even if she's confused by our connection and the natural reactions we have to each other. They're all still there inside her, there to be uncovered.

"I'm going to fuck you to—"

I'm interrupted from finishing my promise when the door of the office flies open. And there's only a split second before a shocked yelp penetrates the room. "Oh my God, I'm so sorry!"

I just catch sight of a distressed-looking Cherry before the door slams, leaving us alone again.

"Oh God, how embarrassing!" Ava scrambles up from the desk with the help of my hand. "Who was that?"

"Cherry." I steady Ava on her feet and push her hair from her eyes on a smile. She's all in a fluster, and it's sexy as hell.

"Who's Cherry?"

"She works for us. Wait there." I head to the door, damning myself for not locking it. Fucking hell, I'm charged.

"Jesse?" Ava calls, and I turn, finding her pointing at my groin area as she dips to collect the things we've knocked from the desk. "You might want to put yourself away. And maybe put your T-shirt back on." She throws it to me and I catch it, looking down at my crotch.

Shit, I'm hanging out all over the place. I hear her chuckle as I continue to the door, tucking my cock into my boxers and fastening my jeans. Swinging the door open, I find Cherry standing outside, her cheeks crimson.

Her gaze drops to my chest, her body visibly softening. "Oh, there it is," she whispers under her breath.

"What?"

She snaps out of her little trance and looks up at me. "Good to see you, Jesse." The tone of her voice is effortlessly husky, and her eyes are flashing delightedly. She smiles, giving me the once-over again, hugging the files to her chest. The pressure pushes her tits up. Again, not that I'm purposely looking. They're kinda just... there.

I ignore her blatant flirting, looking past her down the corridor when I hear the sound of footsteps—heavy footsteps that can belong to only one man. John strides toward us, his signature shades firmly in place. "Cherry," he rumbles, nodding sharply at the woman outside my office before turning his eyes on me. "What are you doing here?"

"We're not staying." I pull my T-shirt on as I back up into the office to let them in, ignoring the grin on Cherry's face.

John spots Ava at her desk, his smooth forehead crinkling a little. "Hey, girl."

"Hey," she says quietly, looking past me to the woman who's on the threshold of her office. She also looks wary. Maybe a little pissed off, and it's not because Cherry put the blockers on our moment.

I quickly move aside when Cherry wanders in, her arm brushing mine. "It's lovely to see you, Ava." She reaches the desk and smiles brightly at my wife, who looks at her with a little suspicion.

"Sure it is," she mumbles, all hostile. "Would you mind giving us five minutes?" she says to Cherry, the question sounding like anything but a question, her tone flat, her smile sickly sweet.

"Of course." Cherry backs away, turning and sashaying to the door. She definitely straightens her back on the way, and she definitely has a little pouty-lips thing going on. Fucking hell.

I roll my eyes and face my annoyed wife. Maybe *annoyed* is an understatement. *Seething* seems more appropriate. She isn't a happy girlie. And I'm thrilled. She cocks her head in question, and I just shrug. What can I say?

"I've given Cherry a few more responsibilities in Ava's absence," John says, maybe a little cautiously. "Sorry if I've upset you, girl."

"Don't worry," Ava grumbles moodily. "It's not like I can remember how to do my job, anyway." She picks up a few bits of paper from the floor and scans them before chucking them back on the desk and dropping to the chair.

"The accounts need to be kept in check, membership fees collected, creditors paid," the big man continues, showing a rare pacifying side.

"You don't need to be worrying about work at the moment." I join John in his attempts to make Ava feel better, because despondency over work isn't good when she's spouting off shit about other jobs. Over my dead body. "We need to focus on getting you well."

Her scowl is pointed at me, though I know she's more annoyed with herself. "I feel fine," she grumbles, pushing herself to her feet. "And I also don't need to be worried about some hussy coming on to my husband."

John coughs, and I smile like a madman on the inside. She's not only being possessive over me, which alone is thrilling, she's also being possessive over her job. This is good. She can quit with the stupid idea of getting another one. "No woman turns my head unless it is my wife," I remind her, wandering over and collecting her hand. "You know that."

Her over-the-top pout is so adorable. She wants reassurance. I'll give it, all day every day. I hope we once again get to the point when she doesn't need it anymore. "I know that." She puts herself in my chest, her arms slipping around my back, her cheek squished against my T-shirt. "For such an old man, you're in high demand, Jesse Ward."

I recoil, and John laughs his laugh that's capable of shaking a building. "Go home," he chuckles, making for the door. "I'm keeping Cherry in check."

"Thanks, John." I wrestle Ava from my front and turn her, leading her to the door. "Old?"

Her shoulders jump under my palms. "Your age doesn't seem to be making the slightest bit of difference to the attention you get. That Cherry must be ten years younger than me."

"You being all possessive?" I kiss her cheek as we walk back to the main floor of the gym, me tailing her, her hands now resting over mine where they lay on her shoulders. "Because I like it."

She comes to a stop, and her body starts jerking a little under my touch. Worried, I round her. She has the biggest smile on her face.

"What?" I ask.

Lifting her arm, she points, prompting me to look over my shoulder. "Rowing machines," she says, definite humor edging her tone, though it's obvious she's unsure why, a small frown marring her smile when I return my attention to her.

"What's so funny?" I ask.

"I don't know." She shakes her head. "Do you like rowing?"

I grin, looking back at the machines, thinking they've developed a lot over the years. There's no way I could execute the perfect *slide* and *hit* on one of those things. I'm so glad I kept my old one. "*We* love rowing."

"We do?" She seems surprised by the revelation. "Am I good at it?"

I chuckle to myself, feeling my eyes spark with revived fire. "You're *very* good at it."

"What, like all romantic, rowing-on-the-river type of thing? Sunshine, peace, and gooey romantic words?" Her eyes gleam. I'm about to burst her idyllic bubble.

My palm creeping across her shoulders, I pull her into my side and start walking us away from the rowing machines. "Not quite like that." I feel her look up at me in question, prompting me to go on. "Our rowing is very unique."

"Why doesn't that surprise me? So, come on, then. How do we row?"

I nod at a few patrons as they pass, the men wiping their sweaty brows with towels. "It involves me sitting on the seat and you sitting on me."

"On those things?" she questions, stopping us and turning to inspect the machines again. "How is that even possible?"

"I don't think it is." I look down at her, grinning, and take her hand, tugging her back over. "Come on, let's try."

Her resistance is instant, her spare hand wrapped around my wrist trying to stop me, her feet digging in. "Jesse." She's laughing, but it's loaded with nerves. "We're in the middle of the gym floor."

"So?" My strength will always win, and I have her where I want her within a few seconds. Her dark eyes scan the length of metal, worry written all over that gorgeous face. Keeping hold of her hand, I lower myself to the seat and pat my thigh. "All aboard," I tease, and she bursts into fits of giggles, the sound saturating the space around us.

"Stop it."

"No." I yank her forward and have her straddling my lap before she can protest again, her torso locked to my chest, our cheeks pressed together. "It goes something like this," I say quietly in her ear, using my feet to glide us down the railing. "Slide." I whisper the word and then launch us back up until our bodies jolt at the other end.

"And hit," she finishes for me. The impact of her chest crushing to mine, her groin rubbing into me, the words that have come from deep within her. It's a potent cocktail, causing wild activity past the fly of my jeans, activity that my wife hasn't missed. She pulls back, her palms on my shoulders, and tilts her head. "Oh dear," she murmurs, wickedly grinding her hips into me.

"Now *you* stop it," I warn, quickly lifting us from the seat before I'm pushed over the edge of control and give endless members of our club a show they won't forget.

She giggles softly and puts herself in my chest, her hand on my nape pulling my lips down to hers. She kisses me hard. Possessively. I'm taken aback, but in no way complaining. "What was that for?" I ask when she slows the roll of her searching tongue.

"Just felt like kissing you." She pulls back, pouting. "I'm allowed, right?"

"Stupid fucking question." I turn us to get us on our way, coming face-to-face with Cherry.

"Oh." Ava moves into my side, clinging onto my arm. "Sorry, I didn't see you there."

Cherry's smile is pushed through gritted teeth, and I sigh, tugging Ava along before she moves into true trampling mode. I flip a tired look down at her as we take the stairs.

"What?" she asks, all innocent and pouty.

"Nothing." I fight to keep my grin contained. It's hard.

Because I've just been marked.

Chapter 31

You need to sleep."

"I want you to finish what you started in the office." There's fire in her eyes. Pure, possessive fire. I smile on the inside. But, and it pains me to say it, she needs rest. I'm taking too much out of her. "Bed."

She gazes up at me as we slowly take the stairs, too many wicked intentions spilling from the depths of her dark eyes. "I want a bath."

"Jesus, Ava, are you trying to finish me off?" Wet, slippery skin won't help my cause.

On a little chuckle, her head meets my bicep, and I notice her steps becoming more labored as we reach the top of the stairs. "You can scrub my back."

"You're evil." Entering the bathroom, I eye the huge marble tub like I hate it. She'll be lost in there all alone. Maybe I could join her, because I could easily get away with not touching her if I stay way on the other side.

"It's massive." She breaks away from me and starts drawing herself a bath, picking up a bottle of bubble bath from the side and taking it to her nose, inhaling before adding a massive dose to the running water.

"We like having baths." I move across to the cream crushed velvet chair that sits in the corner and put my big body in it. "You picked the tub."

She takes in the mammoth thing, humming to herself. "It's very me."

"It's very me, too, especially when you're in it."

She keeps her eyes on the filling tub. "So you're just going to sit there and watch me?" She slowly pulls her sundress over her head and takes her underwear off. Fuck. Me.

I press myself into the back of the chair, every muscle solid in an attempt to stop from shooting up and tackling her to the floor. She's playing games. "Ava, don't tease me."

With her chin on her shoulder, she coyly glances over at me. It's wonderful to see my temptress showing signs of returning to her former glory. Yet it's agony that I can't utilize it to its fullest. "I want you to have a bath with me."

"I don't trust myself."

"Didn't bother you last night."

I scrub my palms down my face, hanging on to my resistance. She wants me. "You're overdoing it."

"I feel fine." Her brown eyes, shimmering and bright, reinforce her claim, and the sense of satisfaction is unreal, but... still.

I shake my head since my mouth refuses to decline, and fold my arms over my chest.

"Suit yourself." She shrugs her naked shoulders and steps into the tub as it continues to fill.

I'm not a happy man. But I just can't deprive myself of the pleasure of looking at her. Admiring her. Thinking about how crazily I love her. So fucking much. Even now, when she's not quite fully mobile, her moves are graceful. She carries herself with a subtle power that has awed me since the day she wandered into my office. She is, quite simply, the most enthralling person I've ever encountered. And she's mine. Beautiful and elegant, with a sprinkling of sass. My head tilts in silent contemplation. A sprinkling of sass? Not if you consider her potty mouth. Then I'm smiling, because I know that potty mouth is enhanced by me. Ironic, really. I'm the catalyst for her foul language—the language that drives me to distraction.

My mind continues to wander as I watch her swishing the water with her feet to build the bubbles. Last night was beyond beautiful. We came together like we'd never been apart, and as she stared up at me while I lazily rocked into her, I knew she felt the overwhelming connection. Maybe I'd hoped our lovemaking would dislodge whatever's holding back her memories, but I didn't dwell on the fact that it didn't. I was too blindsided to care in that moment.

"Jesse?"

I'm awakened from my thoughts by the soft call of my name, and I find her with her hand held out to me.

"Please."

How can I refuse? Simply put, I can't. I get up and strip down, drawn to her by an invisible force that's magic in its power. Taking her hand, I step in the tub and walk her forward a few paces, and then lower myself, bringing Ava carefully down with me until she's snug between my thighs.

"We'll have some tub-talk." I take her hair and push it over her shoulder and down her front. "You think you can resist me?"

"No." Her arms come up over her head and circle my neck, her head resting to the side, her eyes closing. "What's Paradise?" she asks, the question coming from left field. "I keep seeing blue sea and..." She pauses for a beat, thinking. "I think it's a villa."

I recline and slide my hands onto her tummy. "It's a special place. We got married there."

"You told me we got married at your fancy sex club." Her

eyes remain closed, only confirming the exhaustion she's trying to fight.

"We did. We renewed our vows on the beach." I smile fondly. "And then I took you for a swim in the sea."

"Sounds romantic." Her legs entwine with mine, slippery skin on slippery skin. "Tell me how old you are."

Before I can utter a lie again, I give pause, wondering if it will truly mean anything to her if I continue with this game. So far, it hasn't spiked a damn thing in her mind. I chew over my next move for way too long and finally decide to bite the bullet. "I just turned fifty."

I don't know what to expect. Maybe a gasp of shock. Or horror. Or... I don't know, but the silence seems worse, because no shock means I must fucking look my age.

Long seconds pass. Still no reaction. Maybe she's fallen asleep. Or maybe she didn't hear me. Or maybe she thinks she didn't hear me right. "I said, I'm fif—"

"I heard you." Cutting me off, she opens her eyes and looks up at me. "I already knew. I just wanted to see how long you'd keep up the blatant lies."

She knew? "How?"

"Kate told me." She returns to her comfy spot and sighs, while I plot my revenge on Kate. "So I guess that means I don't need to handcuff you to a bed this time?"

Kate is forgotten. Hope is back. "You remember?"

"No, Kate told me." She chuckles, and I sag in disappointment. "I can't believe I did that to you."

"Neither could I," I grumble, absentmindedly tracing circles on her hips with the tips of my fingers, relishing her subtle squirms.

A comfortable silence falls, Ava snoozing peacefully, me staring at the ceiling, happy to let her rest undisturbed.

I have a few precious days before the kids come home to help

Ava find the breakthrough she needs, and my confidence that I can is slipping with each hour that passes. With the twins home, we'll have to readjust all over again. Trivial things such as taking them to school will be an issue for both of us—Ava because she doesn't even know what damn school they go to, or where it is, and me because I never want to let her drive ever again. Never want her to leave my sight. Leaving my family, even for only a few hours, has always been a challenge for me. Stupid, yes. Or maybe not so stupid, given where I am now. The first day of school for the twins was one of the worst days of my life. The teacher didn't take too kindly to me refusing to leave the classroom, and Ava ended up dragging me out by my shirt. And to rub salt into my grumpy wounds, my babies didn't bat an eyelid when I left. I sulked the whole way to work. But, of course, my wife can't remember any of that.

Remember, I demand silently, boring holes into the back of her head, willing the memories to rise to the surface. *Remember me. Remember us.* This helpless feeling isn't getting better, no matter how many new memories I'm building in an attempt to replace the old ones. The old memories are the original memories. Back then, she didn't need to love me. She chose to, even though it could be argued that I didn't give her much choice. Now, I can't help the tinge of worry that this time she *really* doesn't feel like she has much choice. She woke up with that ring on her finger. She woke up with a ready-made family. She woke up to people, people she loves and knows, telling her who I am and who *she* is. My wife. The mother of my children. My fucking world.

My sigh is deep, despondent, and my chest lifts, rolling Ava upon it. I flatten my palms on her hips and stroke gently onto her thighs, making wide circles across her skin. I don't miss the slight tensing of her body, and I notice her nipples have hardened in the steaming water. Her arms, still linked over my head, shift a little, as does her bottom, catching me a treat on my growing cock. I cringe to myself and still my hands. What was I thinking, putting myself in the bath with her? Talk about a glutton for punishment. She shifts again, and this time I growl under my breath, biting down on my teeth to get me through the amazing feeling of her soft arse nuzzling my cock. She's doing this on purpose, trying to break me, wear me down, get the upper hand.

My hands take on a mind of their own and slide a fraction inward, taking my touch to between her thighs. I relax and let my senses guide me, and right now my senses want her in every way they can. My face plummets to her hair and I inhale, my fingers creeping closer to her center. Her legs spread, opening like they could be the gates to heaven. Her face turns out, her cheek resting on my pec, her eyes closed, her lips parted.

"You want me to touch you, baby?" I ask quietly, skimming the swollen lips at her entrance teasingly before withdrawing, going back to circling her thighs. Her body arches on me, her boobs lifting, sending streams of water pouring down the sides of her body. "Is that a yes?"

One hand leaves the back of my neck and reaches down for my hand, trying to put it where she wants it to be. The fact that that's where I want my hand to be, too, is beside the point. She needs to ask. Nicely.

"Tell me," I all but growl, resisting her attempts to move my hand. "You want my fingers where my cock was last night?" I break free of her hold and take my hands to the perfect mounds of her wet breasts, cupping each one.

All she seems to be able to do is mumble broken sounds of pleasure, water lapping her body as she gently squirms on top of me.

"I can't hear you." I dip and nibble at her ear. "Lost for words, lady?"

"Oooh, God."

I smile. "That's better." I move my hands back to between her legs and massage her gently, keeping my touch just shy of her entrance. Fuck, she feels so good. So wet, so warm, so mine. Her whole being goes lax above me, every curve melting into my chest and thighs, her weight perfectly placed, her arms back to curling around my neck. Her head falls limply to the side, eyes drowsy, and I just watch her, transfixed as I play with her, tease her, slowly breach her entrance and withdraw again. "Feel good?" I whisper.

Her answer is a long, breathy sigh. I'm fucking solid, but I have no desire to roll us over and sink into her. I just want to watch her take the pleasure I'm giving.

All. Day. Long.

Her swollen flesh slides across my touch divinely; her soft walls suck my fingers in insatiably. The tips of her nipples beckon me. She is gorgeous. The only sign of her slow build to orgasm is the increasing tension in her body, subtle but obvious when she's spread all over me, her back slipping across my chest. Half of me wants to maintain this level of pleasure for her, where she's teetering on the edge, ready to roll over and seize her climax. But the other half of me wants to hear her scream my name.

My control is taken away from me when she suddenly spins, her position putting the juncture of her thighs perfectly level with my raging dick. Hands above my head, clinging to the edge of the tub, she reaches forward, nuzzles my nose, my cheek, my chin, and then her hips shift slightly, sending my cock plunging with ease into her. I cough my surprise, gritting my teeth, every inch of my skin suddenly tingling. Breath is hard to find, control even harder. "That was sneaky," I pant against her cheek, my cock pulsating wildly, desperate to lunge forward.

"Be quiet," she warns, attacking my mouth with a firm but gentle force, whimpering happily when I put up no fight. She has me just where she wants me, and rather than obsess with how *un*easy she's taking it, I relish in the knowledge that she clearly finds me irresistible. She wants me. Fifty years old, and she wants me.

Taking my hands to her arse, I cover her cheeks with my palms and guide her in slow, amazing circles, grinding her onto me while she hums into my mouth, her tongue fighting delicately with mine. What would I ever do without this? Without her? I pull back, needing to see her face, needing to check she's real. "Give me your eyes." My heart's beating, hard and steadily; I know she's here, but I need to see those eyes. It's an effort for her, but she drags them open, her lashes wet and heavy, her brown gaze drenched with yearning. Or is that love? "I love you." I whisper the words, my head dropping back against the tub, the muscles in my neck failing me. "Words have never been enough, Ava. I've always had to show you."

"Are you showing . . ." She fades off, her forehead falling against mine on a groan. "Now?" she whispers. "Are you showing me now?"

"I'm showing you every second." Our eyes are so close; our lashes are touching. "With no you, there is no me." I'm not telling her this to frighten her, or to make her feel bad. It's not emotional blackmail. I'm telling her because it is a fact. "I'm dust without you. Hollow." I roll my hips, driving deeply. She loses the ability to keep her eyes open, and her lids drop, her fingers now gripping my hair. "Open," I demand, and she does. "You are etched so deeply in my heart, it cannot beat without you there."

"Because it only beats for me," she whispers, and I nod. She gets it. In this crazy situation she's in, she completely gets it, and it's the ridiculous connection neither of us could stop when we met that's happening now and confirming it. It's telling her what we have. Guiding her.

"I don't know how I know, but I know." Her fingers tighten in my hair, and the tiny clenches of her internal walls stroke my cock, taking me closer to that special place. "Together." Her murmured demand brings tears to my fucking eyes.

"Always together, baby," I confirm, my arms crawling up her back and taking her in a hug as we carry each other to release, our bodies crushed together, our hips flexing in sync, our eye contact never faltering. And when we go, we go together, me holding my breath to restrain my roar, Ava panting into my face, her jaw tight.

"Oh Jesus." Air bursts out of me, the sensitivity becoming too much, though I endure it, seeing she's still riding the waves of her orgasm.

And when she's over it, she collapses on my chest in a heap, gasping for breath. "You are the best sex I've ever had."

I don't know whether to laugh or flip my lid. "For the sake of my health, let's just say I'm the *only* sex you've ever had."

"Possessive?"

"You got that, huh?" I jolt through a laugh when her teeth sink into my shoulder. "You're a savage, Mrs. Ward."

She settles and I settle, too, relaxed, sated, and happy. And that's exactly how we remain until the water is far too cold for my liking, and definitely too cool for my wife. She has goose bumps, no matter how much I rub my hands all over her back. "That's enough tub-time."

She resists me when I try to get up, becoming a dead weight on my chest. "I'm comfy."

"You're cold." I rise from the water with ease, Ava attached to my front. "And I need to feed you."

"You think you can manage that without injuring yourself?" She points to my hand, a look of dismay clouding her features.

"That wasn't my fault." My curled lip returns, along with my resentment. "You know, your mother really has mastered the art of winding me up." I place her on her feet and take a towel, smothering her with it, rubbing at her wet hair while she stands motionless before me, letting me do what I'm gonna do.

"Something tells me it doesn't take much to wind you up."

I ignore her and turn her by her shoulders, leading her to the dressing room. "I like the black knickers. There's a matching bra just there," I tell her, opening her drawer.

"And what's this?" she asks, reaching in and pulling something from beneath the tons of lace. I'm suddenly facing my nemesis.

"That's nothing." I swipe the vibrator from her hand and hide it behind my back, my face contorted with the contempt I really feel for the damn thing.

"Is that thing mine?" She looks alarmed. Welcome to my world, honey.

"Nope."

"Then what's it doing in my drawer?" She tries to reach around me to claim it, frowning at me when I step away, keeping a firm hold.

"No idea." I turn and stalk away, set on finally throwing it in the trash. The last thing I need right now is a machine replacing me. Never. I need all of her pleasure. And I need her to need it, too.

As I make it to the stairs, I take the first step, but stagger to a stop when my arm is jolted, the vibrator suddenly gone from my hands. I swing around and find Ava inspecting it, her eyes running up and down the sparkly shaft. "Give it back," I warn, with all the threat I really mean.

Eyes flicking to mine, she smirks. "But it's mine."

"No," I correct her, cupping my cock and mildly thrusting my hips forward, delighting in her eyes falling to my groin. "*This* is yours. That thing isn't needed."

With her lips pressed together, she gives me a wicked smirk. Then she flicks it on. The buzz. That fucking buzz has haunted me for the past twelve years. When is the damn thing going to die? "Do I use it much?"

I'm not having this conversation. "Never. Give it to me." I make a grab for it, but she's speedily taken it behind her back.

There's a playful glint in her eye, one that I would pay endless amounts of cash to see permanently. I'm not the kind of man to pass up an opportunity, and standing before me is an opportunity. One that is goading me.

Clearing my throat, I stand tall and roll my shoulders, my head cocked, my smile cunning. "Three," I state clear and low, taking one step forward, encouraging Ava's one step back.

"Oh, like that, is it? Your silly little countdown?"

"Silly?" I chuckle, if only for effect, briefly looking down at my bare feet, scuffing the carpet with them casually. "No, no, lady." I peek up through my lashes, nibbling on my bottom lip. "You think it's far from silly when I catch you. Two." Another step forward for me, another step back for Ava. I'm not worried. She could put a mile between us and I'd still catch her.

"Remind me what happens when you catch me."

"One," I counter, lunging threateningly, smiling like a crazy man when she jumps back, startled, before quickly composing herself.

"Then I guess I'll find out for myself." She shrugs, blasé, and flicks the vibrator off. "I'm a fast runner."

I fall apart on the inside. Her bravado is cute. And a complete waste of her time. "Baby, I always win. If you remember anything, you would do well to remember that."

She scoffs.

I grin.

She narrows her eyes on me.

I grin harder. "Zero, baby," I whisper, and she's off, though not as fast as she would like, her limp evident. And I suddenly wonder what the fuck I'm doing encouraging this. She'll do herself damage, and all because she wants to prove a point. "Ava, stop!"

"No way, Ward." She hobbles off down the stairs, and I mentally kick myself repeatedly for being such a careless fool.

I don't run after her, I walk, though I walk fast, ready to shut down this game immediately. "Ava, I'm not playing." I see her round the corner at the bottom of the stairs, the vibrator waving above her head, now buzzing again. She's laughing. I'm not. I'm not in the least bit amused. "Ava, for fuck's sake, stop running!"

"Not so you can catch me. I know your game, Ward."

I speed up, my pace now urgent. "Ava!" I roar, my patience fraying. Has she no fucking self-awareness? "I swear to God, if you don't pack it in, I'll—"

"What? Give me the countdown?" She cackles. "That ship's sailed, Ward."

I throw myself down the final few steps, now fuming fucking mad, mixed with a ton of panic, too. If she doesn't kill herself with this recklessness, then I'll do the fucking job myself. I hear the back door slam. The garden? "Ava!" Flying through the house like a hurricane, I just manage to yank the door open before I throw myself through the glass. I see her running across the lawn toward the trampoline. I'm gaining on her, and she looks back over her shoulder, her smile splitting her face. "Stop," I warn, running after her.

"I can't believe you'd get so worked up over my Weapon of Mass Des—" Her words scream to a halt, and so does her body, so quickly that I nearly charge her down. I catch her arms, and she looks at me, her face vacant. "Destruction," she breathes, half-unsure, half-exhausted, her stare stuck to the vibrator in her hand. She drops it like a hot potato, like it could be on fire, and takes her palms to her temples, squeezing her eyes shut.

My heart rate rockets. "Ava? Ava, baby, what's wrong?"

She yells, her body bending forward, like she's trying to make herself small to protect her from something. What? Pain? Fuck, my heart's going to fall at her feet any moment. "Ava, for fuck's sake." I take the tops of her arms and bend, trying to get her face in my sights. And when I do, I hate what I see.

Her expression is agony, contorted with pain. Oh Jesus, something's seriously wrong. Instinct steams forward and has me scooping her from her feet and running back to the house, set on calling an ambulance, a doctor, or maybe even racing her to the hospital myself.

"Jesse, stop!"

Like she could have turned me off, my feet slow, and she wriggles from my arms, taking her hands back to her head and closing her eyes. "There's too many." She balls her fists, obviously frustrated.

"Too many what?"

"Things. Things happening in my head."

My heart that was racing only gathers more speed. Memories? Is she talking about memories?

"Urhhhh!" she yells, and bashes the side of her head, and I move in, seizing her hands and pulling them away.

"Stop," I demand, forcing her arms to her sides. "Just stop it!" She looks up at me, squinting, her forehead wrinkled with the effort it's taking her to think. "Take your time, baby." I pull her down to the grass and hold her hands, letting her have a moment to straighten out everything in her head. "Just take your time." I'm trying so hard not to get carried away. Trying desperately not to let my hope run away with me. "Tell me what you see."

"I don't know, it's all fuzzy." Her hands crush mine, her eyes wide and wild. "It's you."

Oh my God. My head drops back, and I look to the sky, thanking God for this breakthrough. "Where am I?" I drop my sights back onto her, gently encouraging, moving in closer on my knees.

"I don't know, but you're mad. *Really* mad."

If it was appropriate, I'd laugh. "Ava, there are many times in our history that I've been crazy mad. You need to be a bit more specific."

"You can't move."

My forehead becomes heavy with my frown as I rack my brain for something that'll clue me in on where she's at. I have nothing.

"Thirty." Looking up at me, she searches my face for anything to suggest I'm following. I'm not, and I feel awful that I can't offer any insight. It's cryptic. "Thirty," she repeats, now louder, and there's a bit of excitement building. And then she's quickly standing up, looking down at me, virtually shaking with exhilaration. I don't know why. Thirty means nothing. Not being able to move means nothing. Together, they mean nothing. I flinch when she claps her hands, holding them together in front of her delighted face. "I'm thirty-fucking-seven!" she wails. "You can't move because you're handcuffed to the bed! You're thirty-fucking-seven!"

Jesus Christ. I breathe out, overcome, feeling like the sky is falling and blanketing me in pure, unrelenting happiness. It's too overwhelming, and I plummet to my back on the grass, looking up to the heavens in gratitude.

"I remembered something!" She dives on top of me, grabbing my face and forcing me to look at her. "Not just words, but I saw you there! Going fucking ballistic!" Her lips land on mine, kissing me hard.

Of all the things she remembers, it's that. "Typical," I mutter, feigning sulkiness when I'm actually fucking ecstatic. "And watch your mouth, Ava." She's dropped enough f-bombs in the past two minutes to kill me off.

"I will not." Her lips leave mine, and her face appears above me veiled by her damp locks. The smile on her face is enough to make a grown man weep. "Fuck, fuck, fuck, fuck. You're thirty-fucking-seven!"

I fucking wish. "I hate to break it to you, baby, but I haven't been thirty-fucking-seven for a long time."

"I don't care." She blinks, once, twice, and then rapidly, stilling above me, her smile falling. "You were mad. And then I'm mad. Why was I mad?"

My lips press together when she casts her eyes back to mine. I know exactly why she's mad. "Maybe because you thought John freed me, when it was actually Sarah."

"Another woman saw you naked and handcuffed to the..." She fades off, blinking again. "Wait, why am I handcuffed to the bed?"

Jesus, she's suffering a serious bombardment. I reach for her left hand and lift it between us, pointing at her ring. Reminding her. "This, maybe?" I already told her the story of my proposal. She forgot?

"You can't propose when I'm handcuffed to the bed!" she sings, thrilled.

"Wrong," I counter, and she looks at me, all care for the fact Sarah freed me gone. She's smiling. "I could, I would, and I did."

"You're a case, Jesse Ward."

"And that's just one of the reasons why you love me." I refrain from saying *loved*. "Tell me more." I roll us a little, taking her to the grass so she's on her side facing me. "What else is there? What else do you remember?" I'm hungry for more, anything more.

I can see the effort it takes her to think, trying to pluck more memories from the black pit that is her mind, and I'm quick to stop her, placing a hand over her hip so she looks at me. I don't want her straining. "Don't force it. More will come."

"I want them now." Her whiny voice and slumped body make me smile. I'd love them all now, too, but patience is a virtue and all that bollocks. Which is a joke, coming from me. But, for the sake of Ava and my sanity, I mustn't push her more than she's already trying to push herself. If anything, I should take comfort in the fact that she desperately wants to find me in that mixed-up head of hers.

“Come.” I get us up and sling an arm around her shoulders, snuggling her close. “That’s enough exertion for one day.” Her mind and her body must be beat.

I walk her back into the house, following the sound of my ringing phone. I can’t disguise my tenseness when I see the number, because I just know who it is.

“You okay?” Ava asks, looking up at me with concern.

“Just a sales number.” I reject the call and block the number.

Done. I can’t risk Sarah knocking Ava off her high. Too much progress has been made today. Great progress.

I’m feeling hopeful, and dirt from my past isn’t going to tarnish it.

CHAPTER 32

I open my eyes the next morning to Ava beaming at me from where she's lying on her side, mirroring me. Her hand is on my hip. Mine on hers. "What's got you so happy at this time of the morning? Because I'm yet to put my cock inside you."

She chuckles, moving in closer until her breath is spreading across the skin of my chest. "I love watching you sleep. You look so angelic."

I smile sleepily and close my eyes again, wrapping an arm around her naked back and pulling her closer. "Angelic? You mean godly, right?"

"Right. And I'm happy I remembered something."

She's on a high, so happy with herself, just for remembering that small thing. I forbid myself to dwell on the fact that she might not be so thrilled when everything else comes back to her, the good, the bad, and the downright fucking hideous. It's kind of crazy. On one hand, I'm willing the memories forward, begging they come to her. On the other, I'm dreading it. Part of me is hoping they continue to drip through, little bit by little bit, giving her a chance to grasp it all, rather than them flooding back and probably sending her head into chaos.

"Is that your phone?"

I frown, listening. "I must have left it downstairs." She's out of my arms speedily, and I'm not too pleased about it. "Hey!"

"It might be the kids." Her naked back disappears out the door, her urgency hampered by that lingering limp.

On a groan, I drag myself up, not bothering with any boxers, and make my way downstairs. I find her with the phone to her ear. "That FaceTime thing isn't working," she says down the line, her fingers in her hair.

I grin when I look down her naked body, grabbing the coffee down from the cupboard. "Put it on loudspeaker," I demand.

"Hey, Dad!" Jacob sings, followed by Maddie.

"Hey." I grab the cups down and Ava fetches the milk. "You missing us?"

"A little." Maddie sniffs, and I smile. "Nan said we're coming home on Monday."

"That's right." I look at Ava and see she smiles to herself. 'What have you two been up to?" *Don't ask about the boy. Don't ask about the boy.*

"I've been shell hunting on the beach with Hugo," Maddie declares, bold as fucking brass, almost proud, because she knows she's well out of trampling distance. I grind my teeth and throw a glare at Ava, one that suggests she should take the reins before our daughter ruins my mood.

She takes the phone quickly and walks off, getting herself away from my bristly presence. Hugo. Fucking Hugo. "That's nice, darling. What about you, Jacob? Caught any more fish?"

"A twelve-pounder today, Mum!" He sounds so excited. Why can't Maddie find something she's passionate about—something other than boys.

They chat happily for a while as I busy myself with the coffee, and then she says her good-byes, a sad edge to her voice. I look up as she disconnects and sighs. She's falling into despondency. I need to distract her.

"Hey, eyes up here, baby." They instantly flick up and find me. "I have a surprise for you."

"Oh yeah?" She gives a cheeky grin as she places the phone down and wanders over to me, and it fills my heart with all kinds of feel-good shit.

"You have a one-track mind, lady." And I'm so fine with that, but for today I have a date planned.

Resting her hand on my chest, she beams up at me. "Is it any wonder?" Her hands stroke down toward my…

"Whoa!" I laugh, quickly snatching her hand, stopping it from making it to my already growing cock. I'll be doomed. Shit, where the hell is this resistance coming from? "Stop it."

I sit her on a stool, smiling at her pouting face. She shrugs. "I can't help it. I only have to look at you and—"

"You're wet. I know," I finish for her confidently, and massively smug. "You'll get used to it." I flash her a wicked smile.

"So what's my surprise if it isn't that?"

"I'm taking you shopping for a new dress."

"What for?"

"Drew and Raya's engagement party on Saturday."

Her eyes light up a little, but very quickly fade. Then they narrow. I know what's coming. I'm prepared for it. "Do I get to pick the dress?"

"Nope." I smile, smug, and head to get some more coffee.

"I don't think so," she retorts indignantly.

"I do."

"No way."

I turn and find her strutting out of the kitchen, her long

hair swaying across her naked back. "I'll find something in my wardrobe, thank you very much."

"Think again, lady," I yell after her, smiling. And because I feel like reinforcing my authority around these parts, I yell some more. "End of!"

Chapter 33

I'm watching her trawling through her dressing room rails in search of a dress, anything she can wear for a posh engagement party at Café Royal. She has plenty of options, loads of beautiful gowns and dresses, mostly lace... she just can't see them. Because I hid them while she was in the shower.

"Found anything?" I ask casually as I slip on my white Ralph polo shirt, flipping the collar up a bit too cockily as I inspect my fresh face in the mirror.

Slowly, she turns to face me, her eyes raging as I spritz myself with her favorite cologne. "What have you done with them?"

"What?" I ask past my reflection, all innocent. I'm not fooling her. She's been through her wardrobes enough since she was discharged to realize there are piles of things missing. Namely, anything she could wear for an engagement party.

Pointing back to one of her wardrobes, her jaw goes all tight. "All my dresses are gone."

I turn and crane my neck, feigning interest as I look past her to the sparse wardrobe. "That's a damn shame. Then we'll have to go buy you a new one."

"You're impossible." Nostrils flaring, she grabs a pair of jeans and yanks them up her legs before throwing, quite literally, a shoulderless top over her head. "How have I lived like this for so many years?"

Baseball bat, meet my stomach. I very nearly launch into a rant and remind her that she loves me choosing her clothes, yet the shred of reason I have holds me back. Because I'm not dealing with my wife, per se. I'm dealing with the woman I met who fought me at every turn. Yet I was a lot younger then, had more energy. And though I felt the stakes were high, they weren't quite on this level. My reason is fraying fast. "There's no fucking need for that," I snap, turning on my heels and walking away before I lower both our moods further and lose my head. "I just want to buy you a new dress. So fucking kill me," I growl at thin air as I stalk toward the stairs. Just a fucking dress. A simple fucking dress.

"Jesse," she calls after me, appearing across the landing when I reach the top of the stairs. I glower, and she sighs. "I'd love it if you were to buy me a dress." She's pacifying me. Good. I need it. "Any dress you choose."

"Any?" With no argument from her at all? There must be a catch.

"Any." She pushes the confirmation through her tight jaw with a ton of effort.

My smile isn't victorious, just genuinely happy. She's flexing. It's a huge step in the right direction, a step closer to the dynamics of our relationship that keep me calm. "Your Punishment Fuck is canceled." I extend my hand in offer, and on a small shake of her head, she comes to me. "See how happy you make me when you comply?"

Her quiet laugh as we take the stairs together only increases my happiness. "Why can't you just graciously accept my gesture and not be such an arrogant, unreasonable twat about it?"

"Because me being an arrogant, unreasonable twat is all part of our normal." Grabbing my keys from the cabinet and handing Ava her bag, I walk us to the car. "I'd be a fraud if I tried to pass myself off as anything less." I open the car door and sweep my arm out in a gesture. "My lady."

Resting her forearm on top of the door, she sits her chin on it, eyeing me up. "So basically our normal is you throwing your orders around and me obeying?"

"If the shoe fits."

"What if it doesn't?"

I dip and startle her with a forceful, lingering kiss on her lips. "Oh, but it does, lady. And I know you feel it deep inside you. Stop fighting it." She'll never stop fighting it. And I don't want her to. She keeps me on my toes, as I keep her on hers. It might send me wild, but every pound of my heart when we're sparring with words is the sign I need to tell me that I am alive and she is with me.

* * *

The boutique I chose is the very one I followed Ava to all those years ago, the one where she bought that wretched dress that I cut off her body some days later. My choice isn't an accident. I'm hoping it might nudge something for her, anything to give me another rush of contentment when she remembers something.

The store is full of endless suitable options. Yet Ava seems to be passing each and every one of them up. "I like this one." She pulls out a micro cream thing, not too dissimilar to the poor excuse of a dress she bought the last time we were here. It wasn't suitable twelve years ago, and it isn't now, either. And it has nothing to do with her age.

"I don't," I counter dismissively, taking it from her hand and hanging it back on the rail.

"What about this one?" A peach strappy thing is presented to me. I shake my head, and Ava rolls her eyes. "This one?"

"Nope."

"This one?"

I toss her a dark look, and she flops to a nearby velvet couch in exasperation. "Surely I have *some* say in this."

She's purposely pulling out dresses that she knows will send me batty. Driving me crazy is obviously ingrained into her. "You love everything I choose." I flick through the rails and home in on something lace, pulling it out and looking it up and down. It's fitted, will showcase her every perfect curve, and it'll sit just below the knee. "Perfect," I declare, handing it to the assistant. "She'll try this one."

"Yes, sir." The assistant scuttles off to place the dress in the changing room, and I smile, all happy with myself. Until I find I'm being glared at. "What?"

"You didn't even ask if I liked it."

"You said I could choose." I laugh, pulling her up from the couch. Her resistance is pathetic.

"Yes, but you didn't even consult me." Snatching her hand back, she marches off to the dressing room, pulling a few random dresses from the rails on her way, just to prove a point. I inhale some patience and follow on behind. She's being defiant for the sake of it. "Do you like the dress?" I ask, being quickly flashed by very displeased, puckered lips over her shoulder. But I get no answer, making me smile. "Well?"

"That's not the point."

"Yes, it's the point, Ava. I have good taste and I know exactly what'll look lovely on my wife. That dress will look lovely." I point to the others in her hand, the unapproved dresses. Yes, they'll look lovely, too, but I'm likely to be arrested for murder if she wears them. "Those are a no-go." I take them from her hand and toss them aside.

Scowling at me, she yanks the curtain closed, but no sooner have I lost sight of her, I have it back again when she whips the curtain back across, her eyes wide, some kind of recognition on her face. "We've been here before."

"Yes!" Both of our gripes are forgotten with the promise of another recollection. I move in closer, waiting for her to give me more.

Her head tilts, and she looks down the corridor to the store. "I bought a dress."

"Yes. Go on."

Turning her eyes onto me, she brings her hands to her face, the strain from thinking so hard clear. "I bought it here! The dress you cut off my body, I bought it here in this very shop!"

"Yes!" Fuck me, it worked!

"Jesse, I remembered something else!" She virtually dives at me, and I catch her, hauling her up my body and holding her tightly. "That dress cost me a bomb." Her face in my neck, she laughs against my skin, her arms wrapped so tightly around my neck.

"And you wearing it cost me a few heart attacks, lady." I'm smiling through my scolding words, absolutely beside myself with joy.

"There's something else." She wrestles free of me, her front rubbing mine as she slides down my body, her palms resting on my pecs, her eyes darting across the material of my Ralph shirt.

"What is it, baby? Take your time." I walk us across to a chaise and sit her down, holding her hands while she thinks. I'm all hunched over, trying to see her eyes as they jump across her lap.

"You're in your boxers."

I shrug. "Not unusual."

"But you're outside." She looks at me, the corners of her lips tweaking. "You're chasing me." A full-blown smile breaks. "I'm in the dress and you're chasing me down the street."

It was across a car park, actually, but whatever. She's nearly there. "And then..."

Her smile fades and she frowns. And then she gasps, jumping up from the chaise, looking down at my groin. "I'm pinned to the bed? You're..." Her mouth falls open. "You pleasured yourself and ejaculated all over me?"

I'm so fucking happy, my face could split. "Yes, yes, I did that." Except that was before she escaped in the dress. Not that it matters. It's all a little jumbled in her head, but it's all still there.

There's another gasp, except this time it isn't from Ava. We both look to the side and find the assistant staring at us in horror, before she realizes we've seen her and makes a mad dash for the shop floor, her cheeks on fire. I look at Ava, my mouth forming an O. Ava looks at me, eyes sparkling happily. And we laugh. We laugh so hard and so loudly, the shop must be shaking under the force. Ava falls into me, catching me by surprise, and takes us crashing to the dressing room floor, where we roll and chuckle like a pair of silly kids, not a care in the fucking world. Ava's not horrified by her newfound knowledge. Just amused, and so pleased she remembered something. I'm fucking delirious with happiness.

The sound of someone clearing their throat pulls us from our hysteria, and I prop myself up on my elbows, finding another lady looming over us, this one older than the assistant, her arms crossed over her chest. "I'm the store owner. Can I help?" What she means is, can she help with ejecting us from her lovely boutique.

"We'll take all the dresses," I declare, immediately wiping the look of disapproval from her face. She starts falling over her feet to help us, though not up off the floor.

"We have a lovely pair of heels that complement the cream dress beautifully, sir," she says, gathering the dresses from the hook, stepping over our splayed bodies on the floor to reach them.

"We'll take them."

She's delighted. "And a stunning purse to match."

"Pack it up."

"And would madam require any accessories?" she asks, beaming at Ava.

I push myself off the floor and retrieve my tittering wife, holding her up while she continues to chuckle. I haul her close and smother her with wet kisses for a few moments before pulling back and giving her a soft smile. "The only accessory my wife needs is me."

"Yes, sir." The owner disappears with our purchases, and Ava turns to mush in my arms, reaching up to kiss my cheek.

"You're so romantic when you want to be."

"I'm always romantic," I counter, leading her out to the front desk. "In my own way."

The young assistant's cheeks are still flaming red, the poor thing unable to look at us. And then she does, and I flip her a cheeky wink. She disintegrates on the spot, shoving the card machine toward me as I chuckle. I see to payment and take the bag once the dresses have been precisely wrapped in tissue paper.

"I haven't tried any of the dresses on," Ava points out, letting me guide her out of the store.

"I know this body like the back of my hand." I squeeze her hip, and she jolts on a little yelp. "They'll fit, trust me."

Eyeing the bag, she bites her lip thoughtfully. "All of them?"

I know what she's getting at. The lace number I choose isn't the only dress I just paid for. "I'm only showing some leniency because I'm fucking thrilled that you've remembered something else. Consider yourself lucky."

"I *do* feel lucky." She's behind me in a second, climbing onto my back, her face squished to mine. "Thank you for the dresses."

"Thank you for letting me spoil you." I leave the store and walk down the road with Ava clinging to my back, my heart swelling in my chest. Some of this she might be finding hard to wrap her confused mind around, but she's taking quite well to our normal. It's more progress. More light in our darkness.

Chapter 34

AVA

When Jesse insisted on taking me to yoga today, I didn't argue. I could tell he was stunned. But I have a motive. Taking the keys from his hand, I open the car. "I'll drive."

He snorts, obviously finding my declaration amusing. "Absolutely not." Reclaiming the keys, he directs me around to the passenger seat.

"Why not?" My resistance doesn't even dent his fortitude.

"You're never getting behind a wheel again."

Ever? Not ever again? "What? Why?"

"Because you don't need to." He jingles the keys under my nose as he pushes me down into the seat and then buckles me up. "And I'm looking into getting you a driver." He plants a chaste kiss on my cheek and quickly shuts the door before I can protest. And when he lands in the driver's seat, he keeps his attention forward, ignoring the glare I'm shooting at him. There will be no argument over this. I will be driving again.

Flicking some music on, an obvious ploy to kill the silence, he races off down the street with "Sweater Weather" blaring, tapping the wheel in time to the music.

Until there is no music. He peeks out the corner of his eye as I turn in my seat, my face twisted with disdain. "Are you telling me you're never going to let me drive again?"

"Yep." He flicks the music back on and I quickly turn it back off. Is he mad?

"No way, Jesse. You can't stop me."

He half coughs, half laughs. "Watch me." He presses a button on the steering wheel and fills the car with The Neighbourhood again.

"Watch *me*," I counter over the music, throwing myself back in the seat. "If you won't let me drive anywhere, then I'll make my own way around, starting today. I'll get the Tube home. You're being unreasonable. It was an accident. A one-in-a-million chance. You're being stupid."

"Stupid?" he coughs. "Well, that one-in-a-million chance was my wife, so forgive me if my protective instinct has taken on new heights." He slams the button on his steering wheel and shuts the music off, then pulls the car over to the side of the road, prickling from top to toe. *So* unreasonable. He reaches for my slighted face and turns it toward him. My eyes are thin slits of pissed off. His are narrower.

"Listen to me, lady," he orders, nostrils flaring and all. "It is my job to protect you. There's nothing irrational about wanting to keep you safe, Ava." His voice has softened to a mere whisper, his eyes clouding, and I know it's because he's thinking about what could have been. "Every fear I've ever had nearly became a reality. I nearly lost you. So don't you tell me that I'm being unreasonable or irrational or stupid, do you hear me? You have to let me do my thing or I'll go crazy mad."

"And I'll go crazy mad if you suffocate me. I need some space,

Jesse. If you want me to fall in love with you again, you need to let me do that without stifling me." I hate the hurt in his green eyes. Hate it.

His handsome face is splashed with agony, and he swallows, anger mixed up in his expression, too. "You can get the Tube."

I *can* get the Tube? Like I need permission? Fucking hell, he really is crazy mad. But I still nod, despite being staggered on the inside. "Good." I sit back and stare out the window as Jesse gets us going again. And I wonder...

How did I fall in love with such craziness?

I don't know. But it's happening again, and I couldn't stop it if I tried.

* * *

The usual peace blankets me when I arrive at Elsie's. Zara is already waiting in the studio, sitting on her mat. She looks like a pro, all geared up in what I expect is designer yoga gear. "I'm feeling a bit frumpy," I say, rolling out my mat next to her.

She laughs, soft and low. "You look anything but frumpy, Ava." She rolls her eyes. "I was just passing through the shopping mall and they had a huge sale. Oh!" She jumps up and scrounges through her bag. "I got you one, too." She flaps out a black top. "You look about the same size as me."

"Zara, you shouldn't have," I say, taking the shirt from her hand and kissing her cheek.

"Give over," she brushes it off. "It was a fiver in the bargain bin."

"I love it." Something comes to me. "Hey, we should go shopping sometime." I *will* pick my own clothes. My recent shopping adventure might have turned out wonderfully, but that was only because my brain decided to let me remember something. I realize it could have been very different.

Her eyes sparkle. “Oh my God, yes.”

“Come on, chatterboxes.” Elsie floats across the room, giving us a playful, disapproving look. “It doesn’t sound very peaceful in here today.”

I give Zara an oopsie look, and we both settle on our mats and close our eyes.

Peace. It’s quickly found again, and I let it roll over me.

Toward the end of the session, I’m flat on my back, sprawled out, my body weightless. I’m completely zoned out, so calm, so when images start to flicker through my mind, I don’t jerk with shock or panic. Instead, I remain still, absorbing the distorted, blurry visions as if I’m watching them from an old-fashioned projector. Visions of Jesse, and for the first time, of Maddie and Jacob. I feel my eyes squeezing, trying to hold on to the picture of them lying on Jesse’s chest, tiny little bundles, their daddy’s face buried between their heads. I feel a tear trickle down the side of my face, swishing around in my ear. And then the images are gone. But they’re not gone. They will never be gone.

“Ava?” A gentle touch rests on my shoulder, and I blink my eyes open, finding Zara suspended above me.

It takes me a while to grasp my bearings, and I see Elsie leaving the room. “I think I fell asleep.” My voice is thick, and I’m unsure if it’s with emotion or sleepiness.

Zara smiles, her friendly face so happy. “You’re right. Elsie is amazing!” She rises to her feet, pouting, now looking disappointed. “I was hoping we could do coffee, but I just picked up an e-mail from work. Some silly problem with a project I have to get sorted.”

“That’s fine. I can’t do coffee today, anyway.” I can’t? Why can’t I? I can, and I should, though today I’ll be doing it on my own. I can go for a coffee on my own, no problem. I should do something on my own.

"No?"

"My husband..." I stop myself from saying something that would give entirely the wrong impression. "We've had a rough time lately. He's a bit protective. He worries about me." I shrug.

"Oh no." She pouts. "I'll call you. We'll make those plans, and you can tell me all about it."

I smile, though I'm not too enthusiastic about her suggestion. The thing I love most about coffee with Zara is the fact that I don't have to talk about my woes, because she doesn't know of them. "That would be good."

"Thanks so much for letting me hijack your session, Ava. It means so much." She kisses my cheek and breezes away, leaving me in the room alone. Maybe it's silly, but I close my eyes again, hoping the memories will come back to me. But after a good five minutes, I give up, telling myself to be happy with what I got.

I leave Elsie with a grateful kiss and head outside, set to go and process the session on my own with a coffee, but when I make it into the fresh air, I find Jesse waiting.

He's pouting at me from where he's standing by the car, his puppy-dog eyes pleading with me not to be mad at him. I stop in my tracks and cock my head, pursing my lips in fake disapproval.

"I love you." He gives me a stupid goofy grin, like those three simple words are the answer for everything. Truth be told, they are.

I can't possibly be mad with the big softy. I'm too elated by the effect the past hour with Elsie has had and the fact that something came to me. So instead of ripping a strip off him, I step into his big body and hug him fiercely. I can tell he's shocked at my easy acquiescence because it takes him a couple of seconds to return my cuddle. "Where the hell is my wife?"

I smile and pull back, beaming up at him. "I saw you!" I have to stop myself from springing around the street like a jackin-the-box. "I was so spaced out, and I saw you in my mind. It was so clear. I saw you holding the twins when they were born."

"Really?" His face is ablaze with happiness as he picks me up and swings me around in the middle of the street. I laugh, not feeling in the least bit dizzy. Because my eyes are on his.

Chapter 35

It's Saturday, the day of Raya and Drew's engagement party. As I swish the bubbles in the tub, I run over my plan again, from beginning to end. Every bit involves spoiling my wife rotten. Lavishing her with affection and attention. Making her feel like the queen she is to me.

When the tub is at the perfect level of water and bubbles, I flip off the tap and strip down to nothing. Then I wander quietly into the bedroom, watching her nap peacefully atop the bedcovers as I approach. It pains me to wake her, but I need to kick my plan into action or we'll be late for Drew and Raya's party. Kneeling by the bed, I take the single calla lily from the vase on the night table and rest my lips on hers. She stretches and moans, reaching for my naked shoulders. Her touch creates instant flames on my skin. Opening her eyes sleepily, she smiles at the flower and takes it, smelling it lazily before resting it on the bed next to her.

"Time for a bath, baby," I whisper, sliding my arms under her and lifting her from the bed. She snuggles into me as I carry her to the tub, sleepy and warm in my arms. She feels lighter, and as I think back over the time since I brought her home from hospital, she hasn't once finished a meal. In fact, she's mostly just pushed the food around her plate. Damn, we need to fix that. I should have been more forceful.

I set her on her feet and start stripping her down, being slow enough to give her time to fully wake before I lower her into the bath. My eyes are scanning every inch of her flesh that's revealed, searching for signs of protruding bones. There. Right there. I reach forward and brush my palm across her hip, frowning.

"What's wrong?"

"You've lost too much weight." She's still beautiful, the most beautiful thing I've ever set eyes on, but she's definitely thinner. How could I have let this happen? "I need to feed you." I break away and find her robe, opening it up for her to slip her arms in.

She ignores the material hanging from my hands and gives me her eyes. "But I'm not hungry."

"I don't care. You need to eat." I drape the robe over her shoulders, but she pulls away, giving me a warning look. "Stop it."

"Stop what?"

"Worrying. If I'm hungry, I'll eat." Taking the robe from my hand, she tosses it aside, never taking her firm stare from my affronted one. "Don't curl your lip at me, Jesse Ward." A finger comes up and points at my mouth, and I recoil, trying to get my wayward lip under control. I can't.

Seizing her hand, I wrestle it back down, replacing it with *my* finger pointed at *her*. She isn't winning this one. No way. "You're eating, end of." I swoop in and claim her, to hell with the robe. She'll eat naked. You won't hear me complaining.

"Jesse!" Her naked flesh rubbing all over my naked flesh does nothing to help me keep my focus. Food is my focus. Lots of food. Though my dick doesn't agree, clearly hungry itself. My scowl is now pointing to my groin, demanding it behave, as I hoof Ava out of the bathroom.

"Put me down!" Fingernails find my arse and sink in.

"You fucking savage!" I half yelp, half yell, hearing her giggling, her claws going to town, digging further in. "Ava!" I'm forced to release her and rub away the soreness, while she titters before me, flicking her hair over her shoulder.

"I'm not hungry," she affirms, passing me, heading back to the bathroom.

"Ava!"

"Fuck you, Jesse. I'm not damn well hungry."

My rubbing hands stop, my dick now totally limp. Stalking after her, fuming mad by her disregard for her health, as well as her vulgar mouth, I charge into the bathroom to find Ava has one foot in the bath, her eyes on me at the door. My scowl deepens. Her smirk widens. It's adorable and infuriating all at once. "Watch your fucking mouth."

That smirk gets even wider, and my fury is diluted some more by the sight. "Fuck you," she whispers. She's playing the game, testing me. Silly girl.

"Three..." It just comes right on out, my smirk now matching hers.

"Fuck." Another whisper.

I take one step forward, now too thrilled by her playfulness to let her language bother me all that much. "Two..."

Taking her foot from the water, she folds her arms across her chest, wedging her boobs up high, creating a cleavage that serves as a magnet. My eyes fall, my mouth suddenly watering, my cock hardening. "Next?"

"One," I answer, my stare still firmly on her chest.

"And next?" She unfolds her arms and cups her boobs.

I hitch an eyebrow, looking up to her face through my lashes. My smile, the one reserved only for my girl, spreads across my face, and she delights in it, eyes beaming at me. Fucking hell, I love this woman so much. She has the ability to distract me, with only a simple smile. Now I just want to eat her up myself.

She reigns supreme. She is my world. My life. My day, my night, my air, water, and fire. Fuck, what would I ever do without her? I'd die of a broken heart, I just know it. Turn to dust. Fade to nothing. My damn heart slows just thinking about it, and in a moment of brief panic, the feelings very real, I move forward, stealing a kiss, if only to reassure myself that I still have her. And I keep my eyes open, too, as does she, staring deeply into mine. It's a peaceful kiss. A lazy, soft, searching kiss. It's the coming together of two people who are on the same page, and then she speaks and confirms we really are.

"I'm here," she assures me, and I welcome the cuddle she takes me in, maintaining this all-consuming kiss.

"Let me take care of you," I beg, slowing down our pace until our lips are simply touching, the heat still raging. "Let me spoil you and love you with all the power I have."

"But I'm not hungry." She sighs, feeling across my back as I pout at her, showing my true disappointment. "Not for food anyway. And when I am, I'll eat, I promise."

"Ava—"

Her finger lands on my lips, hushing me. "But I'm constantly hungry for you. For your voice, your words, your need to take care of me." She smiles a little, almost shyly. I keep my mouth firmly shut, desperate for more of this. Her hunger. "I know exactly why I fell in love with you, even if I don't remember doing it. Because it's happening all over again."

There's a wobble in her voice, and I'm certain there would be in mine if I were to speak. She's falling in love with me. I gulp down the relieved emotion crawling up my throat.

"You are the most passionate man I've ever met, and you keep it all for me and the children. I can see that. Everything you do, you do it with such intensity. Whether you're mad. Or if you're playing. Or making love to me. Or simply loving me. It's all so passionate, and I love it. I love that the children and I are the center of your world. That you love us with a power that's sometimes a little overwhelming. What woman wouldn't want to be loved with that much intensity?"

Her palms land on my cheeks, her thumb catching a single teardrop as it tumbles. I feel suffocated by my happiness, because for the first time, I see true hope past the possibility of her never finding her memory. She *can* fall in love with me again. Our love flourished because it was supposed to. Because we were meant to find each other. That hasn't changed.

"You are the man of my dreams, Jesse Ward." She kisses the very edge of my mouth. "And I imagine you're the man of many other women's dreams, too."

"Well they can't have me," I vow, as if that would ever be a worry for Ava. "I belong to you, as much as you belong to me. That's just how it is."

Her teeth sink into my bristly cheek, her arms locked around my neck. "Now that we've cleared that up, are you going to spoil me like you promised?"

"Yes," I affirm, pulling back. "Right after you've had a relaxing soak." I carry her to the bath and place her gently down, kissing her forehead, and then leave her to get herself ready. I can't bathe with her. We'll never make it to the party. "Wear the lace dress and meet me in the hallway at seven thirty." I shut the door behind me, satisfied, because I just know she won't disappoint me.

CHAPTER 36

My frame of mind is positive. My heart is hopeful. My trimmed stubble just the right length, my face fresh. My charcoal three-piece suit fits like a dream, and my body in it looks fine. She won't be disappointed, either.

As I wait for her in the hallway, refixing my hair in the mirror, I hear the bedroom door close.

I move to the bottom step, sliding my hands into my trouser pockets. I can't see her. "Ava?"

"I don't think you'll approve." I hear her, but I still don't see her. And now I'm worried. Has she defied my request for the lace dress?

"Let me see you," I order, containing the annoyance threatening to break in my tone. Tonight has to be perfect. Ava not wearing the dress I requested won't get it off to a good start.

"You sure?" she calls. She sounds nervous.

"Get your arse in my sights now, lady."

She appears, cautiously. And I'm utterly blown away. "Jesus." I exhale my wonder, my eyes following her around the gallery landing to the top of the steps. If there's an example of perfection, then I'm looking at it.

The dress. Shit, the dress. Lace, everywhere, and the subtle cream tone brings memories of her stunning wedding gown gushing back. The hem just below the knee is perfect, the material clinging lightly to every wonderful curve she has. I ignore the fact that those curves have reduced somewhat in recent weeks, and move up to her face. Pink on her lips is the only subtle pop of color. It's all this dress needs. The Bardot neckline reveals the smooth lengths of her collarbones, her hair fixed in a sleek knot at the nape of her neck. Understated elegance. My wife has always had it, and it never fails to render me thunderstruck.

Her smoky eyes are taking me in, up and down, her teeth latched onto her bottom lip. "Do you like what you see?" I ask, sure of the answer. Every inch of her is glowing with appreciation, in her eyes the most.

"You're the most handsome man I've ever laid eyes on." She swallows and looks up at me. "Do I look okay?"

"Okay?" I counter, taking the stairs up to her, drinking her in. "You are beauty personified, lady. And you're mine." I reach her and take her hand, kissing her wedding ring. I peek up at her. "Who do you belong to?"

"You." She doesn't stall, doesn't protest, as she smiles down at me. "Always."

"Come." I lead her down the stairs slowly, never taking my eyes from her profile as she watches her feet. "I have something for you." I stop at the bottom of the stairs and reach into my pocket, circling her slowly. My hand on her hip makes her spine lengthen, and she looks over her shoulder at me.

"What do you have?"

"This." I take the diamond necklace over her head and let it settle on her skin. She looks down, her hand reaching up to feel the stones as I secure it. "You only wear it on special occasions."

"Oh my God," she whispers, moving away from me toward the

mirror. Staring at her reflection, she fingers the precious jewelry, lost in thought. Does she recognize it?

"It's beautiful." She looks past her reflection to me. "Thank you."

I smile, unable to be disappointed by her lack of memory. "It's been yours for twelve years, baby." I move in behind her and circle her waist with my arms, bending to get my chin on her shoulder. Our eyes lock in the mirror. "It's beautiful, yes, but it isn't a patch on the woman wearing it." The woman wearing it shines brighter. Is more precious. More valuable to me than anything in this world.

She turns her head to find my lips and blesses me with a delicate, consuming kiss.

Love. It's radiating between us, filling me with happiness. We can do this. Get through this. Because we're *us*. Jesse and Ava. "Let's dance." I turn her in my arms and reach for my phone, pulling up the Sonos app.

She laughs lightly, bemused. "Please not to Justin Timberlake."

My finger pauses on the screen of my phone, and I look down at Ava. It's just another one of those moments, when she says something without a clue of why she's saying it. I won't let it tarnish what I plan on being a perfect evening. "Something a little more romantic." I find the track in mind and turn up the volume. "Like this." "Nights in White Satin" fills the air around us, and she listens with me for a few moments. "Recognize it?" I sound hopeful, though trying my hardest not to be.

"Of course." She steps into my chest and rests her cheek there, curling one arm around my waist and taking my hand. "We danced to it one time."

Placing our clasped hands on my chest beside her head, I start to slowly move us in lazy circles, laying my head upon hers. "You don't remember, do you?" I ask, knowing she's grasped my plan. A mild shake of her head is expected, but the tears soaking through the material of my shirt are not. "Don't cry," I gently scold her, clenching my eyes closed before I defy my own order. "We make new memories if we can't find the old ones."

"I want both." She follows my lead as we unhurriedly pivot on the spot, going so slow, we're hardly moving at all. But we're touching. Everywhere, we're touching, and the most significant place we're touching right now is our hearts. Her heartbeats are sinking into my chest, serving as a power surge, increasing my own heart rate. "But I have you and the children," she whispers, her voice barely heard over the music as it reaches the crescendo. "And that's all that matters."

I breathe in, long and deep, and sink my face into her hair. She's right, though it doesn't make the loss any easier to accept. "Always," I affirm, my voice evidently broken.

The track slowly fades out and we continue to slowly turn on the spot, our hands held tightly against my chest, her body held tightly to mine.

"Time to go, baby," I murmur reluctantly, feeling her hold of me constrict everywhere. Arranging her into my side, I walk us to the car.

"Am I allowed a drink tonight?" Her question is laced with a little mischief, and definitely some hope. I realize that she maybe feels the need for a little Dutch courage. I can't deny her that, but I'll be keeping a very close eye on her.

"One or two," I agree, opening the car door for her. She lowers into the seat and I move in, fastening her belt. As I back up, I stop, my body bent, my face nose to nose with hers. She smiles. I smile. "I hope you have a lovely evening, Mrs. Ward."

"My date is a god. Of course I will."

I land her with a soft kiss. "I fucking love you."

Chapter 37

The foyer of Café Royal sparkles, the grandeur impressive.

We enter the small ornate elevator, both of us quiet as it slowly carries us up. Ava peeks at me a few times, never releasing my hand. When the doors open, the rush of sound hits us—music, chatting, laughter. I step forward, but feel Ava's resistance behind me. "Everyone is looking forward to seeing you," I say, trying to build her confidence. "And I'll never leave your side."

"What if I need the ladies?"

"Then I'll come," I say matter-of-factly, because it is definitely a fact. She smiles, knowing I really will, and leaves the elevator. "If it's too loud, you must tell me." I don't want her getting a headache.

"What will you do? Demand everyone be quiet and order Drew to turn off the music?"

I smile down at her, not needing to answer. She knows I'd do that as well.

"Silly question," she says on a shake of her head. "Of course you would."

We cross the threshold of the room, and I feel Ava's hand squeeze mine, her other hand coming up and clinging onto my bicep. "Relax," I tell her gently, taking a glass of fizz from an offered tray and peeling her hand off my arm. I give her the champagne. "Small sips."

"Right." She sinks the entire glass, stealthily moving back when I reach to seize it. "Too slow, Ward," she murmurs, placing the empty on the tray.

The woman is impossible. "You'll pay for that."

"Can't wait." Her hand raises in a wave, and we're soon joined by Raya. "Congratulations, Raya. You look gorgeous," Ava tells her, taking both her hands and holding them out to admire Raya's dress in all its glory.

"This old thing?" She rolls her eyes and moves in to kiss Ava on the cheek. "Thank you for coming. It means a lot to me and Drew."

"Wouldn't miss it for the world." Ava peeks up at me and jerks her head a little, her way of telling me to give some attention to the lady of the moment.

"Really stunning," I all but grunt, peeling my eyes away from my devious wife just as Drew joins us. His suit is pristine, as expected. He gives his fiancée a loving kiss on her cheek, before moving in on Ava. I will him not to make a big deal of her presence. Everyone commenting on her actually being here won't help.

"Ava, you look sublime." Drew drops a gentle kiss on her cheek before rejoining Raya. "Thank you for coming. Now, if you wouldn't mind me stealing my beautiful bride-to-be."

"Of course, you go." Ava shoos them away and takes advantage of the passing waiter as I shake Drew's hand.

"Easy," I warn as she takes the glass to her lips.

It rests on her bottom lip for a few moments as she regards my increasingly bristly form. Then she makes a show of taking the smallest, slowest sip she possibly could.

"Don't push me, lady." I collect her hand and push through

the crowd, making sure I clear the way first as I pull Ava along with me.

"There's John," Ava says, pointing toward the bar. "And Elsie."

He's brought a date? I change course quickly, heading their way. The big guy is smiling, probably wider than I've ever seen before, and he's made a real effort. His black suit is new for sure, his white shirt stark, and his bald head is supershiny, undoubtedly freshly polished. As soon as he spots me, his bright smile turns into a filthy glare. One that could shrink every muscle I have, and I have a lot. But, of course, I completely ignore his suddenly threatening stance, my body becoming taller.

"Don't tease him," Ava warns.

I scoff. I've waited forever for this. "John." I slap a firm hand on his solid shoulder. He doesn't move an inch. "You look like you're here to impress." His eyes darken, only making my grin widen. I turn it onto Elsie and blind her with it. "And you look ravishing. I hope John has told you so." I can't imagine him paying a compliment.

"Oh, he has." Elsie's hand reaches for John's. "Quite a few times, in fact."

John's still glaring at me, and I'm still totally ignoring it. "How romantic of you." His eyes are telling me to fuck right off before he smashes me in my smug face, but he would never tell me so in front of his new lady friend. "So you two official?"

"Jesse." Ava sighs, sounding tired by my game. Tired? I've only just begun. "Let's go find Kate and Sam."

"Good idea," John growls as Ava pulls me away. I just can't wipe the grin off my face. "Have a nice evening." John sounds less than sincere.

"You too," Ava calls, her yanks of my arm getting firmer. "Jesse, for the love of God, will you behave?"

"This is monumental stuff, baby." I relent and turn, letting her pull me through the crowds. "I've only known him to be goo-goo over his bonsai trees."

"He has bonsai trees?" Her wonder is warranted as she glances back to the colossal, mean-looking man who I adore with all my heart.

"If he pays as much attention to Elsie as he does those trees, she'll be feeling pretty special." I spot Sam with Kate, who's shoving a canapé in her mouth. "Hungry, Kate?" I ask, alarmed as she follows it up quickly with another.

"Oh my God," she mumbles around her full mouth, closing her eyes like she's tasting heaven. "I just can't stop eating." She collects another and holds it while moving in to give Ava a hug. "Food. Just give me food and I'll be happy."

Ava laughs over her shoulder as Sam shakes his head in amusement. "Shall we get some seats?" I ask, mindful of Kate's huge belly, *and* of my wife's dodgy leg.

"No." Sam shakes his head, pointing his beer to a passing waiter. "She's figured out the route to the kitchen. This is the prime spot to bag the good stuff before everyone else gets to it. We'll be here all night."

"You need to sit down, Kate," Ava moans at her, reaching for her tummy and giving it a little rub. "How are you feeling?"

"Hungry," she replies, seizing another canapé and stuffing the whole thing in her mouth.

Sam looks entirely exasperated as he takes one for himself. "And I'm coming out in sympathy. This baby needs to come soon before its mum and dad run out of food and eat each other."

Ava laughs, looking relaxed as she observes our friends munching their way through canapé after canapé. I'm not standing here all night. Besides, Ava needs to sit down. I spot a waitress entering the room, heading this way, and as soon as she makes it to us, I take the tray from her hands. "It's an emergency," I say to her startled face.

"Oh God." Kate's on me like she needs me to breathe, ramming food into her mouth.

"Come on." I usher them all onto the balcony, following with the tray.

The traffic on Regent Street is clear, the lights glowing, the bustle of London a perfect backdrop. Stone columns close us in, prisms of fire warming the nighttime air. It's beautifully idyllic, this little private haven above the busy streets of London.

As soon as Kate's sitting down, I put the tray in front of her, smiling at Sam when he rolls his eyes. "Sips," I whisper in Ava's ear as she lowers to a chair, taking a water for myself. "You hungry?"

"Even if I was, I don't think I'd dare take one from her," she quips, making Kate's chewing slow to a stop.

"Oow...ohhh...usstt." Her hands wave at the tray as she splutters a load of nonsense at us. And then Ava reaches forward, taking one of the little flatbreads as Kate groans happily on. "I don't know what it is about them, but I can't get enough."

I'm thrilled to see Ava pop one in her mouth without any pressing from me. But it isn't in her mouth for long. She coughs, grabbing a napkin and holding it to her mouth. "Fucking hell," she splutters, emptying the contents of her mouth into the material.

"Ava." My bark of her name makes her jump a little, though I get no apology for her foul mouth.

"I know, right?" Kate grabs another and rams it in. "Serious...eeee...est...ings."

"I need water!" Ava starts fanning her mouth, frantically searching the vicinity. "Quickly! Oh my God, my mouth's burning!"

I hand over my glass as Sam falls apart across the table, and she grabs it, slurping it down ravenously.

"Spicy?" I take a wild guess, smiling as she nods over the glass.

"Delicious," Kate corrects.

"You hate hot food." Ava's face is red, a mild sweat dampening her skin. She looks at the platter with disgust.

"Oh, Kate's developed a bit of a craving." Sam takes one of the canapés and holds it out to Kate, whose mouth falls open like she's begging for a treat. "She's draining the local Indian restaurant dry." He slips it past her lips and wipes a little bit of sauce from the corner of her mouth on a fond smile. "I won't miss the midnight demands for a curry, but I will miss these." He cups one of her swelling boobs on a grin. Ava doesn't know where to look, diving into her fizz, whereas I laugh. She got used to Sam's cheeky nature over the years. Now she has to start all over again. "Drinks, anyone?" Sam asks, releasing Kate's boob and rising.

"I'll have a grapefruit juice." Kate waffles around her ever-full mouth. "With a dash of tomato juice and some Worcester sauce."

"Jesus, Kate," Ava breathes, grimacing. "Pregnancy is doing weird stuff to your appetite."

"Tell me about it," Sam says. "Jesse?"

"Just a water for me."

"You go," Ava suggests, nodding when I look at her in question. What happened to never leaving her side? "It's fine. Kate's here."

I sense she wants some alone time with her friend, and I'm honestly not sure how I feel about that. What will be said? I don't know, and that's a killer. But crowding her when she's asked for a little space will do me no favors. "Five minutes," I agree reluctantly, leaning in and pushing my mouth to her cheek. "You're going to talk about me, aren't you?"

"Don't have such a big head." She smiles, and it's fond. It doesn't make me feel any better. I study her for a few moments, trying to read her mind. "Go," she orders, pulling on my sleeve. "And bring some canapés back that aren't going to blow my head off."

It's like she knows the promise that she'll eat will entice me to leave. And I hate that she's right. "Fine."

"And some more of these," Kate adds, tossing another into her mouth. "I'm running low."

I'm out of my chair fast, laughing as I walk away with a chuckling Sam. "Hey, look at that." I nudge his shoulder, and he looks across the bar with me where John's romancing his lady friend.

"He's gonna plant that big knuckled fist on your nose if you don't pack it in," Sam laughs, waving the barman over.

"It would be worth it," I order some water. "And some grapefruit juice with . . . " I fade off, trying to remember the foul concoction Kate requested. I look at Sam, who takes over, reeling off his order.

"Hey, boys." Drew joins us, a hand on each shoulder as he peeks his head through the middle of us. "What the fuck is that?" He eyes up the glass of God-knows-what.

"Don't ask." I turn away from the bar, leaning against the wood. "So not long until you're nailed down, too. Excited?"

"Yes, actually. I know that surprises you."

It doesn't. From the moment he met the lovely Raya, he was smitten. It might have been a surprise at the time, but you only have to see them together to get it. Who would have thought back in the day that this is where we'd be? Sam preparing for the imminent arrival of his firstborn, Drew ready to walk down the aisle. And me with twins and a wife who doesn't know me. I flinch, knocking myself out of my own depressing thoughts, and it doesn't escape the boys' notice. I swallow and shake off the melancholy.

"Hey, how's things?" Sam asks, and I look past them both to see

Ava has moved to the other side of the table to be next to Kate. She must sense my watchful eyes, because she looks up as she collects her glass, and then proceeds to take a cheeky, very measured sip. But the volume of alcohol she's drinking isn't foremost in my mind. What she's saying to Kate is.

Chapter 38

AVA

How are you feeling?" I ask, resting the stem of my glass on Kate's pregnant belly.

"I'm pregnant, fat, and I'm eating like a fucking horse." She blows her cheeks out and motions popping them. "Tell me how *you* are. How's yoga going?"

"Great." I smile, reminded of the image I had. "It beats therapy by a mile. At my last session, I was so spaced out, and I saw Jesse and the twins when they were babies."

"That's great!"

I nod, sipping my drink.

"And how are things with you and Jesse?"

I inhale and take a quick peek into the bar area where my husband is standing with his friends, but his attention is far from on them. "Good."

"And?" she prompts.

I shrug. "He's being very attentive. In between his rants about dresses, drinking, and anything else that displeases him. Which is a lot."

Kate laughs, holding her belly, and then flinches. "Ouch."

I immediately bolt forward, my hands over hers on her tummy. "What is it? You okay?"

She shuffles in her seat, grimacing. "It's nothing. Just the baby lying awkwardly." Brushing away my hands, she settles and gives me her undivided attention again. "It's—"

I hold my hand up, stopping her. "I know what you're going to say. I've figured out very quickly that he's a bit of a control freak."

"A bit?"

"A lot," I relent, taking my glass to my lips, thoughtful. "It's just... weird, isn't it?"

"What is?"

I wave my glass through the air, indicating everything around me. "Up here." I tap the side of my head. "I'm still early twenties, rocking youth and pursuing my career." I look down my lace-clad body. "But here I'm thirty-eight, married to what can only be described as an ogre, and I have eleven-year-old twins. Eleven!" I flop back in my seat, once again utterly shell-shocked by what is my life.

After way too long of a silence, I sip my drink as I look at Kate. She's smiling. "You know, I saw all these emotions in you one time before." She waits a moment for me to ask when, but I don't. I don't need to. "Ava." With one hand on mine, the other on her gigantic belly, she shuffles in closer. I look Kate straight in her vivid blue eyes, wondering where she's hiding the past sixteen years because, frankly, she looks no different. The pregnant belly aside. "For the record, you look fucking fabulous," she says. Reaching up, she pushes a stray strand behind my ear, her smile knowing. She's read my mind, but I still pout, a little put out that I'm much older than I want to be. "How do you feel about him?"

"Jesse?"

"No, the Lord Almighty." The roll of her eyes is dramatic.

"He *is* the Lord Almighty." I laugh softly, casting my gaze to him at the bar. He's still watching me, though something tells me the glass of bubbles in my hand isn't the reason why. I can see curiosity scattered across his face, the signature creases that I've become familiar with spanning his forehead. I breathe in, unable to help admiring the fine form of a man who is my husband. He has a sexy, magnetic appeal that demands attention, and for the most part, he knows it. He's a god, no denying it, and I am married to him. Though past all his cocky arrogance, there's a vulnerability. A weakness. I am the cause of that weakness. His love for me.

I study him as he studies me, his big body relaxed against the bar. My eyes go off on a tangent, roaming the vast length of him, all the way down to his Grensons, and back up again until I get to his face. That face. I sigh, relaxing, a smile breaking free when his green eyes shine, glimmer, and sparkle madly, his devilish smirk faint but apparent. He's aware of the inspection he's under, and, as always, he's taking too much pleasure from my inability to keep my damn eyes under control. I shake my head faintly on a little laugh, and he winks, kissing the air. "Arrogant pig," I mouth.

"I love you, too," he mouths back, making me laugh out loud and quickly return my focus to Kate before I inflate his huge ego even more. The man's a case. When I find my friend, I also find a cheesy grin around another one of those bloody canapés.

"Tell me you don't adore that man," she demands. "Tell me it isn't ingrained into you like every one of your internal organs. Tell me you don't need him to survive."

"I can't," I admit, though the idea is crazy if true.

I look at him and feel electric inside. He touches me, and my veins charge with heat. In his arms I feel at home. Like nothing can hurt me. And I know for sure that it can't.

"I didn't know what I felt at first," I admit. "Attraction, for sure, but trying to get my head around this man being my husband was frightening." I smile when Kate takes my hand and holds it in a sign of support. "I saw something in him, something that I should have been wary of, yet I was more intrigued by him. He's told me things that are unbelievable, yet I believe them." Kate doesn't ask what things, as I suspect she knows. "I just feel myself leaning on him in all ways, and I know it's the right thing to do. I can't explain it. I feel protective of him, even though I know he can more than look after himself. But more protective of his ways, like a need to defend how he is. Because I know why he's like that. The Manor, his uncle, his brother. The scars on his stomach, just the thought of him being hurt, no matter in what way." At the mention of the scars, Kate inhales, flinching. "I know," I agree. "I was so mad when he told me how he'd sustained the injuries. I know he claims to have been nothing before he met me, empty and lost, but still. He shouldn't have been so careless with his life."

"Careless?"

"Not wearing his leathers when he rode his bike," I prompt, and she nods slowly, looking across to Jesse with the disappointment I feel myself.

"He's a silly man," she muses, starting to get up from her seat, the effort too much, even with my helping hand. "I need to pee for the thousandth time in an hour."

"Want me to come?"

"Trust me, you don't want to hear me pee. I sound like a cart horse."

"So you're eating like a horse, peeing like a horse. You gonna start galloping?" I smile when she chuckles.

"Sam's gonna have to roll me out of this joint." She stretches, standing tall, her palms in her back pushing her hips forward. "Oh, God," she groans, the sound pure pleasure. "I'll be back in a minute. You want a drink?"

"Yes, but don't let Jesse see it."

"I'll smuggle it through in my gigantic knickers." She wanders off, and I fall into thought again, at the same time admiring Jesse. Falling in love with him so quickly seems like an outlandish possibility.

But it happened once before.

And it's happening once again.

Chapter 39

I watch as Kate half wobbles, half marches toward me, though it's plain to see she's trying to execute the latter with grit. It doesn't matter if she's failing. The look on her face is like thunder, and I'm puzzled as to why.

"Oh shit, who's upset the she-devil?" Sam mutters under his breath, spotting his girlfriend steaming toward us. "Hey, gorgeous!"

"What the fuck, Jesse?" She launches right in. "Your scars. You told her you had a motorcycle accident?"

"Oh," I say, her grievance suddenly crystal clear.

"*Oh*? That's it, *oh*? You can't keep that kind of shit from her!"

What? I can't keep that kind of shit from her? Fucking watch me. Only because Kate's expecting do I hold back from getting up in her face. I don't fancy a scrap with my mate, not that Kate would need him. She's a firecracker all on her own, more so since my mate put a bun in her oven.

"I know what I'm doing." I breathe through my statement, calm as I can manage when on the inside I'm livid. *I* know what's best for my wife. *Me.*

She's the one recoiling now, and Sam's quick to move in, a

pacifying arm placed on her back. And Kate's quick to shrug him off. "You're lying, that's what you're doing."

"I'm protecting her." I can feel my teeth grinding, my jaw aching in an instant.

"By lying?" She laughs, and it's sarcastic as fuck. "Haven't you learned? Look what happened the last time you kept her in the dark." Her face is getting redder by the second, her rage probably matching mine, though I'm containing it far better than Kate.

"Kate, calm the fuck down." Sam tries to encourage her away. She's having none of it.

"You can't lie to her. It isn't right."

I swallow and reach for Kate's hand, taking it in a firm grip and looking her square in the eye. I hope she sees how sincere I am. How determined. "Kate, lies are necessary when you know the person you're lying to can't handle the truth." I breathe in more oxygen, and Kate snaps her mouth shut, so I push on while she's been silenced. "Ava can't handle the truth, Kate. Not now. Maybe never. I don't know, but in this moment I'm not telling her all that shit. It pales into insignificance, anyway. What matters to me, to Ava, is *us*. Our family. The kids. I want all of her energy on me and the twins. Not a nobody who's not in our lives anymore."

She's staring at me, absorbing my speech. "I think you're mad."

"I feel it," I say. "But she's falling in love with me again, and now more than ever, I don't want anything to jeopardize that." I flick my eyes to Sam. He still has hold of Kate, but his eyes are on me. Sympathy is emblazoned across his face. And his small nod tells me he understands the angle I'm taking here. I'm grateful.

"Oh shit," Kate blurts, her welling eyes overflowing when she blinks.

"Hey." I move in to comfort her, to make sure we're all right. "Don't get upset."

"I'm not upset." She looks down, as do I, finding a puddle around our feet. "My water broke."

"Oh, fuck." I step back, cringing, feeling all kinds of guilty for more or less inducing her labor.

"What?" Sam shoots a fire stare at his girlfriend. "That's what happens when you get stressed out!" He takes her cheeks and moves in, smacking a big kiss on her lips. "If you weren't in labor, I'd spank you stupid."

"Save it for later, Samuel." Kate gazes at him as Sam gazes back. "We're going to have a baby."

And like the news might have just sunk in, he flips to panic mode. "Fuck! I'm going to have a baby!" He looks at me, and then to Drew. "We're having a baby!" he shouts, silencing the room. "Call an ambulance!"

"Someone calm him the fuck down," Kate mumbles, and then that mumble turns into a moan, her body bending at the waist. "Ohhh, shit, there it is."

"What's going on?" Ava rushes over, looking to everyone, and then down at her feet. "Oh."

"Oh, your pretty shoes," Kate whines, clinging to Sam's arm. "They're ruined."

"Give it a rest, woman," Sam chides as Kate flings her other arm out and grabs me. I hold on to her as she pants, her red face now red for other reasons. Flashbacks, tons of them, steam forward and swamp my brain—visions of Ava in the latter weeks of her pregnancy, fooling me into believing she was in labor to wind me up, and then the moment she wasn't playing anymore. The moment it actually happened. I look across to my wife as I help Sam hold up Kate, a crowd of people growing. I watch as my wife throws out instructions, before taking Kate's arm from me. I'm in a world of my own, rendered immobile by my memories, a useless heap of man amid the pandemonium.

"Jesse!" Ava's sharp shout of my name snaps me back into the room. She's looking at me in question. "You're the only one who hasn't been drinking." She must catch my confusion, because she pushes on urgently. "You need to drive us to the hospital."

"Right."

"An ambulance!" Sam yells, frantically looking around the room, like he might find one in Café Royal.

"Will someone shut him the hell up," Kate spits, forgoing the help of her boyfriend and putting all of her trust into Ava, clinging onto her friend. "Oohhhhhh God!" Over she goes again, bending at the waist. "Shit, shit, shit."

Ava starts walking Kate toward the exit, me and Sam following like the useless men we are. "Sam, I need you to time the contractions," Ava orders over her shoulder, helping Kate along. "Jesse, bring the car around."

Kate takes slow, tentative steps, Ava matching her pace. "How bad does it hurt?" Kate asks, looking to Ava for reassurance.

"Like a bitch," Ava answers automatically. I find myself inhaling, a little stunned. "And when that baby's ready to come out, you're gonna feel like you're trying to push a flaming watermelon out of your fanny."

Kate laughs, and then stops, shouting at the doors of the elevator. "Motherfucker!"

"About sums it up," Ava quips, accepting a wet cloth from Raya and dabbing at Kate's forehead.

"You're stealing my thunder," Raya jokes, nothing but fondness in her tone as she takes Kate's other side, the trio of women in a line before us, taking the ropes, putting us to shame.

All that's left for me to do is put an arm around Sam and walk him on behind while I watch Ava talk Kate through it. Like she's done it before. Because she has.

* * *

Five of us sit in the waiting room—me, Ava, Drew, Raya, and Georgia. We insisted they stay at Café Royal and enjoy their party. They insisted on coming. It's past midnight, and Georgia is asleep on Drew's lap, Raya's head resting on his shoulder. The consistent moans and screams of women are leaking out of the doors of the maternity unit. It's only been a few hours since we arrived, and I know more than anyone that it could be a long night. But not one of us is prepared to leave. This is a monumental moment in our friends' lives. We all want to be here for it.

I peek down at Ava. She's sitting next to me, her gaze fixed on our held hands in her lap.

"You okay?" I ask, wondering if she's thinking about when she had our babies. Looking up at me, she sighs, her head falling onto my shoulder. I reach around with my spare hand and cup her cheek. "Does it really feel like you're pushing a flaming watermelon out of your fanny?"

Her jerking body against mine makes me smile, her laugh soft. "Yes."

"Ouch," I quip, shuddering for effect. Her hand reaches for mine on her face and holds it there.

"I don't know where it all came from," she says, almost sad. "It's the story of my life at the moment."

I breathe out, my arse slipping further from the seat. I'm not sure whether I like these little flashes of recollections anymore. They don't excite me, more make me sad. Sad that the instinct is there, but the memory and the essence of that memory isn't. I close my eyes, feeling so tired.

I have roughly two seconds of shut-eye before I hear some doors open. Shooting my stare toward them, I find Sam standing outside the maternity unit, looking like shit, his face washed out, his eyes bloodshot. For a moment, I'm terrified that something has gone wrong. Then a lazy grin creeps across his exhausted face, and my heart works its way back to a safe pace.

"It's a girl," he croaks, his voice like gravel. "We've gone and got ourselves a little girl."

I'm up in a heartbeat, seeing he'll collapse with a mixture of happiness and exhaustion if I don't reach him quickly. He practically falls into my arms. "Fuck me, I never want to do that again."

I smile, knowing exactly how he feels. "Congratulations, mate." I give him the biggest bear hug, taking most of his weight. A girl. I laugh under my breath. That's it. Sam has joined Drew and me in girlie hell. I fucking love it.

I release him only when Ava makes it to us to take over the hug, though I'm on standby to catch him if his legs give. "Well done. How's Kate?"

"Knackered."

We all come together, hugs and kisses given all around. And it's beautiful. A beautiful moment in our lives. My only wish is that the twins were here, and as I look at Georgia, rubbing at her sleepy eyes, that wish turns into an ache. Only one more day, I tell myself. Then I see my babies.

Once we've said our good-byes, I walk an exhausted Ava to the car, practically holding her up. I buckle her in, kiss her neck, and linger there for a time, just feeling her on my skin. She's dozy.

"I love you." Her whispered confession is drowsy, but her deeper nuzzle into me tells me she's aware of what she's saying. My heart could burst.

"I know," I whisper back, kissing her hair, holding my lips there forever.

In this moment, such a perfect moment, I decide what I must do in the morning.

Chapter 40

Ed Sheeran's "Give Me Love" plays quietly, a soft background noise in our bedroom, the tones calm and relaxing. Ava's lids peel open gradually, blinking as they do, her pupils shrinking before my eyes as she becomes accustomed to the morning light. I know the second she finds me straddling her waist, because she smiles. And that smile falls the moment she tries to reach for me.

Because she can't move her hands.

Her eyes dart up to the headboard, where her wrists are securely shackled. A few jerks of her arms later, she returns her eyes to me. I raise my eyebrows. Her mouth drops open.

"Morning, baby," I chirp, resting my palms on the insides of her upper arms, pushing them into the bed.

"Oh, no you did not," she sputters, having a little futile wriggle beneath me.

"Oh, yes I did." I lower my face, slowly getting closer and closer to her lips. She stills. "Remember what your last words to me were last night?"

Her eyes slightly widen, and I know, I just *know* she's going to deny it. She shakes her head mildly, a smile tickling her lips. Oh, she knows damn well.

"Have it your way." I sigh loudly, dropping my head until my chin meets my chest. "I'll start at three," I warn her, my voice loaded with the craving consuming me. "And when I get to zero, baby—"

"What? Are you going to force me to marry you again?" The cocky edge to her tone is thrilling.

"Three," I begin, not blessing her with an answer as I rise to sit up straight on her waist.

"Jesse . . . ," she says slowly, cockiness fading and concern creeping forward.

"Two." I hold my fingers up and lazily lower them to her stomach.

She stills, hard as steel. "No."

I walk my fingers south, purposely slowly, prolonging her anticipation. "Do you remember what you said?"

Her lips press firmly together, my stubborn little temptress.

"No?" My fingertips reach her tickle spot and stops. "Fine by me. One."

"Jesse." She exhales my name and then quickly sucks in air and holds her breath, ready for it.

"Zero, baby," I whisper, removing my hands from her hips and falling forward onto her, catching her mouth and startling her with a smoldering, hot, consuming kiss. Though I catch the surprise in her eyes, she falls straight into it, matching the deepness, plunging her tongue far and wide. There's not a piece of my mouth she's not finding.

"Marry me," I say softly into her mouth.

I feel her smile around my lips. "You've married me twice already."

I pull back, a little scowl escaping. "Is that a no?"

"I didn't say no." She looks up at the cuffs, pulling a bit. "Will you release me?"

I have no idea why I bow to her order so easily, especially since she hasn't technically said yes, but I find myself doing exactly that, reaching up and freeing her, leaving the cuffs dangling from the bed. She sits up and pushes me to my back, now straddling me. And then she takes my arms in turn and cuffs me to the bed. And I let her.

It's official. I'm crazy.

"What are you doing?" I ask as I watch her spread her body the length of mine, looking up at me as she starts to lazily pepper light kisses across my torso. My head drops back, a rough moan spilling free, my eyes closing in bliss. This could be a trick. She could be leading me into a false sense of security. But right now, with her mouth gliding across my flesh, the warmth of her licks and bites leaving fire in their wake, I couldn't give a fucking shit.

I don't fight the restraints. I don't lose my mind that I can't touch her. I don't worry about the potential of her trying to extract information from me. I'm lost. A slave to her worshipping mouth. Every nerve ending alive, every vein pumping with hot blood.

"This is the Truth Fuck, yes?" she asks, her voice husky and low as she kisses her way up my body, onto my chin, and then my mouth. A wave of panic comes over me. There's no expression on her face, just pure, potent lust.

"Yes... ohhhh..." I choke on my groan, her hips grinding into my groin. "Shit, Ava."

Rising a little, she frees my cock from where it's pinned to my lower stomach, and it pings up, the tip brushing over her entrance. I jerk. She jerks. And then she lowers herself onto me, taking all of me on one slow plunge. I clench my teeth, breathing through my nose, as she starts to work her way up into a mind-blowing rhythm. I stare up into her eyes, brown eyes that are spilling desire all over me. She's killing me over and over with each and every swivel of her hips, her palms resting on my chest. I find the will to break eye contact, my gaze falling to her breasts as they bounce lightly, and then to her stomach, where evidence of her pregnancy with the twins looks back at me.

Beautiful. Every inch of her is beautiful.

Falling forward, she encases my head with her arms, her face a fraction from mine. Her pace never falters. My pleasure never dips, remaining consistent, taking more of my breath with each grind.

"You want some truths, Jesse Ward?" she murmurs, weaving her fingers through my hair.

I just nod, ignoring the ache developing in my arms and focusing on easing the ache in my cock that's being stroked by her warm walls.

"I *do* love you." She kisses me and alters the swing of her hips, turning it into more of a soft rock. That move, those words. It's my undoing, and it's Ava's, too. "Together," she orders softly around our busy mouths, and with that word, I tip the edge and tumble with her, maintaining our kiss the whole time we're riding the waves of pleasure together until our kiss slows to a stop, as well as our moving bodies. Though her constricting walls and my pulsing cock go on for far longer. I feel the release of her muscles when she sighs, her body melting over mine. "Marry me," she breathes, turning her lips onto my cheek.

If there was ever a moment in my life that I could bottle and store away forever, this would be it. Because she's just told me she's all in.

"You can't ask me that when I'm handcuffed to the bed," I whisper, feeling her immediately move and release me. The second my hands are my own again, I flip her to her back and crowd her.

"Marry me?" she repeats.

"Stupid fucking question."

And I kiss her.

Chapter 41

It feels like D-day. The kids will be home later, we meet Sam and Kate's baby girl for the first time, and Ava has her follow-up appointment with her doctor. Two of the things on our list I'm elated about. The last not so much.

I'm dreading hearing Dr. Peters tell us that he's happy with her progress, because I definitely wouldn't say I'm happy. With the progress we've had in terms of our relationship, yes, I'm delighted. But in terms of her memory, I'm disappointed. I might sound ungrateful. I probably am. Like my mother said to me earlier this morning, I should be thankful that I still have her at all. The thought alone makes my blood run cold each time it enters my head.

As we wander down the corridor toward the maternity unit to see Kate before heading to Dr. Peters's office, I can feel Ava's nerves spiking. I wonder if she can feel mine. I sway between asking her if she's all right or not saying anything at all.

"I'm fine," she says, peeking up at me. "At least some things are coming back to me. Wouldn't you be more concerned if I had nothing? An empty head?"

"I just wish you would remem—" I stop myself in the nick of time, mentally thumping myself. Why would I even dream of saying that?

I'm walking one second, and standing still the next, Ava having pulled me to a stop. Turning into me, she finishes for me. "The kids?"

Damn, she's good. But after Kate's labor Saturday night, it's not surprising her mind is on her own children. Ava had relayed every pain her friend should expect. Like a pro. And I think the notion comforted her. Made her feel even more maternal.

Stepping into me, she lifts on her tippy-toes and kisses my stubbled cheek, and I push my face into it, throwing my arms around her and squeezing her to me. "I can't wait to see the kids," she mumbles into my shoulder, probably struggling for breath. "We need to get on with things, and we can't do that while we're incomplete."

She's putting me to shame, but one thing I know is that the time away from the twins, the most painful time in my life for more than that reason, wasn't entirely wasted. I made my wife fall in love with me again. Mission accomplished.

"I love you." I refuse to let her go, people having to sidestep us in the middle of the corridor to get past. I don't care. Wherever, whenever. Always.

"I know," she answers, fussing over me with kisses like I need to be fussed. "Come on. We have a baby to meet." At that moment, the doors to the maternity unit open, and Sam appears with a bundle of blankets in his arms. And beneath the piles of soft cotton, his baby girl.

Christ, my eyes begin to well, my throat clogging up on me. I cough to clear it, and Ava gives me a knowing look. I scowl out of principle before my wife thinks I've transformed into a complete sappy twat.

Sam grins, so wide. "Guys, meet Betty."

"Oh my God." Ava melts at his feet, going totally goo-goo over the baby. I'm alarmed, stepping forward to take a peek. Yeah, she's cute all right. My wife swoons all over Sam's arms, cooing and oohing, clucking and smiling.

"Don't get any ideas." It's out before I can stop it, and she looks up at me, her fingers playing with Betty's little hand. Sam's quick to fall apart, and Ava's quick to put me straight. "I'm happy with the two, thanks."

I know I visibly sag before her, and I can't help it. Imagining going through pregnancy hell again makes me sweat. The worry. The anxiety. The constant fear that something small, a twinge or something else, meant something was seriously wrong. And then the labor. "Good," I confirm, rolling my shoulders, making Sam laugh harder.

"You're too old, man." Sam sticks the knife right in and twists it repeatedly.

"Fuck you," I spit, moving on, keen to divert *that* conversation. "How are you, anyway?" He looks knackered.

"I thought I'd seen every intimate part of my girlfriend." He shudders. "I was so wrong."

I laugh, looking toward the door when Kate comes wobbling through.

She looks surprisingly fresh, considering. "I snuck out because it's not visiting time and they won't let you in." She reaches Ava, who is fast to take her in a hug.

"I'm so happy for you."

"Don't be," Kate gripes. "I'm walking like John Wayne for all the wrong reasons." Her joke, delivered flat and dry, sets all of us off laughing.

Sam places Betty in Kate's arms. "Yeah, how long until . . . you know . . . " He nods down at Kate's hips.

Her look is pure filth. "I only have enough energy to stab you." She drops a light kiss on Betty's head, all the while keeping daggers on Sam, who's grinning like a fool.

"It'll be a month at least," I tell my clueless mate, relishing his horrified look. I feel his pain. That month after the twins were born was the longest fucking month of my life. Giving him a slap on the shoulder, I sigh, raising my hand and gesturing some wanking action. "Meet your new best friend."

He groans, and slips his arm around Kate's shoulders. "It's a good job I love this crazy woman. Let's get coffee before I fall asleep here and now."

We start to wander toward the small café at the end of the corridor, Kate wobbling along with the help of a very attentive Sam, me and Ava following. I look down at her, finding her thoughtful. I'm speaking before my brain engages. "You know, if you wanted another..."

I have absolutely no fucking clue where that just came from. What the actual fuck? Who put those words in my mouth? I know who. That bastard thing called decency. Or is it guilt? Desperation? I don't know, but what I do know is that if she really *really* wanted to have another baby, I'd find a way to deal with it. If only just so she could be pregnant and remember it again, to go through birth and have that experience to remember. To be a mother to a baby and a toddler. To have the first tooth and the first day of school. Pain churns in my gut. It's only now it dawns on me just how much she's missing from our children's lives, and while I would love nothing more than for her to have those memories back, I have to accept that they may not come. So maybe I could give her some in another way. Am I being gallant? Or have I completely lost the plot? I conclude, quite speedily, that it's the latter. What the hell am I thinking? The sweat beads on my brow are instant.

"Don't worry," Ava chuckles, clearly noticing my suddenly awkward form. "I don't."

"Thank fuck," I breathe, all kinds of relieved. I don't think I've ever suggested anything so dumb. I'm fifty, for fuck's sake. I'm done making babies.

Chapter 42

We're back to silence as we sit outside Ava's doctor's office, my foot nervously tapping the carpet until Ava's forced to reach forward and place a firm hand on my knee to stop it. "I'm sorry." I sigh, taking her hand and bringing it to my mouth, kissing the back. My knee starts going loopy again, adrenaline making it bounce. I can't stop it.

Ava sighs, exasperated, jumping up and sitting on my lap, a last-ditch attempt to get my shakes under control. It's a ridiculous plan. Her weight. My strength. She starts jerking away on my lap like she could be vibrating. "Fucking hell, Jesse."

My trembles stop, just like that. "Will you watch your fucking mouth?" Her swearing won't help me, and neither does her insolence in the form of rolling eyes.

"Ava Ward," someone calls from behind us before I can unleash more displeasure on her, and I look to see Dr. Peters standing at his office door. He smiles, taking in the sight of my lap full of Ava. "Please, come in."

We walk into his office and take a seat in front of his desk. I flick Ava a look, trying to read her disposition once again. She looks perfectly cool. Content, even.

"How are you, Ava?" the doctor asks, slipping his glasses on and scanning her medical file on his desk.

"I'm good," she replies quickly, reaching for my hand and squeezing.

"And the headaches?" He looks up over his glasses and smiles a little, noting our held hands.

"They've subsided."

He starts jotting down notes. "What about physical movements? Your coordination, for example?"

All I see in my mind's eye is Ava's hand finding my cock with perfectly steady hands. Her coordination is just fine, though I refrain from telling the doc that. "She still has a slight limp," I say, knowing Ava won't. "And her head is still fragile around the wound."

"To be expected." He gets up and circles his desk, taking a small penlight and bending to shine it in Ava's eyes. "And your sensory functions?"

I raise my brows, and Ava flicks a coy look my way. "I can feel, see, smell, hear, and taste."

I smile back at her, despite it being inappropriate. "I'll vouch for that." I flip her a wink, letting my muscles relax for the first time since I walked into this office.

"Good." He slips the light into his jacket pocket and checks the site of her head injury, nodding happily, before checking her leg, too. He returns to his chair. "Any breakthroughs in your memories?" Resting back, he taps his pen on the palm of his spare hand.

She shrugs, glancing at me. "Small things here and there."

"No matter how small or insignificant they may seem, they're all important." Another smile. "Your symptoms are classic to traumatic amnesia, Ava. I'm very hopeful that given time and patience, your memories will return. The brain is an immensely complex organ, and the function of our memories engages many different parts of it. In your case, a blow to the head has damaged the structure of your brain and the limbic system which controls your emotions and memories."

Patience. The stuff I'm not well furnished with.

"Obviously we're focused on retrieving your memories, Ava, but may I ask how you see your future?"

I feel my forehead furrow with a frown, and I look across to Ava. She's staring at the doctor, seeming just as confused by his question as me. "I'm sorry, I don't follow," she tells him.

Good. Me either. I redirect my attention across the desk to find the doctor smiling again. All these smiles are beginning to irritate me. What's there to be so pleased about? "It's common for sufferers of amnesia to find it hard to imagine their future when so much of their past is missing. The past and our futures are linked heavily in our memories and the people in our lives, so it's common for patients to struggle with the prospect of their future."

"Ava is not struggling with the prospect of her future," I pipe up, unable to stop myself. What is he suggesting?

For the first time, the doctor looks wary of me. Good. He should be. "Ava?" he says, keeping his eyes on me.

"I don't see my future," she says quietly, and I throw a look her way, deeply injured, and very worried. *What?* "I feel it more than see it," she finishes. "With Jesse and the twins. It's hard to explain." She shakes her head, frustrated. "At first I was frightened and confused. I didn't know him." I shrink into the chair, my hand coming up to my forehead and rubbing gently. "But it didn't take long for me to realize that I do know him. Every sense I have recognizes him, even if my stupid brain doesn't. And as for my children, I feel like I have a huge piece of me missing right now, and it isn't the memories. It's them. Their presence."

I close my eyes and swallow, feeling the doctor looking at me, judging me. I swear to God, if he passes comment on my way of dealing with this, I'll launch his arse across the hospital. "I understand," Dr. Peters replies quietly, going back to his pad. "When are the children home?"

I clear my throat and pull myself together, pushing back my anger. "They're on their way now."

"That's good. The sooner Ava gets back to real life the better. Routine is key." Going to his computer, he starts tapping away on the keyboard. "Try to weave some relaxed time into that routine. There are a few ways we could move forward. I would recommend an occupational therapist who can work with you to acquire new information to replace some of your lost memories. A personal digital assistant may be helpful, too, in helping you with day-to-day life."

"A personal assistant?" I ask, trying my damn hardest not to sound affronted. I know I fail when Ava squeezes my hand, her way of pleading with me to keep my cool. I'm struggling. "She doesn't need a personal assistant. She has me."

"Mr. Ward, you're misunderstanding. I'm talking about a device of some sort. A phone or iPad. There are some really helpful apps that would be great for Ava." The doctor leaves his keyboard and hands me a pile of pamphlets, which I take slowly. "Ava will want to gain some independence back, I'm sure." He looks at Ava, though I don't. All she needs is me. "She may forget things, small things that happened just a day before, or even an hour. It's common." He smiles reassuringly, though I'm far from reassured.

There have been a few occasions when she's forgotten things. Small things. Things I have told her that have disappeared from her mind, and I've had to tell her again.

"With the help of a smartphone or similar, Ava can set herself reminders for key commitments, make notes, et cetera to help her with everyday tasks. I'm sure she doesn't want to rely on you for everything, and it's important for her to have a sense of self-awareness and worth. She has to get back to her life, whether the memories come or do not."

I'm fucking staggered. "Are you suggesting I just leave her to figure this all out on her own?" The man's a twat.

Dr. Peters smiles. I'm close to wiping it from his face. "Mr. Ward, if there is one thing I know for sure, it's that you will never let her figure it all out on her own. But you must give her space to breathe." With that, he stands, and it's all I can do not to jump across the desk and take him out. Is he having a dig? "I'd like to see you again in a few weeks, Ava. Have a look at the literature I've given your husband. There are support groups available to you, people you can talk with who are in the same boat. We'll discuss at your next appointment once you've had a chance to read the information."

Support group? Meet new people who understand? I'm hating this more and more each minute. She doesn't need new people, she has me. I'm her support.

Ava's up before I am, encouraging me to stand. "Thank you."

"Very welcome."

I don't thank him but rather wander out silently, my head ringing. Space to breathe? That's never been my strong point, and it's something Ava has gotten used to. I'm set in my ways, and changing that has proven tricky since the moment she came around. I've struggled, but held out hope that it was temporary. That we would return to our normal eventually. The prospect of having to adapt and permanently change my ways is daunting. And I honestly question whether I'm capable. Where does that leave us?

Chapter 43

The journey home is silent. Uncomfortable. I draw breath a thousand times to ask Ava what's whirling around in her mind, but each time I think better of it. Maybe because I'm worried about what she might say. Does she want more space? Does she think I'm crowding her too much? Does she hate me for sending the kids away so I could focus on discovering *us* again? Question after question mounts until my head is pounding. "Ava—" I'm interrupted by her phone ringing, and she answers rather than letting it ring off and giving me her attention. My hands flex around the steering wheel, irritation heating my bloodstream.

"Hi!" She sounds happy all of a sudden. "Yes, definitely." She laughs, and I frown, wondering who's on the line. Kate's in hospital. "I'll see you there." She hangs up and looks at me. "What were you going to say?"

My mind is blank. "Who was that?"

"Oh, Zara." She slips her phone into her bag. Zara. The friend from yoga. The woman putting stupid ideas in my wife's head about getting another job. "You must meet her. She's fab."

I bite my tongue before we end up in an argument. It's probably best I never meet Zara. I can't guarantee I'll hold back from putting her straight on a few things. "Sure."

When we pull up the driveway, I'm about to unleash some of the questions mounting, but Ava speaks first, stopping me in my tracks. "Whose car is that?" she asks, pointing forward, spurring me to look.

Ava's parents' Land Rover is parked up, and the front door is wide open. "The kids are home." Excitement mixed with apprehension swirls in my gut as I roll to a stop. I have no idea how this will play out. How will Ava be? How will the kids be? "You okay?"

"Yeah." Her answer is quiet as she gets out of the car, hovering by the door for a few moments after she's shut it. I remain in my seat, bracing myself for the reunion. I mustn't get emotional. I mustn't give the kids any cause to worry. On a deep breath, I exit the car and circle it to collect Ava. She smiles at me when I take her hand. "Ready?"

Her inhale is far deeper than mine. "Ready," she confirms, letting me lead her up to the front door. Each step she takes is measured, each breath audible. She's doing exactly what I'm doing. Bracing herself. The hallway is a mess of bags and shoes, the house alive with the sound of the twins from the kitchen. It's normal. Peeking down at Ava as we head toward the sounds, I find her smiling, a certain new lease of life in her eyes. That life gives me life, too, and I squeeze her hand, prompting her to look up at me. "Just tell me if it gets too much," I say. "If you need some breathing space."

"From you or the children?" she asks on a cheeky hitch of her brows.

My scowl is playful as I drop her hand and wrap an arm around her shoulder. "Sarcasm doesn't suit you, lady."

"So you keep telling me."

We enter the kitchen to find the kids sitting at the island while Ava's mum faffs around the space and Joseph follows, taking orders. Maddie is on her iPad. Jacob has his finger wedged in a jar of peanut butter. It's like they were never gone. We both stand in the doorway for a few moments, silent and taking in the scene. Because it's chaos and it's normal and it's beautiful. "Kids are home," I quip, and Ava chuckles a little, looking up at me with eyes full of love.

"Thank you for the time we've had together." Leaning up, she pushes her lips into my cheek. "It's truly been some of the best in my life."

I don't know whether the twinge in my heart is hurt or happiness. We've had some amazing times in our lives. And she can't remember any of them.

"Mum! Dad!" Maddie's off the stool like a whippet, racing toward us. I watch as she throws her arms around Ava's body and hugs her fiercely, Jacob soon joining her.

"Charming," I grumble, giving them each a rub of their heads. "You missed me, too, right?" Neither of them breaks free of Ava, and I don't hold it against them. Besides, I'm taking too much satisfaction and pleasure from watching the mother of my children embracing their attack, her eyes closed, her arms around their backs, her face buried in the tops of their heads. She's smelling them, breathing them in. I don't think I've ever seen anything so wonderful. Glimpsing up at me, Ava smiles faintly, and I see a bit of apprehension in her dark brown eyes. I wink at her, my own silent way of telling her she's doing great.

Releasing her hold of Maddie, Ava motions for me to go to her, and as soon as I'm in touching distance, she pulls me in and I surround them all with my arms. My wife and my children. My world, all bundled safely in my arms. I have to swallow repeatedly to keep myself together.

The twins, usually allergic to any kind of affection from me unless they want something, stay put, uncomplaining, until Ava and I are ready to release them. It's a job and a half, but I finally find the will to pull out, letting them all breathe again. Though my breath is still short, my heart still thumping. Overwhelmed. I'm so fucking overwhelmed.

Ava's mother and father move in only once I've broken up our cluster of bodies, and Elizabeth nods at me as she takes Ava in a hug. "How are you, darling?"

"The doctor's very happy with my progress," she replies, because that is all there is to say. "I'm just glad the kids are back and we can try to get on with things."

Joseph moves in and shakes my hand as the kids stand close by, their faces eager for some information. What to tell them has my mind twisting. "Good to see you, Jesse," Joseph says, following up his handshake with a firm slap to my shoulder.

"How were the kids?"

"Terrible," he mutters, though his tone is joking. "Disobedient, no manners, and constantly moaning."

"Oh, Joseph," Elizabeth laughs, giving my arm a little rub as she passes me. "I noticed you had nothing in the cupboards so I popped to the supermarket." She starts emptying bags, stocking up the fridge. "Milk, bread."

"Thanks, Mum." I point Ava to a stool. "Sit."

She settles at the island while I help Elizabeth unload the groceries, and I listen as Ava walks the kids through everything the doctor just told us. She smiles the whole time, telling them she's happy and they should be, too. "And now I have you two back, we can do exactly that," she chirps. "Get back to normal."

"What about your memories?" Jacob asks, reclaiming his peanut butter. "Will they ever come back?"

"The doctor is very positive," Ava replies, looking up at me. "And if they don't, then we make new ones."

I smile, despite myself, feeling Elizabeth's hand on my arm. I look at my mother-in-law and see encouragement reflecting back at me. "Thank you for having them," I say sincerely.

To which she smacks my arm before taking the empty carrier bag from my hand. "Shut up," she orders, stuffing it in the bin.

I roll my eyes, wandering over to my wife and kids and getting in on the excited conversation. I put myself behind Ava and curl my arms around her waist, resting my chin on her shoulder. Her hands land on mine, and she cranes her neck to get me in her sights.

"Oh, Dad, please," Maddie sighs, losing all interest in the conversation and going back to her iPad. Whereas Jacob looks completely and utterly thrilled by my public display of affection. Of course he is. It's normal for Dad to be all over Mum. He grins around his peanut-butter-covered finger, his attention set firmly on us.

Ava sighs, leaning back into me a little. "It feels right already," she says, looking a little sad, like she now appreciates how much she's missed them.

"Because it is right." I kiss her hair before breaking away. "Now, what am I doing for dinner?"

I get three different menu choices thrown at me all at once. And I smile. Because this is us.

CHAPTER 44

It takes me one second flat to figure out what's not right when my brain wakes the next morning. Ava's not in bed with me. Then another second to break into a panic. Where is she? And another second to get myself out of bed and out of the bedroom. I sprint around the landing and down the stairs like a loon, skidding into the kitchen.

I find Maddie at the island eating her breakfast. "Oh my God!" Her horrified screech pierces my ears, her spoon halfway to her mouth. Her eyes are wide for the brief moment I see them before she swings back around on her stool, away from me. "Seriously, Dad!"

For a moment, I'm confused. Then I register the reason for her alarm. On a cringe, I look down my front. My naked front. *Shit!*

"Where's your mum?" I ask, taking my hands to my groin and cupping myself. I die a little on the inside, though I don't beat a hasty retreat. I'm too worried.

Her arm shoots out toward the utility room, just as Ava appears with a basket of washing in her hands. I get the same reaction from my wife as I do my daughter. The basket full of washing hits the ground, followed by a shriek. "Jesse, what the hell?" Ava snatches a tea towel off the counter and rushes over, making quick work of covering me up.

"You weren't in bed," I snap, letting loose an unhappy scowl. "I was worried."

Dark chocolate strands of hair frame her face as she gives me a tired look. "The kids are back at school today. I needed a head start."

"You should have woken me up. I just had twenty heart attacks between here and the bedroom, Ava."

"You were tired."

"I'm not tired," I retort, while she continues to arrange the small square of cloth over my nether regions. "Never leave our bed without telling me. You'll kill me off."

"Stop being so dramatic." While she's down there determinedly trying to conceal my dignity, her hand brushes the underside of my cock, waking the frisky fucker up. I inhale sharply, as does Ava, watching as the material moves with the help of my growing erection. Biting her lip furiously, she shakes her head. And here we are, back to that blessed thing called self-control.

"For fuck's sake," I mumble under my breath. "Are there any shorts in that basket?"

Snapping to life, Ava darts across to where she abandoned the washing and rifles through. "Here!" She pulls out a black pair and chucks them across to me. Making sure Maddie remains facing away from me, I replace the pathetic towel with the shorts. "I'm decent, baby girl," I tell her.

"You're sooooo embarrassing."

I plonk myself on the stool next to her and chuck the tea towel at Ava. It hits her in the chest and falls to the floor, her hands not even coming up to try to catch it. Because she's too busy indulging in my chest. I pout and look down my fine front, peeking up at her through my lashes. "Breakfast?" I ask, my question bringing her eyes to mine.

They roll as she picks up the basket, before warily flicking to our daughter. "Behave," she mouths, disappearing back into the utility room.

I laugh under my breath. Behave? Never. "How long have you been up?" I call, searching the island for a pot of coffee. No coffee.

"Six thirty," Ava replies as I make my way to the coffee machine and fire it up, not allowing the fact that it's not prepared already bother me. "But Maddie was down here before me."

She was? I look back at my daughter on a raised brow, and she shrugs around her mouthful of cereal. She usually needs a rocket up her arse to get her out of bed.

"Thought I could get my own breakfast this morning."

I smile fondly, flipping her a wink. "Good girl." She's trying to help, anything to lessen the pressure on Ava's shoulders. I'm about to switch on the coffeemaker when I hear cursing from the utility room. I sigh and look up at the ceiling. Lord, give me strength. "Ava," I warn. My day isn't getting off to the best start. Heart attacks. Swearing.

"Shit, it can't be that hard," I hear her grumble as I head her way, finding her staring at the washing machine.

"I won't tell you again, watch your damn mouth," I hiss, resting my shoulder on the door as she stares at the buttons embellishing the front, completely ignoring me. "What's up?"

She sighs. "I don't know how to use the washing machine." She proceeds to smack buttons on the front and twist knobs randomly, getting increasingly annoyed. "How hard can it be?"

I join her by the machine and take her hand gently before she breaks the damn thing. "Take it easy," I say, all soothingly. "We'll figure it out together." I bend and scan the millions of buttons on the front, Ava joining me. Jesus, what do they all do? What's all this rinse and spin business? I bite the corner of my lip, wondering where the manual might be.

"You don't know how to use it, do you?" she says, a little teasingly. I honestly don't.

"Not a fucking clue," I admit unashamedly, slowly casting my eyes to hers. "The washing has always been your area of expertise."

"You cheeky bastard!" she gasps, outraged, smacking my arm.

"Mouth!"

"Shut up. And what's your area of expertise?"

My irritation dissipates, and I laugh, seizing her and mauling her neck for a few precious moments, sneakily flexing my hips into hers. "What do you *think* my area of expertise is?"

She chuckles and tries to swat me away, with little success. I have a firm hold, and I'm not letting go. "So you're good for one thing and one thing alone?"

Picking her up, I sit her on the counter and take her hips. Her smile is dreamy. Gorgeous. And her eyes bright, considering the time of day. "I'm an expert at most things I do." I'm not boasting. I am. I tug her forward until her crotch hits mine, reawakening my dick. I look down and sigh. "Oh dear."

"Oh dear," she counters, pulling my face up and covering my mouth with hers, encasing my naked shoulders in her arms. Good fucking morning. And welcome home. "I need to get the kids ready for school," she murmurs, nipping the end of my tongue.

Right on cue, we hear the sleepy call of Jacob from the kitchen.

"They're snogging in the utility room," Maddie informs him tiredly. "Looks like we're back to normal."

Back to normal. Not quite. But knowing the kids get reassurance from seeing me and Ava up to our old tricks does something sweet to me. Is it that simple for them? Just to have their mum and dad here together, loving each other, being their normal selves, even if we're not? I was starting to feel guilty about sending them away. Now, I'm more sure than ever that I did the right thing by them. Those first few days after I brought Ava home were hell. The emotions, the screaming, the distress. I wouldn't want them to see their mum so lost and their dad so hopeless. That time with us alone was precious. It was needed. For Ava to discover who I am and what I stand for, and for her to accept it. And she does. Thankfully, she does.

I'm pulled from my thoughts by a gentle tap on my shoulder and I breathe in, looking into the eyes that have ruled me from day one. I spend a few moments rearranging her dark waves over her shoulders before picking her up off the counter and setting her on her feet. "You are relieved of duty." I swat her arse and send her on her way, her coy look over her shoulder doing nothing to help the situation behind my shorts. I flash her a warning look, but she just grins in the way she does. As soon as she's gone, I give the washing machine a good whack, and nod, satisfied, when I hear water rushing into the drum.

"Morning, Mum," I hear Jacob chime when Ava enters the kitchen, me following behind. He's scanning the boxes of cereal on the island, all six of them. Ava must have got every type we have from the pantry, covering all angles, I guess. "Where's my favorite?" he asks.

All angles, except Jacob's favorite. Ava's face falls, along with my heart, and Maddie gives her brother a quick kick in the shin. "Stupid," she snipes.

I die a little on the inside when Ava looks across at me, her eyes watering. "It's nothing." I shoot to the cupboard and snatch down Jacob's Pop-Tarts, quickly shoving two in the toaster. "See? Done."

"I'm sorry, Mum." My boy's face is so remorseful, and I'm torn between comforting him or going to Ava. My decision is made for me when Ava hastily escapes the kitchen. My shoulders drop, and I look to the kids as they watch their mum rush away, her hands wiping at her face. Fucking hell. After a quick, reassuring rub of their heads, I go after Ava, finding her in the downstairs bathroom snatching tissue from the roll.

"Ava, baby." I step in and close the door behind me. "It's no big deal." My heart cracks clean in two when she turns to face me, her bottom lip quivering, tears rolling down her cheeks.

"I don't even know what my son's favorite breakfast is." Her voice cracks and her chin drops. "What kind of mother am I?"

That right there sends me into the realms of crazy mad before I can stop it, my hand reaching forward and snatching away the tissue that's on its way to her face. "You stop that now," I order, more harshly than I meant. Her wide eyes watch me warily, the tears still streaming down her cheeks. Crowding her, I grab her face and push my forehead to hers, drilling into her with pissed-off eyes. "Never, ever, doubt your abilities as a mother, do you hear me?" She nods. "Good." I push my lips to hers and kiss her hard. "Now wipe those eyes and get your arse back in that kitchen."

"Okay." She doesn't argue or protest, sniffing back her emotion and pulling herself together. "Can I have the tissue back?"

"No." I take my thumbs and drag them across her cheeks, clearing up the evidence of her tears. "Off you go." Turning her by her shoulders, I walk her back to the kitchen, only releasing her after I've squeezed a little reassurance into her with a flex of my hands.

She nods in understanding and goes to the cupboard to get a plate for Jacob, taking his Pop-Tarts from the toaster and sliding them across the island to him. "Thanks, Mum." He bites his lip, flicking his eyes to me nervously.

"What?" Ava asks, looking to me, too.

"Nothing." I scoot over to the fridge and grab the peanut butter, handing it to Jacob, who proceeds to smother it over his Pop-Tarts.

"Oh." Ava's shoulders sag as she watches, a grimace growing across her face. "Of course he smothers his breakfast in peanut butter."

"You're disgusting," Maddie snorts as she leaves the kitchen. "I'm going to get showered."

"And I'm going to make lunchboxes." Ava swirls around and scans the cupboards.

"Top left," I remind her, going about finishing the coffee I started. When I'm done, I take a seat next to my boy and open my mouth for him to share, smiling as he pushes the last bit of his breakfast into my mouth. "Go get a shower," I tell him, and he's off quickly, leaving me and Ava alone in the kitchen.

I look across to my wife, thoughtful as I devour the jar of peanut butter. I've been so transfixed on all the major things she needs to learn that the simple things, such as the kids' favorite breakfast, never crossed my mind as something to get upset about. So trivial. Yet so eye-opening. One minute I'm high on hope, feeling the love and feelings pouring out of my wife, the next I'm being brought back down to earth by something stupid like Pop-Tarts. But, as I keep reminding myself, this is a marathon. Not a sprint.

I take a sip of my coffee as I watch Ava standing before the open fridge. She's still. Staring ahead. I frown and set my mug down, watching her shoulders begin to jump up and down discreetly. Concerned, I get up and go to her, turning her around until I have her face. Tears are gushing from her eyes, streaking down her cheeks, and splashing her T-shirt. "I don't know what they like in their lunchboxes, either," she sobs, each word a helpless croak.

"Hey." I lower my face to hers, nuzzling, coating my cheeks in her tears, too. We're in this together, stress, love, despair...and tears. Even if I'm not crying them, they're mine, too. I don't get the chance to pick her up; she grabs me first, throwing her arms around my neck and practically crawling up my front. What can I do? There's no easy fix. It's just a matter of time and that fucking thing called patience.

I carry her to a stool and get her comfortable on my lap, her legs straddling me, her face hiding in my chest, her tears soaking into my skin. With my face in her hair, I sigh, cuddling her close. Just giving her the time she needs to get this out of her system. It's just another part of this excruciating process. One more bump in this rocky road. How many more bumps, knock-backs, and cries are to come is daunting. But I need to be strong.

The man she married.

"Maddie loves Marmite in her sandwiches," I say into her hair. "And Jacob likes—"

"Peanut butter," she sniffles, dragging her heavy head up until she has my eyes.

I smile, taking her hands and holding them between our chests. "I'm with you all the way, baby. Highs and lows, good and bad, I'm here by your side. To help you, to wipe your tears, to love you. I love you so fucking much, lady." I kiss her cheek, hovering there for a few seconds, inhaling her into me. "Never give up, do you hear me? We have too much to fight for."

Her little sob is one full of emotion *and* relief. "Falling in love with you again was easy," she murmurs, so quietly. "This, though. The children. I love them. I didn't need to fall, I just looked at them and knew. But part of being a good mother isn't just loving them unconditionally. It's knowing them inside out. What they like, what they hate." Her eyes close, her reality too much to bear, and I clasp the back of her head gently and tug her into my embrace. "I feel more lost now than ever. Just the look on their faces when I get something wrong."

"Stop it," I order. "Right this minute."

"I just hate disappointing them."

"You don't disappoint them by forgetting what shit they like in their sandwich or what they have for breakfast. The only way you could disappoint them is by not loving them. By giving up. Am I going to have to take you upstairs and give you a Reminder Fuck?" I'm deadly serious, too, so she better not question my threat.

"A reminder?" Looking up at me, she sniffles through a little laugh.

"Yes, a reminder." I stand and she slides down my front to her feet. Slowly. Her palms on my bare chest. Her gaze there, too. Lust-filled. I smile on the inside, because no matter how shit the timing is, I've distracted her from her downheartedness, and for that I will never apologize. Distracting her has always been my area of expertise. I'm so thankful that's not lost. Placing my hand between her thighs, I cup her, forcing her to breathe in deep.

"Jesse." Her voice cracks with the fiery passion displayed in her brown eyes, though she makes no attempt to escape me. I drag my hand up to her hip on a smile and clamp lightly down on her tickle spot. That breath she was holding spills free, though she doesn't move a muscle.

"Tell me you'll never question your capabilities as a mother again," I command, flexing my hand just a fraction to give her a hint of the torture she's about to endure should she deny me. "Go on, baby."

"I'll never question it again." The words pour from her mouth fast, hardly audible.

I pinch down and she bucks on a sharp squeal. "What was that?" My smiling face gets close to her scowling face. "Say it again. Slowly so I can hear you."

"I'll. Never. Doubt. Myself. Again." The second she's spelled out my demand, she sucks in more air and holds it, waiting, bracing herself.

I hold her on the cusp of anticipation for a few moments, before shifting my hand to her thighs again and going in for the kill, slamming my mouth to hers and walking us to the nearest wall. This weapon, my ability to bring her back around, to distract her from some of her misery, is all I have, and I'll use it with no remorse or hesitation. The feel of her soft boobs squished against my hard chest, every curve she has melding into every sharp muscle on me, ramps up my need.

Not great when the kids are within screaming distance. Not great at all. It doesn't stop me attacking her lips with force, though, exploring her mouth as keenly as she's exploring mine, her fingernails ravaging my shoulders and back, her whimpers of pleasure sinking into my brain and making my head spin with want rather than frustration.

"Later." I bite on her lip and tug back, until it pops free of my teeth. "You are at my mercy, lady."

"Aren't I always?" Firm fists grab my hair and yank, pulling me back onto her mouth.

"And don't you forget it." We're all clashing lips and teeth, rushed and clumsy. She thrusts her hips forward, catching my tented shorts.

"Dad!" Maddie's shrill shriek lands in the kitchen with a bang and bats down my throbbing cock. Just like that. "Dad!"

I fold, unimpressed, though Ava laughs, taking the edge off my annoyance. Having her to myself, albeit traumatic at times, was a rare treat. Being able to indulge her when I wanted was a blessing, especially given the circumstances. That connection was key. Not having to worry about being caught by the kids was a weight off my mind. A light wave of guilt passes over me for being so selfish.

Growling, I yank myself away from Ava and push her hair off her sticky cheek. "No more tears," I order, heading to the kitchen door. "What's up?" I call to Maddie.

"I can't find my school uniform."

"Me either," Jacob chimes in, appearing at the top of the stairs in his boxers.

I wouldn't have a fucking clue where to start looking for school uniforms. And I just know Ava won't now, either. When she joins me at the bottom of the stairs, I half expect her to break down once more, and so do the twins, judging by their wary expressions. But instead, she breathes in and starts making her way up to them. "If we can't find them, you'll just have to go naked."

"Urghhhhh, gross!" Maddie laughs, watching as Ava passes, her eyes sparkling in happiness.

"Wouldn't bother me." Jacob shrugs and looks down at me, like *What's the problem?*

"He clearly gets his confidence from you," Ava calls, sending me a pointed look.

And I grin, so fucking proud of my wife. And of my kids. Of all of them. We're a team. We can get through anything.

Chapter 45

AVA

I wake this morning like I've woken every other morning for the past six weeks since the kids got home: with Jesse pressed into my back, his lips kissing down my spine slowly and lazily. It's blissful, mind-blanking. And, as always, I melt under the warmth of his mouth rousing me from my dreams. I close my eyes again and let him take me to paradise, let my body soften, and let my senses take over. The friction of our skin rubbing together takes me from warm to blazing. The feel of his morning arousal brushing my thighs and arse takes me from wanting to silently begging. The feel of his breath layering every part of my skin it touches takes me from hungry to starving. I reach back, pushing my fingers through his morning mess of hair, sighing my contentment, bowing my body into his.

"Morning, lady," he murmurs between nibbles of my shoulder, rolling his hips into my arse. "You ready for me?"

"Always." It's the truth. My body responds to him instinctively. My need for him is unrelenting.

One sharp thrust puts him inside me, deep and high, my fingers gripping his hair as I cry out, his teeth nipping my flesh as he grunts. I'm floating. I feel like I'm on cloud nine, just seconds after waking, and I know that's Jesse's intention each morning. To start my day being reminded of how wonderful we are. It really isn't necessary.

I look at this man and sizzle inside. I listen to him, no matter what he's saying, and take huge comfort from the deep baritone of his rough voice. I feel him touch me and just know we were always incomplete without each other. We are one.

Our bodies move in perfect sync, flowing together softly and carefully, like they're so familiar with each other. Because they are. I could never question the sense of right when we're intimate like this, even on my bad days, when frustration gets the better of me, when a whole day passes without so much as a speck of a memory to encourage me on.

Those days have turned into weeks. It's been six weeks without anything, no memory, no flashbacks, leaving me with only the scraps of what I have, of what I built before my brain decided to grind to a halt where my past is concerned. Like a cork has been wedged in the hole, stopping the flow. It hasn't escaped Jesse's notice. His keen eyes are always watching me, his ears always listening. I've given him nothing for weeks. I can see the disappointment on his face no matter how hard he tries to disguise it with love.

I feel under pressure. The only relief I'm getting is when we're making love, when he manages to blank my mind completely, or when I go to yoga with Zara. She's still unaware of my accident and condition, and that's great, because she's my other source of escape. I never feel like I'm disappointing her. I never feel like she's looking at me as if I should know something. My new friend is respite that I so need.

I know Jesse and I are building new memories, wonderful

memories, but every day I still stare at that huge wall of photographs in the family room and wonder where the hell it's all gone.

"Stop it," he whispers, pulling out sharply and flipping me onto my back. My heavy gaze lifts to his green eyes, eyes that scream a thousand emotions each time I look into them, reflecting worry back at me this morning. "We're still us. We still have the children. I still love you, and you still love me. That's all that matters." On a swivel of his tight hips, he enters me again, falling to his forearms. The weight of him calms me, reminding me that I may have lost many memories of this man, but at least I still have him in the flesh. The unrelenting pain that strikes me when I think of being without him is enough to tell me that where I am is where I'm supposed to be. Not that I need a reminder. Not when every fiber of my being is telling me so.

I reach for his back and run my palms across the tight planes, feeling him. "That's all I need," I affirm, swallowing when he withdraws slowly, purposely slowly, his eyes on mine as he drives forward again, exact and smooth.

"Nothing can break us." He sweeps in and takes my mouth gently, and my legs come up to his waist to hold him everywhere I can. "That's it, baby. Hold tight." The change in pace, from grinds to deep drives, has me struggling to maintain our kiss, my tongue becoming erratic in its movements, almost frenzied.

"You nearly there?" He pulls back, not needing an answer, but wanting to see my face when I tip the edge. Wedging his fists into the mattress, he ups the ante, mixing plunges with swivels, flexing sharply and then slowly. I'm lost in him, amazed through my pleasure of the heights he takes me to. To the places where I can forget. Where nothing exists except him and me and the passion we share.

The sweat on his brow sparkles in the dusky light, his face

beginning to strain as my release surges forward and detonates, instantly making me shake with the force, the tingling sensations too much, my flesh too sensitive. And he knows, because his movements stop and he puts pressure where I need it, stemming the sensitivity, as he comes hard, his roar suppressed, his face red with the pressure of blood rushing to his head. My internal walls grab him greedily and milk him dry, the heat of his essence pouring deeply into me.

Jesse drops onto me in a heap of exhausted male, crowding me, still buried deep, where he will be for the next ten minutes while he snoozes on me, sporadically nuzzling and kissing my wet neck, whispering sweet nothings in my ear. And I hold him and savor the moment I cherish each morning before I have to get up and face my day.

I breathe into his shoulder as we settle, constricting him, getting him as close as I possibly can. In my own silent way, I'm telling him that I'm happy to remain where I am. It's not like I have much else to do. Work isn't on the cards for me just yet.

I tried a few weeks ago, convinced Jesse to let me go back to my office, and he did, albeit reluctantly. It took just ten minutes for me to realize I was out of my depth—ten minutes of staring at the paperwork on my desk, ten minutes of Jesse watching me from the couch while I demanded my brain to tell me what to do, and ten failed attempts to enter my password on the computer, before I finally crumpled and gave in to the fact that I was of no use at the club.

I didn't like it, not one little bit, and it wasn't only because I felt so useless. That woman who works for us can't keep her eyes off Jesse, and I could see clearly that my presence wasn't welcome. I squeeze my eyes, trying to remember her name. Small things, simple things that I'm learning are slipping from my memory as fast as they're put there. Like names. *Cherry.* I exhale, thanking my brain for giving me the information I'm looking for. I only wish it would give me my memories, too.

Am I any use at all? I scold myself the moment I question my worth, because there's one valuable job I'm doing. Being a mum as best I can, though I sometimes question my ability there. Like when Jacob brought home some simple maths homework. Simple equations that I know how to solve from my school days, way before the cutoff in my memory. Yet I couldn't do them. My brain simply wouldn't work.

And like when Maddie and I went shopping for a dress for Raya and Drew's wedding. I picked out many outfits, and each one was rejected. I didn't even know my daughter's style. That day is one I'd like to forget, made worse by the fact that when we flagged a taxi to take us home, I couldn't even remember our damn address. It was gone, out of my head like Jesse hadn't repeated it to me a thousand times in recent weeks. Thankfully, my daughter saved me.

But she couldn't save me from the wrath of her father when we rolled up in a taxi. I was supposed to call him to collect us, but I had hoped that I could use the ride home to shed my melancholy mood. I did a good job, until Jesse went off the handle. And then I folded, crying, while Maddie showed her father *her* wrath. It's all so fraught. We're all tinkering on the edge of complete meltdown, and my stupid fucking memory is the cause, my brain's refusal to give me what I need, what we all need, to carry on with our lives with any sense of normality.

And then there are the moments like just now. Moments when my brain is wiped clean of the shit tarnishing it. Moments when Jesse helps me escape. And there are moments with Maddie and Jacob. Moments when I look at those beautiful kids and try to come to terms with the fact that they are mine. How lucky I am. How wonderful they are, how they can make me smile even on my darkest days. Their little jokes about their father, how they relay the stories they know of our love affair. I could listen to them for hours.

"That's enough of the downheartedness today." His voice, muffled in my neck, is still stern. "It's Raya's hen night tonight."

I'm surprised he's reminded me. I just know he's battling his instinct to hold me back. To not let me go. And I know he's read Kate her rights. Silly man. That woman hasn't had a drink for nearly a year. She'll be even more ravenous for some girlie time and alcohol than I am.

"You mean to say you're releasing me for the night?" I tease. I shouldn't poke him. I'm looking forward to this evening so much, just to spend some time with Kate. If he withdraws his consent, there will be fireworks.

Emerging from his hiding place, he cocks one eyebrow, his lips forming a straight, displeased line. "Are you testing me?"

I stiffen when his hand slides to my hip. "Never," I say, quickly holding my breath. He gets me every time. I don't have a hope of fighting him off, his powerful body laughing in the face of my small frame.

"And you will be sensible, won't you?" A tiny dig of his wicked fingers into my flesh jolts me, and I nod frantically. "And you will stay in contact with me, won't you?" Another dig, and another jerk of my body and head. "And before you leave, you're going to let me pin you down and come all over your gorgeous boobs, aren't you?"

I can't find it in me to agree. Not that he desires my agreement. He does what he damn well likes *when* he damn well likes. "You want to mark me?"

"Actually, you like to mark me." He points down to his pec. "I miss it."

I can't help my frown. "Miss what?"

"The tidy little bruise on my chest that has kept me company for the past twelve years. I feel a little incomplete without it." The slight tilt of his head spells out his want. "Suck, baby." He rolls over and points to the area he wants me.

I'm bemused, but I'm getting kind of used to some of the bizarre shit I'm learning about our marriage. And to be fair, I won't deny myself a few more minutes of us in bed together. So I straddle his waist and latch onto his solid flesh, sucking him into my mouth as I look up through my lashes to his satisfied face. The man is a nut. And so am I, since I'm going along with all the madness he throws at me. "Happy?" I ask, inspecting the perfect purple circle.

"Delirious." He gets up off the bed and tucks me in. "I'll sort the kids for school."

I watch him pull on some boxers before he leaves the room, my eyes nailed to his solid back until he disappears.

I relax and think forward to tonight. I need a good drink. To numb myself of feeling. And that's just what I plan to do.

Chapter 46

I sit in the kitchen trying not to think about Ava upstairs getting ready for her night out. Lots of women together, backed up with lots of alcohol. And one of them gave birth six weeks ago, and according to Sam is champing at the bit for a night of freedom since she's finished six weeks of breastfeeding. I forced myself to agree. I'm regretting it now. Grabbing my phone, I dial Ava's mother.

"What's wrong?" she answers in greeting.

"Nothing's wrong." My face twists. "What are you up to tonight?" I ask, all casual, catching the kids' eyes where they're sitting at the island finishing off their dinner. They know my game. I raise my finger to my lips, a sign to keep my secret.

"I'm out," Elizabeth declares. "Bridge and cocktails."

Fuck it. "Okay, have a lovely time." I hang up and beat the marble worktop with my fingertips, thinking. "Ah!" I quickly dial John. "Hey, big man," I chirp down the line.

"No." His gruff, flat reply has me frowning.

"What?"

"It's Raya's hen night. No, I won't watch the kids so you can stalk your wife."

I snarl. "Some friend you are."

"Fuck you. Have you heard from Sarah?"

My mood plummets further. "No, why? Should I have?"

"Just checking. I'm hoping she's gonna fuck off soon, because, frankly, I'm sick of looking at her miserable face."

I flinch on Sarah's behalf. "Tell her to go, John."

"I can't do it. I've fucking tried, but your damn uncle Carmichael is in my ear like an annoying fucking gnat, telling me to do right by her or he'll haunt my motherfucking arse."

I smile a little, but I'm mad, too. "You owe her nothing. Uncle Carmichael owes her nothing."

"Tell that to a dead man," he grunts, hanging up.

I fall into thought, going back to my past briefly. Then I catch the kids giving me wary looks. "What?"

"Don't do it, Dad," Maddie singsongs. "She'll tear your head off and use it as a football."

"You'll regret it," Jacob warns.

Scowling at my kids, I march out of the kitchen and head upstairs where Ava's getting ready. So what am I supposed to do? Sit home all night worrying to death?

I find her in her underwear standing in the mirror. I groan. What's she trying to do to me? "You look lovely," I grunt, slumping my arse on the bed.

She looks at me in the reflection, a smile playing at the corners of her nude lips as she tweaks her hair into position. "I'm not dressed yet."

I shrug, pouting like a moody schoolboy. "You still look lovely."

"You come to mark me?"

I look to the door, hearing the kids in the kitchen downstairs. My scope for marking is limited.

"What do you think of this?"

I return my eyes to Ava, finding her holding up a little black dress. I just shake my head. Negative. "What about this?" A green thing appears, and once again I reject it. She sighs, sweeping her arm out to the wardrobe. "Choose a dress, any dress."

Good. She's getting the hang of this. It takes me five seconds flat to find something suitable—a high-necked, long-sleeved, full-length jersey dress. "Perfect," I declare.

"I'm not wearing that." The dress is snatched from my hand and put back on the rail. She quickly takes another down and goes back to the bedroom. "And stop sulking."

"You're not wearing that, either," I call, trudging after her. She's pulling the stupid gold thing on by the time I make it to the bedroom, a salacious grin on her face. "Why'd you have to be so damn beautiful?"

My wife is a goddess, and I know every other man on the planet must think so, too. And in that little gold number, she's a shimmering goddess. Her cheekbones are also shimmering, and her eyes are smoked out, making them smolder madly. They're "take me to bed" eyes.

"Don't look any man in the eye," I tell her, falling to the chair in the corner of our bedroom. I'm slumped. Moody. I can't help it.

She wanders over and slowly turns, looking over her shoulder at me. With my chin still low, I lift my gaze, dragging it over her exposed back until I reach her eyes. "Zip me up?"

"No," I grunt, eliciting a cute twitch of her lips.

"Please?" It's a purr, one that hits my dick and takes it from semi-erect to rock.

"Why are you doing this to me?" It's a serious question. Just look at her. This beauty, still in her prime, glowing before me like some otherworldly creature. I've tried to reason with myself all day. Told myself she needs to let her hair down and have some time with her girlfriends. Yet that primal, possessive streak in me has only grown by the hour, and now I'm in two minds whether I'd get away with bolting her to the bed. I ponder that for a second, thoughtful, my head tilting as I weigh up the option. I'd get away with it. There's nothing she could do to stop me.

"Don't even think about it, Ward." Her tone is warning. And ignored. I love how she reads my mind.

"And what will you do about it?"

"Divorce." She points to her back again as my jaw drops. "Zip me up."

"No."

"Fine, I'll get Kate to do it when she gets here." She saunters off, all strut and arse. I'm out of that chair like lightning, and I've captured her before she makes it to the door.

"Jesse!" she squeals as I throw her over my shoulder and backtrack to the bed. It's doesn't escape my notice that her screech of my name was more laughed than angrily yelled. She was prepared for my trample.

Flipping her on the bed, I pull off my T-shirt and capture her wrists, pinning her down, straddling her stomach. She blows some stray wisps of hair from her face and blinks up at me. And she smiles. She knows what's coming. I get her hands under my knees to secure them, and pull my cock from my shorts.

"Tell me you love me," I demand, my voice already displaying the hunger in me.

"I love you." She complies in a heartbeat, and I smile.

"Tell me you only have eyes for me." I pull a long stroke down my shaft, watching her as she watches me.

"I only have eyes for you." She licks her lips, flipping her gaze up. "Fuck, you look lethally sexy when you get yourself off."

"Watch your mouth." I drop one hand to the mattress, slowly starting to pump my fist, electric energy sizzling all over my skin. And I dip, taking her mouth greedily. It doesn't take me long to find my rhythm, my body stiff with pleasure.

"Dad! Mum! Everyone is here!" Maddie's yell hits my hearing

like a foghorn, followed by the sound of her feet pounding the stairs. *No! No, no, no!*

"Fuck!" I drop my cock, hissing when it springs back and hits my lower stomach. "You have to be fucking kidding me."

"Quick!" Ava starts scrambling off the bed as I rearrange my shorts, sitting on the edge to conceal my mammoth erection behind the thin material. I'm sweating, and not with worry. I feel like an unexploded bomb. *Motherfucker!*

My baby girl lands in the bedroom, full of excitement. "Betty's here, too!" Her face drops when she finds me on the edge of the bed. "What are you so grumpy about?"

"Nothing," I all but bark. Ava chuckles and puts herself in front of me, indicating her zip again.

"We'll be down in a tick." She looks over her shoulder and raises her perfect brows. "Once your dad has zipped me up."

I pout, taking the fastener and slowly pulling it up. "I'm not happy," I declare, making sure my displeasure is voiced, no matter how plain it is on my face. "You'll pay for this later."

"Yeah, yeah." She breezes out of the room, leaving me to talk my dick down and get my T-shirt back on. Torture. Fucking torture.

I make my way downstairs once I'm decent, wandering into the kitchen to find the whole gang here. Sam has Betty suspended from his arm in her car seat, and Maddie is cooing over her. Drew is helping himself to a beer, and the girls are in a gaggle by the island, praising each other's dresses.

"What's crawled up your arse?" Drew asks, handing me a beer as I dump myself down on a stool.

I don't need to tell them. Sam laughs, followed by Drew. Everyone in my life knows how bad I struggle. I tip the bottle to my lips and almost spit out my beer when Kate swooshes around to face me. "Fucking hell, Kate!" I choke, wiping at my mouth. Her strapless dress is a decent length, to the knee, but her boobs are a bench under her chin. I blink rapidly and look away, finding Sam. He's okay with that? I cock my head in question, but he just smiles, studying Kate's epic rack.

"If we can keep them, that would be fine by me." He places Betty's car seat on the island, joining me on the next stool.

"Too much?" Kate asks, pulling her red tresses over her front so they splay on her chest.

Raya laughs, pouring wine into three glasses. Now, Raya, she looks perfectly presentable, her long-sleeved dress scooping her neck at an acceptable level, the black material a stark contrast to her light blond hair. My approval is short-lived. She turns away, revealing the back. Or lack of it. Her entire back is exposed, all the way down to her arse. I sigh, wondering if it's that unreasonable side everyone's always telling me I have, or if it's simply age.

"Easy on the wine," I grunt, waving my bottle at Raya as she dishes out the glasses.

She smiles as she takes her first sip. "You're not going to invade my hen night, are you?"

I scowl, casting my eyes to my supposed mates. Neither of them look at me. "No." I would, if I had someone to watch the kids while I invade.

"Good." Kate chinks the girls' glasses. "I've done six weeks breastfeeding. My nipples can't take any more. I'm going to get so pissed." She looks at Sam, who rolls his eyes, though doesn't refute her intention. "If I'm still standing by the time I get home, I want you to slap me to the ground." She takes a glug of wine. "Because I'll feel like an underachiever if I'm not flat on my face."

I'm coughing again, looking to my mate to sort her out. But, again, all I get is a roll of his eyes. This is ridiculous. Wine, the dresses, the talk of getting plastered. I rack my brain for someone, anyone, who I could call on to pop over and watch the kids. I come up blank. Maybe I could take them with me. A little adventure around London.

Drew nudges me in the side, his lips straight. "They'll be fine."

Easy for him to say. Am I the only one who's worried? "Someone needs to stop this circus."

"I value my life too much." Drew slaps my shoulder with a firm thwack, making my teeth chink on the top of my bottle. "Come on, then, girls." Clapping his hands, he starts rounding them up, herding them to the front door.

"She'll be fine, Dad." Jacob appears by my side, offering up his jar of the good stuff.

I strain a smile at the cute little fucker and plunge my finger into the pot. "I know, mate," I say, if only to reassure him. She'll be fine. How many times have I told myself that over the years? And look what happened.

"I wish I could go." Maddie's statement has the lick of my finger faltering, my alarmed eyes looking down at my girl. Christ, that's a whole other form of stress. The thought alone sends me cold. Or colder than I already am. Now I really wouldn't think twice about locking my baby girl in a cupboard. "Not until you're fifty," I tell her, following Sam out of the kitchen, softening when I catch sight of Betty sleeping peacefully in her car seat. It seems like only yesterday that my two were that big. Where has the time gone?

The kids race upstairs to their rooms, while I head to the door. I catch Ava before she steps out of the house, pulling her back. The look on her glowing face is a sure sign that she's ready for me. She looks bored. Crowding her, I kiss her cheek. "Don't talk to strangers."

"I won't."

"Put your belt on in the car."

"I will." She reaches up on her tippy-toes and kisses my cheek.

"Drink safely."

"Yes, sir."

"Sit down if you feel woozy."

"Okay."

"Call me if you need me."

Pulling back, she smiles, stroking my cheek affectionately. "I'll be fine."

Why does everyone keep saying that? "Answer me when I text you." I'm annoying her now, though she continues to humor me.

"I will."

"Good girl." I smother her with my lips, my arms refusing to let her go. "Have a good time." I sigh and force myself to release her. The anxiety inside me, it's never gone, but now it seems to be worse than ever. "I love you."

"I know." She dances off to Drew's car.

"I'm dropping them off and picking them up," Drew says. He knows I need to hear that. "Will call you when we're on our way home."

I nod and quickly shut the door before I give in to temptation and race after her to drag her back to the house. The ache inside me may be unreasonable and my mood overboard, but after we've been through what we've been through, I don't think it'll ever leave me. It's a curse. A weight around my neck.

But I mustn't let it pull me under.

CHAPTER 47

I have not one hope of sleeping until she's home. So I sit on the couch flicking the channels, restless and constantly checking my Rolex. The call I've been waiting for finally comes at one in the morning. I scramble to answer it and listen to Drew tell me they're all drunk but safe and that he's on the way to drop off Ava.

A huge weight lifts from my shoulders, and for the first time this evening, I relax. And then I do something utterly stupid. I race upstairs, strip, and hop into bed, turning off the lamp. Because of course she'll believe that I've been sleeping peacefully while she's been out tearing up the town.

It's almost a half hour later when I hear the front door close. And a few moments after that, the sound of her shoes hits the tile floor. Then... silence. I fight the urge to go down and find her. She's home. She's safe. Nothing can happen to her now.

Then I hear a bang and I'm like a bullet out of our bed, pulling my shorts on as I fly down the stairs. I crash into the kitchen and find it empty.

"Ava?" I call, backing up, listening. Nothing. My heart rate shifts a few gears. "Ava?" My attempt not to sound frantic isn't working. "Ava, where the hell are you?" I hurry down the hall, peeking in every room, finding them all empty.

Until I arrive at the family room. I breathe out when I see her standing at the foot of our wall. "Baby?"

She doesn't turn, just raises a finger to a picture, a picture of us on our wedding day, and traces the edge of my face. "I remembered something earlier." She's slurring. She's definitely slurring. Drunk? Plastered, maybe. But she had a flashback? Turning her eyes onto me, heavy eyes, drunk eyes, she points at my bare chest. "You stole my birth control pills."

"Ah."

Guilty. As. Charged.

I hold my finger to my nose, trying to think of a way to wriggle out of this. Of all the things she could have remembered? "'Stole' is a very harsh word." There's no way out.

"What word would you use, then?" Her bare feet are treading the carpet.

"Do you need the toilet?" Or is she starting to stagger?

"Don't change the subject." Her mumbled words are getting hard to decipher. "Why'd you steal them?"

This again? I force my eye roll into hiding and go collect her before she face plants on the carpet. Lifting her into my arms, I take her up to bed. "Because I was madly in love with you and I thought you'd leave me when you found out my dirty little secrets."

Her scoff takes some effort. "You mean your sex club. And the fact you're an alcoholic. And the fact that you were a manwhore?"

"Yes, all of that," I say, taking the stairs. And a whole pile of other shit, too. "Now, are you done?"

"I had a wonderful night!" she sings, throwing her head back and her arms up, forcing me to shift my hold or risk her tumbling from my arms. I guess that's a yes. "And do you know what?" She levels a straight face on me.

Do I want to know? "What?"

"I fancy you so much," she mumbles, her head falling onto my shoulder.

"I should hope so."

"Why, because you're my husband?"

"No, because I'm fucking hot."

A hysterical bout of laughter erupts, and I'm forced to shush her before she wakes the kids. Too late. We meet a sleepy-looking pair when we get to the top of the stairs. "Go back to bed," I tell them as they mirror each other, rubbing at their drowsy eyes. "Mum's just a little drunk."

"A little?" Jacob looks as disapproving as I feel, though Maddie seems amused.

"I'm a lot drunk," Ava declares, wriggling free of my arms. I grumble as I set her on her feet, holding her arm tightly. "And I love you two!"

"Oh God." Maddie cringes when Ava lavishes her with affection. "Mum, please!"

"You're the best things that ever happened to me." She turns her attention onto an alarmed Jacob.

"Don't tell Dad that," my boy quips drily, letting Ava do what she's going to do. "I think it's your bedtime, Mum."

"I think so, too." She pulls Jacob into her chest and squeezes him, his cheeks all squished against her chest. "You're just as handsome as your dad."

"I know," he mumbles, rolling his eyes at me. Maddie can't contain her amusement, chuckling to herself.

"Come on." I claim my drunken wife before she makes even more of a show of herself, flicking my head to the kids for them to get back to bed. Their smiles are fond as I walk Ava to the bedroom, her steps clumsy. "In you get." I unzip the back of her dress and lower her to the sheets. She proceeds to writhe around the bed. "Keep still."

"Are you going to fuck me, Jesse Ward? I'll scream real loud."

"Behave, lady." I chuckle, dragging the gold material down her body and casting it aside. "Underwear."

Her arms catapult upward, landing on the pillows. "Strip me bare."

"I did that years ago. Right down to your soul."

She quiets down a little, squinting to look at me. "I missed you tonight."

"Good." When she's down to just her skin, I remove my shorts and climb in beside her, ignoring the stench of alcohol oozing from her pores. I remain still while she finds her favorite place on my chest, flopping down heavily on a deep sigh. I wrap her in my arms and smile to myself as her breathing becomes shallow.

"And now I'll miss you while I'm asleep." Her murmured words are just what I need to hear. She's glad to be back. With me.

CHAPTER 48

Ava had a terrible hangover the next day. I was smug. Couldn't help it. But a few days later she still looked washed out. Of course, I put the call in to her doctor to check I wasn't missing something, and he assured me all was well. Just something going around, apparently. She's now been laid up for nearly a week, though she managed to go to yoga yesterday. I was skeptical, but she insisted. I even let her go for a coffee with that new friend of hers. See? I can be reasonable.

I look at the kids as they eat their breakfast, thinking they look a little pasty, too. Or am I being paranoid?

"You two feeling okay?" I ask.

They both nod, barely even looking at me, their eyes glued to their iPads instead. I wander over and snatch the tablets from their hands, earning a couple of disgruntled moans. "Shower. We have Uncle Drew's wedding to go to."

They grumble, both dragging their feet as they go.

"Good little children." I smirk as they both give me the death stare before they disappear. Ava's phone rings, and I swipe it up from the side table, looking at the screen as I make my way upstairs to my check up on my wife.

"Zara," I muse, connecting the call. Time for me to introduce myself to this new friend. "Hi." I hear a few rustles, and then the phone goes dead. I frown down at the screen as a text message lands.

Call me when you're free. Just checking how you're feeling.

I take the liberty of answering for Ava.

It's Jesse. Ava's husband. We're on our way to a wedding. I'll get her to call you tomorrow.

Ah! The famous husband. I've heard lots about you ;-)

Did she just fucking wink at me? I give the phone a dubious glare, wondering what exactly Ava's been telling her that warrants a wink. I don't know, but I make a mental note to ask.

I'm surprised when I find Ava sitting in front of the mirror, straightening her hair. "You look perkier." I chuck her phone on the bed and lower to the floor behind her, framing her with my knees, shifting in close until my groin is wedged up close to her lower back. "Your yoga friend just texted you. I told her you'd call her tomorrow."

"You read and answered my message?" she asks in shock.

"Yes." I show no remorse, because I have none. "So what have you been telling this Zara about me?"

Ava's eyes narrow playfully as she sweeps her cheeks with a makeup brush, adding a glow to her cheekbones. "That you're a god. That you're possessive, unreasonable, and controlling, but it's all because you love me with every bone in your body."

"And every drop of blood in my veins," I add, giving her a

devilish smirk, but it falls when I notice she doesn't return it. She's looking pensive. "Hey, what's up?" Is she worried about the wedding? The public appearance in front of so many people? I don't think it could be that. She's seemed okay this past week, her bug aside. Sometimes quiet, but that's to be expected. I've gotten used to her losing herself in her thoughts every now and then, concluding that she's trying to recall something. There have been no monumental breakthroughs in her memories. We've just kind of fallen back into life. And it's been good. Relatively normal, aside from the odd thing she forgets every now and then. According to her doctor, that's normal, too.

I can't deny, though, I still feel so uncertain about so many things. Yet one thing I'm sure of is our beautiful, unrelenting love. But love isn't always beautiful. Sometimes it's tragic. *Most* of the time it's tragic. It cuts you up, tears you apart, fucking suffocates you, but it's the only thing that can put you back together again. It's a sadistic bastard as well as the most enriching, comforting thing in this world. And that's what I've survived on—my love, our love, because if I've learned anything, it's that time stops for no one. Life continues no matter if you're happy with where yours has been or where it is heading. You can't stop it. You just have to tilt the scale and make it the best it can be. Change the direction toward somewhere you want to go.

And that's exactly what I've done. And I thought I'd done a good job. So why is she looking so unsure all of a sudden?

Placing her makeup brush on the floor, she stares at me in the mirror, biting her lip, thinking. "Is it your head?" I ask. "Do you still feel off?" Oh shit, has she had a breakthrough and not told me, maybe because she's shocked? Horrified? Or, worse still, questioning why she's in this marriage? Piles and piles of reasons for her despondency all land on me at once, and I filter through the barrage, trying to dwindle it down to anything obvious.

"I'm pregnant."

Everything except that.

There's some kind of blockage happening between my brain and mouth, rendering me unable to speak. Pregnant? How? The blockage suddenly dislodges, and I immediately start shaking like a motherfucker, my body cold. "I'm sorry, what?"

Her eyes, sharp but cautious, study me in the reflection. "I...am...pregnant." This time, she spells it out, as if I didn't catch the bombshell the first time.

Pregnant. Pregnant. Pregnant.

"Pregnant," I finally manage, swallowing hard. "How?"

She shrugs, looking a little timid. "The antibiotics, I think. Sometimes they interfere with the pill."

"Fucking hell," I all but breathe, slapping the ball of my fist into my forehead. The irony doesn't escape me. It doesn't escape Ava either, going by the slight twist of her lips. When we met and she turned my world upside down, I spent weeks sneakily stealing her pills in a wild and reckless mission to get her pregnant to ensure I could keep her forever. It was no accidental pregnancy, not on my part, anyway. And I wouldn't change a damn thing, either. I adore my kids, wouldn't be without them. But it doesn't mean I want more.

"I knew you wouldn't take it well." Her soft murmur breaks into the bedlam that is my thoughts.

I'm astounded by her calmness. Why isn't she spiraling into meltdown with me? "I'm fifty, Ava." I get up and start pacing the room. "I'm way too old to be a dad again."

"No, you're not." My wife sounds irked, and I look to find she really is, her face bunched, annoyed. "Parents are getting older all the time." She shrugs. "At least that's what my midwife said."

"You've been to the midwife?" Without me? "When?"

"I got a taxi to the doctor's office after you dropped me at yoga yesterday. I needed to be sure before I gave you the news that I knew would send you into orbit."

Orbit? How about another fucking galaxy? "Pregnant!" I bark for the sake of it. "I can't believe this." It's really sinking in now, visions of Kate and Sam's weary faces since Betty arrived popping into my mind.

I've done my time. My days of shitty nappies and sleepless nights are done with. "Oh my God," I sputter, marching to the bathroom and punching the shower on, muttering all kinds of nonsensical shit as I strip down. I get under the spray and hope the cold water will wake me up from my nightmare.

"You're taking it rather well." She quips, appearing beyond the shower door, watching me scrub every inch of my body.

"Ava, let's put this into perspective." I get close to the screen so she can see *just* how fucking panicked I am. "When this baby is ten, I'll be nearly sixty-one." I shudder. Fuck me, I've only just got used to fifty. That's a lie. I'm not used to it at all, and, in fact, in my mind I'm still actually forty. Sixty? I'll blink and it'll be here. "The twins will be in university and I'll be taking our youngest to school on a fucking mobility scooter."

I want to cry, whereas Ava just sighs, letting me babble on. Good. I have plenty to say. "And I'll have to make at least three stops on the way to piss because my old bladder won't be able to hold a cup of coffee for longer than ten minutes." I stagger back, out of breath, half assisted by my panic, half assisted by my spew of words without catching my breath. This is awful!

"You're being ridiculous." She stalks off, leaving me heaving like a worn-out racehorse, all alone in the cold shower. "I have the scan on Tuesday. Come if you want, and if you don't want to that's fine. Don't think I can't do this on my own."

And just like that I'm snapped out of my meltdown. She'll do it on her own? Without me? I flinch, the thought *more* than stinging.

And then I frown to myself, wondering what on earth has gotten into me. And I think *real* hard. I think about what the actual issue here is, and it isn't another baby being around. It's me. My issue. That damn fucker called age. That's the problem. That's what's got me all in a pickle. It has nothing to do with being a daddy again. But everything to do with my stupid complex.

And maybe another factor is the thought of having another someone to worry about. More anxiety. Fuck, another person to obsess about will be a strain that could finish me off. My heart's speeding more just thinking about it.

I breathe in and breathe out, trying to talk myself down. And I think about Ava's face just now. How calm and serene she seemed, even when I tipped the meltdown scales.

"Fuck," I mumble. Can I do this? I look to the bathroom door. Can I do this for Ava? Good Lord, I have to. I can get over all of my issues because I want my wife to be happy. Especially now. Especially after everything. She needs this. Maybe I do, too. And the kids. Something special and new to focus on.

I drag my hands down my scratchy cheeks. "God damn you, Ward," I say to myself, stepping out of the shower and grabbing a towel. I have some serious sucking up to do. I feel like a total wanker.

"Ava?" I say timidly, creeping into the dressing room. She has the wide-leg trousers of her navy Ralph Lauren suit on, a cream silk shirt held against her front. And she's watching me. I'm about to launch into my apology, but she beats me to it.

"We may have laughed about it that time when we visited Betty, but you know what? I'm happy this has happened. I'm thrilled, in fact. Maybe this is just what we need. All of us. Me, you, and the kids. A new life to channel our energy and attention on. Something to look forward to. Something to distract us from the shit storm of the past couple months." She breathes in and shoves her arms through the sleeves of her shirt, while I remain still in the doorway, feeling so ashamed. She's thinking the same as me, though she got there a lot quicker than me, clearly. She's been sitting on this since yesterday. She's been scared to tell me, and I've just demonstrated every reason why. "But don't you worry your fifty-year-old head, Ward." Reaching out, she yanks the cropped jacket of her suit down and shoves it on, fixing the collar of her blouse. "We'll be fine without you."

"Jesus, enough with the knives to my fucking heart, woman. The first did enough damage." But every man at some time in his life needs putting in his place. And for me, no woman on this planet could ever do it better than my wife.

"You asked for it." She storms past me, but I just catch her wrist, jolting her to a stop. Both of us silent, I take her by the waist and lift her onto one of the cabinets, muscling my way to between her thighs. Her face is sulky as I claim her hands and put them on my shoulders. "Snap out of it."

"That's rich coming from you," she snorts, flexing her fingers on my wet shoulders, her eyes focused there. I inwardly smile. "Imagine life without me," I tell her, and she physically jolts. "Not nice, is it?"

"What's your point?"

"My point is you shouldn't say you'll be fine without me, because you won't be. And neither will I without you."

She breathes out, exasperated. "Anyone would think I'd just told you I have one month to live." Her twitch is immediate, and so is my growl. "Sorry," she squeaks, lips pressed together, probably a ploy to stop her saying any more stupid shit.

"Don't think because you're pregnant I won't slap your arse silly."

"Wouldn't be the first time," she grunts, and then she gasps, her eyes wide. "Oh my God!"

My head drops back, my eyes closing. "Yes, I did that," I confirm. I don't get all excited at this morsel of a memory, and I don't search for more. This is how it is now. How it'll always be. Little pieces here and there, and maybe one day in a few hundred years, she'll have the whole story. I'm hoping minus a few not so pretty parts. Like Lauren. And the accident. And the... I let my thoughts trail off there and bat back the growing guilt. I have more important things to think about. Especially now.

"You animal," Ava teases, and I laugh. She never fucking fought me. "So what now, then?"

"Now," I say, slowly bending at the waist, keeping our eye contact as I lower my head. "Now we have another baby." It's that simple. I drop a kiss on her tummy and take pure pleasure from her happy beam. How could I deny her this? Bottom line, I couldn't. And I won't.

"When should we tell the twins?" she asks, losing her delight for a split second. She's worried. There's no need. I saw Maddie with Betty the other day. She was besotted. And Jacob is so laid-back he's nearly horizontal. They'll be fine.

"Let's focus on Drew and Raya for today." I lift her down and drop a light kiss on her forehead. "Let's not steal their thunder."

She smiles, and her eyes sparkle brightly. It's the sparkle that's been absent for far too long. So I'm gonna be a dad again? I roll my naked shoulders and smooth my hair in the mirror. I must be the best-looking fifty-year-old dad who ever lived.

Chapter 49

The ceremony was beautiful, the small church in a village on the outskirts of the city crammed with white orchids and a few dozen guests. Kate and Ava cried like a pair of babies. And Raya looked out of this world in a long satin gown. I don't think I've ever seen Drew smile so wide. The man looked like he was walking on clouds the entire service, and little Georgia was grinning from ear to ear.

We finally make it to the elaborate tent in a field in the quaint village after being accosted for photographs and ordered into various groups here and there. I'm not surprised when we break through the billowing voile sheets at the entrance to find Sam with a beer in one hand, Betty in the other. Maddie is off like a rocket when she spots Georgia helping to ladle punch into glasses for guests, ever willing to help, and Jacob goes about finding our names on the place cards around the tables.

I leave Ava to use the ladies and approach Sam, my eyes nailed to the bundle of joy lying across his left arm. One minute my hands are empty, the next they're full of a baby. I look at Sam, alarmed. "What are you doing?"

"Just give me a minute; I forgot to bring in Betty's changing bag from the car." He's gone before I can protest, leaving me to fend for myself.

Like a big oaf, I carefully negotiate her into the cradle of my arm. *So* carefully. I'm all nervous. I did this a million times with my own, but that was a long, *long* time ago. I look down at her adorable little face. Her hair is Kate all over, red and vibrant, even now, but she has Sam's cute nose. She's awake, her hands at her mouth. I remember the signs. She's hungry. And the flakes of skin scattered between the red strands of her hair are signs of cradle cap. I remember that, too. I smile, taking my index finger to her cheek and stroking her baby-soft skin.

A million memories come back to me, times I'd forgotten recently amid the chaos of our lives. The times the twins would lie on my chest and snooze, Ava curled into my side. The times I juggled feeding both of them, getting it down to a fine art. How quickly I figured out that Jacob was more patient than Maddie, so I'd see to her dirty nappy first. The joy I used to get at bath time, watching their little limbs splash the shallow water. And that smell. The smell I couldn't get enough of. Pure, perfect baby scent. It was like a sedative, could send me to sleep. And it often did.

"Hey, man, you okay?" Sam's question rouses me from my reflections, and I pull back my finger from Betty's cheek, coughing my throat clear as I hand her back to her dad. Sam lowers his mouth to his daughter's head. "I think Uncle Jesse is getting broody."

I scoff for the sake of it, to mask our secret. "My baby days are done." Total lie. "Where's Kate?"

"She's just using the ladies before she finds somewhere quiet to feed Betty."

A riotous applause breaks out when Drew and Raya enter the marquee, all attention turning their way. And when Drew dramatically dips Raya and kisses the living daylights out of her, the noise ramps up a few thousand decibels.

Betty starts squawking, the shrillness piercing the cheers. "Oh, fuck, it's dinnertime and she's pissed at the noise." Sam heads off to find Kate, and I head to Drew, pulling him away from a playfully scowling Raya.

"Your turn in a minute," I assure her cheekily, landing a kiss on my mate's cheek. "Congratulations, you great pussy."

"Fuck you." He laughs, his blue eyes sparkling happily. "How's Ava?"

Pregnant! My head screams the announcement, but my mouth refuses to say it. Not because I don't want to, I kind of do, maybe to get some reassurance from my pals, but because this is Drew and Raya's day, and the shine shouldn't be taken off of that. "She's good. But just you worry about giving your wife the day she deserves."

He smiles, looking across to the gorgeous Raya, a section of her platinum blonde hair plaited and pinned, forming a pretty band across her head, flowers woven throughout. "Doesn't she look gorgeous?" Drew muses as she joins us, tucking herself neatly into his side.

"Beautiful," I agree, bending to kiss her cheek before returning my attention to Drew. "Hey, do you remember that time when you turned up at my house in a state because you'd made love to a woman?" I very nearly have to dip to miss the daggers coming at me.

"What's that, then?" Raya asks, interested.

"Nothing," Drew says lowly, his dark stare on me.

He knows me. Too well. "For the record, the woman he'd made love to was you."

"I'd hope so!" she laughs. "Since before me he only fucked with those chains of his."

Drew moans, claiming a glass of water from a tray and placing it in his wife's hand. "Yes, I was a fucker before I met you and now I'm a lover." He pecks her lips. "You've turned me."

"Who's turned who?" Ava asks, joining us.

As the waiter passes again, I take a glass of water from the tray and put it in her hand. "Raya turned Drew from a fucker to a master lovemaker. Not dissimilar to you and me." I smile bright and cheekily.

"You still fuck, Ward," she says drily, smiling at Raya when she laughs, each of them taking a sip of their wa—

Hold up.

My eyes meet Drew's, and I know we're thinking the exact same thing. "Why isn't your wife indulging in champagne on your wedding day?" I ask.

"Why isn't yours?" he retorts.

"She's thirsty."

"So is Raya."

I feel my lips twitching, prompting Drew's to tweak at the corners, too. "Oh my God," Raya breathes. "Me and Drew are pregnant!"

"Us too!" I yell, way too loudly, earning a knock of my arm from Ava.

"What the fuck?" Drew balks.

"Oh my God!" Raya sings.

"What?" Sam asks, scanning us all as he rejoins the group. I look to Drew, to Raya, and then to Ava. And shrug. I'm not leading on this one.

Drew sighs, but his smile isn't containable. "We were saving it for after the wedding, but doesn't look like that's happening." He wraps his arms around Raya's shoulder. "We're having a baby."

"No way!" Sam's on them with enthusiasm, knocking Raya's water all over the place. "Congratulations, you two!"

"Thanks." Raya blushes somewhat, pointing her empty glass to us while she wipes down her dress. "And congratulations to Jesse and Ava, too."

"Huh?" Sam swings around, looking at us in turn. "What are you two celebrating?"

I look at Ava. She looks at me. "The medication she's on screwed with her pill."

Sam is silent for a few uncomfortable seconds, looking between us. And then he falls apart, hands on his knees and everything. "Fuck, Jesse. Say hello to karma."

My situation makes me the laughingstock of the whole group, including my wife, who reaches for my face and gives it a sarcastic pat. "Poor baby."

"Be quiet. I've got my head around it now."

"Head around what?" Kate asks, handing Betty to a laughing Sam.

He just can't contain himself, jerking his girl in his arms as he wipes at his eyes. "Raya's pregnant," he tells her.

"Oh God, you guys!" Kate gushes.

"And so is Ava."

"What the fuck?" She swings around, blue eyes wide, her red hair whipping her face.

"See." Ava chucks a heavy hand in the air. "This is exactly why I didn't want to tell anyone today. Now I feel like I've stolen two lots of thunder."

Raya muscles me out of the way and puts a comforting arm around Ava's waist. "Are you kidding me? I can't wait to be expecting with you. You're a pro. I'm gonna need all the help I can get."

I could kiss the woman. She couldn't have said a nicer thing at a better time. "We'll be the baby club!" Kate sings, delighted.

"We haven't told the twins yet." That worry I don't like passes over Ava's face. Everyone looks across to the drinks table, where Jacob is cracking the caps off bottles of beer for the men, and Georgia and Maddie are still happily pouring punch. "Does Georgia know?" I ask.

"Yes." Raya beams. "She's more excited than Drew."

"Here's to babies," Sam whisper-hisses, raising his glass as he bends toward us.

"To babies," we all chant quietly, leaning into our little circle and laughing.

* * *

Good food, good company, amazing venue, superb occasion. It's been a fucking brilliant day, everyone together, and after Drew and Raya have had their first dance to Eric Clapton's "Wonderful Tonight," the other guests are invited onto the floor to join them. I look across the table to Ava, her attention split between the happy couple and Betty sleeping in Kate's arms. It's how she's been all day, distracted. She's imagining our family with one more person. I am, too.

The song fades off, and another begins. My heart skips too many beats as Ava darts her eyes across to me, and I wonder if this is a purposeful move on Drew's part. I shoot him a look on the dance floor, his expression telling me everything. My eyes thank him as I slowly return my gaze to my wife, my heart booming nervously.

I smile when I find her still watching me, and I nod mildly, telling her that the recognition happening in her head is right.

I rise to my feet and walk slowly around the table, holding out my hand to Ava as "Chasing Cars" plays. "If you have no better offers." I raise a cocky eyebrow, blinded by her shy smile as she gets to her feet.

"Never will."

I walk her onto the floor, nodding at Drew to tell him today is a job well done as I pull Ava into my chest, one arm around her shoulders, my spare hand resting on her waist. "Hey, Mummy," I whisper down at her, starting to slowly sway us.

"Hey, Daddy."

I feel an overwhelming sense of contentment flourish inside me. It tells me that this is right. I won't ever argue with the Fates, and the Fates want to give us another baby. "I love you, woman," I say, pulling her closer, her head settling in my chest. I rest mine atop of hers, continuing to move slowly on the spot, taking an age to turn a full circle.

"So you'll be there on Tuesday? For the scan?"

"Just try to stop me." I smile into her hair. "And when do you want to tell the kids?"

"I don't want them to think I'm replacing them. Or replacing the memories of their baby days with new ones."

"Don't be daft. They'd never think that."

I feel her chest press against mine, her inhale long and deep, as I catch the twins across the way watching us. Both of them are smiling, Jacob with his arm around his sister. Me and Ava, we make them happy. Just being together. I flick my head at them, ordering them over. I expect a protest, but neither does. In fact, they're quite speedy across the floor.

"We have company," I say to Ava, gently nudging her from my chest. She looks around and finds them, smiling and opening one arm as she keeps her hold of me with the other, inviting them in. Maddie and Jacob join us, and our little huddle continues to turn on the spot, mine and Ava's heads above the twins, her eyes on mine. Love. It's blasting through me unstoppably, lighting my veins, warming my soul. This is just about fucking perfect. And then Ava reaches across and presses a kiss to my mouth, a soft kiss, a lingering kiss. And I'm proven wrong. Now, *this* is perfect. And it's the perfect time to share our news.

"Maddie, Jacob," I say, pulling both their little faces up from their hiding places. "Your mum and I have something to tell you."

Ava's eyes widen a fraction, but I make sure she sees the reassurance in mine.

"What?" the kids ask in unison, heads swinging back and forth to me and Ava.

"What is it?" Jacob's face falls. "Is Mum okay? Are you okay, Mum?"

"I'm fine, darling." She kisses his head, and he settles immediately. "Trust me, I'm so fine."

"Then what's up?"

I breathe in and release our announcement on a stream of air. "There's going to be another someone for me to go crazy over."

Frowns. Two very deep frowns. And Ava laughs, though doesn't correct me.

"What your dad means is"—she takes over, clearly thinking she can break the news better than I can—"I'm having a baby."

She holds her breath, waiting for their reactions. *Please, guys, don't go off the deep end.*

"A baby?" Jacob asks, flipping a frown to me. "Like a little brother or sister?"

I don't mention the fact that I'm praying, proper *praying*, that it's a boy, because any more women in my life will be the death of me. "That's right."

They're quiet, obviously mulling over the bombshell. And then "Chasing Cars" fades to nothing and it's silent, except for the light chatter around us. Good Lord, they need to say something quick before Ava has a meltdown.

"A baby," Maddie hums.

"A baby." Jacob tilts his head, ever the one to really ponder things.

Then they look at each other and grin. And they laugh. They laugh so fucking hard. Ava and I toss bewildered looks at each other, silently asking one another if we have any clue what's so funny. We don't. So I ask, "What's tickled you two?"

"Oh my God, Dad, you're so old!" Maddie chuckles. I've never sworn at my kids. Not ever, and it's taking everything in me, and then some, not to break that rule now. Ava doesn't help when she snorts unattractively, holding her hand over her nose. But Jacob, God bless my boy, comes straight to me and shakes my hand. "Congratulations, Dad."

I have to swallow before I speak. "Cheers, mate." I could cuddle him as he throws his arms around his mum and hugs her with force.

"I love you, Mum."

Fuck me. I blink to keep the tears at bay, but Ava doesn't manage to. She's full-on crying as she pulls Maddie in, too, her face going straight between their heads. "I love you both. So much."

I'm a big fat mess of a man. Totally fucked, and I don't care who sees as I haul my family into me. My life is held in my hands in this moment.

My wife, my babies.

And a new life.

Chapter 50

As I drive Ava to her appointment on Tuesday, my mind is reeling with constant questions. Should we tell Dr. Peters about the pregnancy? Are the risks higher given her condition? She's forgetting things all the while. Small things, but still things. Will she need another CAT scan and will it risk the baby's health if she does? And her age, not that I would ever mention that to Ava. She's not in her twenties anymore.

My head begins to ache.

"Stop it," Ava says across the car, looking at me like she knows what I'm thinking. She undoubtedly does. My wife can read me like a book. Now, given the dam holding back her memories, I'm even more amazed at her ability. Her hand lands on my thigh. I breathe out deeply and squeeze her fingers. "Why don't you tell me about our first scan with the twins," she suggests, clearly trying to distract me from my worry. It works.

My sharp bout of laughter fills the car. That moment. The lack of feeling in my legs when the doctor pointed to two heartbeats. I didn't know whether to laugh or cry. But my amusement fades when I remember how we came to be in hospital having an unscheduled scan. A scan to check if my babies were still alive. My stomach turns, endless flashbacks assaulting my mind—Ava's accident, my stolen car...the sight of blood trickling down her bare leg. I shudder, and I know Ava feels it because she shifts in her seat, facing me, looking at my disposition with a roadmap of lines on her forehead.

"What is it, Jesse? You're white as a sheet."

"Nothing." Shit, I need to pull myself around. I summon a smile to reassure her. There will be no mention of my stolen car or how the driver ran Ava off the road. That was the beginning of the events that would lead to the worst moments of our lives. She doesn't need that information. Not now. Maybe never. "The day of our first scan," I muse, refocusing my attention on the road. "You didn't know I was a twin back then."

"I didn't?" She sounds surprised, and that shouldn't be surprising. "Why?"

I shrug a little, all casual. "You know by now that I had a past. That was one of the most painful parts, and talking about it wasn't high on my agenda." I turn a smile onto her when she tightens her grip around mine. "When the doctor told us there were two heartbeats in that tummy of yours, I went into shock."

She chuckles lightly, the sound so sweet and pure, her hand lowering to her stomach and circling.

"I never anticipated twins, and when I found out we were having them, I was catapulted back to a time I always kept buried." Now her smile is sad, as is mine. So I decide to rid us of the downhearted atmosphere, because, ultimately, it was a wonderful moment. Once I'd got past the shock. "The doctor told us he could hear two perfect heartbeats. Just like that. Two. It came from left field." I laugh a little, remembering with perfect clarity the weightlessness of my body in that moment, because there was a heartbeat to be heard, and that was a relief beyond no other after the accident, but there was also a sense of utter confusion that came with it. "My brain must have malfunctioned, because all I remember thinking was, *my baby has two hearts?* I think I actually said it, too."

Ava bursts out laughing. The sound and her clear amusement has me laughing, too. This is what it's all about. The good stuff, the happy memories. I keep questioning my decision to hold back on the crappy shit, but when I see her like this, so joyful and spirited, that questioning is masked by the sight of her looking so contented.

"You thought it was rather amusing at the time, too." I flash her a devilish smirk. "You savage."

"So that was when you told me about your brother?"

I nod, pulling into the car park of the hospital. "It seemed like the right moment. We had a bath, you lay on me forever, and I shared the story of me and Jacob." I flip her a wink. "Then we came together in the tub."

"Seems like a damn fine way to finish off an emotionally stressful day."

Oh, she has no idea. "When I'm lost in you, there's no room in my mind for anything else. You're the best kind of relief, Ava. Always have been, always will be." I zip into a parking space and turn off the engine, turning to face her. "As long as you always remember that, you and I will be just fine."

She doesn't protest my claim, doesn't even flash me a displeased look. Instead, she crawls across the car and puts herself on my lap. Her dark eyes are shining, true contentment reflecting back at me. Pushing her forehead to mine, she sighs into my face as my palms hold her waist. "I will always remember that," she vows, and I wince, hoping she didn't misinterpret my statement.

"I wasn't suggesting you should give up all of your memories just if you remember that."

"I know you weren't." Her hands lay over my cheeks, her gaze sinking into mine. "But you're right. I may have to accept that I've found all the memories I'm going to find, and you have to, too, Jesse." Her words are soft, pacifying, and the fact she's right strikes me painfully. That's the reality of it. "I've got the most important things. You, and the twins. And my life."

I glance away, a pain so intense bolting through me, making me flinch. "Ava, don't."

"But I'm right." She forces my face back to hers. "I've thought about nothing *but*. I know this is where I'm supposed to be. With you and those two gorgeous kids. The love I have inside me is fierce, and it tells me above all things that I'm home. I can sacrifice a few memories for the sake of that feeling. You need to be with me on this. Continue to tell me the things that matter, but don't beat yourself up when it doesn't trigger anything. You'll kill yourself off with stress. I need you. Now more than ever."

Fuck, I have a wobbly lip. How can she be so together? I absorb her every word, but there are a few in her statement that resonate deeply. *Continue to tell me the things that matter.*

"I will." My voice is thick with emotion, and my head is thick with a nasty mixture of shame and determination. It may seem cowardly, but I ignore the former and kiss her deeply, taking the relief I find in our intimacies. "We'll be late." I nibble the corner of her mouth and break away, opening the car door. "Let's go meet our baby." The happy gleam in her eyes pulls me back from the brink of some confessions. It's my job to protect her, and that is exactly what I'm doing.

* * *

She's turning the pages of her magazine at an epic rate, telling me they're not being read, just skimmed. It's something to keep her occupied while we wait to be called. Something to busy her fidgety hands. The moment we sat down, any semblance of her calmness fled. It's got me all nervous. I place a hand on her magazine, blocking the next page turn. She looks up at me.

"What's up?" I ask. She tosses the magazine on the table in front of us, closes her eyes, and starts to breathe in long, carefully controlled breaths. "Ava, baby, what's the matter?"

"Look around, Jesse," she practically whispers, making a quick scope of the waiting room herself. "All these couples."

We're one of six couples here. You'd think given the condition of these women, they'd give them something a little more comfortable than these plastic chairs to sit on. With that thought, I collect Ava from the hard chair beside me and put her on my far comfier lap. "I don't follow," I admit, ignoring the interested looks of the other men in the waiting room. They should take a leaf out of my book. Their wives' arses must be numb. Mine's not far from it.

"They're all so young."

Well, ouch. She may as well have just kicked me in the gut. I glance around, noting she's not far off the mark. With the realization comes another bout of doubt. Doubt. It's a bastard thing, can worm its way into the most confident of men and eat him alive from the inside out. Well, I won't let it. My chest swells and my chin rises. And I glare at all the twenty- and thirtysomething fathers-to-be, unable to stop myself. I might be fifty, but I'm more man than any of them.

"They might be younger, baby, but we have experience." I nod decisively.

"You do, perhaps." Her counter is quiet, unsure, and I realize my error in a heartbeat. Fuck. *Shut the fuck up, Ward.* "I can't remember a thing."

My face softens. "Stop that now," I order harshly, hating the sound of this sudden doubt in her, too. "When Kate went into labor, you knew just what to do. Like everything, it's all still inside you." I reach for her nose and circle the end with the tip of my finger. "Pack it in."

Softening on my lap, she nods, grabbing all of my reassurance with everything she has. I give myself a swift mental slap, telling myself to never let her see my uncertainty again. It's full steam ahead.

"Ava Ward."

We both look across the doctor's waiting room to see a white-coated lady with wild purple hair and a few too many piercings in her ears. Her look is harsh, though her smile is friendly. "Up you get." I put Ava on her feet, patting down my pocket when my phone rings. "It's the school." I doubt there is a parent in the land whose heart doesn't miss a beat or ten when they take a call from their kid's school. Mine just missed a hundred. I connect the call, working hard to keep my voice stable and my stress level out of heart attack territory. "Hello?"

"Mr. Ward, it's Mrs. Chilton."

"Is everything okay? The kids?"

"Everything is fine, Mr. Ward. No need to worry." Those words are fucking golden, and I nod to Ava's worried face, silently telling her not to stress.

I'm aware of the sonographer waiting for us and hold up a finger in indication that I'll be just a moment. "Then why the call?"

"Maddie seems to have developed a bit of a headache."

I still, staring down the line, my eyes narrowing to suspicious slits. Ava cocks her head in question, so I quickly cover the mouthpiece of my phone to enlighten her. "Maddie has a headache."

"But she was fine this morning."

"Yes, she was. She was also rather put out that she couldn't come to the scan." I raise my eyebrows, telling my lovely wife to catch up.

"Oh, the little minx."

She's got that right. "Mrs. Chilton, can you put her on the line?"

"Of course. One second." There's a few crackles down the line, and while I wait for my fraudulent baby to prep herself to speak to her father, I give Ava a little nod. "You go. I'll be there in two secs when I've sorted out our girl."

Ava shakes her head, dismayed, but with a fond smile as she disappears into the room. "H...ell...o," Maddie says, sounding like she's swallowed acid and a pile of rusty nails.

My girl needs to remember there's not much that gets past me. "Hey, baby," I coo.

"H-hey Daddy."

Daddy? Oh, she's working it better than any Oscar winner I've known. I move to the side of the room, leaning a shoulder against the wall. "What's up, baby girl?" I play along with her, smiling as I do. "Tell Daddy."

"My tummy aches."

My eyebrows jump up. "That's funny. Mrs. Chilton said you have a headache."

"B...b...both," she croaks.

"And having a headache and an achy tummy makes your voice poorly, too, does it?"

Silence.

"Well?"

"I have a sore throat, too!" she snaps indignantly, each word perfectly clear.

"My, my, you are in a pickle." Pushing my shoulder off the wall, I make my way to the room where Ava's waiting for me. "Listen here, madam. Ever heard of the boy who cried wolf?"

"No."

"Google it. Don't think I don't know your game, missy. I have to go. Your mother's waiting for me."

"I want to see the new baby," she whines down the line, fake crying after. "It's not fair."

"I'll get pictures," I assure her. "I promise." Really, I'm just grateful both of them have accepted this news with no major drama. Except, of course, fake illnesses. "Baby girl, there's really not much to see at the moment. It's a peanut. You can come to the twenty-week scan, okay?"

"Really?" The delight in her voice pinches my heart. "You promise?"

Smiling as I take the handle of the door, I give her what she wants. "Promise." I push my way into the room, finding Ava already on the bed with her T-shirt pulled up around her bra. "Now get back to class, you little scoundrel." I hang up after she's sung her good-bye and join Ava, standing by the side of the bed. "Sorry about that."

"No problem, Mr. Ward. We were just getting set up." The purple-haired sonographer presses a few buttons and squeezes lashings of gel on Ava's abdomen. "Are we ready?"

Good question, I think as I stare at the blank monitor, feeling Ava squeeze my hand. I smile, returning her gesture. "Ready," I say as a loud swooshing noise fills the room. Ava's head drops to the side to see the screen, my spare hand joining the one holding hers.

For a long, long while, the sonographer works in silence, moving the scanner around Ava's stomach while flicking dials and pressing buttons, her attention centered on the screen. I don't remember it taking this long before. Is there something wrong? Anxiety grows within me, silly thoughts running rampant in my mind. What if the tests have been wrong? Could there have been a mistake? What will she do if we're told there is, in fact, no baby in there? She'll be distraught. This pregnancy has given her new hope. I can't see that snatched away from her. Fear of the cruelest kind slithers through my veins as I glance from the screen, to the sonographer, to Ava, over and over.

"There." There's a few clicks of buttons, and the motions of the scanner pause on Ava's lower stomach. My muscles relax a little, and Ava's grip tightens around my hand. The sonographer points at the screen, smiling. Or is she frowning? It's hard to tell from her profile.

"What? What is it?" My body goes rigid. *Please, God, tell me everything is okay.*

"Is the baby okay?" I hear Ava ask through my fog of panic.

"Yes, the baby is fine." She looks at us, half-smiling, half-shocked. "And so are the other two."

Someone must have just poked me with high voltage, because I fly back, getting my feet all tangled in the legs of a nearby chair. I throw my hands out as the wall gets closer, only just saving myself from nutting the damn thing. "What?" I barely push the word out through my crippling alarm. The other two? What does she mean, the other *two*? Two plus one. "Three?" The one-word question is jagged and broken. "Thr... ee?"

"Yes, Mr. Ward. Three perfect heartbeats."

What the fuck? I feel dizzy. I need to sit down. But I miss the seat of the chair, landing on the floor with a thud that seems to wake me from my nightmare. I quickly scramble up, but have to grab the wall to steady myself, my legs like jelly. "Three?"

"My baby has three hearts?" Ava asks, and I look up at her on the bed, finding a dirty smirk on her cheerful face. My brain is clearly on the lag, because all I'm thinking is that's the stupidest fucking question that has ever been asked. My wide eyes jump from my wife to the sonographer, their faces a picture of amusement. What? What's so damn well funny?

"I don't und..." I fade off as realization begins to dawn on me, and my face screws up in disgust. They got me.

They're fucking playing with me. If I weren't so relieved, I'd be fuming fucking mad. My jaw tight, I feel my round eyes slowly shrink until they're angry slits. "That is the *un*funniest joke that's ever been played." I find it in myself to release the wall I'm still clinging to, all but stomping my way to the bed while Ava cackles like the demented witch that she is. "Fucking cruel," I add, crowding her vibrating body on the bed and smashing my mouth to hers. That soon shuts her up. Yes, I'm mad, but I'm so fucking relieved, too. More relieved than mad. Pulling away, I scowl down at her chirpy face. The satisfaction staring back at me diminishes my slight, so much so, I soon find myself smiling back. "Think you're funny, do you, Mrs. Ward?"

She nods, the remnants of her amusement still evident in random, short, sharp chuckles as she works to calm her jerky body down. "I couldn't resist," she titters as she looks at her accomplice. "Thank you."

"Yeah, thanks." I fire a playful, filthy look across the bed to the rogue sonographer. "Where do you make a complaint around here?"

Her face drops, and Ava whacks my arm. "Don't be mean. She was just doing what I told her."

"Mr. Ward, I'm sorry if…"

I hold a hand up to stop her words *and* her panic. "Don't sweat it. My wife has a wicked sense of humor." I poke Ava in the soft sensitive spot on her hip, making her jolt off the bed with a girlie squeal. "You'll pay for that, lady."

"I know." Her simple reply makes me smile as she clenches my hand. "But now you feel a whole lot better about only having one, don't you?"

I can't deny it. I really do, and I beat myself up for a few moments for making her resort to such tactics in an attempt to make me feel better about this unexpected pregnancy. "I would have gotten used to the idea of another three," I say, all blasé. I'm lying through my teeth, shuddering at the mere thought. Another three? "There is really just one in there, isn't there?" I ask the purple-haired joker opposite me.

"Just one, Mr. Ward." She goes back to the screen. "I'm sorry, but when your wife mentioned your first scan with your twins, it did make me laugh." Smiling at the white blip, she starts rolling the ball on the machinery, clicking here and there. "Baby, *singular*, looks perfectly healthy. You're six weeks into gestation, Mrs. Ward."

"Can you tell the sex yet?" I ask, knowing full well it's way too early.

"At the twenty-week scan, maybe. Depending on baby's position." The printer to the side kicks in, spitting out pictures of my baby.

"You don't want to know, do you?" Ava asks, a bit disappointed. "Why?"

"Because if it's a girl, I need as much time as possible to prepare. Buy armor. For her and for me."

"Jesse!" She whacks my arm on an exasperated gasp, and I chuckle, swooping in and crowding her.

I grin, she scowls. "I never told you this morning how beautiful you look today."

"I never told you how handsome you look today."

I shrug. "A god among men." I kiss her delicately. "And now I'm taking you home and giving you the king of Retribution Fucks."

Her eyes widen, glancing to the side, where the sonographer is collecting the pictures from the printer, doing a terrible job of playing ignorant to our light banter. She's smiling fondly.

"Wherever, whenever, baby." I help wipe up her tummy and get her to her feet, collecting the pictures from Miss Purple Hair before guiding Ava to the door. "I hope you're ready."

"Maybe later."

Huh? My steps stutter behind her. What does she mean, *maybe later*? I don't need to ask. She looks over her shoulder, a definite knowing smirk forming. "I'm going to yoga and then having coffee with Zara."

"I don't think so." It's out before I can stop it, my declaration hostile, my ego put out.

She rolls her eyes and continues on her way toward the exit. It's condescending as hell, and it only serves to rile me further.

"You're not going to yoga." I need to rein myself in before she slaps me silly. I should know by now that demanding she not do something just makes her all the more determined to do it, if only to prove a point, whatever that is. We've just shared a lovely moment. I'd planned on taking her home and delivering on that Retribution Fuck, and then picking the kids up from school together. She's ruining all of my plans. And on top of that, she's now pregnant. Even more fragile. Even more delicate. Yoga is a stupid idea. Besides, I'm not letting her out of my fucking sight. "No way, Ava."

"Piss off, Jesse." She pushes through the doors into the sunshine, leaving me a heaving, bristling pile of male standing like an idiot in the hospital entrance.

"You're not going!" I yell, earning startled looks from many passersby. I growl at each of them in turn before stalking out, muttering and cursing under my breath. "Ava!"

"I'm not arguing with you," she calls over her shoulder. "So you may as well quit. I'm going. End of."

End of? "That's my line," I bark childishly, catching her and blocking her path to the passenger door. I push my back up against the car as she stares at me tiredly. "I don't think yoga is a good idea in your condition."

"I've checked with the doctor. It's actually a very good idea."

Damn. Okay, then. "I don't think you should be out and about on your own."

"I won't be alone. I'll be with Zara."

My lips straighten. She could be with anyone. But she won't be with me. "I'll come, too. I'll watch your session, and you keep saying you want me to meet this new friend of yours anyway."

"No." She tries to reach for the handle of the door, but I cover it with both hands. "Jesse, stop being so fucking unreasonable."

"Watch your fucking mouth! Don't make me give you the countdown, woman. It's not beyond me."

"And what will you do to me in the middle of the hospital car park?" She laughs, thinking she has the upper hand. She doesn't.

"You tried me once before in this very car park," I inform her. "I did it then, and I'll do it now."

"Do what?" she asks, folding her arms over her lovely boobs.

I push my face close to hers and smile on the inside at her grit. She doesn't budge one inch, squaring up to me. "I'll throw you over my shoulder, slap that gorgeous arse of yours, thrust my fingers into your warm pussy, and work you up until you explode in midair in front of all these lovely people." I give her a forced, satisfied smile, and she gives me a huge gasp. Wait, has she remembered?

"You wouldn't dare!" She hasn't. Her gasp is shock, not recollection.

It doesn't beat me down. I'm not beyond reminding her. "I fucking would and I fucking did. Are you daring me?" I want her to. I want her to double dare me. Triple dare me.

"I'm going to meet Zara." Her little nostrils flare dangerously. "You can't keep me nailed to your side forever."

"Wrong." I almost laugh. I thought we were past this silly power game. "You're coming home with me, and that Retribution Fuck just got changed to an Apology Fuck." So there.

Another gasp. "You're an ape!"

I scratch my armpits in some kind of pathetic confirmation. "Old news, lady."

"Urghhh!" She turns and stomps off. She doesn't get very far. Swooping her up onto my shoulder carefully, I take her back to the car, slipping my hand beyond the hem of her skirt and up the inside of her thigh. "Jesse!"

"What, dear?" My fingers glide past the seam of her knickers and plunge easily into her. She's drenched. Even boiling mad with me, she's sodden. I smirk, satisfied. Nothing's really changed. She goes floppy on my shoulder, her moan broken, like she's trying to hold it back, trying to hide how turned on she is. It only fuels my fire.

"Don't fight me, Ava." I stop by the car, pulling the door open. "You're wasting valuable energy." Keeping my fingers submerged in her warmth, I negotiate her down into the passenger seat, kneeling by the car as I do. "Relax, baby." I walk on my knees, closer to her, and withdraw my fingers slowly, watching her chest expand and her eyes widen. And then I drive them back in, putting weight behind me, achieving maximum depth. She may be mentally pushing me away, but her sweet pussy has other ideas, greedily dragging me deeper, the muscles of her passage massaging my fingers easily. "You like that, baby?"

"You don't play fair, Ward."

"Do. You. Like. That?" I retreat and surge forward, my own sounds of pleasure filling the car and mixing with hers. "Tell me."

Her head falls back, eyes infused with need. I sacrifice my need for a verbal answer when she places a hand over mine between her thighs and starts working with me to bring her to climax. Her back arches against the seat and she stiffens, her clit beginning to throb under the pad of my thumb. She goes quietly, but boy does she go, trembling in the aftermath of her orgasm, her lids becoming heavy. I'm so enthralled by the sight, I forget what brought us to this moment. Until she speaks.

"I'm still going to yoga," she breathes, going limp in the seat.

I laugh a little under my breath, pulling my fingers free of her clenched thighs and taking my time licking her sweet juices from them while she watches. "You're not going."

Her lips twist, her eyes becoming mischievous. Then I'm quickly swallowing when she strokes over my jeans, stirring my raging cock further. She smiles when I solidify from top to toe, inhaling. "Later, I'm going to smother my boobs in peanut butter and you're going to lick it all off."

"I'm dropping you off and picking you up," I all but squeak, resting my hand over hers before my dick bashes its way through my jeans. How'd she know that's her ace card? I don't know, but I'm not arguing. I can kill the time at the club. I really should show my face there, anyway.

Her face beams, satisfied, as she drops me. "Hurry up, then. You've made me late." Pulling her skirt down, she ushers me back so she can shut the door. It feels like I've just been played. Like she has learned again that to get what she wants, she has to catch me at my weakest moments, like bribing me with peanut butter and her boobs. My plan just backfired, and when she fails to hold her grin back as I round the car, my eyes burning through the windscreen, I know for sure I have definitely been played.

Yet that tiny shred of reason within me tells me to let it go. She's right. As much as I want to—feel like I need to—I can't have her nailed to me for all eternity. She has to rebuild other parts of her life. I'm just going to have to get used to the nervous breakdowns while she does that.

CHAPTER 51

AVA

When Jesse pulls up at the curb, he releases my belt, turning to get me in his sights. "Be careful," he warns. "And I'll pick you up at this exact spot in a couple of hours."

"Okay." I barely contain my eye roll as I lean over and peck his cheek. "See you later." I slam the door and jog across the road.

"Don't run!" he yells as I turn to face him from the other side of the road. "Might shake up the baby."

I laugh. The man is a nutcase. I spot Zara up the street near Elsie's and wave as I make my way over. She takes me in a big hug. "Is your husband waiting for you?"

I pull out of her embrace and look over my shoulder, seeing Jesse still idling at the curb. "He's probably checking I get in the building without injuring myself," I joke, returning my attention to Zara when he eventually pulls away. "He worries about me, and now he'll be worrying even more."

"Why?"

"We just came from the hospital." I take the scan picture from my purse and hold it out, and her blue eyes fall to it. I don't get the reaction I was expecting, her eyes taking on a sad edge. My proud smile falls. "Zara?" Oh, shit.

She looks up at me, a bit vacant. "I'm sorry." She shakes herself to life.

"What's up?" I quickly get rid of the picture, concerned.

"I'm being silly. It's just, I can't have children myself."

"Oh my God." I kick myself hard, moving in to give her a hug. "I'm so sorry."

"It's not your fault. It's not mine either, in fact. Just a rare genetic thing that they can't really explain." She embraces my offer of comfort and returns my squeeze. "My ex blamed me, hence his handy fists."

I wince. "What an arsehole." Pulling away, I push a wet strand off her cheek, and she smiles sadly. "You're happier without him, right?"

"Of course. My job's going great, and there's talk of a promotion already. Things really couldn't be going better."

"That's fab."

"Hey, as a matter of fact, I have a date later," she tells me, an excited sparkle in her eyes. "I need a dress. Fancy a quick trip to the shops after yoga to help me choose?"

"Sure." I don't hesitate. She needs me. I'll call Jesse and let him know. He'll be fine.

"Congratulations on the baby, Ava." Zara nudges my shoulder, flipping me a genuine smile. "You're clearly so happy."

"On Central Jesse Cloud Nine," I say without thought, frowning as I do.

"Sounds like an amazing place to be."

"You have no idea."

Chapter 52

For a Tuesday afternoon, the club is heaving. I wander through the reception area, nodding to people as I go. They all seem surprised to see me. Or are they wondering where Ava is?

I'm just heading upstairs when Sam calls. "Hey," I answer.

"Sleeping pills. Where can I get them?" He sounds urgent.

I smile, hearing the exhaustion in his voice. "Do I look like the local dealer?" John spots me halfway up the stairs, surprise on his face, too, before pulling an about-turn and flanking me on my way up. I point to my phone and mouth "Sam," making John grin a shit-eating grin. "Knocking yourself out isn't a good idea when there's a baby around."

"Fucking hell, I've never been so tired. I'm walking dead. And Kate's turned into a demon woman."

I remember those days not too fondly, though we had two to deal with. I don't point that out. Sam wouldn't appreciate it. Instead, I do something any decent mate would do. After all, a bit of practice and refreshing my skills would probably do me well, plus Ava will relish in it, I'm sure. "Hey, how'd you think Kate would feel about letting us have Betty for the night so you two can catch up on some sleep?"

"Argh, mate, you'd do that?" He sounds perkier, just like that, just with the promise of some downtime. "She'd be fine."

"Hadn't you ought to ask her first?" I ask, remembering that first time we left the twins to have a date night. Ava was fine, mind you. It was me who was fretting. I reach the top of the stairs with John, breaking onto the gym floor. I point to Ava's office and he nods, holding a finger up to indicate he'll be there in a tick.

"Trust me, she'll be fine," Sam assures me. "And if she isn't, then I'll come and stay with you."

I laugh, pushing my way into Ava's office. I find Cherry sitting in Ava's chair, and my laughter fades. She looks all wrong. There's only one woman who belongs in that chair. "Speak to Kate and get back to me."

"We'll be there at seven pronto," he counters, hanging up.

"Oh, hi." Cherry beams at me, looking past my shoulder. "No Ava?"

"No Ava," I confirm, heading for my wife's desk. I scan the surface, noting many things out of place. The pen pot is on the wrong side, the mouse mat is different, and the in-and-out trays are all askew. Perfectly neat, but still askew. Ava didn't have them like that, pushed neatly into the back corner. Not that my wife will know that.

"Can I get you a drink?" Cherry gets up, tapping a pile on papers on the edge of the desk to tidy them.

"A water, thanks." I drop into the now-vacant chair and scan the room while Cherry makes her quiet exit. It feels empty. Lacking life. I rest back and wedge my elbow into the arm, drumming my fingers on my cheek, thoughtful. And I smile. A new baby.

"What are you grinning at?" John asks, stalking toward the desk. It occurs to me in this moment that one of my oldest friends is in the dark over the past few days' revelations.

"I'm going to be a dad." I sound stable, and I'm proud of myself for it.

"You're already a dad, you stupid motherfucker." He drops into the chair opposite me. "I thought Ava was the one who lost her memory."

Had anyone else said that, I would have beat them black and blue. But this is John. He'd beat *me* black and blue. "*Again*," I add. "I'm going to be a dad *again*."

The white of his eyes expand. "What?"

"Ava's pregnant."

I see the laughter bubbling up from his toes and wait for it to work its way to his mouth and shake the whole damn club. But he doesn't laugh. Somehow, he contains it, though I see his amusement plain as day. "Was it planned?"

I chuck a pen across the desk at him. "Stupid fucking question, John. What sane fifty-year-old bloke would volunteer for that, for fuck's sake?"

His huge shoulders jump up casually. "I would have, had the opportunity passed me by."

That shuts me up. And makes me shrink. I've never asked John about his past, and he's never volunteered it. Something inside me, maybe caution, just warned me not to. I've often wondered if he'd wanted children if he found the right woman. And he's just answered that. I shouldn't be surprised. He's great with the twins, always has been. Like an adopted pap, in a way. "Was there ever a Mrs. John?" I ask him.

He smiles his big white-toothed smile with his signature hint of gold. "What's taken you so long to ask, boy?"

I inwardly laugh. "Maybe the hostile vibes I get any time I've ever even *thought* to pry."

"There was one woman once upon a time." He shrugs, like it's nothing. It most certainly isn't nothing.

I lean forward in my chair, intrigued. "Really? Who?"

He eyes me for a few moments, clearly wondering whether he

should spill. "It doesn't matter now. It's dead. History." Clearly he's decided against it.

I sigh, mentally plotting my advances, how I can coax the information from him. "Before I knew you?"

His glare is deadly. "Drop it."

"What if I don't?"

"Face the consequences."

"Which are what?"

"Rein it in, you relentless motherfucker," he warns, the threat in his tone no joke, but something tells me that he really wants to share. Yet I do as I'm told, even if my mind is spinning, rewinding through the years, all the way back to when my uncle took me under his wing. John was there then, my uncle's best friend. In fact, he's always just been...there. I hum to myself, racking my brain. I know her. That's why he's being cagey and reluctant.

I flick through all the women who used to frequent The Manor on a regular basis as we stare at each other, for what seems like years, his eyes dark, mine curious. And then he draws breath to speak. "Falling in love with your best mate's girl isn't ideal." His eyes don't move from mine.

His best mate's girl? Uncle Carmichael was his best...

Realization slams into me like a giant wrecking ball to my gut. "Sarah?" I blurt, my heart taking the second shock of the day, except this one is no sick prank. He nods his confirmation. Fuck me. Sarah?

How has he kept that hidden all this time? "John, I don't know what to say." He watched it all, close by, Sarah, me, and Uncle Carmichael, the wretched love triangle and all the tragedy that went with it. And the years that followed, Sarah constantly pining for me, going to epic lengths to try to win me. How did he do that? Face it? Endure it?

"Say nothing and move on," he warns, obviously watching my mind go into overdrive.

All this time he's been in love with Sarah? And I never knew? Never saw it? "How can you love someone who's so destructive?" I ask, baffled.

He looks at me like I'm stupid. "Ask your wife."

I wilt where I sit, going over and over the years, searching for any clues that I missed. Now, I realize there were millions. His calmness with her. His occasional attempts to defend her actions. His anger when she lost the plot all those times. He wasn't entirely mad with her for what she was doing to me. But what she was doing to herself, too.

"You can't help someone who doesn't want to be helped," he says, strangely reminiscent. "*You* wanted to be helped."

"Shit, John," I breathe, throwing my hands up a little. Then something comes to me. She's staying with him, has been for weeks. "Why would you set yourself up like that, and what the hell does Elsie think? Wait, what does Sarah think? Does she know how you feel?"

"How I *felt*. And no, she didn't and doesn't. Neither did your uncle. You think I wanted to add to the fuckup that was you, her, and him? And I stopped loving her when she stopped loving herself. And the reason she's staying with me is because she can do me less damage than she can do you."

"I..."

"You'll keep this to yourself." John's tone is as threatening as threatening can be as he gets up from his seat. "It's history."

"Of course." He doesn't need to tell me twice. "What about Sarah? How long is she staying with you?"

"Until she's back on her feet."

The man is a saint in disguise. "And what about Elsie?"

"She has some holistic therapy shit she wants to try on Sarah."

He looks back, rolling his eyes. "Who knows? Might straighten her out."

The door closes behind him, and I sit there alone in the silent room for a long time, trying to get to grips with this news. The truth is, I can't. No matter how long I try to wrap my mind around it. So many years to be assessed, too many occasions in history to be analyzed to find what I'm looking for. I won't find anything. John did too good a job of hiding his feelings from Sarah *and* the rest of the world. He's put himself at the bottom of the pile every time. It isn't right. Pulling out my phone, I find the number I blocked, unblock it, and dial, and the moment I hear her voice, my skin prickles and I'm out of my chair, pacing the office.

"You need to leave town, Sarah," I say bluntly.

"Jesse?"

"Yes. You need to leave."

There's a pause, and then a sigh. "How's Ava?"

"I didn't call you to chitchat about my wife. I called you to tell you to leave town."

"I can't go anywhere, Jesse. I'm broke."

My feet drag to a stop as I recall John telling me the same thing. She has nowhere to go. Nowhere to stay. So she's putting on John, and John will never say no. "Send me your account details," I order. "I'll transfer some money, and then you leave. Do you hear me?" John's waited decades to meet a woman. Now he's met one, and I'm not having this poisonous bitch ruining what could be his happy ever after. "Do you hear me?"

"I hear you," she whispers, her lack of argument maddening. Because she's that selfish. She doesn't care about John. Or me. She cares about herself.

"I'll do it now. Send me your details." I hang up, and in the two paces it takes me to get back to Ava's desk to log on to my banking, her details land on my phone. I laugh a disbelieving laugh.

She didn't waste time. A few clicks sends a clean hundred grand her way. We didn't talk numbers, but I want her to have enough to ensure she'll never have to come back. Resting back in my chair, I stare at the screen as I kiss good-bye to the best money I've ever spent.

My phone buzzes on the desk, and I glance down to see two missed calls from Ava. Heart in my throat, I go to dial her back but notice a voicemail alert.

I click the icon and bring my mobile to my ear to listen to her message. "I've tried calling you twice and you're ignoring me," she says. "I'm still with Zara. I've had a lovely time! We popped to a store next door and bought her a new dress for a date she has tonight. We couldn't find shoes, but I have the perfect pair, so we're going to go pick up the kids and head back. She's driving, so don't panic. I'll meet you at home."

My knee-jerk reaction is to call her back and put her straight on a few things. But, somehow, I stop myself. I breathe in and relax back in my chair, closing my eyes. She's checked in. She's fine, and she's picking up the kids. I should let her do that. I *must* let her do that. She *needs* to do that. I'm just forcing myself to put my phone away when someone walks in—Cherry with my water. Took her long enough.

She smiles, all bright and willing, as she paces toward me, a definite, deliberate sway to her hips. And if I'm not mistaken, she's undone an extra button on her shirt since she left to fetch my water. My suspicious eyes follow her all the way to the foot of Ava's desk, where she perches her arse on the side, crossing one leg over the other. "Anything else?" she practically purrs.

I sigh. Time to put her in her place. "Cherry," I begin, and she smiles brighter, her eyes dropping down my torso. "Let me explain something to you."

"Umm-hmmm," she hums, starting to nibble her bottom lip.

"If my wife catches you looking at me like that, you'll be choking on your high heels."

My words seem to have zero impact, her eyes crawling up my front until she's gazing at me. "And what about if you catch me looking at you like this?"

I'm staggered by her boldness. "I just did."

"And?"

I lean forward, resting my elbows on the desk. Her eyes sparkle more at my closeness. "*And* I think you're brave," I answer lowly. "You're also stupid."

She shrugs. "No one gets what they want by being reserved."

"You're fired."

Her eyes widen. "What?"

"I said, you're fired." I smile, a blazing smile, one that would knock her to her arse if she wasn't already there from shock.

"You can't fire me," she spits indignantly.

I laugh, sitting back in my chair. "You just disrespected my wife, who also happens to be *your* boss. You think I'd forgo her for you?" I chuckle, the sound wicked. "Let me give you a bit of advice to take on your way."

She slips down from the desk, rejection making her cheeks red, but not with anger, more embarrassment. "What?"

"If you wanted to learn how to be sexy and seductive, you should have spent more time admiring my wife rather than me. Good-bye."

Outrage. It's splashed all over her face. "But you owned The Manor."

I look at her like she's stupid, because she fucking is. "Leave," I all but growl before I flip my lid. Wisely, she takes note of my anger, quickly stomping to the door. Her parting gift is a filthy glare tossed over her shoulder before she slams the door with brute force.

Stupid woman.

My phone rings again, and I quickly snatch it up and answer as I stand and head for the door. "Hey, baby." I'm expecting high praise for leaving her to do her girlie stuff and not calling her back.

"What the hell are you playing at, Ward?"

I stop halfway across the office, racking my brain for what I could have done. I resort to asking, since I'm fucking clueless. "What did I do?"

"You didn't call me back! All I keep getting is your voicemail!" She's wild, frantic, and I grin the biggest grin.

"Aww, baby, you worried about me?" Welcome to my world, lady.

"A bit," she sniffs down the line. I can't help the deep satisfaction.

"My phone must have dropped its service," I tell her, carrying on my way. I'm thinking it's probably not wise to tell her that I was on the phone to Sarah.

"Where are you?"

"At the club." I hear her bristling at the mention of me being here, alone, without her. I put her mind at rest. "I just fired Cherry."

"What? Why? Oh my God, did she make a pass at you? The sneaky little bitch!"

"Well, you know. Your husband is a god among men. I can't blame her."

"You're intolerable."

"And I love you, too. Where are you?"

"At home now. I've just seen Zara out, and the kids are on the trampoline."

"I'm on my way." I hang up and jog to my car, feeling like it's been years instead of hours since I've seen them.

Chapter 53

Pulling up the driveway, I hear the kids before I see them, their shouts of delight reaching me from the garden, the springs of the trampoline going loopy. I rush to the house in search of Ava so I can soak up some of that praise she owes me. I find her sitting at the island in the kitchen staring down at something. My approaching steps don't distract her, her focus engrossed. I realize what's holding her rapt attention: the picture of our new baby. Her fingertip is tracing the edges of the paper. Her eyes look a little dreamy. I hate to disturb her.

"Boo," I whisper in her ear, and her palm slaps on her chest as she startles.

She turns on her stool and glares at me, fisting the front of my T-shirt and yanking me forward. "Next time I call you, ring me back, Ward."

"Fuck, you're sexy when you're mad."

Her scowl turns into an impish grin. "Then kiss me."

"What do you say, baby?"

There's no hesitation. "Please."

I pounce, lifting her from the stool to the island and utterly ravishing her bones. God, is there anywhere I'd rather be? Nope.

Just glue my mouth to hers and let us be done with it. She is like the finest of wines, and I am an expert in that wine. "Spread your legs." They open and I move in, our mouths wild on each other. This is what happens when we're apart too long. Starvation. I can't get enough of her.

"Jesse," she pants, her voice full of warning, though her relentless tongue doesn't let up. "The kids."

I'm about to say *fuck 'em*, getting a bit carried away with myself. But, instead, and very reluctantly, I pry myself from her lips before I take it a step further and push her back down onto the island. "Have you shown them the picture?"

"No, of course not. I wanted to wait for you."

"Over dinner, or now?" Truth be told, I want to do it now. I'm excited.

"Now."

I grin, knowing she read that in my eyes as I help her down. "Did you find shoes for your friend?"

"Yes, a perfect match for the dress. She hung on for as long as she could to meet you, but she was going to be late for her date if she waited any longer."

"Another time." I try not to sound too casual. I know how much this new friend means to her. I need to at least pretend I care. "Maybe when I drop you to yoga?"

"She'll love you, and you her."

"Of course she will. I'm the fucking Lord of The Manor." Flipping her a cheeky wink, I find my stride and take us out to the garden. The creak of the trampoline with each jump grows louder as we walk, my smile growing with it, until it comes into view and I see my boy and girl springing up and down, laughing. And there's another person. "Who's that?" I ask, my eyes set on the woman, her dark hair flapping in the air and around her face.

"Oh." Ava sounds surprised, but not concerned. "That's Zara.

She was coming out to say bye to the kids. I thought she'd left already."

I smile at the woman's back. She's a bit overdressed for playtime on a trampoline. "She's got some energy."

"Why is she wearing her new dress?" Ava asks, confusion now creeping into her tone.

I look at the black lace number, something uneasy settling over me, a weight on my shoulders that I can't shake. My feet slow as we approach. Along with my heart.

And then it stops completely when the woman turns toward us. It's a moment in time when I think I know what I'm seeing, but it's so far beyond my comprehension, it takes my brain a moment to catch up. But the second I see her deep-set blue eyes, there's no doubt. They look as troubled as I remember, and as she stares at me, they fill with hatred.

"Oh fuck."

She's changed her hair color. The blond is gone, replaced with a harsh shade of mahogany that doesn't suit her complexion at all. She's always been pale, but now she looks bloodless. Heartless. Emotionless.

"Lauren." Shock and fear has paralyzed me.

Why didn't I know she'd been released from the institution? We should have fucking been told! I need to get my kids off that trampoline, away from her and her murderous, fucked-up clutches, yet I can't fucking move.

"What a surprise." She walks toward the netting around the edges of the trampoline, poking her fingers through the holes to hold on, a little breathless, but her words are as clear as day. "Nice to see you, Jesse."

"Lauren?" Ava asks, confused. "This is Zara. You know each other?" She drops her hold of me and takes a few steps back. I dare not take my gaze from the woman who nearly sent me to the grave twice. My babies are a few feet away from her, their bounces now slowing, too, their instinct telling them that something isn't right. Fucking hell, how did this happen? Ava's new friend, the one she's been doing yoga with all these weeks, having coffee and going on shopping trips with, is my murderous ex-wife? I swallow, my body starting to shake. It's a result of a bit of anger, but mostly, it's fucking fear.

I need to play it cool. Not give the kids anything to worry about. Fucking impossible when faced with this woman. I know what lengths she'll go to in order to ruin me.

Lauren casts her eyes over to Ava, a salacious smirk on her lips. "Oh, you mean of all the things he's reminded you of, he forgot to mention me?" Her cold eyes fall back onto my motionless form. My veins freeze. "Oh, Jesse, you have a habit of leaving your ex-wife off your list of priorities. And your dead daughter."

Ava gasps, and I force myself to face her. She's brought her hands to her head, her face twisting in agony. And then she screams. And I realize what's happening. She's remembering. "Ava, baby." I go to her, catching her as she falls to her knees.

"No!" she sobs. "No, no, no!" She starts yanking at her hair, deranged and inconsolable. "Make it stop! I don't want to know!"

"Oh, Jesus." I fight back my tears, roaring to the sky, begging for someone up there to stop this insanity. I'm torn, needing to comfort my wife as she's attacked with every tiny detail of our history all at once, the dams opening and flooding her fragile brain.

But there's a psychotic woman a few feet away on the trampoline with my babies. I know what she's capable of. I know the hatred she harbors for me. Yelling, I break away from Ava to face my nemesis. Lauren's smirk is wider. Sicker. Uglier. The kids are staring at their mum, shocked and confused at her hysterics.

Opening my arms, I swallow down my fear, working on

keeping my face sure and strong. They need to see me strong. "Kids, come to Dad."

They both take one step forward, but before they can go any farther, Lauren puts an arm around each of their shoulders, pulling them in tightly. They flinch, their eyes round now, but they don't struggle. I'm so proud they're smart enough to keep their cool.

"They're quite happy here with Auntie Lauren, right, kids?" She kisses both of their heads in turn, her eyes on me. "Adorable, Jesse. Really adorable. And now you have another on the way! How exciting for you. Another addition to your perfect family. Ever wonder what our Rosie would look like if she'd have made it to this age? If you hadn't killed her?"

The pain that bolts through me is excruciating. It makes me physically retch, my stomach twisting nastily. The kids remain silent, unmoving, but the shock on their faces is undeniable. I just need to get them away from her. "Lauren." I keep my tone level and sure, taking slow, careful steps toward the trampoline. "You don't want to hurt my children. You're not evil. Think about what you're doing."

"Of course I don't want to hurt them." She laughs, almost hysterically. Whatever the fuck they've been doing in that psychiatric ward all this time sure as shit hasn't fixed her.

"Then take me," I say. "Wherever you want to go. We'll talk. See if we can work this out."

"Can you bring Rosie back?"

"No one can bring Rosie back, Lauren." I reach the foot of the trampoline, threading my fingers through the netting myself, getting my face closer. I see that hatred in her eyes amplify. "Take me. You want to hurt me. They don't deserve to suffer for my mistakes."

Painfully, I silently acknowledge that either way, my children are going to suffer here. There's no escaping it. Either this lunatic woman will hurt them—and I'll go to the ends of the earth to prevent that—or she'll hurt me, and that in turn will hurt them. I can't win. But the latter is the lesser of two evils. I'm between the devil and the deep blue sea.

"No, Jesse." Ava's voice comes from nowhere, pulling my eyes to the left. She's staring at Lauren, eyes almost crazy, and I know it's because all the madness that's just ransacked her head has made her that way. I've made her that way. "She's already tried to kill you twice."

"Third time's the charm?" Lauren smirks.

"You're not getting the opportunity ever again." Ava's head starts to shake, her eyes falling to me. "I'm not going to that level of hell again. I'm not praying for weeks upon weeks for you to wake up. I'm not letting her hurt you again. You'll have to fucking kill me first."

"That's sweet." Lauren laughs again. "But you're forgetting I have something you both cherish right here." She hugs the kids closer. "Don't get ahead of yourself, *Ava*." She casts her cold eyes over to me. "Seems your husband *wants* to come with me." Releasing the kids, she collects a bag from the soft cushioned edge of the trampoline and reaches inside.

I get a glimpse of the handle of a handgun, and air enters my lungs so fast, I stagger back one step. "I'll come."

"No!" Ava glares at me, furious. I ignore her and walk around the edge of the trampoline, unzipping the entrance. "Jesse!" She's losing it, and I flip her a death stare, silently asking her what fucking choice I have. She has our kids, for fuck's sake. Ava's so panicked, so overcome with what's transpiring, she's not thinking straight. She snaps her mouth shut and diverts her attention to Jacob and Maddie. And then it hits her. Her duty. I see the lioness in her rocket to the surface, accompanied by a newfound hatred for the woman now coming down the ladder of the trampoline, her gun pointed directly at my chest.

"Dad?" Jacob's voice is ragged and cracked as he collects his sister and walks her to the farthest edge of the enclosure, as far away from Lauren as he can get them. "Dad, no."

"It's fine, mate." I force a smile at him. "Everything is going to be all right, I promise you." I don't make promises I can't keep, and I'm ignoring the voice inside my head that's telling me I just broke that rule.

Lauren reaches the bottom of the ladder and stares up at me as she slips her feet into a pair of heels I recognize. Ava's. The hair, the dress, the shoes. It's all been planned. I'm her fucking date. "You can drive," she says, reaching into my pocket. Every muscle I possess freezes as she feels around inside. I hiss when she skims my limp cock. "We'll fix that, I'm sure."

"Get your hands off him!" Ava screams, the wild in her eyes reaching a whole new dangerous level.

"Pipe down, *sweetheart*." Lauren pulls out the keys for my Aston and thrusts them into my chest. "Let's go."

My limp hand takes the bunch, my eyes darting quickly to Ava. She's made it to the kids, and they're huddled together in the middle of the trampoline, my babies' faces in their mum's chest, hiding from this horror scene. "I'm driving." I say the words as clearly as I can, praying Ava hears my silent message. "In *my* car."

"Yes, in your car." Lauren wedges the gun painfully in my rib. "Go."

I'm forced to turn before I get the opportunity to check for any recollection on Ava's face. I fear she's too lost in the new memories to realize what I'm trying to tell her.

As I'm guided to my car by the gun held at my back, I tussle with the temptation to turn and wrestle it from her hands. I'm big enough to easily overpower her. But that gun. One tweak of her finger, no matter how fast I am, and I'll be gone. And then Ava and the kids will be helpless. No way am I risking their lives. Fuck mine. Fuck this. I deserve it all. Had I enlightened Ava, grown some balls and told her everything, she would have been aware of Lauren. Would have maybe seen some signs. Instead, I was the coward I was years ago, and I've put the most precious people in my life at danger's door. My feet are heavy, my heart slowing with each step I take. She won't need to kill me. I'm dying little bit by little bit the farther I walk away from my family.

Chapter 54

My attention is divided between the road and Lauren's lap, where the gun is resting lightly, her finger curled around the trigger. I know fuck all about guns. I wouldn't be able to tell you if it was loaded, or even ready to fire. This could just be a show. I'm unwilling to test *could be*. All I know for sure is this woman wants to make me suffer. I don't know where we're headed. I'm taking instructions as she gives them, following the road out of the city.

I don't know whether to talk to her. Attempt to make her feel at ease. I have not one fucking clue how to handle this.

I'm just so thankful Ava and the kids are out of harm's way. And yet Ava must be terrified—by what's happening now, and by the flood of memories. My knuckles go white on the steering wheel, my heart pulsing with pain. I could go on a rampage. Destroy everything in sight, starting with *Lauren*. But I have to stay calm and sensible if I'm going to get through this.

As my phone persistently vibrates in my pocket, I mentally talk to Ava, telling her over and over to think about what I said as I left. I beg for the penny to drop through her despair and fear.

"Right at the roundabout." Lauren breaks into my thoughts

with her curt order, and I follow her instructions, taking the country road farther out of the city. Every time I catch sight of her, I feel sick.

"You like?" she asks, scrunching her hair when she catches me looking. "You're into brunettes, right?"

"I'm into my wife and my wife alone." The venom in my tone is savage but unstoppable.

She ignores my scathing retort and proceeds to pat down her black lace dress. "She picked this for me." One foot comes up and rests on the dashboard. "And these are hers. You must like what you see."

What I see makes me want to vomit. "You look very nice, Lauren," I say carefully, silently running through my options. There are three, as I see it: Fight or flee being two of the obvious, though that gun she's holding like it could be a vital part of her outfit is rendering those options redundant. Then there's the third option, the one I'm going to take. Pacify her. Draw her into a false sense of security. "How did you find us?"

"Well, there I am enjoying my morning coffee reading the paper and suddenly I'm staring at *her*. She lost her memory, they said. Such a shame. They kindly mentioned that Ava and her husband ran a health club. It wasn't hard to find you." She sighs, pointing the gun to the signpost up ahead as I bristle and curse the fucking journalists to hell and back. "Left there."

It's the area where we grew up. "Why are we here?" I take the turn and keep my speed at thirty as we drive down the narrow country road toward the village.

"A trip down memory lane." She turns in her seat. "Remember the barn where we first kissed?"

"Yes." I remember the barn, but I have no recollection of the kiss. She could be making it up. Or not. Over the years, I've successfully eradicated most memories of Lauren from my life.

Cleansed my mind and left space for only the things that mean something to me. Like Rosie. Like my brother. I want to ask when she was released from the nuthouse. I also want to ask what imbecile deemed her safe to the outside world. Though I know bringing that up would be unwise.

Besides, I know she's safe to most people. It's just me and my family she has a vendetta against. She's volatile. I shouldn't say anything to push her over the edge. We were assured that if she were ever released, we'd be informed. And it was a massive *if*. How the fuck did this happen? Why didn't we know? More questions mount, tearing up my mind as I stare ahead.

The clouds on the horizon are dense and low, giving the illusion of an impressive mountain range. Though however dull the sky is, the surroundings are beautiful. Fields stretch for miles, a patchwork of yellows and greens, though my appreciation is stunted by memories of my childhood and teenage years.

We approach the small, idyllic village church where I married the lunatic now sitting next to me. Flashbacks hit me from all directions, my hands now bloodless, my jaw aching terribly from the force of my bite as I fight the memories away. I see me, barely a man, standing at the entrance of the church, Lauren's parents talking me into entering. There's a sea of faces, all smiling. I see the priest up ahead, his Bible resting in his open hands. I hear myself asking him to pray for me. To help me.

He couldn't have heard my silent pleas. That, or he and the Mighty One decided I was getting what I deserved. That I would pay for the rest of my life for being so reckless with my brother's life.

And I have. I've paid tenfold. When does it stop? When will the punishments end?

"Fond memories. We could have been so happy." Lauren sighs dreamily as we pass the ancient place of worship, the car jumping from the endless divots in the old road. "Until you ruined it. Turn down the next road on the left."

I say nothing, for fear I might say the wrong thing, and take the next lane as instructed. I see the barn up ahead, the ramshackle building barely still standing. "What are we doing here, Lauren?"

"Shut up, Jesse," she spits as I roll to a stop outside the deserted barn. "I'm surprised you haven't asked me about my delightful stay courtesy of Her Majesty the queen."

"What does it matter?" I turn to face her, enduring the face of pure evil. "You're here now."

"I was such a good girl." She smiles, as if thinking fondly. "The doctors knew I wasn't bad to the core. Just terribly hurt. Assessments proved it. They put me on a program. I was an A-grade student, the perfect reformed example. So they released me." She smiles proudly, while I force my frown into hiding. She fooled them? Made them believe she's stable so she could come out here and finish a job she started over a decade ago? "That's when I became Zara Cross."

"They gave you a new identity?"

"The good old justice system. I was vulnerable, Jesse. You see, I'm not crazy. I know damn well what I'm doing, and I know that as soon as I rid this world of your despicable life, I'll be carted back to a padded cell to live out the rest of my days." She pokes me in the arm with the barrel of the gun. "Except I don't want to live anymore. I'm done with this life."

My eyes lift from the gun to her empty dull pits of fading blue, and I comprehend immediately that she means it wholeheartedly. "Lauren, it doesn't have to be like this." I try to work on her reason. "You can be happy again."

She laughs. It's cold and it's fake. "You mean like you? You think I should replace Rosie and pretend she never existed? No, Jesse. Never. And do you honestly think I'm willing to stand by and watch you wash away her memory with a few more kids and that wife of yours? Our daughter deserves justice." Another poke of my arm. "Get out."

I blindly reach for the handle, pulling myself from the car as I keep an eye on Lauren getting out of the other side. Her plan now is crystal clear in my head. She'll pull that trigger on me, and then turn it on herself. She's not going back to prison.

As she rounds the car, she struggles on the uneven ground in Ava's heels, having to hold the bonnet of my car for support. She eventually kicks the shoes off, motioning with the gun toward the barn. I silently lead, looking up at the filthy wooden planks that make up the derelict structure, seeing endless broken slats hanging off, most cracked.

Once we're inside the huge empty space, I look down at the concrete floor scattered with old strands of hay from decades ago, my steps echoing around us. "Up the stairs."

There's a rickety staircase with one or two steps missing. I honestly doubt the rotten wood will take my weight. "Lauren, that doesn't look safe."

"Argh," she coos, jamming the gun in my lower back. "Are you worried I'll injure myself?"

I think for a moment, considering another way through this nightmare. How long has it been since someone showed her any compassion or love? How long since anyone actually worried about her? Her parents disowned her. She's had no one except the professionals poking at her mind. I flinch where I stand at the bottom of the stairs, sick at the thought of it. Can I do it? Can I fool her into thinking I actually care? My stomach turns, my mind reels. The words I should say are thick on my tongue.

She loved me once. And something deep and disturbing inside me warns me that she still does. That's why she's so fucked up. That's why she's on a mission to destroy me. If she can't be happy, then neither can I. If she can't have me, then no one can. There's a fine line between love and hate, and I think Lauren is straddling that line. The question is, can I tip her in my favor? I don't want to. What I want to do is rip her apart piece by piece until she's nothing but a pile of body parts at my feet. But no matter what, no matter how I get there, I need to make it back to my wife. Preferably in one piece. I can't put Ava through the agony of thinking she's lost me again. I've been there myself recently. It's lower than hell.

I slowly turn to face Lauren and conjure up the words my heart forbids me to say. "Yes, actually. I do care." I keep my eyes on hers, searching for anything to suggest this might work. It's my only hope. "Would that be so hard to believe?"

It happens so fast, I nearly miss it. A flash of surprise, followed by a frown. "You care?" She's on the verge of laughter, though I hear hope, actual hope, and it drives me, confirms I'm bang on the money. I feel like I'm selling my soul to the fucking devil, but I'll buy it back. One way or another, I'm making it home.

"I never stopped caring, Lauren. Look at my life before you. I lost the person I was closest to in the fucking world. It fucked me up. I did things I regret. Said things I didn't mean. It wasn't personal. You were just another casualty on my road to self-destruction." It's now I realize that most of what I'm saying is true. There's just one small bit that isn't. The caring part, but the truth is, I only stopped caring, stopped feeling guilty, when she turned on Ava all those years ago. At that point, she was dead to me.

I see doubt in her eyes, but I also see the need to believe me. And now I believe her. I don't think she's crazy at all. I think she's broken. I think she needs closure, and I think the only way she feels she can get it is by destroying me and then herself. I can make her see differently. I *have* to make her see differently. I take one careful step toward her and she lowers the gun just a fraction.

"Why'd you do this?" I ask, motioning up and down her body. "The dress. The hair. Why, Lauren?" There's only one explanation. She wants to be Ava. She wants to be mine.

Her lip quivers. "It hurts me how much you love her. It killed me to listen to her tell me over yoga and coffee how devoted you are. Why couldn't you be that for me? Why couldn't you love me with that much passion?" Her voice finally cracks. "When I was ill, like Ava has been, why couldn't you do whatever it took to make me better?" Tears form a river down her cheeks. "You will do anything for that woman. What is it about her?"

And there we have it. "I'll help you, Lauren. I promise I'll help you." I'm surprised I really mean it. I don't know how I can help her, but, honestly, if it means I get back to my family, I'm prepared to do anything.

"Will you love me like you love her?"

The words she wants to hear won't come. I can't say them. I'll help her, but I can't love her like she wants to be loved. "I..."

She smiles, but this time it's not malicious. It's sad. "You can't, I know." She points to the stairs.

I take a long breath, pinching the bridge of my nose. "Lauren—"

"You've said enough. Just go."

I close my eyes as I turn, looking up to the heavens as I take the unstable old staircase to the hay store above. "Don't do this, Lauren, I beg you." It's all I have left. Pleas.

I don't get a reply. What I get instead is the clicking sound of the safety being disengaged. The barn is empty. There's nowhere to take cover if she gets trigger-happy. I look over my shoulder as I reach the top of the stairs, finding her a few steps behind me. Not too far, but far enough to have the upper hand, far enough to fire before I make it to her should I fight. I'm fucking snookered.

She swallows as she points to a huge opening in the wood looking out onto the countryside. I've heard funny things run through your mind when you're staring death in the face, and currently running through my mind is how beautiful that view is. How lush and green the land is. How this might be the last thing I see.

I approach and widen my stance, my back to Lauren. My mind settles, but determination fights forward. Here, I'm a sitting duck. I'm a dead man. No question, her aim is clear. If I charge her, she'll be shooting in a rush. She'll be clumsy. She might hit me, but the chances of her getting her aim right under pressure are reduced.

I turn, every muscle in my body readying. Her head cocks, and she must see the determination in my gaze because she flexes her two-handed grip on the gun. "Don't do anything stupid," she warns.

"Then just fucking shoot me, Lauren," I goad. Why is she dragging this out? One would assume her sick head is enjoying the anticipation of my death. Or could she be searching for the strength she needs to kill the man she loves? I don't get the chance to reach a conclusion on that. I hear a noise downstairs, the sound of a piece of wood snapping.

My gaze shoots to the gaping hole in the floor where the stairs drop. More wood snaps, the sound echoing through the barn and ricocheting off the walls. I see something emerge from the opening, and it takes me two seconds to recognize who. There's no mistaking the shiny, bald, black head. My heart lurches as Lauren swings the gun in his direction. And he's completely unaware. "John!" I yell, making Lauren spin around to face me. I raise my hands in the air and back up until I'm forced to stop or plunge fifty feet from the opening to the concrete below.

"Motherfucker," John breathes once he's made it safely to the top of the stairs. He slowly pulls off his sunglasses. His nostrils flare. His huge chest heaves. "Put the fucking gun down, Lauren." Most would heed the threat in his booming voice. Lauren isn't most. She moves a few paces to the right, putting her at an even distance between both of us, the gun swinging back and forth between our bodies. My head twists and warps, my panic rising. Did Ava click? Did she realize what I was telling her? Then why the fuck didn't she call the police? Not John, the police!

"You should go, John," Lauren warns. "This is between me and Jesse."

"I'm going nowhere." He's resolute, and I know he means it.

"Then you can watch."

Before I can even register, the gun is on me, her body turning in what seems like slow motion. And she wastes no time pulling the trigger. The loudest bang pierces the air, and my body jolts as John throws himself across the barn toward Lauren. My vision blurs, but I manage to see her turning the gun on herself, taking it toward her temple. John roars, and Lauren crashes to the ground. I hear another bang as they roll across the dusty floor. It's only the sound of Lauren's screams that tell me she missed.

Numb, frozen, I look down my torso, searching for the dark crimson soaking my T-shirt. There's nothing. Then there's something. Pain, fuck me, pain. I hiss and grasp the top of my arm, the blood now found, growing rapidly on my sleeve. The bolts of pain only keep my attention for a microsecond, a grunt from John realigning my focus. Lauren's made it onto her feet, and she's still holding the gun. She walks back, struggling for breath, wild eyes darting. She looks disoriented, unsteady as she backs up, the hole in the floor getting closer and closer, the wood all crumbled around the edges. I see what's about to happen, and for the life of me, I can't think why I try to warn her.

"Lauren, no!"

I'm too late. The floor cracks, and she loses her footing. She screams. It's a bloodcurdling scream—a scream that will haunt me for the rest of my days. A scream that tells me she doesn't really want to die. Instinct has me rushing forward as her arms flail and she plummets backward, the gun firing again before the floor completely gives. I flinch and look away when her head crashes against the edge of a jagged piece of broken wood as she falls through the floor, the impact silencing her. I know she's dead before she hits the concrete below. But I still wince on a helpless, broken sob when the thud of her body meeting the ground penetrates the air, the sound of cracking bones torturous.

My breathing diminishes, my blood running cold, as I fight to get air into my lungs, the pain kicking back in. My arm begins to throb, becomes lead hanging from my shoulder. Forcing my eyes back to the gaping hole in the floor, I carefully tread to the edge of it and peer over. I don't know why. I'm in conflict, relieved, sad, angry. Lauren's mangled body lies in an unthinkable position, her dead eyes staring up at me. I hiss, jumping back from the edge, a low, pain-filled moan piercing my muddled head.

But the moan doesn't come from me.

I whirl around and find John on his back, a pool of dark red growing around his big body. His bloody hand is resting on his abdomen. Shock stills me. Panic finds me again. I'm a mass of useless muscles. My mind has quit thinking, my head an empty mess.

"Help me, you stupid motherfucker." His words are all but a gargle of pain, his eyes rolling in their sockets.

His weak demand wakes me from my inertia, and I bolt across the barn, dropping to my knees by his side. His breathing is shallow. His black skin paling. My hands go to my hair and pull, panicked. "Fuck!" I yell, finally finding the sense to get my phone. I dial 999, demand an ambulance, mindlessly reel off where we are. "John." I grab his face, squeezing tightly. "John, keep your eyes open, buddy. Just keep your eyes open."

"Fuck you," he breathes, trying to focus on me. "There's ten of you, you bastard."

"There'll be a thousand of me if you don't keep your eyes open, big man, and every one of them will be kicking your big black arse." My voice is breaking, my hope dying with every second that passes, his eyes closing for longer each time. A lump the size of a small planet wedges itself in my throat. "John." I take his shoulders, shaking, and his eyes drag open with effort. The whites, usually stark and bright, are bloodshot. "What the fuck, John?" I lose control of my emotions and spill tears all over his face. "What the fuck have you done?"

He smiles. It's tired and his body goes limp in my hold. "I...I...," he gasps, sucking in oxygen. "I told...I told Carmichael..." Drawing air, he winces. "Motherfucker," he breathes, straining to keep his eyes open. "I told him I'd always look out for...you." His confession splits my heart clean in two.

"John," I choke, struggling to see him through my flooding eyes.

"It's...it's time for you to go it alone, boy." His eyes close, and I release a ragged sob, shaking him harder, desperate for him to stay with me.

"John, you bastard, open your fucking eyes!"

But he doesn't.

Because he's already gone.

"No!" I drop his shoulders, falling to my arse and crying like I've never cried before, relentless pain ripping through my broken body. "John," I mumble, squeezing my eyes closed, unable to see him like this. Lifeless. Limp.

This man has sacrificed everything for me. Love, happiness, freedom. He's been there at every turn, good and bad, and now he's gone. Gone because of me. He's given the ultimate sacrifice. His life for mine.

My sobs come, thicker and faster. My guardian angel. He's been by my side through good and bad, has never faltered in his loyalty.

He's kicked my arse and picked me up when I've been down. And the space inside me, the special place in my soul where John belongs, is gaping wide open.

He's my fucking hero.

And he's gone.

Chapter 55

Sirens. Lights. Shouts. The chaos in the middle of the pretty countryside is ugly. Voices are speaking to me but I'm hearing no words. Regret and guilt leave no room for anything else.

"How was she granted release?" I ask the police officer who's been trying to speak to me as a paramedic inspects the hole in my arm. "All this is because some clever prick was hoodwinked by a crazy woman." I shrug my arm, knocking the paramedic's hands away.

"Mr. Ward, I know nothing of the circumstances surrounding your ex-wife's release from hospital."

"Hospital?" I stare at him in disbelief. "No, a hospital is where you go when you're ill or injured. Not when you are a fucking psychopathic, merciless woman with a fucked-up vendetta." I feel hands on my arm again. "Get the fuck off me!" I bellow, making her back away vigilantly.

"Mr. Ward, please, calm down."

"Calm down?" I wouldn't be able to find calm if it dropped at my feet. Anger is consuming me. I feel dangerous. "My wife and kids were threatened. I had a gun pointed at me for over an hour." I throw my arm out toward the barn. "My best fucking mate has just been murdered!" I stagger back with the force of my roar, feeling all control escaping me. "You better leave me alone," I warn. "Just leave me the fuck alone until you can give me answers."

I back away to the wall of the barn and slump against the wood, lowering my arse to the dusty gravel before it can fall there. I sit, fighting to rein myself in. If Lauren weren't dead already, I would kill her with my bare hands. It wouldn't be quick. It would be long and torturous. I should have acted earlier. I should have listened to my gut and intervened before John got there.

I look up when I hear someone shout for space, and see a body bag being stretchered out of the barn. The size, the way the two women at each end of the stretcher move it with ease, tells me it's Lauren in that bag. Then another follows, this one negotiated by two men. My bottom lip quivers, my face falling into my palms. I can't watch. It's too final.

"Jesse!"

I look up and find Ava scrambling out of a car, her face frantic. I choke on nothing, bringing my balled fists to my temples and pushing into my skull. I want to go to her, shorten the time it'll take for her to make it to me, but my body refuses to function. So I remain on my arse, watching as she runs full pelt across the gravel toward me. I see her catch sight of the body bags. I see the falter in her stride. And when she finally makes it to me, she stops at my feet, looking down at my broken form. I'm struggling to keep my head up, but now she's this close, now I can see her, every perfect detail on her face, my body finds some life and manages to push its way up until I'm standing. She's biting her lip, her eyes brimming. I have nothing for her, only the agonizing news. "She fucking killed John."

Her inhale is sharp, the tears instant. "No," she whispers, looking back to the stretcher. "I tried to stop him." Her voice is breaking. "Oh my God, Jesse." She chokes over her words.

"I'm so sorry." Her palms come up to her face, like she's hiding, ashamed of herself.

I snatch them away. "Don't you fucking apologize," I warn, at risk of flying off the handle again. "Don't you dare, Ava."

"The app. The trackers on the cars. I realized what you were trying to tell me, and then John showed up and I told him. He took my phone. I couldn't stop him. I called the police from the house." The impact of her body hitting mine when she throws herself into my arms nearly takes me off my feet. "I'm so sorry." She sobs, and I shake my head into her, holding her as tight as my aching shoulder will allow. "I thought I'd never see you again. I thought it was the end of the road."

I hold her tighter. Fuck the pain. It's nothing compared to the agony in my heart. "Our road never ends, baby." I close my eyes and sink my face into her soft neck, searching for the comfort I know I can find. "Never."

"I remembered." Her sobs are loud between her words. She's not bothering to try to restrain her emotions. I'm glad, because I'm fucked if I can. My tears are unstoppable, soaking my cheeks and her neck. "I remembered everything."

"I know." I'm soul-destroyed that her avalanche of memories was triggered by such a bleak, distressing moment in our history. Absolutely destroyed. There are a million wonderful and pinnacle moments in our lives together. Why did it have to be Lauren? "I'm just so sorry it happened like that."

She pulls out of my hold, shaking her head mildly. "It wasn't her that triggered it all." Reaching for my face, she tenderly feels down my wet cheek. "It was the pure terror in your eyes. I'd seen it before."

I choke on my emotions, dropping my gaze until she forces my chin up. "John's gone," I choke. I can barely see her through my blurry vision.

Lip wobbling, she collects me in her arms and hugs me with the force and love that I so need. "He would never have let anything hurt you," she says, her voice thick. "The man was a fucking warrior, and a stubborn one, too." I can't even bring myself to pull her up on her bad language. "He's gone because he knows how much I need you. How much the kids need you." She takes my hand and lays it over her tummy. I'm not sure who's leaking the most tears now, her or me. I furiously wipe at my face, sniffing back my sadness. "He's my hero, too." She takes the top of my arm and rubs, frowning when I suck in air. "What's this?"

"A graze." I brush her off, not wanting to worry her. Not that she takes much notice. The short, bloody sleeve of my T-shirt is thrust up, revealing a tidy hole in my arm.

"Oh my God!"

"It's fine." Once again I fight her off and once again she wins, slapping me away. "Ava, for fuck's sake, it's fine. Stop flapping."

"Have you had it looked at?"

"I'm in no mood to be poked and pulled about."

She snorts, pointing to the paramedic hovering nearby. "Now, Ward, or so help me." Her expression is fierce as she scrubs at her wet face, and I shrink where I stand, thinking better of arguing back. I don't speak, and I also don't move, so Ava seizes my hand and all but manhandles me to the ambulance. "Don't make me hurt you, Ward."

Wide-eyed, I let her shove me onto the back of the ambulance and onto a waiting bed. She's taking no prisoners. And through my crippling hurt, anger, and guilt, I manage to locate some gratitude.

My wife is back. All of her is back, and it's back with a fucking bang.

Chapter 56

Eight months later

Nothing can prepare you for the loss of someone you adore with every fiber of your being. Nor the grief or heartache that accompanies that loss. A big hole has been left in my very existence by the loss of John, yet my heart is bursting with joyful memories. He was never far away, always there to pick me up when I fell down. His life was dedicated to me. To watching over me, to keeping his promise to his best friend. John was a good man, the best, and no matter how I try to angle my thoughts, he didn't deserve to go. It wasn't his time.

Lauren, however, needed to die. That may sound sadistic. Maybe it is. But all I've wondered is how draining and damaging it must have been to live with so many demons. The reality is, I can't. I've been in some pretty dark places. Have wanted to give up. But the victim in my journey through self-destruction was me and me alone. I never set out to hurt anyone. I never wanted revenge.

All I really wanted was inner peace.

As I sit on the steps in the garden, I watch Ava negotiate her pregnant belly to dip and pick up the hose. And I think for the first time in my existence, I really do have that peace. It's a blanket around me, warm and secure. It defies reason, really. More trauma and stress have been stirred into our already overflowing pot of shit, yet now I feel almost tranquil. Initially, after we walked away from that barn, I wondered how we would ever get over what had happened. The elation of Ava finding her memories was saddened by the loss of John. I got myself in a state over the twins, what they saw, what they heard.

It was only when we sat down with a family therapist at the suggestion of the liaison officer that I really realized that my babies truly weren't babies anymore. Not with their level heads, their matter-of-fact approach. I'd underestimated them at every turn. Tried to keep them wrapped up in cotton wool and protected from the world. I failed. My past caught up with me again, but the twins looked at me that day, square in the eye, and told me that they were proud of me. Not ashamed like I feared they would be. They were *proud* of me.

I broke down, didn't even try not to. I'm human. I'm a dad. A husband. My family is both my biggest weakness and my greatest strength. I live and breathe for them, and that will never change. Until the day I die, it will always be about them.

I look over my shoulder when I hear Maddie talking, seeing her wandering back into the house with her phone to her ear. She's talking to some boy. My instinct is to go after her, to confiscate that fucking phone. But I wisely stay on my arse where I'm safe from my wife's wrath. Maddie's twelve. How serious can it be? I growl at her back and shake my head, returning my attention to the garden before I change my mind and go trample her arse.

Jacob's in the distance smacking tennis balls over the net, practicing his serve.

Me? I have a beer in my hand just listening to the therapeutic sounds of my wife and babies mooching about our home. This is heaven. This is Ava's cloud nine. This is where I am supposed to be, and once again, the Fates have brought me here. I want to argue with them this time, though. Ask them why I can't have John here, too. But that would be wasted breath. And John would say something along the lines of "Get a fucking grip, you stupid motherfucker."

I smile, breathing back my unrelenting sadness. Sadness I know he'd be furious at me for spending too much time on. John can go fuck himself. I actually laugh out loud at my bravery for even thinking it. I would never have said that to him if he were standing here before me. Yet I wish I could. I wish I could curse his arse off to his face, and I would welcome the thump to my jaw from his big hard fist.

"What's so funny?" Ava swishes the spray from the hose over the flowerbeds, eyeing me with a curious smile.

"Just thinking." I push myself to my feet and wander across the lawn to her, my gaze taking constant up-and-down trips over her beautiful form. God love her, she looks fit to burst. We're nearly two weeks overdue now, with no signs of baby making an appearance. I reach her and push my chest into her back, circling her tummy with my arms. My hands meet on the front of her pregnant belly with ease, though I still tease her. "Only just." I smile into her neck when she thrusts her bottom into my groin. "Don't do silly things like that." Closeness to this woman always stirs my cock, but contact renders it concrete. That'll never change.

"Why, Mr. Ward, there's something poking into my back." She chuckles as she continues to drench the flowerbeds.

"Maybe I could fuck this baby out of you," I muse, thoughtful. "You've made it too comfortable in there."

"We've had sex twice a day every day for the past two weeks. Not even your penis coming at it head-on is making it want to come out of hiding." Dropping the hose as I laugh, she turns in my arms, her belly now wedged between us. I look down fondly. Yes, she's certainly carrying big, but nothing in comparison to when she was expecting the twins. Laying my palms on the top, I stroke and feel, my heart swelling with happiness when the baby kicks against my right hand.

"He's having a party in there. Clearly he's got his dad's talented dance moves."

Ava's hands land over mine, and we feel together. "You keep saying *he*. We don't know what the sex of Peanut Junior is yet."

"It's a boy," I assure her. It has to be. I've managed to hold on to my hair for this long. A girl might change that. "Jacob and I can't be outnumbered."

"But Maddie and I can?"

"You two have enough spunk between you for us to have ten more boys and still be out-spunked." I shift my hands and take hers, bringing them to my mouth and kissing each knuckle in turn, each and every one. She's beaming at me, her smile so strong with happiness I feel it warm my face. "It's a boy," I affirm.

"Whatever you say, my Lord." She turns away from me and brings my hands back around her tummy, holding them there as she starts waddling across the grass. I follow her steps, my chin resting atop her head. "Let's mooch."

"Mooch away," I reply, letting her lead the way to the bottom of the lawn where we pick up the gravel path through the flowerbeds that leads to the bench swing hidden at the bottom of the garden. The air is cool, but not quite cold, yet the sun could be blazing down from the sky. I'm toasty warm, contented, calm, and serene. And all of that is being absorbed by my wife.

A beautiful air of peace has surrounded her throughout this pregnancy. I've admired it daily as I've watched her, whether at home or at the club. She's been back to work and I've made sure I've let her get on with it, though I've never been truly far. Just far enough for her not to feel crowded, but close enough to sate my need for constant contact, even if that contact is just my eyes looking at her.

This pregnancy has been an entirely different experience for me. I've not stressed, not faffed, not driven her up the wall with my neurotic worry. And she hasn't played me or used that worry as a tool to wind me up. There has been no faking labor to send me into meltdown. Probably because she knows that this time there will be no meltdown. After all, I'm a pro now. I've got this.

As we walk, I notice her leaning back on me more and more, her body getting tired. "Rest?"

Her sigh is heavy. She's truly fed up now, but as I've told her time and again, these things can't be rushed. He'll come when he's ready. Helping her down onto the cushion on the bench, I take a seat beside her and push my feet into the ground, swinging us back and releasing. We rock smoothly, Ava's head resting on my shoulder. "Kate's bringing a vindaloo around later."

"Another?" I relax back. "That baby will come out expecting a curry instead of your boob."

She chuckles, and quickly flinches as she does, her hand going to her tummy and rubbing.

"Okay?" I ask softly, placing my hand over hers.

"Just a twinge." Pulling her head from my shoulder, she gazes up at me. Her lips twitch, her eyes glimmer.

I know what's running through that wonderful mind of hers. Though I humor her. "What's tickled you?"

"Twelve years ago, you would have crapped your boxers at a twinge."

I shrug, nonchalant. "We're experts now. After the twins, this is a breeze, right?"

A sharp puff of laughter fans my face. "A breeze? Speak for yourself, Jesse. You're not the one pushing what feels like—"

"A flaming watermelon out of my fanny." I've heard her cute analogy a few hundred times. "I know." Turning into her, I pout playfully as I cup her boobs, circling my thumbs over her nipples until they pebble. "Tonight you're going to let me ram my deprived cock inside that sweet pussy of yours and stretch it in preparation."

Her grin is thrilling. And wanting. And lustful. That's one of the few things that *hasn't* been different this time around. Her unrelenting craving for all things me. Thank God, because that would be a tragic loss. "You're so selfless."

"Anything for you, baby." I lean in over her belly and rest my lips on hers. The usual sparks of magic happen inside me, my heart thrumming wildly.

"Deprived cock?"

"Yes, deprived. Only a minute after leaving the snug warmth of that special place my dick feels lonely." It's no lie. "You going to challenge me?"

"Wouldn't dream of it." Her smile lays on mine as my hands feel the delicious weight of her amazing boobs.

"Besides, I have to take all I can get because you're going to be out of service for a while."

"You poor thing."

A rustling from beyond the bushes has me pulling away quickly, scanning the area. I cock my eyebrow at Ava, who indicates to the left with a nod of her head. "I can see you," I call, getting comfortable and rocking the bench again when I realize it's stopped. Two heads pop out of the hedge, grinning. "Neither of you would make stealth ninjas."

"We were gonna jump out and scare you," Jacob declares, breaking free from the branches and twigs, pulling a few leaves from his blond mop. "We're fed up of waiting for Peanut Junior." He offers Maddie a helping hand when her blouse gets caught up.

"You're fed up?" Ava laughs. "Try carrying this thing around with you for nine months."

"Don't be dramatic," I quip, patting the bench next to me for Maddie to come sit. "It's not been that big the *whole* time."

Maddie giggles as she jumps onto the bench and snuggles into my side, Jacob taking the side next to Ava. "Dad, seriously. Do you want Mum to hurt you?"

"She'd have to catch me first, and that ain't happening when she's in that condition." I put an arm around each of my girls, looking across to Jacob. His head is lying on Ava's stomach, his ear pushed close.

Ava's hands start threading through his blond hair, stroking while he listens. We settle and swing for a while, all of us quiet and relaxed, legs swinging freely, heads resting on various shoulders. I could stay here all night, but it's getting chilly and Sam will be here soon with his girls, as well as Drew with his. I smile. Raya gave birth only last week to a little girl, Imogen, bang on time. All these girls; by the rule of probability, Ava has to have a boy in there. I pray she has a boy in there.

"Come on, it's getting cold." I nod to Ava's nipples on a smirk, and she rolls her eyes. "The gang will be here soon."

Jacob is first off the bench, helping a puffing Ava to her feet. "Thank you, darling." Her arm goes around his shoulders as they start back to the house together. My boy. My gorgeous, sweet, thoughtful boy. He's overtaken Maddie in height now, clearing her by a good few inches. He's not far off Ava.

I feel the sleeve of my T-shirt lift and look out the corner of my eye to see Maddie inspecting the scar left behind. Though she doesn't look sad these days when she's feeding her need to see it at least once a day. These days, she smiles. "Did your life flash before your eyes, Dad?"

I laugh and dip, hoisting her up over my shoulder and following on after Jacob and Ava. The sweet sound of my girl's squeal fills my ears. "Yes, and do you know what I thought?"

"What did you think?" she asks, bouncing upon my shoulder in time to my strides.

"I thought about how much I'd miss your sass."

"No you didn't," she laughs, slapping my back. "Hey, Dad. Can I go to the cinema on Friday with Robbie?"

Robbie. So that's the flavor of the month. "Sure you can." I set her on her feet when we make it to the house, leaving her behind as I follow Ava and Jacob. "What are we watching?" I call behind me.

"You're hilarious." Her exasperation makes me chuckle as I open the fridge and pull out some Sun-Pat. But that chuckle fades to nothing when it's swiped from my hand. "Hey!"

Ava grins and sashays as best she can to a stool, finger-dipping my jar as she clambers onto the seat. "What's yours is mine," she declares, popping a delicious-looking finger into her mouth and making an over-the-top job of licking it clean.

I hear the kids laugh as I sulk at my wife, wondering why, of all the things she could crave, it has to be my pots of heaven. Sharing my vice is no joke. I've only just got to grips with Jacob pinching my passion. "Share," I order, taking myself swiftly across the kitchen and joining her on the next stool, my mouth dropping open. I may even be dribbling.

Humming, she scoops out a huge dollop and holds it out to me. This part of the sharing process I don't mind at all. My mouth watering, I move in to claim her finger. But she quickly diverts to her own mouth, lapping it up quickly on a satisfied smile and sparkly eyes. I recoil, disgusted by her game, though the kids seem to think it's hilarious.

Only one word comes to mind. "Three," I practically snarl, widening her grin.

"Oh boy," Jacob sighs, collecting some juice from the fridge. "Mum, will you ever learn?"

"Don't mess with the peanut butter," Maddie adds, resting her elbows on the counter and settling in for the show. "You'll pay, and your bladder isn't as strong these days."

I laugh on the inside when Ava tosses her an indignant look, her finger hanging out of her mouth. "Stay out of it, sassy-pants."

Maddie shrugs her shoulders, chin resting in the palms of her hands. "I'm my mother's daughter. Ask Dad."

She isn't wrong. "Two," I say, turning back to Ava, my eyebrows high.

"There's nothing wrong with my bladder." She takes another huge helping of the good stuff, her nose high. "And if there is, it's your fault." She nods at the kids in turn.

"One." I start drumming my fingers, all casual and cool, appearing tired of the light banter. I'm not tired at all. These moments, the simple moments, are some of my favorite family times.

"Mine," Ava whispers, plunging in her finger again and holding it up in demonstration before lapping it clean. "Get your own, Ward."

"Zero, baby." I'm off the stool in a flash, my fingertips homing straight in on Ava's weak spots.

"No!" The jar is quickly cast aside in favor of my arms.

"You asked for it," Maddie sings, going on her way and leaving us to it. "Don't pee yourself."

"Whose is the peanut butter?" I ask in her ear, handling her gently but firmly. "Just say the words, baby, and I'll stop."

"Never!" She laughs, fighting my hands away with little success. "Ohhhhh..."

My torturing fingers stop. That wasn't a regular sound that I hear when I'm tickling her stupid. I release her in a heartbeat, scanning her up and down. "A twinge?"

Jacob's by my side quickly, and Maddie's not far behind. Ava stills while we all wait with bated breath for her conclusion, her eyes focused on her bump as she drops to her feet from the stool. "Yeah, I think...oh my FUUUUCK!" She doubles over and screams, forcing all of us to cover our ears or burst our drums. "Sorry, kids," she adds, starting to pant.

"Bloody hell!" Maddie starts running circles around the kitchen in a panic. "Peanut Junior is coming!"

"Shit!" Jacob yells.

My head could pop off my neck. What's with all this fucking bad language? "Will everyone watch their mouths!" I yell, taking Ava's elbow.

"But the baby's coming!" Maddie shouts, still doing panicked laps of the kitchen. "Call an ambulance. The doctor. Anyone!"

"It's coming!" Jacob covers his face with his palms. "It's because you tickled her!"

Christ, everyone needs to calm the hell down. I take a deep breath. "Don't worry, kids," I say calmly. "Dad's got this." Am I telling them, or myself? "Maddie, you get Mum's bag. Jacob, you get my mobile so I can call the hospital and tell them we're on our way."

We all flinch when Ava lets out another almighty, blood-curdling scream, grabbing onto me with both hands, her nails puncturing my forearms. "Fucking hell, Ava," I hiss, prying her buried claws one by one out of my flesh. "Sorry, kids."

"Does that hurt, Ward?" she pants, bending, starting to sweat.

"Just a bit." I play it down. I shouldn't have. She sinks her nails into me again on an evil look.

"Good."

Jesus, she's turning into a psycho. I watch the kids fly out of the kitchen to fulfill their orders, and realign my focus on Ava. "You want to sit."

"No!"

"You want to stand, then?"

"No!"

"Right." I roll my eyes, accepting my mobile when Jacob thrusts it at me.

"You okay, Mum?"

"Yes, darling." She reaches blindly for his head and gives it a loving, reassuring pat. "I love you."

I recoil, shaking my head in wonder. So she's just a psycho bitch with me, then? Dialing the hospital, I keep hold of Ava as she moans, constantly cursing me and apologizing to the kids. "Hi, my wife's gone into labor. Ava Ward." I watch Ava's face turns bright red. "We'll be around half hour." Her nostrils start to flare. "Yeah, great. Bye." I hang up and hand the phone to Jacob. "Call Nan and tell her to get her arse here quick."

"We can't come?" He looks totally put out.

"Trust me, mate. You don't want to be anywhere near your mother while she's pushing Peanut Junior out."

"I'd rather him than you," Ava spits, going into another scream, grappling at my arms.

"There's no need for that now, is there?" I sound so condescending, but other than dishing out a Retribution Fuck, which is off the cards right now, I have no other option but to humor her. "It's *your* body who rejected the pill." She's not slapping this on me. No way.

"Really, Dad?" Maddie smacks my arm. "You're gonna say that to her when she's in labor?"

So it's gang up on Dad day? Has it escaped everyone's notice that I'm the only calm one around here? "Jacob, call your nan," I order, this time less calmly. Ava's contractions have come on fast, and there's not much space between them. I pull Ava's hair from her damp face and indicate for Maddie to tie it up with the hair-band on her wrist as Jacob dials Elizabeth.

"Nan, it's Jacob." He dances on the spot, eyes on his mother. "Mum's in labor. Dad said get your arse here now."

I hear my mother-in-law's screech of joy. "Tell her to hurry," I call.

"Hurry, Nan!" he shouts, hanging up and stuffing my phone in my pocket for me.

"I love you," Ava tells Maddie while she secures the tie, feeling at her startled face. "You're beautiful, smart, and sassy, and I love you."

"Love you, too, Mum."

If she wasn't in labor, I would think Ava was drunk. What's gotten into her? It's a stupid question. I know what. It's that whole replacement thing. "Come on, lady," I say, breaking up their moment. "Let's get you to the car."

Her answer is an epic scream, her body unmoving when it solidifies in a natural attempt to stem the pain. "Oh my fucking God!" *Pant, pant, pant.* "Sorry, kids." She fists the front of my T-shirt and hauls me forward with a power Wonder Woman would be envious of. Her eyes are wild. "This baby is coming out now, Ward." Yet another scream pierces the air immediately after her statement.

And following that, my panic. "What?" No. No, no, no. "Ava, we just need to get you in the car and I'll have you at the hospital in no time at all."

She starts to fold to the floor, moaning on her way down. I have no choice but to scoop her up and carry her through to the lounge where it's more comfortable. "There is no time," she wails as I lay her on the couch. "Not on the couch! It'll be ruined."

"For fuck's sake." I can't help it. "Sorry, kids." I lay her on the carpet and get her head comfy on a pillow. "Baby, I need to get you to the hospital."

She shakes her head. "It's coming."

"Jacob, Maddie, hold your mum's hand," I order, sending them to the top end. Once they're in position, I reach under Ava's long skirt and pull her knickers down; the material is drenched. "I'm just going to check what's going on down there," I tell her, to appease Ava more than myself. "Then we'll get you to the hospital." I help her legs to bend, ensuring I keep her covered as best I can as the kids look on.

"I need to push," she pants.

"You do not need to push," I assure her as I take a peek between her legs. It's way too soon. "Oh, fuck!" I blurt, seeing the crown of a head breaching her vagina. "Shit, Ava!"

"I fucking told you I need to push!"

"Dad?" Jacob's unsure voice lifts my hollow head, and I find two sets of very worried eyes. This wasn't part of the plan. They're panicking.

I need to take control. "Maddie, go get towels and a cool flannel. Jacob, I want you to get the duvet off our bed and open the front door." I grab my phone as they shoot off like obedient bullets. "Ava, baby, no pushing yet, okay?" I dial for an ambulance as she nods, blowing out short, sharp shots of breath. "I need an ambulance. My wife is in labor, and she most definitely isn't going to hold out until I can get her to the hospital."

"What's your wife's name, sir?"

"Ava. Ava Ward."

"And your address?"

I reel it off as the kids dart into the lounge simultaneously, both their arms full of my requests. "The baby's head is crowning," I tell the operator, trying to push back the urgency I'm feeling and remain calm for Ava. She's huffing and puffing, cheeks blowing out, eyes clenching shut.

"Okay, Mr. Ward, first things first, don't panic."

I laugh. If she'd said that to me when Ava's water broke with the twins, I would have verbally ripped her head off. "I'm not panicking," I assure her coolly. "But I am going to need someone to walk me through this." I take another quick peek under Ava's dress. "This chap is in a rush." Fucking hell, he's stalled making his entrance, and now he's decided he's got jet propellers in his feet. I watch as Jacob plumps pillows and Maddie flaps the duvet out.

"An ambulance has been dispatched and the midwife called."

"Thank you." They'd better hurry.

"Okay. Now who is there, Mr. Ward?" the operator asks.

"Me, my son, and daughter."

"How old are they?"

"Twelve. They're twins." Ava's eyes spring wide open, her head shaking furiously from side to side. Sweat is dripping from her. "Just hold one moment while I get her comfortable."

"No problem."

I drop the phone and slide my arms under Ava's body, lifting her from the floor. "Pull the duvet under," I tell Maddie. "And the pillows there." The two of them work efficiently and calmly, and I know for sure that my coolness is the reason why. I just need to maintain it. But, fuck, this was not part of my plan when I've mentally walked through Ava's labor dozens of times. "Guys, I need your help," I tell them, lowering Ava back to the soft duvet. "Can you do that?"

Both nod, eyes passing back and forth between me and Ava. "Is she all right, Dad?" Jacob asks, the shock not masked in his voice as well as it is on his face.

"She's fine," I assure him, stroking back Ava's hair from her wet face, dropping a kiss onto her forehead. "Aren't you, baby?"

She groans but tries to nod, too, her head jerks uncontrolled and erratic. I smile, grabbing her hand and squeezing. "You ready?"

Blowing out air through her pursed lips, she constricts my hand. "Don't leave me."

"None of us are leaving."

She looks up toward the kids, who are on either side of her head, straining a smile. "This is nothing compared to when I had you two," she assures them.

I laugh when the kids' eyes bug, glancing at each other.

"Maddie, put that damp cloth on Mum's forehead," I order, moving back down Ava's body. "Jacob, hold Mum's hand. She's going to squeeze it really hard, mate, so get those muscles flexing."

"I don't want to hurt him," Ava wails, her back bowing violently when another contraction hits her.

Jacob quickly snatches up her hand with both of his, moving in closer to her head on his knees. "It's okay, Mum. Squeeze as hard as you need to."

My fucking heart melts as I grab the phone and put it on loudspeaker, resting it on the floor next to me. "Okay. We're ready."

"Okay, Mr. Ward. How far apart are the contractions?"

"One minute, maybe two." I encourage Ava to bend her knees more and spread her legs further, taking a towel and laying it over her knees.

"On the next contraction, I want Ava to push and you to apply pressure on her vagina."

My eyes widen, and I look at the kids, who, as I expected, are cringing terribly. I'm not cringing. I am, however, fucking confused. "You want me to push the head back in?" Surely not.

Ava screams as I utter my question, her face going red. "You're not pushing it back in, Jesse! I want it out! Now!"

Fucking hell, the pressure. "Okay, baby. Calm down."

"Mr. Ward." The operator isn't laughing, but she's not far off. "I want you to apply pressure at the top of Ava's vagina." That word again, and the kids both grimace. "The angle will help the baby's head pass through easier."

I blink my eyes rapidly, trying to focus on the part of my wife that I love the most, the part that looks *nothing* like I remember. "Right," I breathe, reaching forward. "How hard?"

"Firmly, Mr. Ward."

"It's coming!" Ava starts panting, her cheeks inflating. "Now!"

"Okay, push, baby!" I do as instructed, applying as much pressure as I'm comfortable with.

"Go on, Mum!" the twins chant together. "You can do it!"

She grunts, she wails, she cries. It's all so familiar, but no less easy to hear. "Jesse!" My name is a drawn-out, high-pitched howl, her head tossed back, her back arched. "Oh my God, it hurts!"

I wince, keeping my eyes rooted between her legs. A head, smeared with blood and goo, emerges slowly but surely, my spare hand resting on the underside. "Come on, Ava," I yell, cheering her on. "He's coming."

She slumps, exhaling raggedly, and the baby's head slowly retreats. I reach to my brow and wipe away the sheen of sweat. "The head came out a bit, but it's gone back in again," I tell the operative.

"Perfectly normal, Mr. Ward. We'll wait for the next contraction and encourage a big push."

"A big push, Ava. Did you hear that?"

"I'm not fucking deaf!" she snaps between quick, sharp inhales and exhales, throwing me daggers. I shrink, but the kids chuckle, Jacob having a quick shake out of his poor hand. "I'm sorry, darling," Ava says, clumsily reaching for his head and patting around in his hair. "Did I hurt you?"

"Not at all." He raises his arms and flexes his nonexistent biceps. "I'm built of steel."

Maddie cackles. "In whose world?"

"Concentrate," Jacob orders, giving Ava back his hand.

"Oh, no." Ava's panicked eyes land on me with a bang. "Here's another one!"

I pull myself together and move in closer. "This time a big push, okay? The biggest you can manage."

"I'm trying." She's getting tearful, her eyes welling.

"Come on," I coo, placing my hand back where it should be. "You pushed two babies out one after the other. This is a walk in the park."

"Screw you, Ward. This one must be as big as Jacob and Maddie put together. I'm going to be ripped in two. Oh, oh, oh!" Her teeth grit, her fists ball, her head shoots forward. "Arghhhhhhhh!"

"That's it!" I encourage her, watching as the head crowns and gradually stretches her opening. "Come on, baby! He's nearly here." The agonizing sound of her screams goes straight through me. "A bit more! Yes, yes! That's it, Ava!"

The head passes the widest point and slips free of her walls, a perfect little profile on perfect display. My voice catches in my throat, my hand stroking over the top of his wet head. Fuck, even covered in slime he's gorgeous.

"The head's out," I say to the operative, grabbing another towel.

"That's great." She's so calm. "One more push on the next contraction, Mr. Ward. When the baby is out, lay it straight on Ava's chest and wrap it in a towel. Make sure the cord isn't caught up."

"Okay." I prepare myself, glancing up at Ava. She's crying now, feeling Maddie's hair as she dabs the flannel across her forehead. "Ava," I call, making her head drop limply. "One more push, baby."

She nods on a big swallow, closing her eyes.

"Just one more, Mum." Maddie pushes some loose strands of hair off Ava's face as Jacob has another shake of his hand in preparation, throwing me a *Jesus!* look as he does. When Ava starts with the semi-controlled breaths again, I know the final push is coming. Leveling her eyes on me, she grits her teeth and nods, her face starting to go beet red. There's no sound from her this time. Just round eyes glued to me as she goes into the final stretch.

He comes out so fast, I nearly miss it, my gaze set on my beautiful wife being helped by my beautiful children. "Oh, fuck." His wet, slippery body falls into my big hands, and his screams start immediately after that. The sound is fucking golden. He's fucking perfect. I'm a fucking wreck, my eyes full of tears. I carefully shift him into one hand, being careful of the cord, and push Ava's T-shirt up, laying him on her chest and covering them with a towel.

I expect the twins to grimace and look away, but they are utterly mesmerized by the sight, their little jaws hanging open. "He's here," I croak, mindful that the operative is waiting for an update. "He's here and he's perfect."

"Congratulations, Mr. Ward."

"Thank you." Emotion ambushes me as I watch Ava hold our baby to her chest, her lips resting on his head, her eyes closed.

"I hardly did a thing." The operative chuckles. "You were a perfect student. I've had confirmation that the paramedics and midwife are just a few minutes away. I'm going to stay on the line until they arrive."

I nod, sniffle, and wipe my nose with the back of my hand as I crawl up the side of Ava to join them. Her face is red and blotchy, her hair a wet mess. But she's stunning. I smile and reach for my baby's little hand, amazed by his tiny fingers. "He's perfect," I whisper, instant love booming within me.

"You keep saying *he*." Ava looks down at the back of his head. "Is it confirmed?"

I frown. No, it's not. I was so enthralled, I didn't look for his bits, or lack thereof. "Wait." I reach for the towel covering them, pulling it up before lifting a little leg a tad so I can see.

"What is it, Dad?" Jacob hurries around to my side, as well as Maddie. "A boy or a girl?"

I smile, looking at each of their impatient faces before cocking my head for them to look themselves. Both their heads dive down to inspect the area.

"Well?" Ava asks, impatient. "Tell me."

Maddie coughs. "It's definitely a *he*." Looking up to Ava, she smirks. "And he's got a bigger penis than Jacob has now!"

I let out a bark of laughter, roughing my boy's hair when he throws an indignant look Maddie's way. "Get lost, Maddie."

I crawl up and lie down beside Ava, my body stretched the length of hers and then some. I kiss my baby boy's sweet little head, inhaling as I do. Lord, I've missed that smell so much. "You did so well." I turn my lips to my wife and kiss her sweaty forehead, taking the opportunity to breathe her in, too. "So, so well."

Sighing deeply, she closes her eyes and nuzzles into me. "You're my superstar."

"That's one I've never been called before," I quip lightly. "What happened to *god*?"

A tired chuckle melts into my ears as I snuggle in close, the side of one finger stroking down his little cheek. "He's a good-looking little fucker," I whisper. "Clearly he takes after his dad."

"Your ego knows no bounds."

"Hey, what are we calling him?" Maddie is already besotted, her attention on the baby and the baby alone.

I stall voicing my preference, like I have for some time. I'm not sure if it's a good idea, or what Ava would think. "I don't know." I shrug mildly. "What do you guys think? What does he look like?"

Both of them crowd him, their heads cocked in contemplation. "He doesn't look like anything." Jacob reaches forward and touches the end of his nose. "He's so tiny."

"I think he looks like a Joseph," Maddie declares. "He's got the same amount of hair as Pap."

I grin when Ava snorts. "What do you think, Mummy?"

Ava breathes in, her chin lowering to her chest to look at his peaceful form. She thinks for a while, and then she looks to the twins. "Maddie, Jacob, meet your new brother." Glancing back at me, my wife smiles faintly. "Baby John-Boy."

Oh, fucking hell. My heart bursts. "Really?" I ask, pushing down the lump working its way into my throat.

She shrugs, as if it's nothing, when it is absolutely *everything*. "He looks like a John to me." Peeking back down at him, she nods to herself decisively. "Yes, he's definitely a John. And if we're lucky, he'll be as loyal, brave, and loving as the original."

Fuck, I'm a goner. I bury my face into her neck and let my stinging eyes release the tears. My emotions are shot, a huge concoction of overwhelming happiness and unrelenting sadness.

I'll make sure baby John-Boy is all of those things. If it's the last thing I do, he'll be everything his uncle John was. I feel Ava's hand in my hair, comforting me. I've held it together for long enough. It's all coming out now.

But then baby John-Boy decides it's his turn to have a wail, putting the stoppers on my intended release time. I peek up, my face wet, and find his fist rammed in his mouth. "Someone's hungry." I look across to the kids and cock my head. "Mum's about to get her boobs out."

"I'll go see if the ambulance is here!" Jacob bombs from the lounge like a spitfire, leaving smoke in his wake. I laugh. He's just witnessed his mum giving birth, not that he saw the graphic stuff, but still. It was an experience. And he's scared of a bit of boob?

"Can I stay?" Maddie asks, a little tentatively. She's so curious, completely bewitched by her new brother.

"Sure you can, darling." Ava reaches for her hand. "But first would you mind getting me some water?"

"Ice?"

"Lovely."

Maddie shoots off, eager to help. It's a great start to the new dynamics of our family. "Shall we?" I ask, helping her lift him to her breast. He latches onto Ava's nipple like a suction pad, his cheeks hollowing and pulling long sucks. "Fuck me, he's definitely a breast man."

"Stop." Ava laughs, smacking my hand playfully before settling her head back down. If there is a more beautiful sight than this, then I'm yet to see it.

"You're a lucky man, John-Boy," I whisper, taking my face down close to his. His eyes are open just a fraction, but they're on me. "I'm willing to share for now," I tell him, dropping a kiss on his forehead as Ava giggles softly. "But be warned, I'm only loaning them to you. I want them back. Understand?" I stroke over his smooth head, smiling down at my new baby boy.

I swallow down the lump closing my throat and look up to the eyes that keep me alive. And looking back at me, her gaze soft and teary, is the beauty that is my life.

Epilogue

Eighteen months later

AVA

The sun is warm, the sky clear. Our house smells like cakes baking and potatoes roasting. It's all mixing up with the drifting scent of charcoal from the barbeque floating in from the garden. It smells like home, our home, and the sounds are perfectly our home, too. Maddie's music blaring down the stairs, Jacob smacking a tennis ball across the net. John-Boy squealing in the garden. I smile and peek out the kitchen window as I rub cream into my hands, seeing Jesse on all-fours chasing him. I say *chase*. He's making all the threatening sounds as he crawls after our lumbering toddler on the lawn. He's just walking. Literally *just*. I was beginning to worry; the twins were both on their feet at twelve months, but John-Boy...oh, no. But then when he's got four people to carry him around wherever he pleases, why the hell would he bother using his own two feet?

Taking my apron off and letting my hair out of its ponytail, I head for the garden to join in the fun now all the food is prepped.

As I make it to the back door, finding them rolling around on the grass, I can't bring myself to interrupt their roughty-toughty fun. Besides, I'm hardly dressed for wrestling. So I stand at the door, my shoulder resting on the frame, and I do something I'll never tire of. I watch them. Jesse and John-Boy. I watch them laugh, roll, squeal. My husband is on his back and currently has our toddler held in the air above him, swishing him from side to side like a diving fighter plane. He's making the noises to match. John-Boy thinks it's hilarious. I do, too. All that fear Jesse tried to hide in the early stages of my pregnancy was wasted effort. I understood his panic. Fifty is quite mature to be fathering a child. But, truth is, it's given him a new lease of life. After everything that happened, John, Lauren, my accident, John-Boy was a pure blessing in disguise.

I breathe in and take a seat on the steps quietly so they don't notice they have a spectator. Jesse rolls over and places John-Boy on his unsteady feet, quickly moving back. "Can you catch Daddy?" he asks, ruffling up John-Boy's blond hair. It's thick and gorgeous, just like his brother's and just like his daddy's.

"Dada, noooooo!" John-Boy bends at the waist and places his little palms on his knees, like he could be telling Jesse off. I stifle a laugh, grinning like an idiot as John-Boy stomps forward with outstretched arms and Jesse walks back on his knees, keeping the distance. "Dada, bad!" He's getting stroppy, his gorgeous little face twisting with displeasure. "Back, back, back!" he shouts. "Back, Dada!"

"You can go faster," Jesse tells him, getting to his feet. "Run for Daddy."

"John-Boy run!" He waddles on, his pace picking up. "John-Boy, run, run, run!"

"That's it." Jesse walks backward, his pace slow, even though John-Boy's little chubby legs are now virtually sprinting. My breath catches when I see him stumble, his hands coming up in an instinctual move to save him before he hits the deck. He doesn't need those hands.

"Oops, there he goes." Jesse laughs, swiping John-Boy from his feet in one swift move. And then he is sailing through the air like a jet plane once again. Jesse's always there for him. Always there for all of us.

I clap, laughing, winning both of their attentions. I'm not sure whose green eyes sparkle more. "Good running, John-Boy!" I call, holding out my hands for him to come.

"Mama!" He struggles free from Jesse's hold and gets set on his feet. God, his little grinning face is just edible. Clomping on his way, he holds his arms out while Jesse keeps close company behind to catch him when he falls. Because he will.

About two of Jesse's strides away, the inevitable trip happens. And once again he's saved by Daddy, who swings him into my arms. "There he is!" I sing, catching him from Jesse's hands and putting my lips straight on his cheek, making him giggle, the sound so sweet.

Jesse lowers to the step beside me, his attention now on me. When his gaze meets mine, he smiles that roguish smile. "I like your dress."

"Of course you do. You chose it." I roll my eyes as I reach over to offer my lips. I don't get a chance to poise them ready for his attack. He's on me fast, delivering a smacker of a kiss. "Hmmm, you smell divine." I hum, feeling John-Boy pulling at the top of my black wraparound dress. That fresh water scent on my husband is still the best tranquilizer, my body folding under the smell, his breath always so minty fresh.

Pulling back a fraction, Jesse circles my nose with his. "Someone wants access," he quips, nodding to John-Boy wrestling with the black material of my dress. "Greedy little sod."

"Someone needs to get used to the fact that Mummy's boobs aren't at his disposal." I take John-Boy's hands and push them away, making him whine and start slapping my chest in protest.

"I know, mate," Jesse sighs, reaching for his chubby cheek and pinching lightly. "She's a tease, right?"

I laugh, repositioning John-Boy on my lap, away from me. He's having none of it, fighting to turn. I moan. This weaning business is exhausting, but with me now setting up my own interior design firm, it's essential. Plus, he's way too big now to be hanging off my boob. "Mummy will get you a bottle."

"Booby, booby, booby!"

Jesse falls apart, chuckling uncontrollably next to me while I fight off our relentless toddler. "Just let him have what he wants." Jesse places his hand on John-Boy's head, rubbing lovingly.

I refuse to give in, and part of me is wondering if my conniving husband has a method to his madness, because he usually does. And this time, I suspect he's cottoned onto the fact that with his son stuck to my breast, there's no way I can go back to work full-time. Well, he can think again. He sulked for weeks when I told him my plan for my new business. Even laid a few of his fucks on me. They didn't make a difference. I held my own, and he finally relented. He's learning. "Jesse," I moan, looking for the backup I need. Jesus, he'll still be attached to my breast when I'm fifty, and I plan on having surgery way before then. Like as soon as these balloons shrink back down to their usual form, which basically means they'll be spaniel's ears again.

"I'm sorry." My wayward husband snorts and gathers himself.

"Why are you finding this so funny, anyway?" I grumble, handing John-Boy over to Jesse. "I thought you wanted them back for yourself?"

He stands John-Boy on his knees and smiles fondly at the little bugger. "But his needs are greater than mine, aren't they, buddy?"

I'm stunned. Never in a million years did I ever expect those words to fall from my husband's mouth. "You've changed," I mutter, feeling absolutely slighted as he distracts John-Boy by blowing raspberries on his belly. The shriek of laughter is ear-piercing and heart swelling all at once, John-Boy's hands yanking at Jesse's dirty blond waves. "If you're feeling that blasé about my boobs, you won't mind if I get them inflated to their former glory." I realize I've just poked the bear with a huge fucking stick. But still...what the hell, with all this casual approach to my assets? Or his assets, more to the point.

Jesse's playful motions still, his face smothered by John-Boy's round tummy. I smile to myself, waiting for the thorough dressing down I'm about to get. Slowly, his face turns toward mine, his green eyes narrow, the cogs of his mind smoking they're spinning so fast. "Take that back right now."

I pout, all innocent, and shake my head. I'm in the mood for a Retribution Fuck. "I'm getting a boob job."

"Over my dead body, lady."

I sigh, rising to my feet. "Get a grip, Ward. I've had three kids ravish these boobs, on top of you. They're knackered." I turn and wander into the house, Jesse hot on my heels with John-Boy thrown under his arm, laughing. Daddy isn't laughing, though.

"Ava!"

"Mama!"

I get to the fridge and pull out some milk for John-Boy, turning with a coy smile on my face as I shake it up. "So whose boobies are they?"

"Mine," Jesse growls, nostrils flaring and all. "I only loaned them."

"Mine!" John-Boy sings, making grabby hands for his milk. My grin stretches my face as I hand John-Boy his milk, Jesse's displeased eyes following me all the way. He shoves it straight in his mouth and pipes down.

"I believe they are actually mine," I declare haughtily, sashaying out of the kitchen, knowing exactly what I'm damn well doing. *These boys*, I think, heading to answer a knock at the front door.

The whole gang marches into the house. Drew and Raya head straight for the lounge to lay a sleeping Imogen on the couch, while Georgia dances off upstairs to find Maddie. Sam and Kate have a verbal spar on the way to the kitchen over whose turn it is to change Betty's nappy, and Mum and Dad, followed closely behind by Jesse's parents, head straight for the kitchen to take the reins.

I follow the troop, meeting Jacob at the entrance to the kitchen. "Look at the state of you." I sigh, pointing to the grass stains on his knees as he spins his tennis racket in his grasp.

"Are Uncle Sam and Drew here?" He shrugs off my fussing hands and pulls a tennis ball from the pocket of his shorts. "We're playing doubles, and me and Dad are gonna win."

I laugh. "Of course you are, darling. Dad always wins." I take his shoulders and push him into the kitchen. "Come say hi to everyone before you disappear back into the garden."

"Hey, Mum?" He stops us from progressing to the kitchen, looking up at me. He gives me his sweet little crinkled forehead that's a replica of his dad's. It's frightening how much our boys look like Jesse. They're like little doppelgängers. It's both highly satisfying that they've inherited their father's obscenely handsome looks, and very worrying, too. How many girls will I be fending off over the coming years?

Which reminds me, Jacob has a guest—a girl he's fond of. Jesse and I agreed to let them each have a friend over for this afternoon's barbeque in John's memory. Neither of us expected them to invite friends of the opposite sex. "What's up, sweetheart?" I know what's up.

"When Clarita arrives, don't embarrass me, will you?"

I feign a shocked face, resting my palm on my chest. "Me?"

"Yes, you. And please keep Dad under control."

I laugh. "You don't have to worry about your father. His attention will be on Maddie and her *guest*."

"Still, be cool, yeah?"

"Yes, I'll be *cool*," I assure him. "But just remember."

"What?"

I smile down at my boy and kiss his hair. "You only need one woman in your life. And who's that?"

"My mother." He sighs on an expert roll of his eyes, one I know he's learned from me.

"Good boy." I leave him to say his hellos to the gang, going back to the front door when there's knocking.

I open and find Elsie with a huge bunch of flowers held in front of her. Her head pops up over the spray, her pink hair blending with the colorful arrangement. "John always bought me big, bright bouquets. He said the more vibrant, the more they reminded him of me."

I smile, a little sadness washing over me. "They're beautiful." I accept them and give her a big hug. "You look gorgeous. Thank you for coming."

"Don't get all sappy on me or I'll cry, and John would not be happy about that." She gently but firmly swats me away, lifting her chin high. "Where are those gorgeous children?"

I laugh and open the way, leading her to the kitchen. "Elsie's here," I declare, smiling when everyone rushes to welcome her. I make my way to the fridge, pulling out a jug of Pimm's.

"What's up with moody balls?" Kate asks, collecting the glasses for me.

Sure enough, Jesse's forehead is a map of angry lines, his scowl pointed at me. I smile sweetly at him as I pour drinks for me and Kate. "I may have dropped the boob bomb."

"Oh, that would explain it." She chuckles and takes a glug of her drink as Raya joins us with Elsie.

"Explain what?" Raya asks, taking an empty and holding it out for me to fill.

"My man is grumpy about the boob situation."

Raya whines a little under her breath. "Oh God, my breasts look like they've been ravaged, and not in the best way." She looks down at them, her lip curling in disapproval.

"Oh, you young girls!" Elsie chuckles. "Grow old gracefully."

I snort. "It's all right for you with your tight little body." I'm still doing yoga with Elsie, though not as often, and I can guarantee I won't have her figure in my midsixties.

"What's going on?" Jesse asks, looking as suspicious as I know he is as he approaches, a quiet John-Boy still gobbling down his milk in his arms.

"Nothing," I sing, taking the jug of Pimm's and topping up the girls.

"Hey." Kate pulls Sam over. "If Ava's getting her boobs fixed, so am I."

"Ava isn't getting her boobs fixed because they aren't broken," Jesse declares, throwing Kate a deadly glare.

"The surgeon's an expert, Jesse," I argue, aware that I'm wasting my time. "I'll be in perfectly safe hands."

"I'm the only expert on my wife's boobs around here, and the only safe hands they'll be in are mine. End of."

Drew smiles as he pops the cap off his beer. "I think John-Boy is more the expert these days, right?" He chuckles around the top of his bottle as I silently will him to stop with the teasing. It just makes the gorilla worse.

At that moment, John-Boy takes his empty bottle and smacks it over Jesse's head, as if in agreement. Everyone flinches, but not Jesse. He's too busy still giving me the death stare.

Elsie, chuckling, takes John-Boy from Jesse's arms. "Come on, children," she sings when Maddie and Georgia come dancing into the kitchen. "Maddie, you get Betty, and, Georgia, you get Imogen. Let's go play." Elsie directs all the kids into the garden, and I smile after her. She'll have them all doing baby yoga in no time.

"So when do you fly out?" Raya asks as the men break away and go congregate around the island.

"Tomorrow." I'm reminded that I still have a ton of things to do before we head for the airport. I haven't even finished packing.

"I can't believe we're not invited." Kate throws me a feigned hurt expression that I find easy to brush off. She understands.

"It's just me, Jesse, and the kids." I can't be made to feel guilty. It's our first holiday for over two years. "And I can't wait to have them all to myself." I glance over to Jesse as he glances over to me. Fucking hell, he's so damn beautiful, even when he's grumpy. My husband. The man who's given me three beautiful kids. I look at them each day and thank all things holy that I found the enigma that was Jesse Ward. I thank my lucky stars that I walked into that posh sex club of his and had the wind knocked out of me by just the sound of his voice. Of course, then I saw him. And then he saw me. At that very moment, when I was standing before him struggling to find breath, and he was looking at me with that heavy frown of his, it was game over. For both of us. Simple as that.

The road was rocky, the secrets dark, his ways challenging. And what's most cruel is that I had to discover all of his secrets not only once, but twice. But every drop of pain and suffering each time was worth it. He's not an enigma to me anymore. Hasn't been for a long time. He's my husband, the most devoted, adoring, gorgeous example of a man any woman could hope to have. Except any other woman can carry on hoping, because this one, this man, he's mine.

I smile the smile only he can draw from me. It's one filled with love of the perfect kind. Because he's mine.

I'll always be with this man.

* * *

JESSE

"I love you," I mouth as she gazes across the kitchen at me, looking at me in the exact same way she looked at me the first time she set eyes on me. With lust. With awe. She's looked at me in that way every single day of our lives together. Well, almost every single day. The accident, her temporarily lost memories, was just a blip on the horizon of my happiness. Yet at the time, it felt like the end of my world. I should have known that our love would prevail in the end. And now I really do know that we're unbreakable.

Smiling that smile that sets my insides alight, she kisses the air toward me before returning her attention back to the girls.

"So, the boobs?" Sam asks, tapping the top of my bottle with his, winning my attention.

"Sam." Drew punches his bicep. "Why'd you have to do it, ah?"

"Just asking." He grins around the lip of his bottle, his always smiling eyes not letting him down.

"Just asking for me to nut you?" I quip, yet somewhere close to serious, and he knows it. "There are no boobs beyond what's already there." She can get that stupid idea right out of her head. "And what's there is perfect." I clink their bottles. "To that motherfucker John."

"The motherfucker John." They laugh, pulling one from me as I head for the garden, stopping at the back door and looking across the grass. "It's like a fucking crèche," I mutter, sounding exasperated at the sight of all the kids, though I'm really not. Elsie has them all lying on their backs, legs in the air.

"I'm off to smack a few balls over the net with Jacob." Drew swipes my boy's racket from his hand and jogs off to the court with Jacob running after him, shouting for his magic racket back.

"Suppose I better go show them how it's done." Sam rolls his eyes like it's an inconvenience. "Coming?"

"No, I'm waiting for some more guests." Just as I say it, the doorbell rings, and I dart back into the house before Ava can beat me to it. I meet her in the hall. She's ahead of me, but a quick, sneaky grab of her wrist and a yank back puts me in front. She knew I'd be lurking, waiting to pounce.

"Jesse, don't you upset Maddie," Ava warns, knowing my game.

I slap on my killer smile and flash it at my wife before swinging the door open. But it drops when I find a young girl. Oh. I haven't a speech planned for Jacob's friend. Not one that won't make her cry, anyway.

"Hello, Mr. Ward." Clarita dazzles me with a smile full of personality.

"Hi." I open the door wider and let her in. I'm handing this one over to my wife. Smiling at Ava, I nod to Clarita's back as she approaches. Let's see how she welcomes this new woman into her darling boy's life. "Over to you," I quip.

Her scowl is barely contained. "Hi, Clarita. Jacob is on the tennis court. Do you want something to drink before you head out?"

"I'm fine, thank you. It was very nice of you to invite me."

Is it me, or is Ava swooning? Yes, she's definitely swooning. What happened to the lioness? "You're more than welcome, sweetheart. Help yourself today, okay? Drinks, food, you name it."

"Why don't you just ask her if she wants to stay the night, too?"

I grumble under my breath as I shut the door, plodding back to the garden. "Dada!" John-Boy spots me and breaks away from the group, clearly fed up with yoga.

"Hey!" I scoop him into my arms and let him pull at my cheeks.

"Maddie!" Ava calls from behind. "Your guest is here!"

I swing around so fast, John-Boy starts giggling uncontrollably, obviously thinking Daddy's playing. I'm not. Damn it, why did I leave the front door? Ava's knowing look tells me she knows I'm mentally kicking myself. I needed a few moments alone with this little twerp my daughter's apparently crushing on. And as I think that, the little twerp comes into view, standing next to Ava. My eyes pop out of my head. Fuck me, how old is he? Panicked, I look to Ava, searching for some backup. I get nothing but a shake of her head. What the fuck? He must be knocking on six foot.

As Maddie passes me, she throws me a look to suggest I should keep my mouth the hell shut. She can think again. I watch as she reaches up and kisses his cheek. Good Lord, someone hold me back. "She's nearly fourteen, Jesse," Ava says to me quietly when she's made it over. "Don't be all over the top about it."

"Why does everyone insist on saying *nearly fourteen*? That doesn't make her fourteen, and even if it does, she's still illegal."

"Illegal to date?" Ava laughs.

"To do *everything*," I confirm.

"She's growing up, Jesse. Get over it. She and I have had *the* talk. She's a sensible girl."

My body starts twitching uncontrollably as I stare at my wife in horror. "*The* talk?" Please, God, tell me Ava's not going to say what I think she's going to say.

"Of course. We had that conversation at least a year ago."

John-Boy's vibrating in my arms now, so much so, Ava must think I'm going to drop him because she takes him from me.

"You need to calm down," she warns.

Fuck that! "If you and Maddie have had the talk, it's only right me and . . . what's his name?"

"Lonny."

"Lonny?" I question. "What the fucking hell kind of name is that? His parents must be morons, too." I sink the rest of my beer, eyeing up the little fucker. "How old is he?"

"Fourteen."

"Give me a break." I laugh. "He must be lying. He's at least twenty."

"Oh, for God's sake." Ava smacks my arm. "Stop being dramatic."

I see Ava in the corner of my eye wandering off across the grass. Dramatic? I don't think I am. Me and Lonny need to have a chat.

My shoulders back, I wander over to Maddie and Lonny, seeing with perfect clarity the warning in my baby girl's eyes. And also the worry, because she knows I'm not interested in heeding her warning. "Hi." My voice is low and rough, just as I intended. Manly.

Lonny smiles at me. "Mr. Ward, nice to meet you."

I recoil. I can't help it. Has he got a vise on his balls? His squeaky voice doesn't match his height. Maybe the shit really is fourteen. I look down at his offered hand, my eyebrows rising. Let's see if his handshake is any manlier. I clasp it hard, immediately disappointed when he flinches in pain. I smile on the inside. "Let's take a walk, Lonny."

"No, Dad." Maddie dives in front of me, like her little girlie figure might stop me. A fucking bulldozer wouldn't stop me.

"I just want to chat with him." I appease her, knowing I'm wasting my time. "You want to chat, don't you, Lonny?"

"Y-yes, sir." He looks afraid. He should. *Be* very *afraid, Lonny.*

"See?" I sweep my arm out in gesture for him to lead on, blinding him with the smile I usually only reserve for my babies. It falls the moment Ava shoves John-Boy in my arms. Oh, she's cunning. I can't very well trample when I'm holding the baby. John-Boy doesn't help my cause of trying to appear threatening when he grabs my stubbly cheeks and squeezes them. Lonny laughs. I do not.

"Let's walk," I tell him, nodding down the path to the swing bench, the most secluded place in the garden.

Stuffing his hands in the pockets of his jeans, he walks on and I follow, eyeballing him the entire way. "You have a lovely home, Jesse." He smiles at me, and I raise my brows. "Mr. Ward," he corrects himself, very wisely. The little suck-up. So, it's compliments all the way, is it? My eyes narrow on him as we stroll, and he quickly darts his gaze to his feet, taking one hand to his hair and running it through nervously. I won't ever admit it out loud, but he's a good-looking little fucker. I can see why my girl is crushing on him.

"Tell me about your grades." He might carry the looks and, apparently, the charm, but it's all a waste if the kid's an underachiever. My girl is bright. She needs someone to equal that.

"My grades?" he asks, a little hesitantly, and I nod. Though my prompt doesn't push him to go on, his cheeks filling with a bit of color. It's as I thought. He's a reject. "I'm top of some of my classes, Mr. Ward."

Oh. Do I have a compulsive liar on my hands? "What classes?"

He smiles, awkward. "All of them."

Oh.

"My favorite is maths, though. And science. I'd like to be a physician someday." He sighs. "But the university fees are steep." He blows out his cheeks, and I conclude on the spot that his parents must be a little hard up. "Who knows, I might win the scholarship I'm hoping for. It'd be real cool if I won that place at Oxford."

Oxford? The boy dreams big, and as I watch him, scuffing his feet as he ambles on beside me, I can't help but think of my brother. He was ambitious, too, full of dreams and determination to make them happen. I flinch a little with the unexpected thought. "Here, sit," I tell him, pointing to the cushion on the bench as I settle and sit John-Boy on my lap. I don't need to rock the swing. Lonny's long legs take care of that for me.

"How'd you meet Maddie?" I ask, probably too shortly.

"Me and Jacob are mates."

Oh, I see. Worming his way into the affections of his mate's sister. The conniving shit. "Your mum's told you it's illegal to kiss until you're thirty, right?"

He glances up at me, alarmed. "It is?"

"Oh, yeah, it is." The poor kid looks terrified. Good. I put John-Boy on his feet on my knees when he starts getting restless and yelling at Lonny. "And your dad's told you about the birds and the bees, right?" I'm completely unprepared for the wash of sadness that passes over his face, his eyes dropping to his swinging feet. Shit, what did I say?

"I don't have a dad, sir."

"Of course you do." I laugh. "Everyone has a dad."

"Mine walked out on my mum when I was eighteen months old. Haven't seen him since." He shrugs, like it's no biggie, and I die on the inside. Really die. I'm a twat. "I looked him up last year, but he wasn't interested. So it's just me and Mum."

I want to punch myself in my stupid face, and I'm pretty sure Ava would if she knew I'd just put my big foot in it. I cast my eyes to John-Boy, who's dancing on my lap, talking a load of gibberish as he claps his hands and yells at Lonny. Eighteen months. John-Boy's age. Unexpected anger rises from my toes and burns my insides. He walked out on his boy? So who's guided him his whole life? Who took him football training and to his first match?

"You don't need a man like that in your life," I tell him, overwhelmed by the respect I have for this kid now. "You're doing fine without him, anyway." The kid has Oxford in his dreams, and something deep, and oddly proud, tells me he'll make it there, too.

"Dream big, fight hard." Lonny says it quietly, his gaze staring off into the distance, as I stare at him, astounded by his attitude. "Make things happen." He looks at me and smiles. "You have to go for what you want and take it."

"I couldn't agree more," I murmur, wondering if his philosophy applies to my daughter, too. I wonder where my fight is, my desire to scare this kid off. It's gone.

"He's so cute." Lonny takes John-Boy's hand and lets him yank and pull at it while both of them laugh.

"Of course he is. He's mine." I flip Lonny a wink when he glances at me. I'm done interrogating the boy. "You go find Maddie."

"Actually, I wouldn't mind having a game of tennis with Jacob." He frowns, looking back toward the house, where, no doubt, Maddie is in her mum's earhole nagging about my trampling ways. She needn't worry. This kid has trampled *me*, it seems. Looking back at me, Lonny's lips straighten. "But I don't think Maddie will be very pleased."

I laugh and stand, setting John-Boy on his feet so he can walk back, jerking my head for Lonny to follow. "Let me give you some advice about the women in my life, most importantly Maddie." His face is pleading for that advice as we wander back up the path slowly, John-Boy stomping along beside me, my shoulder dropped a little so my hand reaches his without stretching his little muscles. "My daughter is stubborn."

Lonny blows out his cheeks, nodding. "Tell me about it."

"Don't back down. She's just like her mother. Defiant and difficult for the sake of it. She'll have you running in circles if you let her." Something tells me Lonny is already dizzy. "Be firm. Stand your ground." I give him a light slap on his shoulder, nodding my affirmation.

"Yes, sir!" He beams brightly as he heads off toward the tennis courts to find his mate. "Thanks, Mr. Ward."

I smile and dip to tie the laces on John-Boy's little Converses. "Lonny," I call, and he stops, looking back.

"Yes, Mr. Ward?"

"You can call me Jesse."

Another beam, but this time no words. He jogs off and disappears around the corner, and John-Boy and I continue back to the house. The moment Maddie sees us, she flies over, her dark eyes frantically searching for Lonny. "Where is he? Oh my God, did you kill him and bury him under the shed? Mum!"

"Calm your knickers, little lady." I continue past, her wide eyes following. "He's on the tennis court with your brother."

"He is?"

I see it in her already. Indignation. She looks just like her mother as she huffs and goes marching off. I laugh, mentally cheering Lonny on in my head. She's going to get a nasty surprise. "Hey, Maddie."

She swings around, her eyes flaming. "What?"

"He's a good kid. Don't be a little cow, or he might dump your stroppy arse."

Her jaw drops open, her face outraged, and I smile, getting on my way with John-Boy.

"Who are you and what have you done with my dad?" she calls at my back.

I don't answer, smiling at Ava when she approaches with curiosity rife on her face. I shake my head and swing my arm around her neck. "I can't wait until tomorrow," I tell her, pulling her in and kissing her temple.

"Me either." Her hands disappear under my T-shirt and glide over my skin, coming to rest over my heart. It's going crazy, thumping happily.

Now it beats for four people.

* * *

The next day…

The familiar smell of the sea air fills my nose as I stand on the seashore in my shorts, the Mediterranean a never-ending blanket of sparkling water under the blazing sun. It's John-Boy's first time in Paradise, and he's mesmerized by the sand under his little bare feet, his toes constantly clawing. "Look, Dada!" he says, over and over, doing little dramatic gasps as he points to the gigantic expanse of blue water before him and the white sand he's standing on. "Gosh," he breathes, bewitched by the sea. "Gosh, Dada."

My fucking heart swells to epic proportions as I hold his hand and Jacob holds his other, our feet getting precariously close to the water. Maddie is dancing in the shallow depths. "Look, John-Boy!" She kicks the water and he chuckles, the sound adorable. "You coming to play in the water?" She drops to her knees and holds out her hands.

"No, Addie." He shakes his little head and turns into Jacob, raising his arms for his brother to pick him up. I lower my arse to the sand as Jacob lifts him and sets him on his hip, though John-Boy's eyes don't unstick themselves from the water. "Oh gosh," he gasps again, pointing out past Maddie. "A oat!"

"Yes, a boat!" I sing, clapping my hands at him, making him jig excitedly in Jacob's arms.

"Oh, here's Mum." Maddie jumps up and frantically brushes the wet sand from her body. "Quick, Dad!" Her hands flap at me, hurrying me to my feet.

"You ready, guys?" I ask, pulling my Wayfarers off and getting my first glimpse of her. "Fuck me," I breathe quietly as she comes down the steps from the villa, her white layered lace bikini perfect against her olive skin, her hair plaited over her shoulder. And she has a calla lily in her hand, just a single calla lily. I smile and reach into my pocket as she approaches. "Mrs. Ward, you look out of this world."

"You too." She holds her wrist out, eyebrows high, and I grin, dragging the cuffs from my pocket. "Shackle me, Ward."

I do as I'm bid, snapping one over her wrist before securing it to me. I don't know how she knew I'd have them. Then again, this woman has always read me like a book. Leaning in, I push my lips to hers. The kids don't say a word. Even John-Boy is silent, probably staring out at the water rather than at Mummy and Daddy handcuffing themselves to each other. "Ready?" I ask her.

"Always," she replies, turning us toward the kids. I laugh under my breath when I find Jacob standing tall in his swim shorts, a book in his hands.

"What's that?" I ask, bemused.

"A Bible. I have to look like I know what I'm doing. This is important." He clears his throat and looks down at the pages, drawing breath to speak. "It's—"

"Wait!" Maddie yells, chasing after John-Boy when he decides that now he'd like to try the water. "John-Boy, no." She lifts him into her arms and returns to her spot. "Sorry. You may resume."

I look at Ava, frowning, and she laughs. "Go on," I prompt, sliding my hand into my wife's.

"Do you, Jesse Ward, take Ava Ward to be your wedded wife?" Jacob asks, a certain posh edge to his voice. "To have and to hold from this day forward. To love, honor—"

"I thought we weren't doing the official thing?" Maddie interrupts, scowling at Jacob.

He leans into her, full of annoyance. "You're ruining their special day."

"Seriously? They've had, like, two already. Who gets married three times?" She rolls her eyes and starts bouncing John-Boy when he starts yelling impatiently, reaching for his new favorite friend, the Med.

"Me and your mum do," I snap, giving her a face that dares her to argue. "You gonna argue with me? And before you answer, think carefully about who will be paying for your wedding when you find *the one*."

She snaps her mouth shut, startled, and probably pleasantly surprised, and Ava cocks an interested eyebrow. "Get on with it, Jacob," I tell him, before anyone has the chance to ask where *The* Jesse Ward has disappeared to. Turning to Ava, I breathe in the salty air and wink.

"Dad, do you take Mum to be your wife?" Jacob spurts out the words tiredly.

"I do."

"Mum, do you take Dad to be your husband?"

"I do." She grins at me, yanking my hand when my eyes drift down to her boobs straining against the white material of her bikini. "Eyes up here, Ward."

"Sorry." I flash her my roguish grin, returning her gesture and yanking her hand when her gaze takes a casual jaunt down my prime chest. "Hey."

"Not sorry." She chuckles, diving at me, her thighs trapping me in their grasp, her free arm around my neck. And her gorgeous lips on mine. "Don't ever tell me I can't admire what's mine." Biting my lip, she pulls back, just a fraction, so her forehead rests on mine. "I love you, Jesse Ward."

"Of course you do." Resealing our lips, I turn and run into the water with her attached to my front.

"I now pronounce you man and wife!" Jacob yells at us, his declaration only just heard over our laughs and the splashing water. "Hey, wait for me!"

As soon at the water is up to my waist, I take us under, rolling us around, our bodies and limbs twisting, the moment reminiscent. Except this time we're not just us. We're not just Jesse and Ava. We're not just man and wife.

We're Mum and Dad.

Only when I'm unable to hold my breath any longer do I push us to the surface, gasping for air when I get there. Ava soon reattaches herself to my front, breathing heavily in my face as she blinks her eyes open. "Fuck, it's cold." She shudders in my arms as Jacob splashes his way to us.

"Watch your mouth," I warn, landing her with a kiss before pulling the cuff off my wrist and pushing her away from me. I'm attacked from behind by Jacob crawling up my back until he's standing on my shoulders. "Off you go, boy." I take his ankles and launch him into the air, just in time for Maddie to tackle me. "Amateurs," I mutter, taking her under the arms and throwing her away. She screams, I laugh, looking to the shore to see John-Boy standing just out of reach of the rolling shoreline.

"Dada!" he yells to me, quite put out that he's missing all the fun. "Dada, gosh!"

I wipe my hair from my face as I trudge through the water. "Touch the sea," I tell him, laughing when his little head starts to shake furiously, knocking his blond curls about. "Dada come get you?" I ask.

"Dada!" he yells, starting to pad the sand with his feet, making grabby hands for me.

I make it to him and lift him into my arms, his little padded nappy trunks dry as a bone. "You always swim in the swimming pool at home," I say, kissing his hair as I walk back into the water, the others up ahead dunking and splashing each other. "Hey, calm down, guys."

They all stop with the larking around and start encouraging John-Boy in, clapping and singing excitedly as he starts to jerk in my arms. The moment his toe touches the water, he gasps, and I decide it's now or never. So I quickly sink us in up to our necks.

"Oooh, cold, Dada!" he moves to my front, clinging onto my neck as he looks back to the others, clearly desperate to join them. I swim over as Jacob climbs onto Ava's back, and as soon as I'm close enough, Maddie is on mine, cooing over my shoulder to John-Boy, who has adopted a chimp-style hold uncannily similar to his mother's. With Maddie lying on my back, and John-Boy plastered to my front, I swim toward Ava until our baby is squished between her chest and mine, the twins dangling from our backs. The happiness radiating from my wife's eyes is fierce, and I know mine is reflecting right back at her. This moment, this precious moment, is what any man should live for.

And I do. I live for them. My heart beats to keep me alive for them.

"Kiss me," I say to Ava over John-Boy's head, reaching forward with my spare hand and slipping it onto her nape, holding his little body to my chest with my other. "And close your eyes."

Smiling, her eyes flutter closed with mine and our lips meet. I taste nothing but love in her kiss. I hear nothing but love in the sound of the twins' laughter. I feel nothing but love in John-Boy's baby skin pressed against my chest. And I smell nothing but love in Paradise.

The only sense I don't have in this perfect moment is my vision. To see my beautiful family surrounding me.

I don't need it. I feel them. With every fiber of my being, I feel them.

Their presence, their faces, their love, is all carved deeply into my soul. It makes me who I am.

My wife. My children. Their love.

It's pure bliss, ladies. Total gratification. Absolute, complete, Earth-shifting, universe-shaking love.

Don't tell me there's anything more perfect than this.

I wouldn't believe you.

End of.

Acknowledgments

As always, my love and thanks to every single one of the JEM team, but a special thanks has to go to you. My readers. To this day, I'm still floored by the response I've had to my crazy, neurotic, nut-job Lord of the Manor. Thank you for loving Jesse as much as I do. Writing his story has truly changed my life. JEM xxx

About the Author

Jodi Ellen Malpas was born and raised in the Midlands town of Northampton, England, where she lives with her two boys and a beagle. She is a self-professed daydreamer, a Converse and mojito addict, and has a terrible weak spot for alpha males. Writing powerful love stories and creating addictive characters have become her passion—a passion she now shares with her devoted readers. She's a proud #1 *New York Times* bestselling author, and seven of her published novels were *New York Times* bestsellers, in addition to being international and *Sunday Times* bestsellers. Her work is published in more than twenty-three languages across the world.

You can learn more at:

JodiEllenMalpas.co.uk

Twitter @JodiEllenMalpas

Facebook.com/JodiEllenMalpas

You Might Also Like...

THIS MAN SERIES

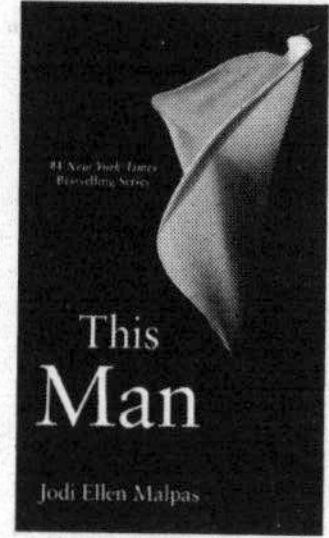

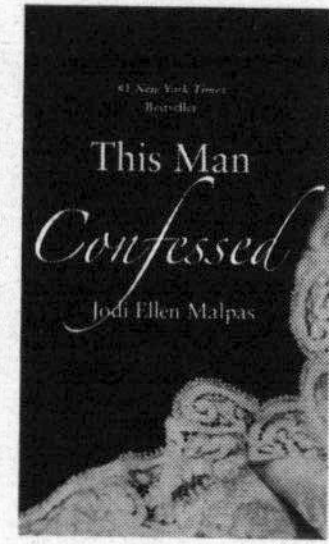

ONE NIGHT TRILOGY

STAND-ALONE NOVELS